THE DEEP AND THE DROWNED

Also by Ian Green

Extremophile

THE ROTSTORM

The Gauntlet and the Fist Beneath
The Gauntlet and the Burning Blade
The Gauntlet and the Broken Chain

THE DEEP AND THE DROWNED

IAN GREEN

An Ad Astra Book

First published in the UK in 2026 by Head of Zeus Ltd,
part of Bloomsbury Publishing Plc

9 7 5 3 1 2 4 6 8

A catalogue record for this book is available from the British Library.

ISBN (HB): 9781804545898
ISBN (EBOOK): 9781804545874

Cover design by Simon Michele
Cover illustration: Marcela Bolívar
Map design: Ian Green

Typeset by Lumina Datamatics Ltd

Printed and bound in Great Britain by Clays Ltd, Elcograf S.p.A.

Bloomsbury Publishing Plc
50 Bedford Square, London, WC1B 3DP, UK
Bloomsbury Publishing Ireland Limited,
29 Earlsfort Terrace, Dublin 2, D02 AY28, Ireland

HEAD OF ZEUS LTD
5–8 Hardwick Street
London EC1R 4RG

To find out more about our authors and books
visit www.headofzeus.com
For product safety related questions contact productsafety@bloomsbury.com

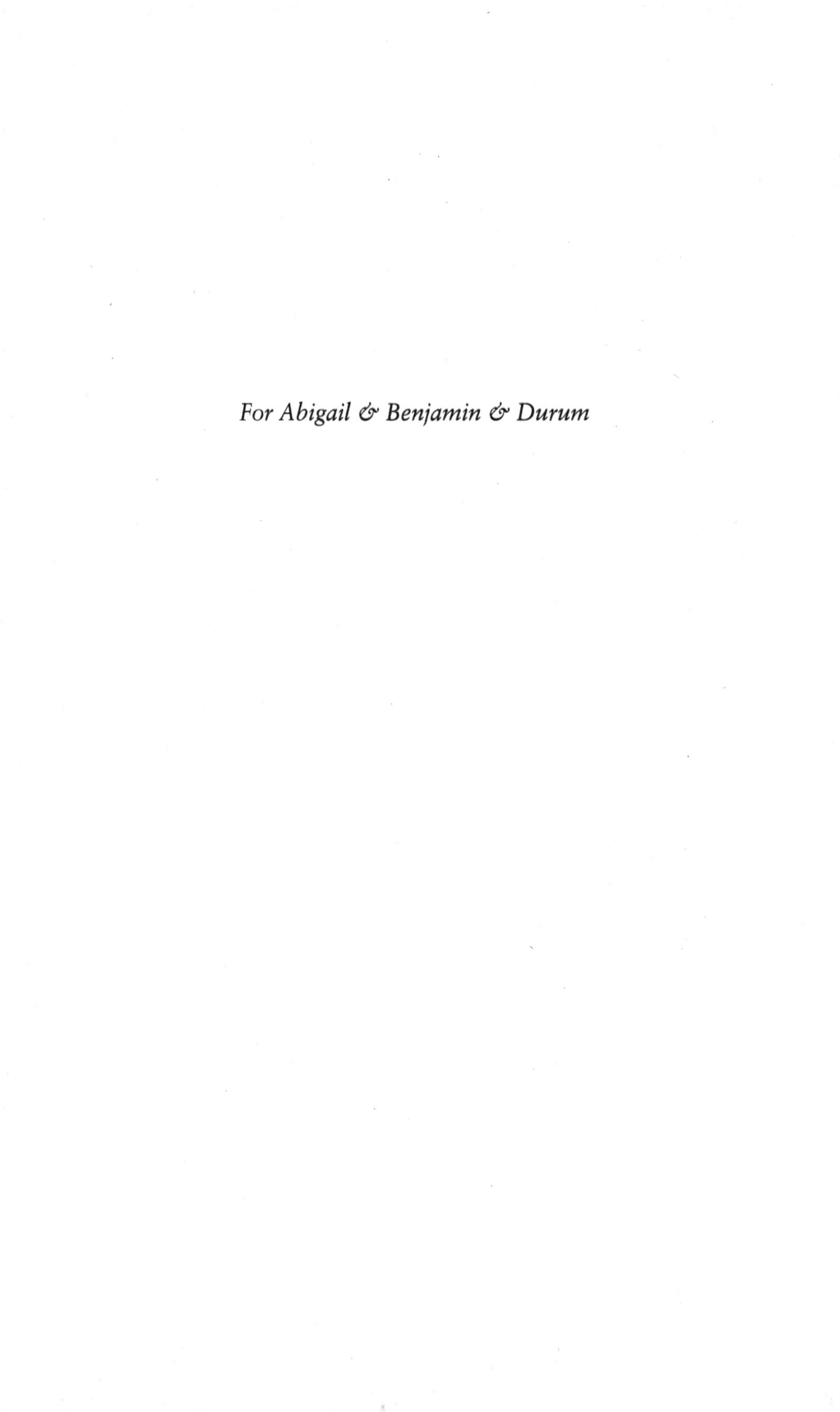

For Abigail & Benjamin & Durum

CONTENTS

CHARTS

CHARTS

World of Morost

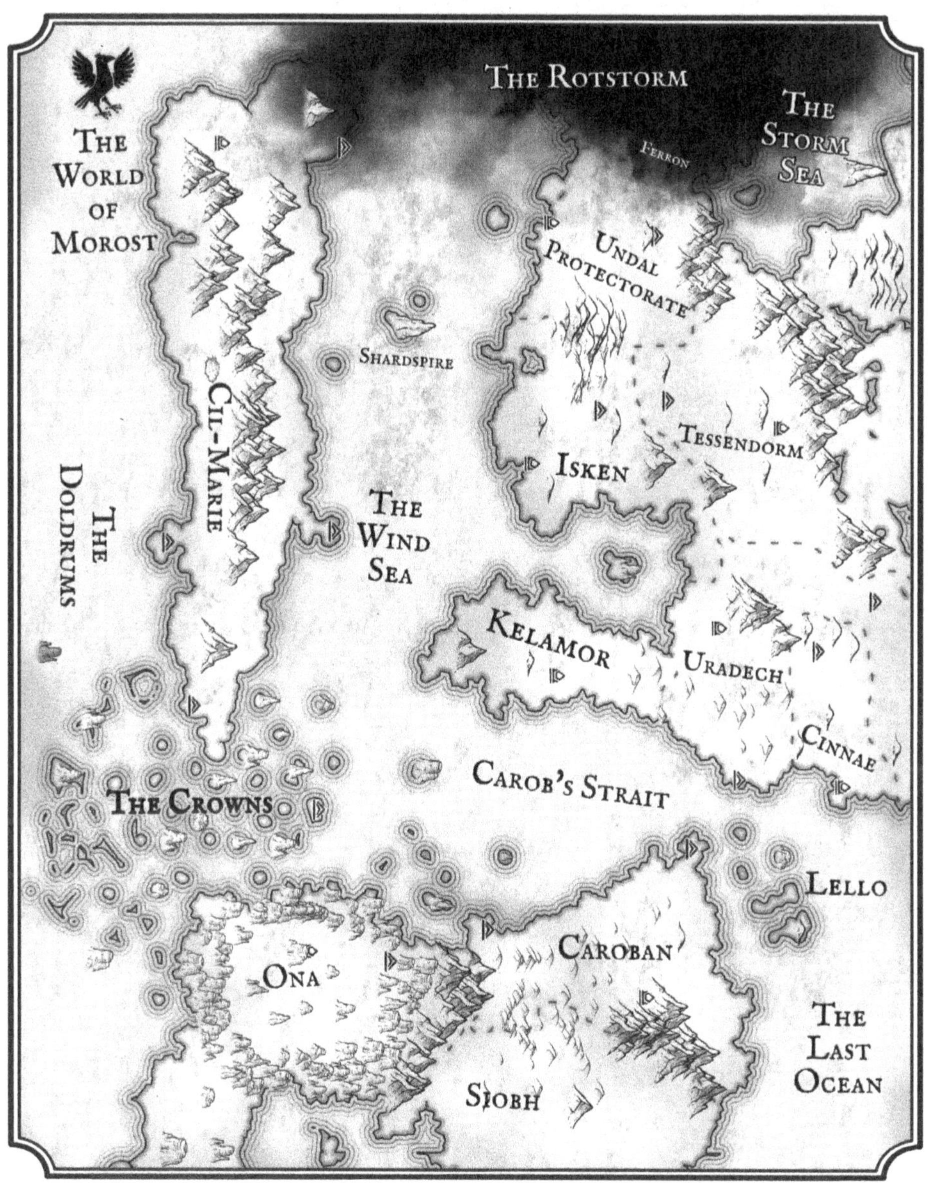

The World of Morost, year 1133 Isken – **From the charts of the *Cutlass Hawk*,** Captain Killian Heroneye

Crown Archipelago

The Crown Archipelago, year 1132 Isken – **From the charts of the *Cutlass Hawk*,** Captain Killian Heroneye

PROLOGUE

BURNER'S RUN

Storm and wave crashed over Marion and the water pulled at her, and for a moment she felt her resolve slacken, felt her fingers slip on sodden rope. How simple it would be to let go, and then the sea would take her. She gripped tighter through no conscious volition – simply an animal desire to continue. There was no space for thought as the ice water hit her with pummelling blows again and again and again. The boat plunged down the wavefront and Marion could not hear herself yelling, could only hear the scream of wind and the skirl of twisting timber as the hull of the *Mendicant Heart* surely began to tear apart below her. She twisted the wrist-thick rope she was gripping thrice around her arm and huddled closer to the railing of the ship and shut her eyes. *This is not how you die, little fool.* The salt spray was everywhere, seeping through her clenched lips and filling her throat. She forced herself to focus.

Up, down. Her body felt each crest as the ship fought through the storm – distantly she could hear sailors yelling, but the soaking ocean spray was freezing her face and the roar of the water filled her skull and she could make out only animal noise, diction and meaning lost in the storm. She was soaked down to her core. Her Blade was belowdecks, though he would be no help to her here. A sword had its uses, but so did a rope. A scream, up, down, and Marion forced herself to open her eyes and began to crab-walk her way along the rail of the ship towards the captain and the wheel. *This is not how you die,* she thought, repeating it over and over in a litany of fear. Her chest was heaving at the exertion of breathing through the spumes of water, every inhalation drawing more of the sea down her throat, into her roiling gut.

The sails were furled and tied tight save a lone triangle of grey sailcloth that strained at the rigging. The ropes were all cinched, and what crew she could still see were huddled over opaque mechanisms and ratchets and lines. Marion was not a sailor – she had no idea which rope would doom them, and which held salvation. The ship was all that remained, all that was left of hope and life – around them, the sea was irate and endless. The sky above was a nightmare of twisted cloud as grey as the sea below, a mirror to the dark water. The gap between sea and cloud seemed impossibly narrow, that slight film in which Marion clung to life. If she fell upward somehow she was certain she would sink into the cloud as sure as she would the water below.

Another wave exploded across the rail of the ship and threw Marion from her feet, and she slid spluttering and cursing until she was brought to a sharp stop by the rope at her wrist. Her elbow throbbed as she scrabbled to the nearest piece of wood that seemed sturdy, part of the ship – not something that could be washed away. They were twisting from side to side as well as pitching, and she tried to picture the ship as sturdy, as steadfast, and she breathed deep and her stomach heaved as again they crested upward, another wave. In the port and for so many days it had been such a heavy thing, this ship, solid wood seasoned by endless miles, but now it was thrown around like a twig in a river rapid. *How many cursed waves are there?* Always the answer seemed to be: *one more.*

The rain was thick enough that she could not tell where the spraying water of the cresting waves ended and the deluge began. The storm had risen in moments from seemingly dead clouds and seas, and now Marion was painfully aware of how far they were from land. She could picture perfectly the captain's thickly annotated map of the Crowns, and the broad circlet of open water that protected the inner islands from civilisation – *Burner's Run.* The place the winds all blew towards.

The nearest land was twenty miles back, or twenty forward. There was nothing else, no scrap of rock in Burner's Run – only mad currents, impossible winds, and circling sharks. *Too far.* Marion spat salt water and with a fluttering heart uncoiled the rope from her wrist and hauled herself up the stairs to the aftcastle where Captain Rulligaunt stood resolute. The man gripped the rail in front of the ship's great wheel, yelling back at a pair of sailors each twice his size, who seized the wheel's wooden bulk between them.

The wheel was fighting them, but the two men were planted firm and straining hard as they tried to keep the ship from taking a swell across its sides that would send them all to the deep. Marion was no sailor, but she could understand that well enough. Rulligaunt's signature tricorn hat was lost and his thinning hair was plastered across his face. His eyes did not leave the water, ever, and he called over his shoulder or down to the deck terms she did not know. *Lines, sheets, points, port, aft,* she thought, *I'm to die on this thrice-damned ship and I'll die hearing this nonsense.* The *Mendicant Heart* was a small ship with only one central mast and no forecastle, only the aft raised above the main line of the hull. Small enough – she was sure one of these waves would turn them to flinders if they did not find land. *Too far.* She knew it was too far for them to reach land, but what else could they do? She wished for a galleon, a Cil-Marie warship with high sides, three masts, two decks of slaves and oars. She wished for rock and stone and immutable dirt.

'Captain!' she yelled, and scrambled across the soaked deck to his side. He did not look at her, and instead yelled something about a 'fore-line' that sent three sailors on the main deck scrabbling towards the central mast. 'Captain, we must make for land! This is madness!'

Rulligaunt turned to her and then back to his wheelmen, and then back to Marion, and his mouth twisted in a grimace. His face was slick with sea spray and rain, and through the dark of the storm his eyes glinted.

'Too late for that. You set us on this course, Lady,' he bellowed, and then he gestured out to the seas around them. 'Across Burner's Run, you said, and I said, no, but your ducats are heavy. So now we are set, aye? There is no turning back! A shore in this storm would mean death, not salvation, and the nearest is not one we'll reach today. The only way is through. I've sailed worse than this.'

Marion clutched at the rail and crouched low as they rode another wave downward, her stomach flipping as the proud beam of wood at the ship's fore pointed ever lower, the bushels of greenery wrapped tight to the wood soaked and ragged. She did not know their purpose, but when they had left port the greenery wrapped around the forward beam had been vibrant, *alive*, and now it was as salt-wrecked and ragged as she. As they reached the bottom of the depression between the previous wave and the inevitable next, Rulligaunt hauled her to her feet and Marion bristled and pushed his hand away, grasping desperately for the railing. *Perhaps I do need the Blade up here.* The captain was forgetting himself. Deference was owed, and she owed her people the duty of ensuring future deference as well as present, regardless of tempest or the temptation of aid.

'Turn!' she yelled. 'We can try Burner's Run another day, when the weather favours. You are under my command, Captain Rulligaunt. Take the *Mendicant Heart* back to where we can ride out this storm.'

Marion heard her voice, so loud, and winced at a brightness. *Sunlight?* The captain was ignoring her, was staring instead ahead where the waves were calming. A few desultory waves crested and fell around the ship, but they were nothing compared to the rolling breakers that had pressed them during the storm. The ship pressed onward, floundering up and down, and Marion ran a hand through her mane of black hair pushing a fresh wave of freezing salt water down her back. She felt bile in her throat as her body readied itself for the next assault, her every instinct clawing against the sudden calming of the storm. The tempest had been raging for what felt like hours, but this ending was as unnatural as its sudden appearance. She kept one hand on the rail but lowered the other to the hammer at her belt. The mark of her rank, black metal inscribed with arcane sigils of powdered silver. It was heavy with potential. Its weight was a surety at her hip, and the sunlight brought her strength. *I will not be ignored.*

'*Captain—*' she began, but Rulligaunt held his eyes to the horizon and simply beckoned for her to follow his gaze.

Marion looked outward. Sea and sea and sea, grey waves still larger than any she had seen before that day, twisting clouds that beams of sun cut through to dance on the mist and surf spray, a diffuse golden light that seemed to fill the air as every drop of mist and rain and spray was caught and ennobled and all was suffused with sunlight. She squinted and felt an ache in her lower back where the cold had reached her inners. She was frozen. *This is madness. All of this.*

'Burner's Run needs a tithe, you said,' Rulligaunt hissed, and gestured at a distant wave. 'Get it ready, Lady.'

Marion's eyes widened and she drew her hammer. In the bulk of that wave beneath the golden glow was *something* – movement below movement, a hint, a blackness that seemed to push back against the gold of the sun. The turning scale of a great serpent below the waves, lost below iron water as soon as she found it, a shadow in darkness. Zalan, serpent of the Crowns. Zalan, the great Judge. Zalan, the shipbreaker. Zalan, seagrave. Guardian of the inner Crowns. Terror of Burner's Run. The mad god of the Russilan. Her mouth was suddenly thick with bile, her breath short. *A Judge.*

'Blade!' Marion shrieked, but she did not take her eyes from the sea. The shadow was gone. *Where is the beast?*

Marion had never seen a Judge. The scale of it was hard to comprehend between the enormity of the waves themselves. She gripped her hammer tight and kept her eyes on where the writhing coils had glimmered darkly beneath the water. Her hammer was fashioned from the bones of the relu, a minor god – the mote in her hammerhead was from a mantis-thing that had hidden in a deep forest glade in the east of Cil-Marie. By all accounts it had been beautiful. Zalan was a Judge, a far greater god that that little mantis – but her hammer was a reminder of the authority she represented. Once, Judges had walked Cil-Marie, but the Sun-Masters had cut them down. *It is only a beast, in the end, no matter from what flesh it is wrought. It is only a greater beast.* The *Mendicant Heart* drifted forward, rising and falling with the waves, and Marion's Blade appeared on deck, dragging his cargo.

Blade Mournchild was clad in matte-black plate armour, every inch of him save his bare head cosseted in heavy unadorned metal. The sailors had laughed at him behind his back when he first boarded – what fool would wear such armour on a ship? If he went over the side, Mournchild would sink faster than an anchor. Rulligaunt's sailors wore salt-spoiled cotton and his soldiers wore boiled leather, with barely a scrap of metal save their heavy blades – even their shields were simple wood. None would laugh to Mournchild's face, though. From the deck he turned up to her, his shaven skull and face painted a stark white, black tear tracks and shadows daubed around his eyes. In one hand he held the Russilan child by the scruff of her neck – there was no fight left in the filthy girl, her face a mess of bruises. Mournchild asked Marion no questions – he simply waited for his instruction, his face a mask, thick lips pursed. The sailors parted around him as they went about their tasks, and if eyes lingered on the child or the Blade, Marion did not spare the energy to notice them.

'That was not a natural storm to be born and die like that,' Rulligaunt said, and he moved closer to her. 'And that is Zalan the bloody *shipbreaker* out in those waves. We are in it now. You wanted to cross Burner's Run, you'd pay the tithe, you said. Russilan blood, you said. So bloody do it, my Lady, or we are all swimming back to the Coracles, by which I mean we are all down to the deep and the dark. *Pay the tithe.*'

Marion's eyes flitted across the water, but she could find no trace of the great snake.

'Be ready to make sail on my mark, Captain, as fast as ever you have,' she murmured, noting to herself to remind him of his manners later, and then she tried to find some sense of grace as she slipped her way down to the main deck. The stairs and deck were flooded with seawater. There was no land visible in any direction, only shadowed hints at the horizon. *Perhaps those are the Coracles?* She could not be sure. Certainly too far to swim to. Marion went to her Blade and Mournchild nodded in deference. His eyes were a putrid red today, iris sclera and pupil all. *Playing with his dyes again.* Marion could not waste worry on Mournchild's oddities. She hauled the Russilan girl from his grasp and strode to the rail amidships, and called out to the sea in the direction she had seen the scale and writhing muscle.

'Great Zalan!' she cried. 'We seek the Deep Crowns! We seek safe passage! In payment, we bring the blood of the Russilan. Grant us your boon!'

She said the words as they had been told to her, as she had mumbled them to herself silently for so many days. The water before Marion rippled, bubbled, and Zalan rose. The head of the serpent was as wide as a cart, with teeth longer than Marion's legs and four fangs at least twice that again. Water poured from it as it rose, cascades of brine and sea foam falling. It had eyes, so many eyes. Two great abysses of onyx on each side of its flared skull, and then dozens of smaller eyes surrounding them, each a different gemstone, each a different sparkling hue, asymmetrically patterned and intricately glinting in the dancing sunlight. All of them focused on *her.* Its mouth was open.

It is just a relu grown fat, Marion thought defiantly, but her heart betrayed her with its fearful rhythm. The Judge Zalan was a creature of the pattern itself, its scales a burnished metal and glittering black that glowed with a woeful radiance, and its teeth the sparkling blue of mountain ice. The serpent hung in the water perfectly still as the ship bobbed, and Marion bowed her head as its crystalline red tongue snaked outward. Crystal, but sinuous as flesh and seeking as Zalan tasted the air. Metal and stone as living meat, spirit made flesh. Judges and relu were manifestations of the skein, the pattern below the world coalescing into something material. They followed their own physics and laws. Marion was no mage, no adept – she could not sense the great skein that bound the world. Yet as the serpent stared at her she could sense something – a concatenation in the air, as if the world itself was *leaning* towards the beast.

Marion held the girl forward to the railing, and at last the little mouse seemed to wake.

'Wait!' the girl cried, but Marion was already bringing her hammer down. A single blow to the back to the head caved her skull and sent the girl limp, and Marion felt the thrum of her hammer's power as she let the girl drop over the side. Her hammer could break stone or steel – bone was no matter.

And then the snake will eat the Russilan, she thought, her gaze set on the serpent's maw, *and the ship will be free to pass.* That was what the sage in Druich had said, what three others had confirmed by rumour. The old god of the Russilan had been mad this last decade, and it hungered for the blood of its people.

The dead child hit the water and disappeared with the softest of splashes and the great serpent dove after it, sinuous lengths of dazzling scales leaping free of the water and then slipping back beneath the waves. In a heartbeat it was gone. There was silence on the deck of the *Mendicant Heart*, and Marion held her hammer out and Blade Mournchild wiped brain and blood and hair on a cloth he then primly discarded over the side.

Marion turned to the aftcastle where Rulligaunt stood expressionless, staring down at her.

'Across Burner's Run,' he called, 'and onward to the Crow's lair! Make all—'

The ship juddered and then the bowsprit buckled upward and snapped, the soaked boughs of willow wand and hazel that surrounded the central beam sent scattering to the salt water below. From the churning sea the great snake Zalan rose upward, and above them the beams of dancing sun died one by one and the rain began. The sky darkened and she felt the boat begin to rock as icy drops fell across her face, and she felt the eyes of the serpent fall upon her, its myriad gaze piercing to her core. The serpent reared back and raised its mouth to the skies and around them the seas began to writhe as the waves danced and fought in all directions. High above, deep in the cloud, pale lightning flashed and a wave of thunder washed over her, filling her entirely. Marion fell to her knees.

'Flee!' she screamed, and then the serpent dove and Rulligaunt was roaring, the sea was rising around them. *This is not how you die, little fool!* Marion forced herself to repeat her master's words in her mind. Her master was never mistaken. Her master had seen Marion's death, and it was not here. Blade Mournchild gripped her under the arms and dragged her across the deck unceremoniously to the captain's cabin, as all around them sailors scrambled and Rulligaunt yelled his orders. In the cabin she threw herself down to her bunk and gripped at the walls as the ship bucked and outside the sea roared. Marion closed her eyes and allowed herself a shaking sob with the certainty of their weakness. *If the snake wishes us dead,* she thought, *then we are dead.* If they died, then her master was wrong, and her master was never wrong. None of it made sense. With trembling fingers she wiped the sea from her face, her eyes, and forced herself to sit up. Another impact against the hull sent her sprawling again.

Blade Mournchild looked at her with his doleful eyes, and Marion grabbed a clay cup that had been stashed in her bunk and threw it at him. He watched it come and made no effort to dodge, no effort to catch. Just another thing to ignore. It bounced from his armoured chest and clattered to the floor, rolling back and forth as the ship pitched and yawed.

'What next, you say, Mournchild? Good bloody question.' Marion fell back to her bunk and the ship heaved and she groaned. If Zalan chose, they would all be dead in moments; even if the snake allowed them to flee, if the captain's skills failed then the storm would wreck them before they could get clear of Burner's Run and back to the calm waters of the Coracles. If they survived, she had failed anyway, and so must try again. *Failure is not an option.* Marion pictured the Russilan girl falling so quickly to the water. *Was she even Russilan? Was that the mistake?* The sage had been clear, and the man who sold the girl had seemed scared enough. *I'll kill them later.* The ship pitched then righted itself and she shut her eyes and gripped her hammer, and Blade Mournchild said not a word. Marion hissed through her teeth as, far below the waterline, something impacted the hull again.

'What bloody next, Mournchild!'

She felt the weight of the water surrounding them, the weight of the storm above, the crushing immensity of the vast miles of ocean between her and land, the immensity of the archipelago of madness between her and home, and she clutched her hammer to her chest prayed to the Sun-Masters and the ghosts of her ancestors and clenched her teeth. Across from her, her stoic Blade sat on the cabin floor and settled one hand on his helm, the other on the long hilt of his sword as if preparing for a ceremonial duel. He stared at her with his reddened eyes so she averted her gaze and cursed the sea, the snake, the child, the sage, the Blade, and the master who had sent her to this fate. Most of all she cursed her prey, the traitor Jean du Cilcan.

'Sun blind you, Jean du Cilcan. I *will* find you,' she whispered. The ship rose, and fell, and when Marion closed her eyes, instead of darkness she saw the face of Zalan. Zalan, serpent of the Crowns. Zalan, the great Judge. Zalan, the shipbreaker. Zalan, seagrave. Guardian of the Deep Crowns. Terror of Burner's Run. The mad god of the Russilan.

She saw him, and she knew that through water and wood and darkness he saw her, and all she could do was pray.

ACT 1

ONE THOUSAND CROWNS

The sea remembers
The rock protects
The stars hold true

– Russilan proverb

Skerry

Skerry, year 1134 Isken – **From the charts of the**
Cutlass Hawk, Captain Killian Heroneye

1

THE SKERRY HAUL

'Notably there is no record of an extant skein-wreck or great mage of the Russilan – indeed, the skein appears to have played little part in their culture from what writings we have found. Unlike the college of mages in Kelamor, the Undal military adjuncts and whitestaffs of Riven, the Isken Guild of the Arcane, and so forth, no note of a specific group or individual of power has been made. Only references to "Starfinders", but these appear to have been some form of priest.'

– ***Notes on the Russilan,*** Gallo Mancinus

Killian held up a hand, and behind him Silver and the Breygar twins fell still. He listened to the forest – Skerry was a small enough isle he could still hear the endless murmur of the sea, but through the pines he thought he had heard some disturbance. He held his breath but all was silent save the creak of boughs, the rustle of needle against needle as the trees brushed against one another. The old forest on Skerry's western shore was a tangle of twisted black pine and briars, and Killian was sweating despite the cool night air. It had been two hours uphill since they left the dog-boat on the beach, and Killian was starting to get the twist in his gut that normally preceded everything going wrong.

Silver tapped him on the shoulder and placed her hands on each side of his head, guiding his vision to a patch of darkness that looked much like any other. She waited, looming at his shoulder patiently, as he let his eyes drink in the forest. *There.* A flicker of light. As he turned to her the light was enough to cast the faintest momentary glow across the pale of her skin, her permanently downturned mouth and her wild mop of hair lit all in red flame for the briefest of seconds as she held her head close to his to track his gaze.

'That'll be the spider crew,' he muttered, and Silver drew back, silent in her agreement. The Breygars each already had their heavy cutlasses in hand – they'd had to chop their way through a dozen briar patches already to reach this point. Silver drew her own sword, a narrow Kelamor rapier, and Killian slipped his shortbow from its sling and pulled the string from his belt pouch. It was still dry, and he rubbed his hands on his shirt to get the worst of his sweat off before he let the string uncoil. As he looped bowstring to bow he glanced upward – it was dark enough his eyes would not help him, and he was practised enough that he did not need them anyway. There was no moon, only stars – a vast ocean of them above dancing over the swaying treetops. He pulled an arrow from his hip quiver and nocked it in the bow, and blew out a breath from his nose as he tried to find a constellation he could recognise. With a squint, he found the Six Dancers, that cluster that always stayed together yet never in quite the same configuration. *Change, or chance?*

Killian dropped his eyes back to the forest and stared in the direction where the light had flickered. Light meant the diggers were still awake, and the sound he had heard was likely them as well.

'Six of them,' said Big Breygar, drawing closer, and Small Breygar sniffed. They were both of a size, but her silent brother was the second born and thus 'small'. In the darkness Killian could only make out their silhouettes, slim and still. He scratched at his chin. Six of them, *if* the information they'd gathered the day before in Skerry port was right. They'd moored up as if they were after a refill for the *Cutlass Hawk*'s water barrels, and he and Big Breygar had spent a while chatting with the locals down by the dock and in a dingy inn with the cover of trying to shift a few crates of lacquered Kelamoran pots. Skerry port was a small town, more wood than stone, walled with a simple palisade of pine trunks, but Skerry was a good stop on the Coracle run for water and so the docks were busy enough he thought they'd raised no notice.

'Likely no watch – they shouldn't be expecting trouble,' Big Breygar continued, and Killian licked his lips and scratched at the scruff on his chin.

'We could try and send them running,' Silver said, and they all stood silent as they considered it. 'A screamer arrow?' Killian shifted his feet and in the forest an owl called mournfully, its cry seeming to fall through the woods from treetop to soil, settling over all of them. He looked up again at the swaying treetops and tried to guess the wind.

An easterly, tonight? He wanted to be back on the water. Closing his eyes, he tried to remember what the Six Dancers symbolised. His mother had told him: *the first constellation you see will tell you your fate that night.* Was the Six Dancers change, or chance? *Luck*, he heard his mother say a lifetime ago, her voice quiet and smooth.

'It's a small tomb if the rumour is right,' he said slowly, considering each word. *Luck*. Silver would want no bloodshed and the Breygars would do as they were told. Screamer arrows were expensive and he only had two of the carved arrowheads in his belt pouch – he did not want to lose them unless he had to. He also did not want to kill six men – but he needed what was in that tomb. *We all need it.* Killian flexed his fingers around the shaft of his bow and then pushed his hair back from his face. 'We won't need long. They'll be at their camp. I say we go quiet. If it goes loud, we scare them if possible. If it goes wrong, head to the dog-boat. At dawn, we sail.'

He did not say, *with or without you*. He did not need to. Silver knew he would not leave her, and the Breygars knew he would do what he had to. They had been with him long enough and seen him do worse. The business with Affy Burngull was still fresh in all their memories, Big Breygar's most of all.

Big Breygar spat and moved forward to take the front position as she always did when they had to move with stealth. She was as sure-footed on the rocky forest floor as she was on a deck. Killian followed, crouching low and watching his feet, stepping on rock where he could and earth when he couldn't, lowering each foot carefully when he had to step on fallen needles or sticks. They moved slowly and Killian focused on his breathing, the feel of his bow, the scent of the pine thick around him, focused on the immediacy of his body and the world rather than his anxiety of what waited for them in the darkness or the burning in the bottom of his gut that told him to go to the fire, to cut and thrust and skewer until there was no reason to be quiet.

Skerry was north in the Coracles and the forest was all towering pine and thickets and stone, not like the Deep Crowns where the trees felt older and smaller, or to the south where they would like as not be traipsing through some Tullioch orchard. The northern Coracles were all ruins and dark forest, straggled freeholds with wooden palisades built on the broken stumps of stone walls. *Russilan walls.* Killian absently raised his hand from his bow to touch the amulet hanging around his neck, a heron skull cast in steel. He did not like Skerry, did not like the rough stone boulders that cut through the forest floor and sent them circling and meandering as they moved, but he clenched his jaw. *We need this.* The Evertree Sisters had been clear on that. If he returned empty-handed again they'd promised to take his ship and his fingers. *See how you fare with your ropes and your bow then, sailor,* they had said.

He pushed the memory from his mind and focused on following the elder Breygar through the underbrush. It was not long before the tang of woodsmoke drifted through the darkness and a dappling light began to dance across the boughs from the campfire. The camp was a simple affair – a heavy canvas canopy strung between three pines with bedrolls beneath it and a sack of provisions, a doleful donkey tied to a tree twenty feet back in the forest. A water barrel sat beneath the canopy, and there were spades and hammers and picks and prybars and empty sacks. The spider cultists from Skerry port (not that he thought they would admit to being spider cultists) were sat watching a dwindling fire, and Killian forced himself not to look at its flame lest it utterly ruin his night vision. Behind him Silver was utterly still, and behind her Small Breygar was invisible in the darkness. With a tense jaw, Killian followed Big Breygar and they moved through the darkness and listened as snatches of conversation drifted to them through the smoke like muttered prophecy.

'*...she won't go, they say, but what other chance do we have...*'

'*...take a week, if ever...*'

'*...fucking size of my hand, swear on her...*'

Silver gently gestured past the camp, and Killian saw nothing, but Big Breygar began to move. They circled the diggers' camp slowly, pausing for a whole minute after Small Breygar broke a twig, and the crackle of fire faded with the conversation as they entered the wood north of the encampment, and Killian saw what Silver had been pointing at. *She must have seen it through the trees.* He had no idea how – to him it was shadow within shadow, but Silver could see better in the darkness than anyone he knew. Rising amongst the forest of black trunks was a ziggurat ten foot tall, made of three stepped tiers. In the weak starlight that broke through the forest canopy the stone was utterly black, but Killian knew it would be granite. Russilan tombs always were, even on isles where that stone was not found.

Quickly they moved to the base of the tomb, and Killian slipped his arrow back into its quiver and set down his bow, adjusted the heavy cutlass on the leather-wrapped sword-hook at his belt. The Breygars took up position facing back to the camp, crouching in shadow with their own cutlasses in hand, heavy sabres with blades weighted at the tip and solid handguards that had both seen long use. With Silver at his side, Killian quickly circled the ziggurat once.

'Type one,' she said, and he didn't respond. Silver loved her types and her classifications, though no Russilan would have recognised them, he was sure. Killian pressed his hand to the stone. The ziggurat was made of square stone blocks half his height tall, and each slotted together with barely a seam. His finger pressed against the stone and found those near-invisible seams, and he felt where the spider cultists had pried and chipped, where they had hammered. They had barely made an imprint, and Killian allowed himself a smile. The tomb was unopened.

'Still fresh!' he called quietly, and heard Silver sniff in response. They began covering the lower tier of the ziggurat, each probing at stones. Killian kept glancing back in the direction of the camp – he could hear no conversation now, could see no flicker of flame, and he could not even see the Breygar twins. The trees surrounding the ziggurat leaned over it as if reaching down towards him, their lower branches snagging at his shirt as he worked his way around, but there was a clearing in the centre of the canopy and Killian could see the stars better. He paused from his inspection and pulled a probing branch clear of his shirt and stared upward until he found the Six Dancers again, and squinted. Had they changed positions? They had names, but he had long forgotten those. His mother had called them sisters, but he had heard other versions over the years. He had sailed long enough to meet people from lands across Morost, and all had their own name for the stars, all had their own meanings. *The stars don't care.* Silver would know. *I'll ask her on the dog-boat, if we make it before sunrise.*

'Here,' Silver called, and Killian went to join her. Silver claimed she could find the keystone by touch, but he could never replicate that and she would tell him no detail. She led his groping hand across rough stone that felt just as the rest did, but after a moment he felt a shivering burn as the stone recognised him, and at once Killian was dropped into the skein. They had found the keystone.

The skein – the pattern beneath the world, above the world, through the world. The connection and concentration of everything: stone and water, sky and soil, life and death. The magic that suffused everything. *At least that is how Starfinder Rurich used to tell it.*

The skein rushed over Killian as if he was falling into cold water and then every sense was magnified, and he could see a layer of vision beyond what was normal – lines of light and darkness and *feeling*, connections between stone and itself, stone and the ground, tree and the sky, tree and the earth. He could see the stone but also where the stone had been, where it might go – that was simple enough with stone until his gaze took in a tree, and then the complexity of the connection within the living thing stunned the breath from him. He could see the endless bugs and creatures, the crow asleep in the high branches, a squirrel in her drey awake and watching, every needle and branch and twig and bough, every movement and potential movement. *Too much.*

Killian focused on the stone. The keystone of the ziggurat was a solid knot of glowing lines a burning purple as seen through a rain shower being lit by a black flame, and he could see inside it, as if he were seeing all sides of it at once from every direction and the interior of it as well, where no light had ever touched, all at once superimposed. The dark forest was illuminated with ten thousand lights of connection, and it was not only his sight. Killian could hear sounds beyond any pitch his ears had ever touched, could feel vibrations on his skin and weight in his heart that hinted at more and more and more. He tasted the air and the sense staggered him, the cold night air, the salt of the sea *so* close and the sweet bitter sap of the pines, his mind sluggish as it tried to make sense of the connection hinted at by taste and touch and smell and sound. He saw the world unfettered by the limitations of his physical senses. He saw his own fingertips, traces of light to his bow, to Silver's hair, to the ziggurat, to themselves. The more he stared the deeper the detail he saw until he felt himself falling, the water that had rushed over him now pulling him down and down like a whirlpool.

It overwhelmed him, as it always did, and Killian sank to his knees and closed his eyes and tried to count breaths the way he had been taught. *Focus on what you can control,* his mother had said. *Be the sea. The tide goes in and out, and nothing will change that.* As a child if he fell into the skein he would panic, would thrash, but his mother would hold him tight. His sister would watch, silent. *Breathe.* The thought conjured her memory to the dark of the forest, and he was sure if he opened his eyes his sister would be at his side as she had been then, ragged and winnowed by hunger and fear, staring. *Breathe.* He pushed Key from his mind and stroked his fingers across the imperfections in the granite. The keystone beneath his hand was different from the other stones – within it was a twist of connection, a knot in the skein. Killian was always good with knots, a sailor had to be good with knots or he would find himself landbound or drowned. Even as he tried to focus on his breath he felt under his fingertips as that knot unravelled under his gaze and suddenly there was movement, sound, movement—

Silver pulled him back by his shoulders and the skein dropped from his senses, and Killian was plunged into the darkness of the forest at night. His sister was not there, and for a moment desolation washed across his mind as his memory of her face began to dim. He sat back into the dirt and rubbed at his knees and waited with Silver kneeling at his side, one hand on his back, and before them the keystone sank inward and the stones around it pushed back and grated to join it, all of them pushed through some unseen mechanism in near silence. Little rocks and earth tumbled down as the stones moved. Killian had seen type-one ziggurats, as Silver called them, dismantled with hammer and drill back in the far Northern Crowns as merchants from Isken and adventurers from the Kelamor Houses tried to plunder their riches. There was no mechanical means that these stones could move in such a way hidden within. It was skein-magic, old Russilan skein-magic to lock away that which was most precious. *And it opened for me,* he thought, and felt that familiar twist in his stomach at what he was about to do.

The stones stopped moving, and there was an entrance four feet high and four feet wide, a darkness deeper than the black of the stone at night. He glanced back towards the digger camp, but there was no sign of movement. Silver was ahead of him, scrambling her lanky body low to the ground and into the tunnel where she sparked a striker and touched it to her bullseye lantern. The little lantern was crafted to shed as little light as possible, with a steel cover to its glass eye that she could adjust. She shielded what little light that escaped from leaving the tunnel with her body, and turned to him expectantly. Killian crawled forward and paused to check again for any break in the silence of the forest, but there was none. He allowed himself a grin.

'Sacks!' he called out lowly, and Small Breygar appeared from the shadow and passed him four burlap sacks with rope cinches. Killian crawled after Silver through the darkness of the entrance tunnel, but the light from her lantern spilling back was enough for him to see the stone beneath his fingers. The air tasted stale, and Killian felt a chill down to his core. He always did after touching the skein, a wave of cold and utter fatigue. He would sleep like a dead man when next he rested, regardless of what treasure they found.

The larger tombs were guarded by fire and magic and traps of all sorts, pits and spikes and runes of power, but the small single tombs never seemed to be. Only locked, guarded by the weight of the stone. For that brief moment as he followed Silver in the cramped entrance tunnel, he let himself feel the weight of that stone, the intention and effort that had been put into making the structure. He understood that it was a mark of respect, to bury someone like this, to work so hard – to quarry stone and ship it across wild water, to carry it through forest and up mountain... He could not make himself believe they did it for the dead – the dead felt nothing; they had gone onward to whatever came next – the endless fire below, or something else again. A tomb like this was for the living, a place to put their loss and give it shape, a reminder. *And there are no more living Russilan.* He pushed his guilt aside and crawled forward.

They entered the central chamber and rose to their feet, and Silver set her lantern on the stone floor, opening its eye to let light spill across the tomb. There was a carved stone sarcophagus at the far end of the room, draped with threadbare tapestries, and to the right a wooden table was covered in riches – jewels, chalices and plates worked in gold, a dagger with a blade of blue stone and a handle embedded with pearls, piles of tumbling shells. Always to the right were the riches. To the left, an identical table held nothing but dust and a few clay tablets of the sort the Russilan had used for writing, thin slate covered in cuneiform scratchings. Killian stared at the gold and smiled.

'Two sacks at least!' he said, but Silver was ignoring him. Her rapier was sheathed and she had one of her sketchbooks out, and she was sketching the room before he ransacked it. Killian's hand twitched impatiently. Spider cultists outside, the Evertree Sisters waiting on his next payment, and here was Silver *drawing*. But that was their deal. She would help him with her books and her maps and her knowledge, her rumours, but in return she could draw everything before he sold it and any writing was *hers* and hers alone. Killian stared at her, wishing her to hurry up. Her mouth was twisted in a frown and her hair was sticking up in all directions where it had escaped its tie behind her head. He felt his breath catch, as it always did these last months when she joined one of their expeditions. Her shirt and trous and boots were all muddied and she was as slick with sweat as he. He went to her and placed a hand on her shoulder gently, stroked a stray strand of hay-blonde hair from her cheek.

'I know you can remember it, dear cartographer,' he said. Silver could remember whatever she had seen, even if she only saw it for a moment. 'Can you at least do the treasure first so I can get to work?'

Silver waved at him absently, and she licked the end of her charcoal again and kept sketching, but after a few moments more she did move off to the table of riches. A table of riches, a table of writings and offerings of food, wine, that would all be dust by now. The ceiling was etched with constellations, careful carving into stone. Killian stared at the tapestries covering the sarcophagus but he couldn't make sense of their faded geometries and patterns; there was no story he could decipher. The dyes had faded, and in the lantern light he could only make out the darkest lines in the intricate patterns. The walls were otherwise unadorned. It was a minor grave.

Silver soon moved on to the table of writing and Killian began filling the burlap sacks, padding each item in a wrap of linen within to prevent *too* much damage. Four chalices, two platters, a string of pearls, that fabulous dagger, three rings. A conch shell with silver filigree across it was full of white coral chunks, and there was a carving of a whale in what must have been jade. It was heavy. There was something that felt like an orb of stone the size of his fist but looked like wood, and in the dim lantern light he could make out no detail. All of it he put into the sacks, along with the rolled cloths next to it that were threadbare and thick with dust. Silver would want to look at those before he cleaned them up and sold them. It was the work of only a few more moments to check beneath the tables for anything fallen, and to cinch his two sacks tight. They had a pleasing heft. Silver was slipping two clay tablets into her satchel from the other table, and she turned to him grinning.

'These are incredible!' she said, and he grinned back and nodded at the sarcophagus.

'Time for the main event,' he said, and she hesitated.

'You will, anyway,' she said. 'You will even if I told you not to.'

Killian's grin faltered. 'I owe—'

'I know what you *owe*,' she said, and then she shook her head and clutched at her satchel. 'I'm sorry. I *know*, Heron. It would not be fair of me to tell, and I cannot ask. So I will not.'

Killian chewed his cheek. The distinction between *not telling* and saying you specifically weren't telling seemed thin to him, and his gut still ached. He remembered the Evertree Sisters and their men, his hand held down flat on a stone table and a chisel pressed above the knuckle until it drew blood. *Your ship and your fingers.* He grimaced and strode to the sarcophagus. His mouth opened to apologise, but he clenched it shut. *I won't apologise for this. The dead are dead.*

'We couldn't bury my mother,' he said, and dragging the tapestries free of the sarcophagus lid he set his hands against the rim and lowered himself down, getting his legs at an angle where they could do the work. The stone of the sarcophagus beneath the tapestries was covered in intricate looped carvings, and within them the shapes of animals, birds, fish, beasts. A horned Carob whale, a great squid. Killian closed his eyes and set his grip.

'I imagine they gave you no choice,' Silver said, drawing close to his side, and Killian heaved. The stone was still, was silent, and he strained and pushed and felt every sinew in his arm tighten until— *There.*

The stone slid free a few inches, and tumbled back to the floor with a thud. Killian rose and shook his shoulders. The interior of the sarcophagus was deep and utterly dark.

'Lantern,' he said, and Silver raised the light high. Within the sarcophagus was a skeleton and around it the usual detritus of the grave – mouldered cloth and hair, a jumble of bone, the occasional twist of flesh or skin wizened beyond all recognition. Methodically Killian began to search with his hands from the top of the sarcophagus to the base, probing gently. A bracelet of jade beads. A ring of silver with a wide face. Ten coins nestled in what might once have been a leather pouch, thick gold pieces with a snake on one side and a bird on the other. A fine chain of gold with a bird skull at its end. He did not recognise the bird from the shape of the bone, but his hand went to the steel heron skull looped at his neck on its leather cord and for a moment the weight of the tomb reached him.

'They gave us a choice,' he said, hands still. 'They said we could have her to bury, but the administration fee was six silver pennies.'

Killian straightened and slipped the necklace into the sack, along with the rest of it, and then rolled his shoulders.

'We should move,' he said. 'Dog-boat by dawn, then on to Samurkan. I want to be far from here before the spider cultists realise they missed out.'

Silver nodded and he led her to the entrance, sparing one last glance around the tomb. *Untouched for how long?* It had been hundreds of years since the Thirst wiped the Russilan from the map, hundreds of years where this tomb was silent and still and whole. A few moments with him and it was bereft. He bowed his head to the sarcophagus.

'Sorry,' he said quietly, and then crouched to enter the tunnel, but Silver's hand stopped him.

'So what happened?' she asked, and she crouched and brought their faces level, her long legs folding like a stork. He smiled at her, because he couldn't think of an alternative.

'What do you think?' he said. 'We couldn't pay, Key and I, so the Cil took our mother. No idea where. Mass grave, maybe. Fed her to the sharks. Compost. Who knows what those bastards do.'

Killian didn't wait for the look of sympathy he knew was coming. *Why did I tell her that?* It was manipulation, maybe. Reminding her of his history in that moment, but it had not been conscious. It had simply felt right to talk of his mother, in this place. He shook his head and crawled forward into the darkness of the tunnel. It was an awkward crawl with two sacks of loot. As he pulled himself to his feet at the other end, dusting himself off as he peered towards the diggers' camp, a torch sprang into light in front of him in a shower of sparks.

Killian's hand dropped to his cutlass and he took a step back and sideways so his body blocked the entrance to the tunnel.

'Thank you,' said a voice he didn't recognise, and in the glare of a burning torch he saw Small Breygar with a blooded face and his arms held behind his back by two of the diggers. Another six were arrayed in a semi-circle around the entrance to the ziggurat, and slowly two of those lit torches from the one already burning until all of them were bathed in yellow flickering light. Silver had not emerged from the tunnel behind him. There was no sign of Big Breygar.

'Thank you?' Killian said, and the man holding the first torch stepped forward. He was a big man in sweat-stained clothes, with thick arms and a bald head and a nose that had seen its share of breaks. As he raised his torch to Killian, he grinned.

'Thought we'd have to break the bloody walls down,' he said, and from his back a tiny creature crawled to rest on his shoulder. A spider the size of Killian's hand, with legs as thick as fingers, its body a deep amethyst blue and its legs a shining metallic black. Its many eyes were rough red garnets, and the torchlight danced across them. *A relu.* Killian had seen a few like this, with people, since the winter the gods went mad. Little spirits once bound, now free to make their own alliances, to live and to die.

'Now you just be putting that treasure down, lad,' the man said, gesturing to Small Breygar. 'We have your watchman. This is our isle; it was empty when we came. Our isle where we can be who we are, and our treasure to find. So you pop that down like a good lad, and get your hands off that bush-cutter.'

The spider twitched its legs in agreement, and Killian raised his hand from his cutlass hilt and grinned. His father always said he smiled too much, but his father was a dour old bastard and wouldn't know salt water if he made his tea with it.

'You've eight,' he said at last, licking his lips. 'Is that a spider cultist thing? Do you always have eight?'

The man's smile faded a little, and from his belt he drew a cudgel of stained wood, dark and smooth, and began adjusting his grip on it.

'This could be easy,' the man said, and Killian just shook his head.

'Life isn't easy,' he said, and the spider cultist grinned, 'but I'll give you a chance. This is your isle, aye, I can see that.'

With one hand he slowly reached up and drew the steel heron skull from beneath his shirt. The diggers fell still.

'It's your isle,' he said slowly, and he took a step forward and held his hands open at his sides. Behind him Silver emerged, and a glance from the corner of his eye showed his bow was gone from where he had left it leaning on the cold stone of the ziggurat. In the flickering torchlight flecks within, the grey stone sparkled as they caught the light, and Killian made himself smile wider. 'It is your island, but this tomb belongs to my people. To the Russilan.'

He gestured to Small Breygar, and then to the dark forest beyond.

'Now I've retrieved the relics of my people – relics it would have taken you, what, a span to dig out? Two span? If you could get past the traps and the curses. If you didn't wake the ghosts. So I have at my feet two sacks. I say, one goes with you back to your town, for your spider – and I mean it sincerely when I say I've no bones with whatever god you truck with. My god is the mad snake, after all. And the other sack goes with us, back to our boat, back to our people. You save yourself a few weeks of pain. No more blood is spilled, on such a fine night. How say you?'

The big man cocked his head and looked round at his team, all of them armed with cutlass or cudgel, three of them with their flaming brands.

'A nice idea,' the man said, and the spider on his shoulder crawled across his neck and came to rest on the other side of his body. 'But as you say, life isn't easy. Why have one for our god, when we could have two? Why don't we take what we like and send you walking home with not a burden to bear, Russilan? And if you've bones about that, we could simply leave yours here – there is a tomb, you see. It wouldn't be so much work.'

Killian's smile faded and he felt Silver tensing beside him. He held a hand to her for calm. He felt the thrum in his blood, the acrid taste of adrenaline at the back of his throat. He wanted to draw his cutlass and leave the forest red with their blood. The familiar thirst filled him, the burning desire to show the threat just how wrong they had been in their choice of victim. He grimaced. *I can't let Silver see me like that.* Killian spat and tucked his heron skull back in his shirt. *Life is never easy.*

'Two reasons, big man,' he said, and hoped he was right. He raised a finger. 'The first, is that you caught the man I left to watch the door, but not the four archers I left in the forest, who right now have their bows trained on your gut. You might get me, but they will certainly get you. Not a pleasant way to go, an arrow to the gut. They might get you back over the Skerry spine to the port. You might even have a halfway decent healer there. But I doubt it. You'll die slow, and you'll feel every second of it.'

On cue from the darkness an arrow streaked and slammed into one of the torches being held by a cultist, sending it spinning to the ground. The cultist cursed and fell back to the dirt, but the big man stayed entirely still. He was still smiling but it was a still thing now, a rictus grimace. The eyes of all the diggers were flitting to the darkened forest, torches waving as they sought their attacker, and Killian exhaled. *Thank you, Breygar.* He tossed one of the sacks forward to the feet to the spider cultist and from it tumbled a golden chalice. Killian straightened up and held up a second finger, and with his other hand drew his cutlass. The torchlight flashed across the burnished steel of his blade, and he held it level and still, tip pointing at the throat of the lead digger.

'The second reason,' he said, 'is that I'm Killian Heroneye. Captain of the *Cutlass Hawk*. I've sailed Burner's Run. I've outrun Cil-Marie galleons, outfought Tullioch spear guard, sailed a rotsurge; I've fought a dozen duels and won a dozen duels. I sate the old Russilan Thirst with blood, not salt water. Whatever you choose to do next, this night ends with me on my ship. One way, you have a sack of gold for your god. The other, you die in this forest and I bring hell to your people. Which will it be?'

The digger squatted down slowly and took the golden chalice in his hand and squinted up at Killian, then nodded.

'With our thanks for your alms, Heroneye,' he said, eyes crinkling, and the amethyst spider crawled down his arm and into the chalice. Standing, he gestured at the two cultists holding Small Breygar and they pushed him forward, tossing his cutlass to the ground after him. Small Breygar grabbed it and scrambled to Killian's side, and Killian picked up his sack of treasure and began to back away to the treeline. The diggers watched them, unmoving, and as darkness covered Killian and his crew Silver leaned close.

'What do we do now?' she asked, and Killian squinted at the figures standing still in the torchlight and let out a shaky breath, felt the adrenaline coursing through every fibre of his body.

'Salt and spit, Silver,' he said, his eye twitching, 'we bloody run!'

2

THE CUTLASS HAWK

'There are of course many more than a thousand islands in the archipelago known as the Thousand Crowns. The island chain runs between Cil-Marie in the west and the mountains of Ona in the east, with the Wind Sea and Carob's Strait to the north and the impassable Doldrums to the south. The influence of the Strait Kingdoms and Cil-Marie is weakly established in the Northern Reach. It is thought that the Southern Crowns are wholly under Tullioch control and Cil-Marie's expanding presence in the Western Isles is a point of concern to many. There are isles with their own mountains and cities, and others where barely a shack may prosper, and every variation in between. Every isle has its king, and every king wants their due.'

– ***The Thousand Crowns***, Alwin Brakspear

They reached the dog-boat as the dawn crested over Skerry isle, the black pine forest softening in pale reddish light that cut through the low cloud. Big Breygar had rejoined them moments into their run, and they had held pace. It had taken them two hours to reach the tomb climbing uphill from the beach, but downhill at a run the time fell away from them as fast as the ground. Killian ran the whole way with a screamer arrow nocked in his bow, Small Breygar carrying the loot and Big Breygar taking the lead, hacking at the underbrush with her cutlass whenever it grew too close. Silver was stoic and silent as they ran, her long legs seeming to eat up the distance, her gait awkward but fast.

The dog-boat was pulled above the high-tide mark – it was a simple thing, a ten-foot-long rowboat pointed at either end with three rows of cramped benches and four oars. The Breygars pushed it down the beach with practised ease as Killian kept his bow on the treeline, scanning for any sign of the spider cultists or whatever beasts roamed Skerry. Before landfall he had searched his charts and notes for any mention of predators and found nothing, but the Crowns were nothing if not predictably chaotic. There were isles scarce bigger than a ship where bone-monkeys would drink your blood as you slept, isles where venomous winged snakes would hunt you through the pine. Skerry had no notes in his charts, but the un-noteworthy fauna were enough to keep his eye on the trees. A century before, the Kelamor had released jaiboar across the Northern Crowns in prelude to an invasion that never came, seeding the isles with their favoured food source, and the spined hogs had teeth that cut through bone like breadcrust and they bred, well, like *jaiboar*.

'How did you know they were spider cultists?' Silver asked, her rapier drawn. She looked near as tired as he felt, her arms covered in scratches from the thick bramble and low branches of the dark forest. There were dark shadows below her eyes, but still there was a glimmer of excitement. *All a game for Silver. Playing at pirates.* He did not think she had ever seen a jaiboar take a hand, a foot. *A face.* She had not woken in the shadow of unknown trees to find a companion dead, all the blood drained form their corpse, bone-monkeys staring down from the trees above, torpid and round with the blood they had drunk. Killian still saw those bone masks when he slept, sometimes.

'Rumour,' he said at last, and he spat on the sand. *No bone-monkeys on Skerry. Get a grip.* 'An inn in Druich, heard they were kicked out of Caroban for worshipping spiders, stole a ship and fled to the Crowns. Rebuilt the old Skerry port. The lad who told me said they were decent enough – no human sacrifices or weird stuff. Just, spiders. They've been keeping their heads down, set themselves up as a water stop.'

The Breygars yelled out behind him and he and Silver ran down the beach and clambered into the dog-boat. Killian welcomed the freezing water of the gentle surf as it soaked him up to his waist, taking a heartbeat to splash water over his face. Then he was in the boat and he allowed himself a moment of calm. Small Breygar helped him haul Silver in, not that there was much of her to haul – for all her height, the scholar was light and lithe. The Breygars began rowing without waiting for an order, pulling on the long oars and speeding the small boat out into the secluded bay. The *Cutlass Hawk* was moored past a rocky promontory to the north. As they rowed, Killian checked the cinch on their haul once more and stared out at the sea as he unstrung his bow. The bowstring was soaked, and would need cleaning and drying if it was to be salvageable. The sunrise turned the flat water to burnished copper, with only the occasional ripple dancing once they got past the surf lapping at the beach.

'*I'm Killian Heroneye,*' Big Breygar said suddenly, her voice husky. '*I once outflew a gull, and then outdrank a fish. I've got a big sword that is so thirsty. Haven't you heard?*'

Small Breygar laughed and Killian felt his cheeks flush. Next to him Silver's perpetual frown twitched a little as she turned to regard him.

'*I'm the best sailor in the whole dog-boat,*' Small Breygar added, and his sister hooted. His face was still smeared with blood, and one of his eyes was swollen and red. The spider cultists had been gentle, all things considered. There were plenty of isles where Small Breygar would be dead, the rest of them likely with him.

'I don't sound like that,' Killian said, and the Breygars both laughed.

'Maybe not now,' Big Breygar said. She had a gap between her teeth and a wide smile, but her dark eyes flashed with something other than humour even as she grinned. Weighing him up. *Always weighing.*

'It worked,' he said flatly, and the Breygars nodded and kept rowing. They knew him well enough by now to understand there were moments for wit, and moments to remember who the captain of the ship was. They'd seen him when his blood was hot. *When the thirst had me.* They joked no more. Skerry fell behind them, the thin spine of little mountains running up its core casting long shadows over the forest and the bay. The boat scudded around the rocky coast and Killian saw the *Cutlass Hawk* and chewed on his lip. *She looks strong.*

The ship was a simple caravel, eighty foot long and twenty-five wide. At its heart the central mast stood proud, and on the raised aftcastle the smaller second mast swayed in unison. The ship was lateen-rigged, with triangular sails running on long wooden yards mounted at an angle on each mast. Both were furled tight, and he could see a single figure on deck – probably his first mate, Pollos Twice-Kissed. The dark wood of the hull caught the morning sun and Killian tried to savour the moment, tried to see the night as a victory. *One bag of loot is better than none,* he told himself, *and nobody died.* But in the back of his mind he pictured the sack he had forfeited – chalices and shells, a platter, a string of pearls. He couldn't help but tally up the price they might have fetched. He pictured the faces of the Evertree Sisters, their jagged teeth and cold eyes. They were Tullioch. They would not care that nobody had died; they would only care what he had brought in.

Next to him, Silver stirred.

'*I'm Captain Killian Heroneye of the* Cutlass Hawk,' she said, lowering her voice and adding a swagger of braggadocio to every word. '*I've got twenty Russilan archers in every tree, and—*'

Killian stopped her with a raised hand.

'Enough, now,' he said. 'We came here for loot; we are leaving with loot. Everyone is alive. You got your drawings. And none of you are paid to make jokes.'

The Breygars lowered their heads and rowed, and Silver frowned at him and sighed, then turned her gaze to the sea. She thought she knew him better than the Breygars, perhaps, but not for as long. She had not seen him as they had. He was not her captain. *She is something else entirely.* In an attempt to make nice he withdrew one of the coins from the sack of loot and handed it to her. Silver nodded her thanks and studied it intensely, her fingertip tracing over the raised lettering surrounding the icons on each side. On one face a glyph of crossed lines, a sinuous curve struck through by five shorter lines. On the other face, a tree and three stars. The only sound was the sea and the soft splashes of the oars, but that was enough. As they drew closer to the *Cutlass Hawk*'s anchorage a current began to pull them south, but the Breygars persisted. Killian was tired, and so he closed his eyes and waited.

They pulled the dog-boat alongside the ship and above them Pollos Twice-Kissed began rousing the crew, his deep voice booming as he yelled.

'Up, loves!' he cried. 'Fast hands and fast heads!'

Killian waited as the Breygars made fast with the haul ropes, and then Pollos dropped a ladder and he scrambled up it, Silver behind him.

'Head south-west,' Killian said as soon as his boots settled on the deck. The ship looked in fine enough order, though a pile of wood shavings sat where Pollos had clearly been whittling. Killian frowned at those and then closed his eyes. He really was exhausted. Pollos retreated into the aftcastle and returned with a skin of water and a map in a heavy leather roll. Killian took a drink and Pollos glanced nervously at the shores of Skerry as if expecting pursuit at any moment. The first mate was a beast of a man, a hulking Undal with shoulders an axe handle wide and hands and face weathered by a life on the water and scarred heavily on one side. *Kissed once by his mother, and once by saltfire,* so he said. Killian wasn't so sure about the former, but the twisted burns were from saltfire sure enough. Pollos's thick hair was tied back in a loose knot and his heavy jaw was clean-shaven as ever, and he stared at Killian intensely. Behind him the crew were emerging out from below deck, moving to help the Breygars haul up the dog-boat and make it fast.

'We do all right, Captain?' Pollos asked, and Killian shrugged and lifted the bag of loot.

'Enough,' he said. The Breygars would surely tell the full tale to the crew. Pollos laid out the map on the top of a barrel and Killian focused and found Skerry, and then traced his finger to Samurkan. 'Take the eastern channel around the Lances, and then pick up on the Horse Water. Wake me if anything strange happens this morning, aye?'

Pollos nodded, but stopped Killian leaving with a touch at the elbow.

'We'll be needing a new tide-mage if we want to sail proper, Captain,' he said quietly, and Killian did not meet his eye. 'Affy Burngull has been dead a moon and more now. We need someone to read the currents and the reefs and the wind. River work, reef work, can't be done with no tide-mage. It limits us.'

Killian chewed at his lip. 'I know,' he said. 'Samurkan will have one. We'll drop Silver, visit the Sisters, get a new mage, and then it's open water.'

'Aye!' Pollos responded, his energy at once rejuvenated, and Killian headed for his cabin. Silver was already inside sat in his chair at his table, poring over the clay tablets she had retrieved. His own effects were pushed aside haphazardly.

'Please,' he said wearily, throwing his sword belt into a lidless sea chest. 'Use my room, Silver. Move my things. Don't worry about the state of your boots, not a worry at all. Do the dead have anything of interest to say, this time?'

Silver did not look up.

'You are always like this after we rob a tomb,' she sighed at last. 'So serious. And I'm the one who is meant to be full of reservations. Is the mighty Captain Heroneye feeling the weight of history?' She gently leaned back and turned her gaze from the tablets to him. He shrugged and went to his washbasin and filled it from a ewer of cold water, and began to undo the ties on his shirt. As he did she rose languidly with the angular grace of a hunting cat and came behind him, her long arms reaching around and embracing him before her dextrous fingers began to undo the final ties on his shirt. There was a tarnished mirror fixed to the wall and he caught her expression as she leaned into his shoulder, a hunger in the set of her jaw. Killian closed his eyes and tried to let go of the image of Affy Burngull, dying, screaming. *We need a new mage.* He tried to let go of the numbers in his head, the numbers he owed the Evertree Sisters. *The Skerry haul won't be enough.* He tried to forget the burning intensity in Big Breygar's eyes, even as she laughed and rowed. *She will never forgive me.*

'Remind me of our deal, Heron,' Silver said in his ear, and Killian stopped moving and took her hands in his, held them still and close.

'When we are going after the Russilan tombs or other historical oddities, you tag along. You get your time when it is first opened. Any writing or artistry is yours; any treasure is mine. In exchange, your knowledge and your expertise.'

Silver pulled the shirt from his back and kissed his neck. He shivered and tried to hold on to his thoughts. Above all, he needed to be free and clear of the Evertree Sisters. The memory of the cold chisel edge pressed into his knuckles, the surety of it, burned in his mind.

'Anything else?' Silver whispered, and Killian shook the Evertree Sisters from his mind and turned to her, and pulled her shirt over her head in a single motion.

'No questions,' he said, and tilted his head up and met his mouth with hers. When she finally drew back, she repeated his words back to him.

'No questions,' she said. 'The dead always have something interesting to say, Captain. But it is not for you to hear it.'

He felt the *Cutlass Hawk* move as the wind caught her sails and heard Pollos yelling at the crew outside, and Silver drew him to his bed.

Blade Mournchild beat the first man to death with his own boots. They were heavy boots. The other man tied in a heap by the cellar wall could not help but watch. The cellar was bright – some preferred darkness for this sort of work, believing it would inspire the imagination of the captive and ensure their cooperation. Blade Mournchild preferred light, as bright as it could be. His vision was a little muddled – darkest blue today – after he added the necessary drops and pigments to his eyes. Lieutenant-yeux du Lune – Marion – made no mention of it anymore. Early in their partnership she had chastised him for impinging his operational effectiveness, in her words, but no enemy had made Blade Mournchild bleed in more than a decade. He took the chastisement, and added drops to his eyes anyway. It was necessary. Mournchild took his time with the beating; after each barrage of heavy blows he dragged the man across the floor to the wall and held up his face to his true captive. Through the blue tint overlaying his eyes, the blood was as black as Mournchild's armour.

'Please!' the tied captive said, many times, and variations thereof. Blade Mournchild did not listen – this was not the time for listening. He did not ask the man he was beating any questions – he was just a man who happened to be in the tanner's shop when Blade Mournchild arrived. A convenience. Better to have an example. The man had his boots off when they had arrived and had been complaining of the leatherwork or something similar, and Blade Mournchild had let inspiration carry him.

Finally, his victim lay utterly still. The boots were ruined. Mournchild threw them onto the body and waited a long moment, listening. There was no sound of disturbance above. The city watch would come, eventually. Even in a city as large as this, such screams would be investigated. Lieutenant Marion was above, drinking the tanner's bitter coffee and reading the man's papers and records.

'I have three questions for you, tanner,' Blade Mournchild said. He wiped his face with a cloth from his belt pouch, and grimaced at the black blood cloying to it. His ceremonial paint was ruined, *again*. Even after so many years it was no easy thing to get it just right, and to be outside without it would earn him another penance. He sighed and drew up the hood to his cloak, lest the tanner see his face without his paint in order.

'If I answer, you will let me live?' The tanner panted, and Blade Mournchild reached down a gauntleted hand and gripped the man's shoulder. He squeezed until he heard the collarbone crack, and then waited for the screams to subside into shaking sobs.

'No, tanner,' he barked, and huffed a laugh. 'If you answer, I will let you *die*.'

He gave that a few moments to sink in and then lowered down to his knees. His armour was heavy steel plate, but the smiths of Uradech had done him proud. He retained near full mobility, and years of constant use made his motion in the armour and the shirt of mail and leather beneath it easier than it was on those rare occasions when he removed it all. He held the tanner's jaw in his hand and considered the bone beneath his fingers. It was such a simple thing, the breaking of flesh and bone. Most did not realise just how little force was required, if you understood the right place to apply the pressure. Mournchild's teachers had been thorough.

'You sold a child to my colleague on the promise she was Russilan. This was not the case. Did you know this?'

'You must believe me! I—' Mournchild gripped the man's jaw tighter and silenced him, and then reached down with his other hand and found the gap in the broken collarbone and dug his armoured fingers in. The tanner writhed against his bonds and his eyes were manic. *Perfection.* Mournchild did not need the answer to the first question. *The first question is simply to focus his mind,* Lieutenant Marion had said.

'The second question,' Mournchild said, 'is personal to *me*. Do you know the five names of Baal, and the endless fire below? Do you follow the great Judges? What sect or creed are you, leather-man?'

The tanner was sobbing and all of the usual things, and Mournchild did not bother listening to the babbling. Again, this was a standard tactic. Show them they are weak; show them you do not really care. Ask them questions unrelated to your true goal, where there is no clear correct answer. Make them desperate to please. Remind them of their god, their afterlife, the punishment that is to come. Do all of this, and then ask your true question.

Blade Mournchild hushed the man and drew his dagger. It was a long piece of black metal, as matte as his armour. The guard was wrapped in thick layers of worn leather, and the blade was impeccably sharp. On its surface etched in the circular script of Uradech the five holy names of Baal, the god above. The glyphs etched into the blade were filled with silver, then rubbed with ash from the morning's fire so as to be all but invisible. *As above, so below.* Mournchild worshipped no spirits, no Judges. They were powers, but there was an invisible power beyond them all. *Baal, Morost, Pendar, Tulu, Salaman. Invisible to those who do not know the portents.* He watched the torchlight dance in the blue of the tanner's eyes, and he traced the tip of the dagger along the tanner's throat and asked the only question the lieutenant actually wanted answered.

'Who sold you the girl, and where do we find them?'

After he cleaned his blade on the tanner's corpse he doused the torches in sand buckets and clambered up the stairs.

The cellar of the tanner's shop stank of raw hides and chemicals, and now fresh piss and blood and death atop the old, but Mournchild ascended and entered clean air once more. He found Lieutenant Marion sat at the tanner's counter leafing through a sheaf of papers, cradling a simple clay cup in one hand.

'Rather a lot of screaming, Mournchild,' she said, and he did not think there was a question and so he simply waited. She soon grew bored with the papers and threw them down. Since their escape from Burner's Run the lieutenant had been on edge – thrice she had yelled at him, and more than once he had heard her weeping in the night during the long voyage home. He did not know why the demon-snake Zalan allowed their ship to leave. He did not care. It was a monster. *These islands are full of demons and monsters.* He had seen Antian and Tullioch walking the streets, fearless – the little mole-dog creatures and the hulking lizard-folk would know their place as lesser beings in Uradech, would defer properly to the children of Baal. *This place is a madness.* When their ship had limped to the nearest isle after escaping Burner's Run, the locals had found them, and to a one they wore elaborate headdresses in the shape of seabirds. Nobody mentioned it, but Mournchild itched at the memory. *Uncivilised,* he thought, *godless, feckless children.*

'A mage from the Arcanists' Guild,' he said at last, and Marion's eyebrow lifted. 'By the name of Darnielle.'

'A leatherworker bought a child from a mage?'

Mournchild shrugged. 'Orphans are taken to the Arcanists' Guild if they have a capacity for the skein-magic. This one failed her classes, and the tanner found the mage wandering the slave markets outside of town looking to sell. He got to the mage before anyone else managed, and got the girl cheap. The mage claimed she was Russilan – that many of the orphans were. Said they were stronger in the skein, if they were Russilan.'

Marion stared at him, and Mournchild pulled his hood lower. His masters in the church in Uradech would be ashamed of him, speaking to a godless one with the paint on his face askew. Mournchild had done many things his masters would find shame in, since they sent him away.

'Samurkan is so *provincial*,' Marion said at last. 'Bloody Isken dogs with their toy guilds. They are children. Back to the inn, Mournchild. I have dinner with the ambassador this evening. Tomorrow we will go to the Arcanists' Guild and find this *Darnielle*. Perhaps they have some lore on Burner's Run, and perhaps another child for us. Gods know there were no Russilan at that pitiful excuse for a slave market. I am loath to try again with nothing but another child and hope, but our time runs short. Jean du Cilcan must be found, no matter the cost.'

They left the tanner's shop burning, and many eyes saw them and many heads turned away. Cil-Marie did not act beyond its borders with any regularity, but when it did those with sense would avert their gaze. Walking three steps behind Lieutenant Marion, Blade Mournchild silently repeated his catechism, the five names of Baal the creator. *Baal, Morost, Pendar, Tulu, Salaman.* He had been sent to Cil-Marie to serve Lieutenant Marion for a reason, and she had been sent to the Crowns for a reason. Strange creatures, monsters, foreign guilds, odd cults. He would not be affected – he would remain pure. *And I will discover why my masters sent me here; why the lieutenant is so important to them.* He gazed at the street hoping for portent or sign, but there was only stone and dirt. With a sigh he pulled his hood down and kept one hand on his sword hilt.

It was three days at sea to make Samurkan from Skerry. The winds in the Coracles were easier than in the Southern or Eastern Crowns, predictable in their uncanny nature. Winds in the Crowns were far less constant than in the Wind Sea or the Carob Strait, but Killian had spent a decade sailing these waters and his charts were as good as anyone else's. The one truth of the Crowns was that wherever you sailed the prevailing wind blew towards Burner's Run, but there were so many isles and there was a saying his mother had taught him: *islands make their own weather*. Killian took the ship south and east past the Lances, a series of tall rock spires of brutal grey full of gulls and puffins and little black-backed skuas. The sharp grey of the stone was broken only by gnarled shrubs that clung to the cliffsides and tufts of mossy grass. There was no safe anchorage to be had and nothing to climb to anyway, in the Lances – no water, no land. Only cliff leading to cliff leading to air.

'Perhaps a nice view from the top,' Silver said, leaning on the rail with her sketchbook, and Killian just shook his head.

'There is no top,' he said, 'only air.'

Silver's sketches were not the artistic interpretations or romanticised drawings one might buy in the more urbane ports – they were hurried, scratched things, thick with annotation. A scholar's reminder, rather than an artist's vision. She ignored him and kept on drawing.

As they drew near enough to attract the attention of the ravenous birds, he set Galli and Nils to throwing nets on lines. The two scampered barefoot, Galli with her mat of silver hair tied back with twine, Nils with his thick brown curls pushed back from his eyes with a strip of cloth. Both the children were sinewy and callused, clad in simple wool, worn and patched, and they chattered and smiled and joked as they set to fetching the nets. They caught a handful of birds that lighted on the rail of the ship in the day whilst the rest of the crew manned the sails and lines. Timmult was perched high in the little crow's nest, ostensibly on watch, but over the persistent thrum of the living wind Killian could hear the thin song of Timmult's reed pipes drifting down. He left Pollos at the helm and Renard and the Breygars hauling lines and retreated to his cabin, and from his sea chest drew a small lockbox and a battered notebook and tried to settle the accounts. There was the water on Skerry, and food as well. New sailcloth, twelve bone sail needles. Provisions fresh and stored, more unguent for Renard's medical store after they used so much of her supplies after what happened with Affy Burngull. He counted the scarce coin in the lockbox and then stared at the notebook where a single number was writ large at the top of the latest page.

EVERTREE SISTERS, 4270 DUCATS

Killian felt the panic rising in his chest, the bile in his gut twisting, and so he carefully put the notebook inside the lockbox, put the lockbox back in his sea chest, and went back on deck and took the helm and lost himself in the minutiae of running the *Cutlass Hawk*.

'Tide-mage,' Pollos said to him when they hit a path of smooth water and constant wind, 'and a ballista on the front wouldn't go amiss, Captain. More corsairs in the eastern reach this year, Blue Darrow's lot, the Crows, the Black Moon gang. They might think twice at that. That or a few good archers.'

Killian shook his head.

'Tide-mage, aye,' he said, 'but a ballista won't stop a corsair. If they are close enough to see that, they are close enough to see we are running a bare crew with no heavies. When we get to Samurkan get word from the docks, find out where the raiding is bad this year and we will steer clear. Maybe Concarneau, if we can find the papers to reach the port.'

As the sun faded they made anchor in the lee of the southernmost Lance, and Killian had Nils and Galli light a single lamp on deck. As darkness fell the sheer height of the Lances was felt only as a presence, a shadow against the darkened cloud beyond. The endless chatter of the seabirds came down to them from on high, a thousand calls all intermingled with the sound of wind over rock and water. Nils and Galli were the youngest of the crew, barely more than children, and Killian left the two of them to it. They spent the night waiting for the skua chicks to land on the deck, flat-footed and unsure. They were attracted by the light. The children netted and clubbed them and by morning they had a barrelful, mainly skua chicks, but some others mixed in that had been fool enough to hope for an easy meal discarded by the ship.

That day the wind held true and the skies stayed clear, Galli and Nils plucking feathers and sorting dead birds, Silver staring at her clay tablets and muttering to herself, and Killian contemplating again the ducats he owed the Evertree Sisters. More than he had seen in his life, more than he could picture. He spent the day chewing his lip and checking the manifest. That night they were on open water – there were small isles visible in all directions, but Killian's charts of the run between the Lances and Samurkan were old, and he didn't know the reefs and shoals well enough to trust the ship close in to land without a tide-mage. That night he broke out a bottle of rum for the crew to celebrate a job well done, even as he scratched his finger with his thumbnail to draw focus from his growing anxiety. The Breygars gave an exaggerated retelling of their boastful escape from the spider cultists, and Pollos Twice-Kissed threaded a wick through one of the skua chicks to make a lamp.

'I learned this from an Antian in the Eastern Holdfast,' he said, and those who had not seen the trick before crowded around to see better. Timmult and Small Breygar did not bother – they focused on their rations of rum.

'Do the Antian sail?' Galli asked, and Pollos smiled at her and chewed on his lip as he tried to force the stiff wick threaded on a sharp stick down further in the chick's gullet. It was gruesome work, his hands already slick with oil from the creature's feathers. The Antian were something between moles and dogs in appearance, furred and snouted but with nimble hands. Their ceramic and metallurgy work was the envy of half the Strait kingdoms, and Killian had noted Galli taking every opportunity to ask after them. They were rare outside their holdfasts, rarer still in the western reach where Cil-Marie held sway. They were afforded no rights by the Cil.

'They sail when they must,' Pollos said at last, 'but they've the under-roads, lass. Far below the water, tunnels in the seabed itself between their holdfasts. Most don't leave, but them that do are no more averse to sailing than any who've grown up on land. Fast hands, too. Mind you, I'd rather a Tullioch.'

Timmult sniffed at that but made no comment. He had lost three fingers to a Tullioch a decade past, though he would not be drawn on the circumstances. Only that he didn't care for them.

Pollos set his prize lamp atop a worn barrel and with great ceremony lit a taper. The little bird was fat and sat crooked, its web feet splayed. Pollos lit the wick and the bird was so full of fat and oil that it burned bright. The firelight danced over the burns on Pollos's face, catching and casting shadow on every ripple of scarred flesh, and the man was smiling. All gathered round – the children Galli and Nils, steadfast Renard and Timmult and Pollos the sailors, and the Breygar twins. The absence of Affy Burngull, their old tide-mage, was not mentioned. Pollos had not mentioned it again since Killian's latest affirmation that they would indeed hire one, and Big Breygar had made no note of his death save earlier in the day when Timmult asked why they were going the long way past the Lances instead of cutting through.

'Captain let our mage get et by goblins,' Big Breygar said, in a carrying whisper. 'Can't cut through the Lances without a tide-mage. We're stuck to the big lanes until we get a new one.'

Killian had ignored that, and as they sat in the light of the skua lamp he stared away from it and up at the stars. The first constellation that night had been nothing special – it was simply the warrior, with his sword and his shield. The warrior was bright and came high in the sky, and so was often seen before the other stars that lingered and danced over the horizon as the moon waxed and waned. *It doesn't mean violence is my fate.* His mother would have balked at so simple an interpretation. *Conflict,* she would have said, *strength.* She would have had readings depending on where in the sky the warrior was first seen – *and did you glance his spear or his shield or his face or his boots?* Each would have a different meaning. *She could not predict her end, though.* He wondered at that. *What star did she see, the night before they took her?*

Silver sketched the skua lamp, and then when the ration of rum was gone Killian spread on the deck the loot from the tomb for the crew's inspection. The crew assessed the wares, and then he gathered them up again and gave each of them one of the heavy gold coins from the sarcophagus, with a snake on one side and a bird on the other. He even gave those to Nils and Galli. The rest he piled back into the sack. Even as he did it, he knew he could not afford it. *But what price can I put on their loyalty?* The children were loyal enough, and Pollos, but the Breygars and Timmult and Renard were hired crew. They were loyal as long as they were paid. *And Big Breygar hates me.*

'That'll get us right,' he said, 'and then on to the next job. We'll stay three days in Samurkan. Pollos will sort lots for who stays with the *Hawk* on which day. Any of you aren't back on deck dawn of the fourth day, we will see you some other journey.'

Killian went to retreat to his cabin, purposefully leaving the rum bottle uncorked next to the stuttering light of the skua lamp. The crew would not want to drink rum with him, and he had to keep his distance, and already the drink he had taken had sent his thoughts down maudlin sea lanes. He saw Silver hesitate, but then she stood to follow him. Before he left he turned back to the stars. He could see the burning lance, faint on the horizon – a trail of a dozen stars ending in a bright red mote, far brighter than the others. His mother had never told him what the burning lance portended – or if she had, he had not listened well enough. Reaching back into the sack he produced the bracelet of jade beads he had taken from the sarcophagus, and tossed it to Big Breygar.

'If not for Big, we would all be spider food,' he said. She held the bracelet and stared at him, eyes unreadable in the light of the burning skua. Killian ducked his head and went to his cabin, and Silver followed. There was a long moment of silence, and then on the deck they heard Renard singing. 'Three daughters of the mist, unkind'. It was an Undal folk song that Pollos had taught her, accompanied only by the creak of line and timber and the endless murmur of the sea.

Kiss your daughters, count their toes,
hear the daughters, wail and woe,
The first daughter, she is a-sleeping,
    the second daughter, she is a-gone,
the mother, she is forgotten, the third daughter,
    she is a-bone.

Heed the story, hear her wail, see the croft in ash,
the daughter of the Mist alone, claws of iron a-flash;
Spare my child, the farmer cries;
back, ye beast! the soldier.
Wail and woe the daughter brings,
and takes the debt that's owed her.
Kiss your daughters, count their toes,
hear the daughters, wail and woe,
Kiss your daughters, sing so sweet,
sate the daughters, peace for meat.

They sat in silence as Renard sang, and then Silver pulled him to his bed.

'The Undal are such *barbarians*,' she said, and he laughed as he kissed her neck.

'You like barbarians.'

On deck, laughter and then the thin sound of Timmult's tin whistle and the scrape of crates as the crew cleared space for dicing.

'What happened to Affy Burngull?' Silver asked, eventually. They lay together in his bed, narrow as it was, pressed close, a thick blanket pulled tight over them to fend off the cold of the sea at night.

'No questions, I thought.'

Silver squirmed against him and was silent, and then tapped her long fingers on his chest until he gripped her hand to stop her. This was their fourth voyage together since they met two years before, their third sharing his bed, and their rules were simple. *No questions, no feelings, no ties.* Her rule and his rule and their rule, in that order. She wanted to focus on her work, not the prying questions of the dubious treasure hunter, and he insisted on reciprocity. When they fell into each other, he wanted to keep her at the arm's length he kept them all. And both had agreed, a voyage was a simple thing, but beyond the bounds of the ship, each owed the other nothing.

'Big Breygar isn't happy about it,' she said, and he let go of her hand to pull her closer.

'They shared a bunk,' he said at last, and sighed. 'A rotsurge got him. One of those nightmare storms that drives in from the west, it rolled across an isle whilst we were on land settling a deal with some pearl divers. Strange folks, big eyes, feet and hands webbed like frogs.'

'I've never seen a rotsurge,' she said slowly, and he could hear the interest in her voice. He turned his head to the wall of his cabin.

'Neither had Affy,' he said. 'Acid rain. Red clouds that eat flesh to bone. Lightning, more lightning than you've ever seen, black and red. Clouds that aren't like any storm the sea ever sent. And then where the lightning hits, beasts and monsters. Goblins – shark-skinned, black-eyed beasts. They ripped Affy to shreds as we were running for the boat. I'd seen one before, Pollos more than one. The pearl divers fled to the water. When a rotsurge comes, you run or you hide. You can't fight a *storm*.'

They lay in silence, and Silver moved her head onto his chest, breath hot on his skin. She did not ask, and so he told her.

'She blames me, because I ordered that we run, and I didn't wait for Affy. She blames me because I'm the captain, and when something goes wrong it is my fault.'

'Was it your fault?'

'Of course it was. I'm the captain. If something goes wrong, it *is* my fault. We could have waited for him, could have gone back for him. I made the choice. Another lesson from the world.'

Silver drew her hand back from him and into her chest, and drew her head from him and lay next to him, together but separate.

'The world doesn't exist to give us lessons,' Silver said, and they lay in silence.

Killian closed his eyes and did not sleep for a long time.

Samurkan

Samurkan, year 1131 Isken – **From the charts of the *Cutlass Hawk*,** Captain Killian Heroneye

3

SAMURKAN BY NIGHT

'In the third moon of the 43rd year of the Stone (year 1124 Isken), in the depths of winter, a madness descended upon the gods. In the Undal Protectorate there was report of a battle of great skein-wrecks, and the bear of Undal Anshuka awoke from three centuries of slumber. The wolf of Ferron, Lothal, was reborn. In the Wind Sea, the Bird and Whale left their waters and roved wide. Amongst the isles of the Crowns, Zalan the serpent began attacking ships. In Ona the Father Dragon brought a storm beyond any seen before that raged a hundred nights. In every land, the great Judges broke pattern and covenant, and the endless little spirits of the world grew wild. In the decade since, the Judges roam with rage, and our caution has been rewarded.'

– ***Letter to the Council of Isles on the Madness of the Spirits***, Anneli Thirdblood of Holt Suolaa

Killian strode down the gangplank of the *Cutlass Hawk* dressed in a preposterous coat of black with ruffles of white lace at every conceivable opening and a wide-brimmed hat to match. There were buttons of pearl and lacquered shell and beneath it he wore his simple leggings and shirt of black and a belt with a buckle of worked silver. His worn cutlass was sheathed awkwardly behind him lest it detract from the ensemble. He had shaved this voyage's beard but left behind a moustache that he had rubbed with oil, and he wore an eyepatch of blue silk over his left eye. Behind him Silver was smothered in something between a priest's robe and a mage's cloak, with a veil of red lace twisted around her face as if she were from Lello. The robe was a deep red, with lustrous silver thread picking out arcane patterns.

At the bottom of the gangplank, the floating dock bobbed in time with the ship behind and the dockmaster waited along with two heavies. He was fat, which Killian took to be a good sign – few were fat in Samurkan on the Isken government payroll unless they were open to the realities of life. Smiling, he swept his hat from his head and cut as regal a bow as he could.

'*Cutlass Hawk*, is it?' the dockmaster said, and behind him the two thugs were cricking their necks in a simultaneous pantomime of threat. Killian felt his gut tighten. *Shit.* With a glance over his shoulder he confirmed that the Breygar twins had indeed scrubbed the ship's name from the hull, and so he simply did what he always did. He kept smiling.

'Haven't heard of that one, Harbourmaster,' he said, and with a flourish he gestured at Silver. 'We are the *Rock of True Blessing*, out of Lello. I am Captain Perrinous Silhat, and this is the illustrious skein-mage Tellactor. We come with silk and wine and had heard Samurkan is the best place to trade with the illustrious Isken guilds, may the sun never set upon them.'

The dockmaster grunted and crossed his arms. Killian bowed again for good measure, and nudged Silver to do the same but Silver just stood in her shambles of a red robe, clearly trying to look mysterious.

'Lello,' the dockmaster said, savouring the word. 'Well. Your ship does rather match the description I was given of one *Cutlass Hawk*, which owes twelve ducats in unpaid docking fees. And whose captain is one Killian Heroneye. That is not you? Brown eyes, scar on his cheek. Something of an idiot.'

Killian smiled again and smoothed his moustache with his thumb, because now he was getting a good feeling. Next to him Silver was stock-still, but Silver always panicked too soon. Killian took a moment to glance up at the city. Beyond the forest of masts in the wide shelter of the bay, the city sprawled in all directions up the mountainsides of the island. Samurkan was the self-proclaimed jewel of the Coracles, the lush group of isles making up the heart of the Northern Reach that were more easily accessible to the powers of the Strait Kingdoms. A pressing wind from the west made the pennants and flags stand proud, and there were so many of them. Each shop and manor was festooned, showing allegiance to one guild or another, or perhaps more than one, each flag intricately painted with sigil or shield or runic design. Samurkan was Isken's lead outpost in the Crown Isles, and the folks here were even more desperate than those at home to show they were loyal subjects of their guilds.

The buildings were all in that ridiculous Isken style, with circular pillars by the dozen and draped canopies casting shadow over the walkways and doorways. The city was bustling and alive and the docks were busy, and nobody was watching the dockmaster and his two men at the furthest corner of the floating dock. Just another ship, in a port too busy for that to be a moment of note. Killian looked for the inevitable urchin, and found two – gaunt children dressed in thick patched wool, lingering by a pile of crates nearby. He did not let his gaze linger. With a glance he could see ships from Cil-Marie, Kelamor, Caroban, Isken, Undal, the Southern Crowns – there was even a Tullioch coral ship, but it was far enough he could not pick out the detail on it. *No need for anyone to notice a little old thing like the Hawk.* Killian looked upward and licked his lips. Herringbone clouds high above, and a pale winter sun.

'No,' he said, returning his gaze to the dockmaster and still smiling, 'not ringing a bell I'm afraid. Sounds like a handsome fellow, though. Is he in much trouble?'

The dockmaster smiled back and smoothed down his tunic, then retrieved and opened up a leather-bound journal from his belt pouch. Killian did not stop smiling as he sized up the two toughs through his peripheral vision – they were both dockside brawlers, heavy in every sense of the word. Scarred and broken knuckles gripping thick cudgels. *At the very least,* he thought, *I can outrun them.* Of course that wouldn't solve the problem of Silver standing next to him wrapped up like a Lello royal on their wedding night, or the *Hawk* behind with sails lowered and mooring ropes tied. The dockmaster was reading his journal, tongue between his teeth. He squinted up at Killian.

'Well,' he said, lingering on the word and smacking his lips. 'He is certainly a man of interest. Three ducats from the Evertree Sisters to hear of his arrival, and two from the Crab guild, two from the Spice guild, one from the owner of the Long Crossbow tavern. That is... eight ducats, simply for saying his name. Not like your name, Captain...'

The dockmaster paused there and waited for Killian to repeat the pseudonym he had used, but Killian had already forgotten it. He stopped smiling for a moment and settled his hat back on his head, rotating the rim so the trailing strand of white lace wouldn't obscure his vision. The hat had belonged to a wine merchant out of Kelamor, and Killian had won it playing chissick, and it was the worst piece of clothing he had ever encountered.

'Well,' he said, 'well well well. I do see, dear dockmaster. I do see your problem, and I applaud your diligence. The Crab guild you say? Nasty, nasty business. Nasty creatures! I never eat them, myself. Too much like spiders. Presumably to confirm my ship, the, uh, *Rock of True Blessing*, is indeed hailing from Lello and my comrade the skein-mage and I are ignorant of this Killian fellow and his presumably *perilous* crew, well, that sounds time-consuming. Is there perhaps a tithe we could pay now, directly to you, to ensure that we are logged correctly and can go about our business?'

The dockmaster smiled as Killian knew he would. *Show me a straight dockmaster, and I've got land in Old Ferron you might be interested in.* From there it was a simple haggle, twenty ducats countered by ten and so on, until nobody was happy but the deal was done.

'You are registered, Captain Perrinous Silhat, skein-mage Tellactor, of the *Rock of True Blessing*. Two ducats per day to be paid upon departure, *and they will be paid* before departure. If you break guild law whilst on Isken soil in Samurkan, you will pay guild fines be they gold, time, or blood.' The dockmaster smiled nastily and leaned in. 'If you do happen upon Killian Heroneye, dear sirs, I would recommend you encourage him to keep a low profile. The docks are always accommodating of an enterprising man, but the higher tiers of Samurkan are full of prying eyes. Good day!'

The dockmaster strode away fifteen ducats richer, and next to Killian, Silver ripped the red lace veil from her face. She was pink-cheeked and sweating.

'What in the burning hell was the point in that, Heron?' she said, and immediately began trying to pull the red robe over her head. 'They made us in about one breath! You might as well have paid the bloody fine, would have cost almost as much.'

Killian shrugged and began to unbutton his jacket, and swung his cutlass from the back of his belt to its usual place at his side. Silver knew her books and her histories, but her understanding of the realities of life was laughable. At the railing of the *Cutlass Hawk* the crew were lined up and they began to jeer down as he and Silver undressed, and one of the Breygar twins let loose a whistle like a steaming kettle. Killian waved them down and dropped the jacket and hat on a barrel.

'Might have worked,' he said, shrugging, and helped Silver untie the back of the wizard robe. They had picked that up in a trunk of costumes from a travelling show in payment for a little help a season back. 'What's the point of costumes if we don't use them? At least this way the Crabs and the Spices and the Evertree Sisters and whoever the hell owns the Long Crossbow don't know we're here, and we can get in and out, simple and happy.'

Pollos Twice-Kissed gave an inarticulate shout from the deck of the *Hawk* and threw down Killian's hat, and he snatched it from the air and pulled it down tight. It was a heavy black tricorn of salt-weathered leather with a single steel pin of a crow perched on a cutlass blade. Killian turned to Silver and smiled. The great skein-mage Tellactor of Lello was now Silver again, a lanky streak of piss with a permanently downturned mouth, skin paler than milk, and hair like a hay bale a horse was halfway through eating. She was shaking her head and settling her satchel with her papers across her shoulder – she must have had it beneath the wizard robe. At her belt hung her thin rapier, and the juxtaposition of the sword and the books hanging on opposite hips made Killian smile. From the corner of his eye he could see the two urchins lingering, just out of earshot.

'We've been two weeks at sea, dear one,' he said. 'Don't worry about bribes, don't worry about the guilds, don't worry about a thing. We are going to get a bath, a bed, a drink. Not necessarily in that order. Tomorrow is for business. First night in town, we need to make some memories!'

Silver sighed and stared up at the town towering over than them, tiers upon tiers and streets upon streets rising from the impoverished to the industrial to the mercantile to the peaks of society, the great guild houses lining the mountain ridges surrounding the bay of Samurkan. One dock over, a gull was fighting a child over a twist of pastry, and all around them the stink of fish and ship's waste and business was a film Killian could taste in the back of his mouth.

'You can afford a high tier, tonight,' Silver said, and Killian just laughed and grabbed her by the shoulder and set off. As they passed the urchins, Killian dropped to one knee on the dock and held a copper penny between his fingers, leaning to them conspiratorially. The two leaned back, hesitant, and he could see the grime thick on them beneath their clothes.

'A penny each,' he said, 'to take a message to Mistress Merrow at the old school by the eastern gate. You know it?'

The two nodded mutely, the nearest reaching her little hand forward for the coin. Killian held it back.

'There'll be a bowl of soup in it at the other end, aye?'

The children nodded mutely again and he handed each of them a copper penny.

'What's the message, Captain?' the one behind asked. He had crooked teeth and a thick wrap of wool around most of his head, and his feet were bare on the wet wood of the dock. Killian stood and took Silver's arm and straightened his hat and his sword belt.

'The message,' he said, 'is that Captain Heroneye will visit tomorrow.'

The children left at a run, and Killian walked on with Silver in silence, and though he could feel her gaze on him he kept his own eyes forward. *No questions.*

The trouble began after the bath, for which Killian was grateful. They were in the baths of a saloon he had not tried before in the mid-tiers, the simply named *Haven.*

'I need to return to my rooms at the guild,' Silver said, and Killian flicked water at her. They were entwined in a large stone bath, steam dancing over the surface of the water.

'Now?' he asked. 'Really, Silver? First night in port should be a celebration!'

Silver stood and pushed water from her body, sending foam and spray across him as he gazed up at her, grinning. She smiled.

'We've *celebrated*,' she said, a finger tracing his nose. 'We've eaten well, we've bathed in this fine place, we've drunk their wine. We've been away a span, *more*, Heron. I need to get back to the guild and show them I have made some progress. I can get prices for those items, if you wish. The guild will pay more than the smiths and the breakers will give you – and those pieces of Russilan history will be intact.'

Killian reached for his wine and finished it – a pale acid vintage from Cil, the sharpness fading on his tongue as he savoured it. Silver had chosen it. The private bath was dimly lit by a single lantern, and he could hear the noise of the tavern below. Silver towelled herself down and he watched, enraptured.

'Intact,' he said, 'in the private collection of the diggers' guild, or some Isken noble. Let us see what the prices are.'

Silver pulled on her clothes and leaned down to kiss him, then belted on her rapier and grabbed her satchel. The diggers' guild was his name for her Archaeological and Anthropological Guild, and normally she would not take kindly to it. Instead she reached for her wine glass and took a final drink.

'It was a good voyage, Heroneye,' she said. 'No death, a little *threat*, and both of us are better off. Not bad company, either.'

He smiled up at her.

'When will I see you again?' he asked, and she shrugged. 'I could come to the diggers' guild?'

'No questions,' she said with a smile, and then left him alone with his thoughts. She did not look back as she closed the door.

'This wine is too expensive,' he said aloud, and then sunk his head below the water. There was something so *off* about being submerged in fresh water. When he was in the sea there was pull; there would be tide and current, wave and surf, the motion of his own body to keep himself afloat. It would be cold, sharpening. This warm bath was a luxury. *A luxury I can't afford.* He re-emerged and fished around the side of the stone tub until he found the dregs of Silver's wine and then Killian lay where he was, deep in thought, and drank from the bottle. When it was empty he sent it bobbing across the water, a little ship with no sails, no oars, no hope.

The tavern below fell silent, and he squinted at the door, and then at the single window. The silence continued, and then the dull sound of heavy footfalls. *Shit.*

Killian threw the sword belt and boots and clothes through the window as the door began to open, and in nothing but his tricorn hat and heron-skull necklace he waited perched on the high sill to see who entered. The door swung open and framed in the light was a hulking Tullioch, nearly seven feet of sinew and muscle. The creature was black-scaled with a fan of dark green behind its head, its heavy jaws open slightly as it tasted the air, looking every inch like one of the salt-water iguanas that lazed in the southern reach, only a foot taller than Killian. Not just a Tullioch – Heavenly Nassin, the Evertree Sisters' top enforcer. He was clad in simple black wool, his clawed feet bare, and a heavy red cloak falling over his shoulders. At his belt was a dagger with blade of pale rock and a handle of mottled coral. The Tullioch ducked under the door lintel and met Killian's eye and clicked his teeth, his equivalent of a laugh.

'Heroneye—' he began, voice thick and raspy, but Killian raised a hand.

'Tomorrow, Nass!' he said. 'I swear it by salt and storm – tomorrow!'

Before Nassin could reach him, Killian dropped from the window. It was ten foot down to the hard cobbles below and his legs crumpled beneath him and he landed hard on his hip.

'Piss!' he said, and struggled to stand. He looked back at the window. It was surely too small for Nassin to follow. He had a few moments before the Tullioch would be downstairs, out of the inn, and finding his way to this back alley. It was thirty yards or more until the main street where the inn entrance was, and behind him the alley branched. Killian pulled on the first leg of his breeches and then stopped at a sharp whistle.

'Well,' said a voice, 'look at that. Wouldn't bother picking any of that up, matey. Just you leave it there and run off now.'

Killian turned to see three figures blocking the nearest end of the alley. Killian let his breeches fall and deftly scooped up his sword and drew it free from the belt, spinning the heavy cutlass in his hand. The three advanced a few steps closer, one man drawing a long knife, another a heavy cudgel from beneath his cloak. The third figure was a woman, her nose squashed tight to her cheek by a poorly set break. The alley was dark, save for the odd flicker of candlelight through the shuttered windows of the inn looming over them.

'At least one of you will die,' Killian said, forcing himself to stand tall.

'Pull your trous up,' a voice rumbled from the end of the alley behind the thieves. *Nassin.* 'This one is mine. Leave now, little fleas.'

The thieves turned to the new voice and the woman spat. Killian pulled up his breeches as the thieves rearranged themselves, standing sidelong to keep both him and Nassin in their sights. The woman cast her hood back and drew two short axes from her belt.

'One or two is easy enough, Tullioch,' she said, and Nassin shrugged and stepped forward. Killian glanced behind him. The alley branched in two, but Samurkan's middle tiers were a warren. It could lead him to a bright street and an easy escape, or a dead end.

'Nassin,' he called, pulling on a boot. 'I really will come by tomorrow. I promise. Just getting some things squared away, aye?'

The night air was cold on his wet hair, and he pulled on his second boot and then grabbed his cloak and satchel and shirt in one hand and twirled his cutlass. The thieves shifted. *Kill them all.* The voice was his own, thick, in the back of his skull. *Three dregs, you could do it in three slices.* Killian worked his grip on his cutlass and glanced upward but the endless lanterns of Samurkan obscured whatever stars danced across the sky.

'Give us your stuff,' the cudgel-wielding man said, 'and maybe you don't die tonight. What ain't you dicks understanding?'

Killian took a step towards the thieves with his sword raised, and at the other end of the alley Nassin stepped forward, his massive clawed hands spread out to each side, letting out a low hiss.

'Tomorrow!' Killian yelled, and he turned and ran. He was at full speed within a few steps, hurtling down the alley. Behind him he heard a scream. *Left, right?* He reached the junction and stopped dead.

'Zalan's scaley arse!' he spat. *I tried.* Both turnings ended with high walls within a dozen feet. It was a dead end. Killian spun back. One bandit was on the ground bleeding out, making wet coughing noises as they tried to crawl away. The other two were harrying Nassin, one with her paired axes flashing and the other jabbing with a long knife. The Tullioch growled and slashed with his claws, and with one hand drew his stone dagger. Killian sighed and dropped his clothes and satchel and made his run.

He barrelled into the knife-wielding man cutlass first, leaping at the last moment and trying to drive all of his momentum into the heavy blade of his chipped and battered sword. Killian's cutlass had hacked bough and underbrush, tangled lines, ravenous beasts, bone-monkeys, jaiboar. Men. Women. Tullioch. Antian. The cloth of the thief's cloak proved little resistance, and the blade sank deep into the meat of his shoulder and drove him to his knees, howling in pain. Killian wrenched it back and brought the guard of the hilt down on the man's skull. It was a heavy metal half-dome that surrounded the hilt, perfect for brawling when quarters below ship were too tight to swing the blade properly. The man slumped to the ground and Killian scrambled back just in time to see Nassin stop a falling axe blow. His clawed hand snagged out and gripped the handle of the axe mid-swing, and as the wide-eyed woman went to draw her other axe back, Nassin's knife flashed and her wrist sprayed blood. The second axe clattered to the cobbles and Killian glanced nervously at the alley past Nassin. He was unsure if he could make it past.

'We didn't mean no trouble!' the woman said, and Nassin leaned forward and ripped out her throat with his razor-sharp teeth. A spray of claret cut across Nassin and the alley, and he let her body fall to the ground and then spat blood and rounded on Killian. He gave Killian a nod, and then pulled a scarf from one of the dead bandit's necks and began to wipe his face, his dagger blade. He looked down at the spray of blood coating his dark shirt, his cloak, and sheathed his dagger.

'Put your clothes on, Heroneye,' he said, shaking his head. Killian mutely began to obey, his eyes stuck on the dead woman, on the red mess of her throat. 'I'll be sending you my laundry bill. The Sisters would like to see you, *tonight*.'

Marion had dressed in her finest armour, black leather bodice and pauldrons and greaves over tight black trous, with a cape of midnight blue. Whilst Mournchild availed himself of their inn's kitchen – she could never get over how *much* the Blade ate – Marion had carefully shaved the sides and back of her skull and brushed her thick mane of black hair with oils until it was proud and glossy. Her clothing and cloak were inscribed with the jagged sigils of Cil, sigils of power mixed in geometric designs, all inlaid in silver over her black armour. Her hammer shone at her belt, and her boots were polished to a high sheen. All of it she had done *herself*, cursing every moment. A lieutenant of the Lune legion had to be used to esoteric tasks and hard living, but after a decade of servants preparing her every need at the academy (and a decade of Antian slaves doing the same in her manor before that) Marion was still unused to the indignity of preparing herself. *I need a hand,* she thought, *some little Cil with no tongue and fast fingers to sort these messes.*

The Arcanists' Guild house was in the top tier of Samurkan, high above the stink of the harbour and the cramped streets of the mid-town. Marion was still musing on her desire for some helper when they arrived – night had fallen and dark cloud masked the stars beyond, and turning to the sea, Marion could see the distant lights on ships bobbing outside of the safe refuge of Samurkan's harbour. She was learning – a night of quiet winds, and many ships would brave the open water rather than pay the dockmaster's tithe. The sea was so placid – it made her fingers twitch. *Zalan is there,* she thought. *Somewhere. He could be here.* She could not fathom why not – all these waters were connected, and the beast had marked her. She had felt its eye upon her. *I still feel it now. Why did it let us leave?*

Blade Mournchild stepped forward and knocked at the heavy gate of the Arcanists' Guild, and Marion forced her mind from servants and serpents. He was in his usual matte-black plate armour, his heavy longsword sheathed at his hip and a hooded cloak hiding his face. She had not seen what idiocy of dyes and paints he had come up with for tonight, in the honour of his silly little god. Mournchild retreated to her shoulder, and Marion took in the guild house.

It was a dozen floors of white stone, limestone perhaps. The entrance was up a handful of steps leading to a long landing lit by brazier and wall-mounted torches, and a dozen columns of marble stood at the base of the steps, each topped with a burning flame of a different colour. They cast odd shadows on the entryway, the single heavy door of oak lined with ornately worked steel. The wood of the door was etched with tiny writing. *Names?* Marion could not tell without peering, and did not want to appear overly curious to whomever was watching. She was certain someone must be – that was the feeling in her gut.

The door creaked open and a person in a hooded robe of pale yellow stepped forward, a sash of green across their chest. From the hood of their robe a thick veil fell, covering their face. The veil was also pale and yellow, layer upon layer of thick mesh that allowed her no sight of the crooked old one's face. Marion waited. After three breaths, the veiled creature bowed low and sniffed.

'The Arcanists' Guild of Samurkan welcomes you,' they said, and they sniffed again. 'What do you seek this night, child?'

Marion's smile was as thin as the edge of Mournchild's knife. 'I am Marion de Guillame du Requin-Port, Lieutenant-yeux du Lune. We seek the mage Darnielle.'

The old creature bowed once more, and wordlessly gestured for them to follow. The interior of the guild was as ostentatious as its exterior – sconces burned with flames of every colour, and tapestries of thick weave and fine artistry hung from every wall. The stone floors were clear and clean, and their footsteps echoed as the old servant led them deeper into the complex. Marion had glimpses of side corridors, darkened rooms, what was perhaps a great hall. There was some sort of dining room where ribald laughter echoed, but the servant led them away from sounds of laughter and life and deeper into stillness. At last they came to an unmarked wooden door with a low bench outside, and the servant gestured for them to wait. Marion stood tapping her toe, Mournchild at her shoulder, and watched as the servant entered the room after a single knock without waiting for a response. She could glimpse no detail beyond the robed figure's frame.

At last the door reopened, and the servant withdrew and gestured for them to enter. They walked into a small room lit by a lantern hanging on one wall. The other walls were covered in bookshelves, all of them overflowing onto side tables, chairs. The room was full of books, papers, and artefacts – weapons, jewellery, stones, clay tablets covered in scratches, patches of tapestry. Amongst this chaos, a figure stood at the back of the room looking out of the solitary window at the dark harbour below. They turned and raised their hands in welcome, and Marion stopped dead.

The figure wore the same yellow robe as the servant, but with a sash of darker green. Dark leather gloves covered their hands, and their face was entirely hidden – not by a veil, as the servant had used, but by a mask carved of pale wood. The mask had two smooth horns jutting upward and a completely smooth face save two dark horizontal slits scarcely wider than a coin over the eyes. It was pulled close to the figure's face, and around it a thin hood and wrap of dark material sat, obscuring every inch of skin or hair.

'Welcome, Marion de Guillame du Requin-Port, Lieutenant-yeux du Lune,' the figure said. 'I am the mage Darnielle. Who is your companion? Will you sit? Would you care for spirits, tea?'

Without waiting, the figure strode to the solitary desk and sat behind it, carefully removing artefacts from the desk's centre and retrieving a bottle and three glasses from a drawer. They gestured at the chairs in front of the desk, and Marion moved a sheaf of papers and sat down. Mournchild went to the door and stood impassive and impressive, looming with his face hidden. Darnielle nodded and placed one of the glasses back where they had found it.

'What brings a lieutenant of Cil-Marie and an Uradech paladin to the Arcanists' Guild?' Darnielle asked, pouring a measure into each glass. Marion took the glass and drained it – it was whisky, smooth and clear. She set her glass down and smiled.

'You sold a Russilan child to a tanner at the slave market outside of town,' Marion said. The mask was impassive. She waited. Darnielle lifted their glass and then set it down again and placed their hands on the desk, spreading their fingers.

'There is nothing illegal or improper there,' they said. 'Isken laws forbid the purchase and sale of slaves, but outside of Samurkan's walls, the laws do not apply. They are a *pragmatic* people, above all. Has there been some issue?'

Marion exhaled deeply. 'Have you heard that to cross Burner's Run, a tithe of Russilan blood can sate Zalan the shipbreaker? We took this Russ child, and made an attempt.' Marion smiled and showed her teeth and crinkled her eyes. 'It did not go well. Why do you hide your face, Mage Darnielle?'

The mage was nodding and tapping their fingers.

'She was Russilan – I am sure of that,' they said at last. 'I've heard this silliness about a blood tithe, but nothing to back it up. I wear a mask, Lieutenant, because in Isken to be a mage is to be *other*. We are tolerated, but not well liked. So we work behind masks, even amongst ourselves, and then we are free to live in our society without judgement of our fellow citizens. We are not the only guild to do so – the Guild of Knives, the Spice Guild, those horse botherers at the Guild of Carriages. It keeps things somewhat less violent, they say.'

Marion let herself sink back in the chair and toyed with the whisky glass.

'We saw Zalan,' she said at last. 'I have great need to reach the Deep Crowns, Mage. *Great* need. We took a ship and we paid this tithe, and it did not work. The beast drove us back, snapped our mast, cracked our hull. It took four days of rowing to reach land, half the crew doing nothing but bailing water, night and day. I have great need to reach the Deep Crowns. There is a man I must find. The Russilan child did not work, and you claim they truly were Russilan. I'll take your word at that. I've consulted mages in Concarneau and Requin-Port and Druich, rumours from those and a dozen ports beyond. Drunken claims of those who say they have crossed.'

'The Bloody Crows,' Darnielle said in response, and Marion nodded. Piratical corsairs who emerged across Burner's Run and disappeared back to the Deep Crowns, leaving chaos in their wake.

'I am at an impasse, Mage Darnielle,' Marion said, and she tapped a finger on the head of her hammer. 'Cil-Marie is not without resources. If you or your guild can aid us, you will be rewarded.'

The mage Darnielle raised a hand up to the wooden mask with the horns, the face that was so reminiscent of the devils of Strait Kingdom mythology. They turned their gaze to Blade Mournchild.

'Why does Cil-Marie not use its flying orb?' they asked. For ten years, Cil-Marie had been in possession of an ancient artefact of the distant Ferron Empire, long fallen. An orb that glowed silver and could fly across the sky. *A closely guarded secret.* Marion smiled thinly.

'Zalan is not constrained by water,' Marion said, 'and the Father Dragon of Ona flies the skies of the Eastern Crowns. Such a resource, if it existed, would be precious indeed, and there are many wars to be fought, many places where eyes are valued. If such an orb existed, to risk it so close to the lair of a mad Judge would… not be prudent.'

The mage shrugged and pushed a clay tablet from the centre of their desk to the side, and dipped a gloved finger in their whisky and drew a rough circle on the stained wood.

'Burner's Run is impassable,' they said. 'Yet I have thought long on this. There are two paths that might lead you to the Deep Crowns. I will tell you one – if you will take me with you. I have research projects that may benefit from such a journey.'

'You will tell me both,' Marion said, and the mage shook their head.

'If I do that, your holy warrior may feed me to the nearest toothy fish. No. I will tell you one, and I will come with you. If we fail, I will tell you the second.'

Marion reached her hand forward and gripped the mage's hand tight. The mage leaned close and Marion could smell the spilled whisky, old parchment, dust.

'There is one man who has crossed Burner's Run who is not one of the Bloody Crows, though he won't always admit to the feat,' they said at last, and they began rifling through papers on their desk until they found a map. They tapped on the Deep Crowns, that circle of islands cut off from the world by Burner's Run, right at the heart of the archipelago.

'Tell me, Lieutenant,' they said, 'have you heard of Captain Killian Heroneye?'

4

THE THIRST AND THE HUNGER

'At some point the Russilan occupied most of the isles of the Crowns, and from contemporaneous accounts we have established that their people fell to a plague of unknown origin first noted around 757 Isken reckoning. The decline was rapid, and within a generation their nation was shattered. The Russilan were a secluded people prior to their fall. Little is left now but great tombs in dark forests. Ancient blood wards in the skein are still extant even now and are of great note to practitioners of the pattern, though the secret of their creation and continuation is lost along with their creators.'

– ***Notes on the Russilan***, Gallo Mancinus

Killian kept flexing his fingers as they descended to the harbour. A taciturn Heavenly Nassin loomed a few steps behind him. The last time Killian saw Nassin, the Tullioch had been the one holding Killian's hand flat on a table as the

Evertree Sisters threatened his fingers. Even then, he knew it wasn't personal. Nassin was not a fellow for holding grudges, though many held them against him for all he had done as the Evertree Sisters' heavy hand.

'You know,' Killian said, 'it might not be great for us if the city guard find those bodies.'

Nassin just grunted and Killian kept his eyes forward. The road descending from the marvellous bath at Haven down to the lower town passed a few guard huts, many inns, and the buildings soon turned from largely residential and commercial to truly industrial. As they reached sea level there were warehouses packed with ice and enchantment for the fishers to leave their haul in, tanning and dyeing sheds and all the stink of a working port. Paint and flame and piss and smoke, and the huge butcher yard opposite the floating dock where great wooden cranes would lift whales and lower them to the bloody slabs below. The whaling port was teeming as always and, as they walked the harbourfront headed to the Evertree Sisters' lair, Killian could not help but watch. Dozens of braziers lit the butcher's slab in sickly orange. The latest specimen was a Carob whale, thirty foot long, blue and mottled grey on its top and pale white below. Its tail fin was long and tapered, nearly as wide as it was long, and on its brow above two dead glassy eyes three horns of shining white jutted proudly, complex antlers with perhaps eight points on each. *A young one.* Killian shivered and turned away.

'Don't your lot worship a whale?' he asked Nassin, for something to say, and then stopped as he heard the footsteps behind him pause. Nassin stepped close.

'We worship the Bird and the Whale,' Nassin said, voice quiet and close. His reptilian eyes flashed in the torchlight that danced across the harbourfront from a dozen sources. 'We worship the great Judges of the ocean, by their true names. *The* Whale is not *a* whale, any more than your snake-god Zalan is *a* snake, Heroneye. Our religion runs back a thousand years, when your people were still squealing in the dirt. When *you* still had a people, that is. Our gods have existed since the ocean was born. Our mythology is deep, our worship as varied as our kin. By my lot, do you mean the kin of the Wind Sea? The Southern Crowns? The shore dwellers? Those in the caverns of the coasts of Ona? I do not call you a Baal worshipper, nor a wolf-botherer, nor a honey-drinker. I do not say you worship a hole in the ground like some gibbering Siobhish. If you are going to live, Heroneye, you must learn that the world is greater than ever you have dreamt, and you must learn *manners*.'

Heavenly Nassin started walking again and Killian fell into step, flexing his fingers. *So much for making conversation.* He let himself smile, just the smallest smile in the darkness of the street when he was sure Nassin wasn't looking. *If you are going to live...* The hulking Tullioch thought there was a chance of that, at least. Killian was inclined to agree. If the Sisters wanted him dead, Nassin could have let the thieves have their way, or simply killed Killian himself.

At last they arrived at a bustling trading yard with a huge tree planted in the front entrance. It was a lithe and springy birch of some sort, Killian thought – he had never been good with trees. The bark was silver and seemed to be peeling in chunks from the trunk, but in a way that looked natural to him rather than sickly. The yard was huge, walled in stone and covered with a thin wood-framed roof high above.

Everywhere there was motion. Nassin led him past bustling stevedores and swearing foremen, meticulous clerks with sheaves of paper and beleaguered sailors. There were crates being hauled by teams of horses, barrels, slabs of stone and carts of raw ore next to racks of amphora, massive clay jars with pointed ends. A hooded mage was animatedly gesturing at a relu in a cage of iron – the relu was a badger with fur of molten darkness and stripes of iridescent pearl. Its eyes were voids of utter absence and it snarled at the mage and the clerk accompanying him, and Killian saw its three lolling tongues of sinuous blue flesh testing the air past teeth of dull stone. He held a hand to his heron skull locket and said a silent prayer to the stars. *Trading in gods, now.* He was certain that would not end well for anyone involved.

Whatever could be traded, the Evertree Sisters were there to be sure it *was*. Of the ships docked in Samurkan each night a great amount would be loaded and unloaded at this very warehouse. The Evertree Sisters were the ultimate brokers of goods in Samurkan and the northern waters of the Crowns. *And secrets,* Killian thought. *And worse.* They existed at once as legitimate traders and members of Samurkan's polite society, but there was no doubt amongst those who plied their trade in the shadows how far the Sisters' interests reached. He kept his hand far from his sword hilt and tried to straighten his hat and his cloak as Nassin led him to the raised tower that overlooked the trading yard. It was open-sided with a wooden platform perhaps fifteen feet across, with nothing but a thin railing between the occupants and the hard-packed dirt of the trading floor below. Killian licked his lips and glanced back at the harbour. He could not see the *Hawk* amidst the forest of masts that gently swayed in the night breeze. He followed Nassin up the worn steps that circled the platform and emerged, bowing with a sweep of his hat before he even glanced at the occupants.

There was a huff and Killian replaced his hat and straightened his back. The Tullioch Evertree Sisters sat cross-legged on wide-cushioned stools. Between them was a low table with a chissick board and a pot of tea, a dancing ribbon of steam escaping its spout. To one side a second table was covered in papers, at which a young man with a shaven head and a thin beard was awkwardly writing. There were lanterns on each corner of the platform, casting a steady glow. The Sisters were both looking at him. Beatrin was the elder. She wore thin metal eyeglasses perched on the end of her snout and a robe of midnight blue, with a shell brooch worked with gold and silver. Her scales were a lustrous dark green and her crest a deep gold. She was taller and broader than her sister, and she moved slowly, as if every motion was considered. She appraised him with sharp eyes, nostrils flaring a little. The younger sister Hallis turned to gaze at him as well. She shared her elder sister's colouration but was shorter and slighter, barely over six feet tall. She wore a tunic in matching blue to her sister and black trous, tailored to allow her long tail freedom of movement. At her belt was a dagger with the same white stone blade and handle of coral that was sheathed at Nassin's side.

'Leave us, Hulp,' Beatrin said, and the young scribe hastily gathered his papers and sped down the stairs. 'You too, Nassin.'

The huge Tullioch waited a long moment, long enough to meet Killian's eye, and then departed as well with a stiff bow. Killian had no doubt at all about what that eye contact had signified. Killian took a half step forward and opened his mouth to speak, but Beatrin held up a finger.

'You are here to listen, *Captain* Heroneye,' she said, and gestured to the floor beside the chissick board. Killian sat cross-legged and watched the match and waited. The crew may think him impatient, but he knew when to exercise his restraint. *They have no idea how patient I can be.* Beatrin moved a white stone forward, onto a square occupied by one of Hallis's black stones. Killian shook his head and the elder Tullioch turned to him.

'You think it a poor move?' she hissed, gently, and he shrugged.

'You are leaving your back line defenceless,' he said, gesturing, and she clicked her teeth.

'The egg is giving lessons,' she said, clicking her teeth again, and Hallis snorted. 'Last time we saw you, Killian, there were raised voices and threats made. You owe us, what is it now? Four thousand two hundred and seventy ducats…'

'With interest,' chirped Hallis, voice bright, and her sister nodded and began pouring tea.

'With interest,' Beatrin continued. 'How did your run to Skerry go. Hunting a barrow, was it?'

Killian bowed his head in deference.

'A Russilan tomb,' he said. 'We made it out with a full sack of gold, opals, pearls. Real treasure. I just got into port – once I've got a good buyer, it should—'

Beatrin silenced him with a raised finger.

'This is good,' she said. 'You see? I prefer this. I prefer, let us count gold, not, let us count fingers, yes? But I am good at counting, whatever it is we count. You bring it here and we will sell it on. Free you up for your next job, yes?'

Killian worked his jaw. They would sell it for half what he could get himself, he was sure, but he could see no choice.

'Of course,' he said stiffly. 'I've a few crates of Kelamoran lacquered pottery – I was going to do a run to Druich to offload it to the market there, some Cil idiot might take it.'

The Tullioch locked eyes with each other and drank their tea, and Hallis moved a black stone towards Beatrin's unguarded back line.

'I have a colleague working on the location of another Russilan tomb,' he said hurriedly. 'There are rumours of a larger one in the north-west of the Coracles, in the forest by the Western Antian Holdfast. The Antian have no interest in Russilan tombs. Should be an easy one, potentially a big score.'

The Tullioch continued to ignore him, and played their game. Hallis was pressing her advantage, but soon enough Killian realised Beatrin's game. She had drawn Hallis's forces deep into her own territory, stretched far from home. With a single move Hallis's strength was cut off, surrounded, and the younger sister sat back and flicked her tongue, tasting the air. She tapped a claw on her dagger handle and then shook her head, waving the game away, conceding defeat. Beatrin smiled and turned her gaze back to Killian.

'You are a young man, Captain,' she said. 'Your ship belongs to us. Your life, to us. You are ours to use as we need. You understand this.'

It was not a question, but Killian bristled. 'I owe you,' he said slowly, 'but my ship and my life are my own.'

Beatrin clicked her teeth dismissively. 'Your people covered this archipelago until the Thirst took them. Tell me, boy. Do you ever look at the salt water and thirst? Do you ever feel the pull to swim until you can't see land and drink deep? I've heard it can affect those of you with the Russilan blood. Do you see the current beneath, like a tide-mage? It is said that every Russilan could see the true current.'

Killian did not answer. Beatrin had asked him all these questions before, more than once. He waited for the blow to come and tried to ready himself. *They will not take my ship.*

'We enjoy these treasures, of the Russilan tombs,' Beatrin said, and she patted his knee. 'We enjoy it a great deal, the taking and the having. You came to us with your sack of treasure and your stolen ship and said, what was it? *Fund my first voyage and I'll repay you threefold.* When was that, Captain? Three winters have passed since that day, but you were so *convincing* and the grave goods you brought so... different. We *like* you, Killian Heroneye. But you are slow in this repaying and more costs are always added, and we are growing old. You will go to Druich with your pots – and more cargo besides. You will go seeking this tomb by the Western Antian Holdfast and bring us its riches. Our well-wishes and our backing and whatever resources you need. You will do this because no other can open these tombs, and you will pay us what you owe. But first, we need you to do something else. We need a ship with a shallow draught and oar sweeps, unarmed and unassuming. A soft-bellied eel, my sister might say.'

Hallis grunted and blinked at him and bared her teeth.

'You will take Nassin and forty blades and you will sail east to Caragh's Point with two of our ships, and then with all stealth you will take your little caravel with its shallow draught right past the corsairs who anchor there, and you will go upriver, and in the dead of night you will help Nassin make war on the corsairs of Caragh's Point. They have three ships, perhaps a hundred men. They are led by a man named Blue Darrow. But you will have surprise, and *surprises*. Do this for us, and the interest will stop accruing, and you and your crew will have a little reward. You leave tomorrow by the noon bell. Do you understand?'

Killian looked down at the black chissick stones surrounded on all sides by the white and he flexed his fingers. He understood all too well.

Killian returned to the *Hawk* and slept as best he could. The butchers from the whaling port were yelling to each other, the hundred ships in port all creaking. There was loading and unloading to be done at night whilst the wind stilled a little, and there were other dealings to be done as well. A hundred crews, all hungry to see people other than those they'd just spent however long crammed on a ship with. Assignations and fights, secret trades and convoluted plots. Killian spent the night restless, stirring at every sound, trying to map the next move. *If* they could survive this stupidity at Caragh's Point, *then* he might be able to convince Silver to hunt for the tomb by the Western Antian Holdfast. *If* the corsair Blue Darrow caught them, *then* he would slaughter them all. *If* he tried to flee, *then* the Evertree Sisters would have his hands amputated, and he would be begging on the streets of Samurkan or grabbed by the slavers that stuck like barnacles to the city walls.

He felt the weight of each *if* and each *then* – not only for himself. He was the captain. *You made yourself a captain.* A captain was a man who did not command only his own destiny, but that of others as well. A crew who trusted him, a ship whose fate would match his own. With a start in the darkness he sat bolt upright.

We cut no fresh bough on Skerry. It was old luck, an old tale, an old wisdom. Fresh boughs cut whenever you leave an island, and if they are still fresh when you next reach port all would be well. Affy Burngull had told him it was a story meant to remind sailors they needed time on land, fresh food, lest they go mangy and rotten like those long-haul seamen of the Wind Sea and the Last Ocean did. He lay back down. He could not remember Affy's face except as a screaming mask of blood. Sleep took Killian in the end, and he dreamed of the rotsurge – the black lightning, the roiling cloud, the acid rain burning his skin as he ran. Grey goblins with skin and teeth like sharks and slavering black tongues ripping into flesh with their bare hands, fingernails like claws, thirsting for black blood. The storm moved on, and he was back in Requin-Port with his mother and his sister Key. The Cil were leading his mother to the gallows, only this time he was close enough to hear her speak. This time nobody held him back. She spoke to him, but he did not understand the words, only the terrible darkness in her eyes. In the dream he held Key's hand so tight and he did not let her go. When he woke he did not feel refreshed, and he stared long into the tarnished mirror hung on his wall.

He called the crew to the deck. The Breygars were on shore, and Timmult and Renard were impatient for their turn. Galli and Nils had been planning to go ashore with Pollos Twice-Kissed later in the day.

'We've a job,' he said roughly. 'Heavy stuff for the Sisters. Four days out, four days back.'

They all waited patiently, but he could see Timmult's and Renard's faces drop. They could see the inevitable.

'We leave at noon,' he said. 'We'll have forty aboard, as well as us. We will need canopies on the deck where we can.'

'Piss,' Renard said, the first word she had uttered in days. Apart from singing folk songs from Undal and Isken after dark the woman did not speak often, preferring the company of the cheap novels she picked up in the harbour markets. 'I've a date the night, Captain.'

Killian nodded. 'I owe you one, then, Renard,' he said. Timmult simply hung his head and then moved off to sulk elsewhere.

'Don't bloody want one from *you*,' Renard muttered, and her shoulders slumped as she returned to her duties.

Pollos came to him quickly.

'Forty men for eight days is a lot of water and met,' he said, scratching at his temple. 'We've still no tide-mage, Captain!'

Killian held his hands up for peace.

'They'll bring their own met and water,' he said, 'and I'm off for a tide-mage now. We'll be sailing in convoy with *Adamant Hand* and *Jade*. I'm sorry, Pollos. No date for you tonight either.'

Pollos simply shrugged his huge shoulders and rubbed at his chin and headed below decks, calling for Timmult and Renard to join him. He would rearrange the little cargo they had to maximise their space. If Killian was lucky, Pollos might even manage to sell some cargo to neighbouring ships if any of their mates were keen enough.

The last job was going to be the hardest. He went to Galli and Nils and stared down at them. They were already dejected.

'You know what a heavy job means,' he said quietly, and Nils nodded but Galli looked up at him defiant. *Is she what, thirteen summers now?* Nils was a few years younger, and softer besides.

'I work on the ship,' Galli said, petulant, and Killian rubbed at his eyes and stared across the harbour to the butcher's bay. There was no sign of the Carob whale from the night before, but the stone slabs were slick with red. He tried to picture himself at her age, rake-thin and salt-sore. His mother was dead by then, three years dead. His sister had been three years gone. *Three years abandoned.* He had found a ship, eventually, but it had been hard before. *Hard after, too.* He had stood with nothing but a bill hook as corsairs boarded, and he had fought with the crew. He remembered drinking rum with the survivors, but he did not remember the names or faces of the dead. The face of the first corsair he killed that day was lost as well. *Too young,* he thought, *all of us too young.*

'You two are my crew,' he said quietly. 'A captain takes care of his crew, and a crew takes orders. We will be back in eight days, and after that on to Druich, and after *that* on to the Western Antian Holdfast. A real Antian city!'

Galli's head came up at that. The mole-dog Antian were reclusive, though a few could be seen wandering the docks of the larger cities of the Crowns. In Cil-Marie they were afforded no rights and kept as slaves, and so they were rare in the Western Crowns and elusive elsewhere – they kept to their own holdfasts and underground kingdoms. Killian knelt down and from his pocket took two copper pins – they matched the one in his hat, a crow perched on a cutlass. He pressed them into their hands.

'You are my crew,' he said, 'and I will be back for you. Trust in me. Now fetch your things. You're to Mistress Merrow for eight days, to see if she can teach you something worthwhile! Knots, navigation, *swordwork*.'

'What does Mistress Merrow know about *swords*?' Galli muttered, and Killian stepped back on the deck and unhooked his cutlass. It was a simple blade, the heavy metal of the hilt engulfing his fist. He moved the blade in slow circles, then faster, left and right, figures of eight, and Galli and Nils tracked the tip of his blade.

'Merrow wasn't always old,' he said, and he cut a series of hard slashes through the air, sweeping his blade wide. Slowing, he pointed the tip of the sword at Galli's chest. 'You saw me duel that fool with the rapier at the solstice festival? I can fight with a sword, can't I?'

Nils nodded, but Galli's eyes were locked on the tip of the blade that held steady a foot from her chest. Killian lowered it slowly and hooked the hilt onto his belt.

'Mistress Merrow taught me,' he said, 'and she will teach you. She is a thousand summers old, I think. You don't live a thousand summers without winning some swordfights. Heed her well, and next voyage we can duel with the practice blades, *all* of us, and a silver coin to the winner.'

He left the children appeased. Killian paid the dockmaster in full – the night before, Heavenly Nassin had escorted him back to the ship along with three toughs and they had taken the sack of loot he had acquired on Skerry isle so he was left with the coins he could scrape together from the bottom of his sea chest. He pictured the dagger with its blade of blue stone, the pearls embedded in its hilt. As the dockmaster droned on, Killian stared at the *Cutlass Hawk* and imagined his ship as it ought to be – fresh sails and new rope, boughs of green lashed to the bowsprit, a ballista on the foredeck, fresh paint on every rail. His crew in matching tunics with his emblem sewn on the breast, and above it all he would stand, resplendent. *A true captain.* That dagger would be in his belt, a Russilan dagger for the greatest Russilan captain the Crowns had known in two hundred years. In his mind Silver was standing next to him. *That is new.*

'Captain Silhat?' the dockmaster was saying, and Killian nodded absently and took the bill of departure he was handed, and then trailed Nils and Galli to Mistress Merrow's. They knew the way. Thrice before since taking the pair aboard he had left them, when a job seemed too foul. The sea was dangerous and full of unknowns, but he could not bring himself to knowingly take them into a straight fight. A ship wasn't so bad a life for a child. *It was good enough for me.* The two of them whispered conspiratorially. They had stuck the copper pins on immediately, Galli pinning hers to her woollen shirt and Nils to the headband wrapped tight around his forehead. He had a wicked scar below that, a jagged long thing he did not like people to see. Killian had never asked after its provenance – the boy had been rescued by a trade ship from a wrecked settlement on an island a few days south of Samurkan, a village trying to establish itself. There had been a handful of other survivors, and Killian had heard the stories – something came from the forest. The torches and fires died when it came near, and it wailed, and the survivors did not know why it passed them by. That island was marked with a red dot on his charts now – *to avoid.* He would wait for the boy to tell him.

Killian followed them, nudging them along with a hand atop the head or a short whistle when they lingered too long. They paused a full minute to watch a Tullioch crew unloading the strangest dog-boat the children had ever seen – it was twenty foot long and the hull was living coral, bright blue and purple though clearly worked and cultivated and shaped. The Tullioch rarely harboured their ships in non-Tullioch waters, but their dog-boats would trade often enough as the bigger ships sat outside of harbour. Killian could not see their ship, but Samurkan port was enclosed as if by a huge crab claw of land, scrubby hills dotted with trees. There was at least one other coral ship in the floating dock he had heard, but he made no mention of it lest the children insisted on seeing it. They would want to see the beast beneath it that pulled it through the seas, and the Tullioch were not keen on observers. He let the children watch until the hulking lizard-folk had finished unloading, and then hurried them onward.

Mistress Merrow's was on the fringe of where the docks met the more reputable mid-tier of Samurkan. The streets turned from packed dirt to cobbles only one road before her door. It was a simple enough place: an old hall that had been the private chapel of a Kelamor noble house. They had settled Samurkan before the Isken came and took it by a mixture of trade and force. The noble's house was long gone, but the chapel where their people had worshipped still stood, even though there was no congregation. The Isken were pluralist and affably agnostic, acknowledging Baal and the great Judges of the world, and the endless fire below, but they did not by and large see any profit from organised religion. It stepped on too many of the other guild's areas of profiteering, and so was kept to a minimum.

The iconography of Baal was long stripped, leaving only vague pentagonal markings on the walls. Mistress Merrow had taken over the space two decades before. When Killian entered she was in the open kitchen at the back of the grand space, muttering over what was most likely soup. She squinted at the door and smiled.

'My boy!' she said, and hustled quickly to the door. It pained him to see the catch in her step, and when she hugged him she felt so slight and frail. He remembered so many afternoons with her and broom handle swords, practising his blocks, his attacks, learning every trick she had to teach. The grey in her hair sent a shiver down his arms.

'Merrow,' he said, and held her for a long moment. She took a step back and gazed at his face, worry flitting over her craggy features, and then she turned to Galli and Nils.

'It simply CAN'T be! You are too big!'

As Nils and Galli showed exactly how much they had grown, and their new pins, and told of the sights they had seen, Killian trailed deeper into the chapel. The children were all out for the morning, of course, taking whatever work they could find. They would return for soup and then lessons in the afternoon, and then more soup with bread, if it could be found or scrounged. He went to the rows of makeshift bunks that were lined up against the back wall. There were more than the last time he had visited. His gaze drifted and he remembered lying under a blanket in the darkness, Mistress Merrow sat on the floor beside him holding his hand. There had not been so many children, then. *What happened to the others? Beres, Nat, Scuttle?* He had seen Gustav crewing a crab-hunter out of Koch Dara, but Gustav had been odd as a child and time had not mellowed them. They had duelled and chased and run through Samurkan, those three long years after his mother died, before he found a ship. *Key should have been there with me.* Killian pressed a hand against the wall.

'Captain Heroneye,' Merrow called, and he blinked and set his face and went to them. 'These children are telling me they've learned nothing of letters and numbers, this last voyage. Skua lamps and knife throwing, Nils says!'

Killian did his most elaborate bow, twirling his hat with a flourish and dropping a leg. His cloak swept behind him. Galli and Nils grinned up at him, and he could only see Key's face. *I had no choice!* He held his composure, kept his voice from cracking, kept a smile for his crew.

'Mistress Merrow,' he said, 'you of all people should know how much children lie. They have been doing nothing but sums and eating vegetables. I must dash. I will return within a span.'

Merrow nodded, and she looked down at her clasped hands and then up at him. She opened her mouth to ask, though it pained her, but Killian put a hand on her arm and squeezed gently. With his other hand he pressed a small cloth bag into her hand. Inside it were thirty ducats, and two of the heavy gold rings he had found in the grave in Skerry that he had hidden in his rooms before they even made land in Samurkan. She felt the weight of it and fell into his arms and held him tight.

'Is anyone bothering you or the children, Merrow?' he asked quietly as Galli and Nils squabbled over empty bunks, and she shook her head.

'They know we've no money,' she said, 'and the guards are good enough near here. They know me well. There is one, lad… a new fetcher for the slave ring outside of town. Scar down his jaw and hair past his shoulder, thin bugger. Mean eyes. Goes by Ralad. He has been watching the little ones. We lost one a span back and if it weren't him I'll be damned. I went out there with a guard but we… we couldn't find her. She'd not been here long. Never gave me a name. She was mine, though, Killian.'

Killian worked his jaw. The guards were as corrupt as anyone else in Samurkan, and he knew some had ties with the slave market outside of town – many an unwary drunken sailor had woken in shackles outside of the city walls. A slaver openly taking one of Merrow's children was different, though.

'I'll deal with that,' he said softly. 'Anyone gives you trouble you need more than a guard; if I'm not here you go to the Sisters. You tell them to put it on my tab. They will make it right.'

Merrow shook her head and clasped his hands. 'I won't deal with them,' she said, and he stood tall and straightened his hat.

'You will,' he said, frowning down at her. 'You will if you need to, Merrow. The Isken don't care for any who aren't in a guild, and the slavers will take whatever they can get. If you have trouble then you get the Evertree Sisters. They don't care a spit for you, but they know I'll pay them back.'

Eventually, he thought.

'Nils,' he called, 'Galli. Check the docks each day after the fifth in case we are back early. Sword forms, footwork, knots, navigation. I want letters and numbers, I want a crew smart enough to sail my ship. Mind Mistress Merrow. This is her ship, aye?'

'Aye!' they both called, and he left before the memory of Merrow's hall could have a chance to overwhelm him. Nightmares of bloodshed, days of hunger, moments of joy – it was too much.

5

THE SLAVE MARKET

'The northern strip of islands known as the Coracles are relatively civil – the larger isles are mapped and patrolled by the great guild ships of Isken and the galleys of Kelamor that seek to control trade and prevent piracy against their peoples. From here the wealth of the isles – be it stone, metal, wood, or flesh – can be traded north to the Strait kingdoms and beyond. Eventually though these influences dissipate, and then there is no law except that of cutlass and arrow. In the Deep Crowns past Burner's Run ravagers await, and the corsairs known as the Bloody Crows. No ship of Isken or Kelamor can cross the Run and its feral god Zalan, and so the Coracles remain the last bastion of civilisation.'

– ***The Thousand Crowns***, Alwin Brakspear

Killian was halfway up the city having just dropped a note in to the Archaeological and Anthropological Guild for Silver. The guild house was a simple stone building festooned with scarlet banners of thick cloth that caught the wind. The doorkeeper was a dour woman with intricately braided hair and a tunic of that same scarlet, and the banners and tunic were all emblazoned with the guild's crest – a pick crossed with a scroll – in a verdant green, which he thought clashed rather terribly. *No wonder Silver doesn't wear the guild robes.* The doorkeeper seemed immune to his smile and his bow but she took the sealed note anyway. It was a simple few lines explaining he had urgent business but should be back in a span to set off for the next dig.

Turning from the guild house, he stopped at a low wall and looked down over the city. From such a lofty vantage the smell of the docks and the lower industries was blown away by the sea breeze, and he could see the harbour in its entirety. A high-sided Isken guild ship was raising its sails as it neared the crab-claw escape from the inner harbour, and beyond he could see a few dozen ships heading this way and that. There were little fishing boats pulling up ropes with pots for crab and octopus, canoes with outriggers laden with sacks moving between long Kelamor galleys that would be heading north back to the Wind Sea. Killian turned his gaze south – the Crowns were so dense he could see a dozen islands before the horizon faded to haze, and the shimmering shapes of what might be ships just at the edge of his vision.

Behind him two guards in heavy capes and steel caps sauntered, talking loudly. From the corner of his eye he followed their progress. One had a cudgel, the other a spear and both thick Isken accents. *Transplants from the mainland*. Killian kept his gaze on the sea and waited for them to pass. He was not sure if Nassin would have dealt with the bodies of the cutpurses from the night before, or simply left them and trusted to his reputation to keep the guards at bay and witnesses absent. Killian let them pass and then headed in the other direction, back down to the docks. The sun was already climbing high, and he knew he should be on his ship sorting the thousand things that needed to be sorted before they set sail.

Killian stepped fast until he reached the Black Hart. It was a street back from the docks, a dingy little inn with a sign of a black-coated deer limned in green flame. Killian pushed in and went straight to the bar, casting an eye over the tables as he went. There were no faces he knew. The Black Hart was the place to find a tide-mage, if any were to be had. The shutters were pushed wide and sun danced across the tables and low stools, all of it worn but none of it as mended as it would be in the sailors' bars. Sailors knew better than to piss off tide-mages.

Behind the bar the familiar face of Petal gazed at him impassively. Her hair was pulled back in a loose tail, and streaks of grey competed with a lustrous chestnut brown for attention. Petal was working at a keg spigot as she stared at him, cleaning it with a rag. Killian drew close and pulled up a stool and leaned forward.

'You got Affy Burngull killed I heard,' she said by way of an introduction, and Killian's smile dropped. He took off his tricorn hat and set it on the bar.

'Petal,' he said slowly, 'Affy got Affy killed. It was a rotsurge. Goblins. Magic lightning, acid mist. Judgement from on high. Nobody is safe in a rotsurge.'

Petal stopped polishing the spigot and stared at him, and then shrugged.

'Maybe,' she said. 'After a new one?'

Killian nodded wearily and turned his gaze across the common room of the inn. There were men and women, some in robes, some in stained leather armour or simple tunics of wool or cotton. One had the runic tattoos of an Undal-trained skein-mage, and another was studying a hefty book inscribed in intricate writings. Every nation and people trained their mages differently, but in the end it was all the same magic. The skein, the pattern, the current – there were dozens of names for it that Killian had heard. When he touched it, when he fell inwards to that strange interpolated world of sensation with such extra *depth*, he thought of it as a thousand spiders' webs of salt water all joined together, through and above and below each other. The Tullioch called it the great current; the Carob called it the one.

'Is Yggrid free?' he asked, and heard Petal snort behind him.

'On a galleon headed south to the Tullioch reefs,' she said. She passed him a glass and he nodded appreciatively.

'So who is?' he asked.

'Nobody,' she responded, and gestured at the common room. 'Skein-mage for the Undal ambassador. Arcanists applying to the guild. A couple of bone-fixers from Uradech. A fire-mage from Caroban who doesn't know a reef from his arse. No tide-mages, Heroneye.'

Killian drained the ale she had passed him. It was sweet and thick and bready. He set down the glass and fished two copper pieces from his pouch.

'I'll poach if I have to,' he muttered, and she nodded and looked down at the coppers on the bar. Killian drew a fat gold coin, a proper Isken ducat, and set it down beside them slowly. 'I need this, Petal, and I need it now.'

'I've one,' she said slowly, a smile tugging at the corners of her mouth and she scooped up the coin. 'New to Samurkan but she knows her tides and reefs, and she is ready to sail. She has all the sight you'll want and a few extras. I'll send her to the *Hawk*?'

'You are,' he said, smiling his thanks, 'a rare being of competence, in this mess of a town.'

He swept his hat to his head, and with a bow burst free of the stuffy confines of the inn, leaving Petal frowning behind him. Squinting at the sun he scratched at his chin. He felt strangely energised. He was under the thumb of the Sisters, and they wanted his help with corsairs of all things – but his ship was in good shape, his crew were healthy enough, and Silver would join them for the foray to the Western Antian Holdfast. *One more job to do,* he thought, *and then it is open water for a few days, at least.*

The slave markets were simple to find. Isken law and guild law covered the island of Samurkan, saving for the spur of land extending from the eastern gate down to the sea. It was a narrow and windswept sweep of dirt and stone that the Samurkan council had decreed a freeport – there was a single jetty, past the safe confines of the crab-claw enclosed inner harbour. If you set your ship there then it was a long walk up rocky shores to reach the thin strip of the island that was exempt from docking fees, taxes, or any law. *A necessary evil to ensure trade*, the council called it.

Killian strode through the eastern gate unchallenged and loosed his cutlass at his belt. The sword had no scabbard – instead it was clipped into a heavy steel hook that fit snug about the base of the blade. The hook was wrapped in worn leather and there was no edge to the blade for the bottom four inches. He let his hand rest on the familiar shape of the hilt and stared at the mess of the slave market. Tents and shacks and long lines of cages edged a maze of paths. There was no delineation he could tell from one owner's property to the next. The only difference seemed to be the manner of bondage. There were leg shackles and chains of iron, simple rope nooses, intricate leather harnesses and everything in between. The slaves he could see were mainly adults and older children. There were no Antian and no Tullioch – every Antian who appeared would be bought within hours by the few who were in Samurkan regardless of cost. The last time a Tullioch was kept in chains in the market a Tullioch crew out of the Shardspire in the Wind Sea had drunk a tavern dry and then set out with cutlass and sword – the city guard had to intervene, eventually, but the cost of the lost merchandise had sunk into the mind of the slavers and no Tullioch was ever seen in the market again.

They will still be chained, Killian thought. The same with the children who were not on display. They would be kept on a ship or under cover, children and Tullioch, where the good people of Samurkan and the Tullioch sailors would not be distressed by the sight. *Though perhaps the Evertree Sisters keep the Tullioch from chains, even out of sight.* His mouth twisted. *Or perhaps they don't…*

There was plenty of foot traffic. It was perfectly legal to *own* a slave in Samurkan. In Isken proper that itself was a crime, but here in the colony things were more relaxed. The sale and purchase were the crime, and then only within the city. It was not only slaves on sale – this was the tattered edge where those who refused to pay Isken's customs fee could try their luck, but without the protection of guard or wall, and with the company of slave traders. Killian walked the market and closed his heart and his ears to the fate of those in their chains, and instead focused on the slavers and their guards, armed with cudgels and long catchpoles – wooden shafts with nooses at the end that they could tighten in a moment. After twenty minutes of asking quiet questions he found the man who must be Ralad, sat on a crate with three others around him, playing dice on an overturned sea chest with a broken side.

Killian walked past. The man was as Merrow had described. Lank blonde hair hung past his shoulder and a thick scar ran the length of his jaw. He was a light man, but Killian could recognise the corded muscle of a sailor, slight but powerful, wiry and tough as the sea itself. The man had no sword, but a crude dagger was sheathed in his belt next to a ring of keys. Killian stopped and a row of men and women chained to a stake in the ground looked up at him. He cast his eyes down and then turned around. He knew there would be a way to handle this. A path of diplomacy. A path of peace. He tried to picture the Russilan captain in his mind, with the bejewelled dagger and the beautiful ship – the *Cutlass Hawk* if he made his fortune. *What would that Killian do?*

'You Ralad?' he called, and the man looked up from his dice and took Killian's measure.

'Who the fuck are you?' he said, and Killian blew out through his nose.

'I'm the man who wants to talk to you about a purchase,' he said, keeping his voice level. '*Privately*.'

Ralad looked at his companions and snorted and as one they stood and began to spread out. He walked forward and made a show of looking Killian up and down.

'I ain't the buying-selling fella, ponce,' he said, and reached a filthy hand up and took the fabric of Killian's shirt between his fingertips and rubbed. 'This is a nice shirt. That's a nice hat. Those're nice boots. What's a fancy boy like you doing here, knowing my name? My name shouldn't be in a fancy boy's mouth. What's it to be? A threat, fancy boy? I pissed you off? Your mum all sad I ain't been to visit her yet today?'

Killian grinned to hide the pulse of fear that shot from his heart to his fingertips. *I should have brought Pollos and the Breygars.*

'A nice hat, nice boots, a nice shirt,' he said. 'You're right. Maybe I *am* a fancy boy. In fact, I have a nice sword, too. And a nice ship full of sailors who call me *Captain* and hop when I say, and some nice friends in the Samurkan guard. And I want to talk to *you*, Ralad. For a moment. It will be worth your while.'

Killian heard the bells in the city toll the hour, dolorous chimes competing with the caw of the seabirds. *Noon. Shit.* He was already late.

'Might be I don't like your tone, boy,' Ralad spat. 'And if you was a fancy captain then where is this crew? Look like a boy, to me, a boy playing dress-up. Damn fool to come here alone. Damn fool to interrupt our game. You ever worn shackles before, boy? You know how to row? Fancy lad like you might have a heavy purse, I reckon.

Maybe we can lighten your load, send you back to your mother's teat. Or maybe we lighten your load and let you pull an oar for a few years 'til you learn who not to piss off.'

Ralad's friends started laughing and Killian heard the last chime of the noon bell fade over the city, and high above the stink of the slave market a murmuration of small birds moved sinuously across the iced bone blue of the sky. *Sparrows?* He squinted down at Ralad and considered the man, considered what he could say or what bribe he could pay to keep this man away from Merrow and the children. He pictured Galli and Nils in chains, in darkness, at the mercy of men like this, and felt a familiar vibration in his chest. Anger, escalation, violence – an easy answer. The answer he had turned to after the Cil hanged his mother. The answer he turned to when he was a boy with a billhook and pirates came for the crew who had taken him in. The answer he always seemed to turn to. *The answer that lost you your sister, you damn fool.* He forced himself to smile. *Control yourself!*

'I don't have time for this,' he said, turning to leave and breathing out. *I'll bribe some guards to keep a closer watch on the school.* One of Ralad's companions reached a hand out and grabbed his shoulder.

'Why you know Ralad, eh?' he asked, and Killian chewed on his lip and his eye caught the gaze of a slave, one of a dozen chained in a row, sat in the dirt. The gaze was sharp. *Fine.* Killian touched a finger to the heron skull at his chest and turned back to the slavers. There was a tall one still drinking from a clay cup, a fatter one with a limp, and a balding one with a scruff of beard and one wandering eye. Killian looked at each of them in turn and took off his hat and tossed it to one side, and then he stepped forward slowly and smashed his forehead into Ralad's nose.

Ralad fell back screaming and Killian wrenched his shoulder free from the grip of the other slaver and drew his cutlass and landed a heavy punch with the hilt guard into the bald man's gut. As the man doubled over, Killian leaned forward and then pulled at his sword, scoring the man's stomach. The bald man fell to the ground screaming and began to scramble back.

Ralad was back on his feet and had his knife drawn. The tall slaver was running back and grabbing at a catch pole; the one with the limp was dithering, looking this way and that. Somewhere nearby a slave started jeering, and then there was cacophony as a hundred voices raised to echo the inarticulate shout. Killian spat and stepped forward and slashed downward at the ditherer, who threw up an arm as he shrieked and fell back. The blade hacked a gouge from the arm and then it was Killian's turn to fall back, quickstepping as Ralad lunged at him.

'I'll have you in a cage, boy!' Ralad spat, thick blood coating his mouth and chin. He lunged again and Killian feinted a parry but then sidestepped and brought his blade down in a brutal chop to Ralad's back. The man fell to the mud and Killian brought his blade down again and again until Ralad stopped moving, and then turned with a heaving chest. The gut-cut man was still down and sobbing, the one with the arm wound had fled. The tall slaver with the catch pole lowered it gently to the ground and took a step back. Killian levelled his blade.

'A nice shirt don't make someone *fancy*,' he hissed, and he wiped Ralad's blood from his face with his free hand. It was hot, and it tasted of salt and iron.

'Boss won't like this,' the slaver said, 'Boss'll have you, man. Best you go. You run, now, hear me!'

Killian swept up his hat and spat. There were shouts and cries beyond the slaves. More of the slaving crew would come, he knew, not just from this group. He cast a glance at the chained slaves, straining at their bonds, and then knelt down and wrenched the ring of blood-soaked keys from Ralad's belt and threw them at the nearest prisoner. The tall slaver turned to flee and Killian was on him in three steps, lunging at his legs and chopping the back of an ankle with the end of his cutlass. The man fell hard and Killian was atop him in an instant, bringing his sword down in hacking chops to the back of his skull, a frenzy of blood and gore. The gut-cut slaver was face down in the mud, a slave on each limb holding him down as another choked the life from him with their unlocked chains. When Killian finally stopped hacking, a hand touched his shoulder and he whirled and drew back his blade, but it was a slave woman, hair matted, eyes wide. Beyond her was chaos, a hundred voices raised in clamour, the shout of the slavers, the screams of the freed.

'Who are you?' she asked. Her voice was rough, her accent was from Cil and she had the amber skin and pale silver eyes common to the people of that huge isle. *The people who killed my mother.* Killian looked down at himself, his shirt and trous thick with blood. It was in his mouth, and his hands and sword were crimson. *I'm a fool who can't be trusted.* He felt his senses return, his fear, and to the woman he just shook his head. He turned and ran in the opposite direction of the shouting. He ran, his mind a desperate thing as he tried to plot his way out of the slave camp, back to the gate, back to the ship. He had gone there to *threaten* and now there were men dead in the mud, more fighting. *Escalation.* He did not even know which of the slave traders he had just made war on. *A bloody fool, same as ever.*

Killian ran, and for a moment he was a boy running through the warrens of Requin-Port, his mother hanged and swinging from the gibbet behind him, a stolen knife in his hand, a black plan in his heart that would lead to nothing but more loss. *Because I'm a bloody fool.* He ran and he forced one thought to drive him onward through the adrenaline-soaked immediacy of his actions, the violence he had wrought. *This is not like that.* When they killed his mother, he had taken his vengeance and fled, and lost his sister in the process. *This is not like that!*

Mistress Merrow is safe.

'Baal, Morost, Pendar, Tulu, Salaman,' Blade Mournchild said, and the Tullioch flitted her tongue from her horrible muzzle of scales. He hated Tullioch. He hated Antian. *I hate most humans as well, to be fair,* he thought.

'Those are the five faces of the great god Baal, in whose image we are made,' he continued. In front of him, the two Tullioch leaning against the wall of the warehouse clicked their teeth. Beside him, Marion shaded her eyes with her hand and stared at the compound. They had asked after this *Heroneye* in four inns this morning before someone said the Evertree Sisters would know. They had been easy to find. *Some little local power.* Darnielle the mage had bid them farewell the night before, with a promise to meet the next morning, yet the mage had not appeared. Now as the noon bell tolled these Tullioch had barred their entry to the Evertree Sisters' compound and asked what they were about, and then one had laughed at Mournchild's eyes.

They stood in the shade of a towering birch tree, and beyond the two Tullioch was a vast warehouse busy with enterprise and movement.

'I asked why your eyes are red, swordsman,' the Tullioch continued. It was a green-scaled beast seven foot tall clad in short trous and a waistcoat of worn leather. 'I don't give a piss about your gods.'

The two Tullioch clicked their teeth again and Mournchild shifted his feet infinitesimally to optimise his position.

'Alive,' said Marion, and she took a step back and folded her arms. Mournchild nodded.

A lunge forward sent the first Tullioch slamming into the stone wall of the warehouse, and before it could raise its arm, Mournchild's plated fist crashed into its temple. The creature slumped to the ground awkwardly and the second Tullioch, brown-scaled and heavily muscled, leapt onto Mournchild's shoulder. He twisted and threw it across him, sending it sprawling in the dirt, and then stomped down with his plated boot into its spine. The beast wheezed and crawled and then stopped still, turning one eye up at him.

Across the warehouse all activity had stopped, and from a dozen different positions Tullioch were stepping forward. Some were armed only with their claws, others with billhooks, and one with the heavy axe it had swept up from a pile of firewood near an unlit brazier. They began to step forward.

'The great god Baal has five faces,' Mournchild said to his fallen enemy. 'My eyes are coloured to reflect this. Five are one, like fingers and thumb become a fist, or a hand. Baal, Morost, Pendar, Tulu, Salaman. White, blue, green, yellow, red. My eyes are red as I pay my respect to Salaman, today.'

The Tullioch were drawing closer and Mournchild stepped away from the fallen beast and lowered his head, standing at Marion's side.

'We seek an audience with the Evertree Sisters,' she said imperiously. 'On behalf of the Sun-Masters of Cil-Marie.'

From amongst the Tullioch waiting with their weapons, a female with scales of lustrous green and a crest of deep gold stepped forward. Mournchild watched impassively as the second Tullioch he had struck slowly raised itself and went to her and spoke quietly in her ear. The female removed a pair of thin metal spectacles from her robe and perched them on her snout, and then nodded slowly.

'The Evertree Sisters welcome the representatives of Cil-Marie and the mighty Sun-Masters, long may they reign. I apologise for the commotion. Will you take tea?'

Lieutenant Marion bowed stiffly and waved her hand in Mournchild's direction.

'My protector took umbrage at a religious matter,' she said. 'No apologies are necessary. Let us take tea.'

Mournchild was left at the base of a tower as the Lady Marion travelled upward to speak with those *lizards*. Those at the base gave him a wide berth, until eventually the brown-scaled Tullioch he had thrown came to him. It proffered a clawed hand and Mournchild stared down at it.

'It was a good throw,' the lizard said, and Mournchild sniffed. 'You said you worship Salaman, today? What does this mean, swordsman? Your god is not ours. My sister and I meant no offence.'

Your existence is the offence, he thought, and forced himself to breathe deeply. The lieutenant would not be well pleased if he got into another altercation. One would be a sign of strength, but a second would signal a lack of control. He shrugged at the Tullioch and planted his feet and set his hand on his sword hilt and waited.

Killian made it past the slave camp and joined the throng of people fleeing the chaos. Behind him, on that thin strip of rock where the sprawling slave lines and shacks and tents had aggregated like flotsam after a storm, there was screaming and smoke – a tent or canopy was ablaze. The guards at the eastern entrance of Samurkan were still in the process of closing the portcullis and Killian drew his cloak tight about him and did his best to look afraid, his tricorn hat and cutlass clutched in his hands beneath the fabric of his cloak.

There were a few dozen rushing the gates, most of them workers with some errand with the slavers, a handful of customers. There were three guards, and two barred the way with spears whilst the third was trying to insert a metal rod into some sort of release for the portcullis. The eastern gate was narrow, just wide enough to let a two-horse cart through – not that any cart would travel the rocky path down from the gate to the slavers' peninsula.

'Let us in!' someone yelled, and the chorus was taken up. The guards were calling for calm, and from the slave camp a shrill scream cut through the tumult. Killian wiped his bloody face on the shoulder of his cloak and pushed his way forward when it became clear the guards were barring the way to all.

'Slave gangs are fighting each other!' he cried. The guard with the metal rod looked up at him, panicked. The woman was young, even younger than he. 'Some of the slaves are getting loose.'

'We need to—'

Whatever the young guard was going to say was cut off by a crash as a two-level shack in the heart of the slave pens came careening down into the tents. As the guards peered at this latest chaos Killian retreated back just far enough to get his hands behind two of the other people clamouring at the gates. He shoved them both towards the gate, and as the guards fended them off with spear shafts and curses, Killian dove between their legs and scrambled up and started to run.

They yelled, of course, but they did not give chase. He had already managed to turn a corner down the first side street he saw when he heard the portcullis drop, metal impacting worn stone. Killian took two more corners blindly, careening, and then forced himself to slow to a walk. He was still bloody, and could see a wending trail of smoke over the eastern wall – some fire in the slave camp had spread. Bells of alarm were beginning to echo through the city. The east gate would be nothing but guards and soldiers and guild men soon enough. *And I'm already late.*

He snagged a bucket of water from next to a washing line dripping with undyed cotton and washed his face, wiped his sword down as best he could, and then dipped his hands. By the time his hands were in, the water was already pink, and the clotting blood on his hands fell away like rust. Killian allowed himself a long moment to try and bring calm.

After drying his face on an unsoiled corner of his cloak, he stood tall and set his hat upon his head and settled his sword on his hip, adjusting his cloak over his shoulders. *Calm and collected,* he repeated to himself. *A captain on the way to his ship.* Samurkan law did not apply outside of the city walls or the reach of the harbour, so there would be no recourse from the guards now that he had made it inside, but he knew whichever slaving outfit Ralad worked for would be seeking blood and gold and retribution. Killian started making his way down the familiar streets of the east ward and then stopped.

The dark door of an inn on a side street, and hanging above it a ludicrous sign. A crossbow, those winched flat bows of the kind they said the Tessendorm favoured, with a ludicrously long stock. *The Long Crossbow.* The dockmaster had said the owner wanted a ducat for news of Killian Heroneye. Killian frowned. There was something familiar about The Long Crossbow, as if he had heard it long ago. A joke or a rhyme or a story someone had told him as a child. He looked down the street towards the docks. The *Cutlass Hawk* was waiting, with Heavenly Nassin and forty soldiers crammed aboard. The Evertree Sisters' ships *Adamant Hand* and *Jade* were waiting out of harbour, ready to sail the next two days in convoy for this ridiculous pirate feud. All of them, waiting for him.

Let them wait. His nerves were still riled from his flight through the lower town, and there was a satisfaction to knowing the Evertree Sisters would have to wait on him, rather than the other way around. The harbour on Samurkan was deep enough that they waited on no tide to leave, only his presence. He grabbed that mote of power and held it close.

Killian strode into the dark inn. The common room was small, half a dozen trestle tables with low benches. The bar itself was stained and scarred wood, and behind it there were no bottles – only huge casks of ale. Killian squinted in the darkness. This sort of bar was common enough in the Crowns. No glass on show, or it'll get broke. The mugs would be unfired clay, and the ale would be awful. He had spent enough time in such places, and worse, and better. Grimacing, he ran a finger across his damp cheek and pictured the bathtub and the sharp wine in the upper city from the previous evening. Killian tugged on his shirt and strode to the bar and called out.

'Hello there! I've a thirst!'

There was a shuffle and a figure emerged from the back room. The solitary window was shuttered and let in only faint diffuse light, but they carried a candle and they used it to light another on the bar top. Killian found himself smiling broadly in recognition. The man was bald and short and wide, a thick wild beard and a round nose set beneath dark eyes and ponderous brows. His skin was utterly pale, reflecting the wan candlelight like a pearl in the light of the moon. He squinted at Killian and then set his candle down with a shaking hand and wiped his eye with the back of his hand, moving around the bar.

'Struan?' Killian said, moving closer. 'It is you, isn't it? You dog. You beast. You absolute joy!'

He reached across and grabbed the man's shoulder, face, disbelieving the evidence of his eyes and fingertips.

'Lad...' Struan gasped, his voice thick with emotion.

'I thought you were dead!' Killian said, and then he was laughing and so was Struan. The man shuffled out from behind the bar and embraced Killian and held him for a long moment.

'I thought *you* were,' Struan said at last. His eyes roved across Killian's face, a twist of pain across his mouth. His voice was the same deep timbre Killian remembered from his childhood. *Before we lost Mum. Before Samurkan.* 'You just disappeared, lad. What happened? I washed up here a year back and heard someone talk about *Heroneye*, the treasure hunter. Something about a duel, something about the captain of the guard's daughter. But you were out and away again before I could find you. Is it true, lad? You've your own ship? Your mother would be so proud, my lad, so happy to see you alive.'

Gently Struan reached up to Killian's chest and drew the iron heron skull pendant forth and held it in his hands.

'Captain Heroneye,' Killian said, and he tucked the amulet back into his shirt and stepped back and gave his best bow. 'Of the *Cutlass Hawk*. A two-mast caravel, Struan! I've my own crew. I've sailed half the Crowns!'

The older man shook his head, smiling, and settled himself down on a bench.

'Half the Crowns.' He laughed. 'Judges' eyes, it is good to see you, lad. When you left...'

Killian sat beside Struan and held his gaze. *When you left…* After his mother had been hanged by the Cil. There were a dozen years and a thousand questions between their last meeting, but when Killian opened his mouth only one question came to his lips.

'Do you know what happened to Key?' he asked, and when Struan turned his gaze to the floor Killian held his breath.

'After what happened to your mother, the rest of us were making plans to leave Requin-Port. You know that. Then you went and, well, disappeared. Key wouldn't leave with us, lad. Wouldn't see it for what it had to be. In the end she did like you did. Disappeared in the night with no goodbyes. We looked a long time, but in the end we had to leave with those who could. I've had no word from her since. Like you, I thought the Cil got her, or she jumped a ship.'

Killian closed his eyes and pictured his sister, a mirror to himself. Just as pale and gangly, just as dirt-worn and scuffed from their life in Requin-Port as their mother tried to keep them alive. Struan was one of the other adults, a half dozen Russilan who had been trying to cobble together something like a community under the boot of Cil rule.

'Where did you go, lad? The governor…' Struan asked, and Killian made himself smile. He remembered the governor of Requin-Port, sleeping in his bed. The governor, unassailable in his manor. Killian, just a child with a stolen knife.

'It was you?' Struan asked, and Killian smiled and held his tongue between his teeth. The older man sighed and shook his head, mouth downturned. In the flicker of the candlelight Killian could read fear in Struan's eyes. Struan didn't want it to be true, Cara's son red-wet and murderous.

'Six silver pennies they wanted,' Killian said, 'to bury mother. Key wanted to do it. I wouldn't let her. I stole a knife from the docks, and I waited until night and then I *climbed.* Hell of a thing, Struan. Not sure any man could have made that climb, anyway. A boy, though… but I was seen, and so I had to leave. I had to leave. Stowed away on an Undal trader; they let me stay when I told them the Cil wanted me for a slave. Got to Samurkan and found some kindness for a few years here, then when I had some legs under me and could hold a cutlass I found a ship and took whatever work I could get.'

He shrugged, as if those brief sentences could cover more than a decade of blood and sail. Struan simply stared and Killian was ten summers old again, bringing a broken sword hilt back to the house, a pot of crabs, a three-legged cat. Struan would look at him that same way: patient, waiting for him to start speaking. *I've learned, though.* Killian held his tongue and they sat in silence. Struan looked so sad.

'We always thought it was you,' he said at last, 'though in truth we assumed you'd died to do it. Bloody business for a boy.'

Killian stared at the candle. 'She was the best of us, Struan,' he said at last. 'I could kill every Cil I meet for the rest of my life and it wouldn't wash away what they did.'

They sat in silence and Struan reached out and adjusted the candle's dish, turning it slightly.

'There are Cil and *Cil*,' he said, and Killian pictured the woman in chains in the slave market.

'I know, Struan. I know.'

'You're young to have your own ship,' Struan said, and Killian shrugged again, felt heat rising in him. *My own ship.* Except he owed the Evertree Sisters a fortune. He flexed his fingers and looked at the knuckle where Heavenly Nassin had held the chisel-tip tight.

'I have to go, Struan,' he said eventually. The older Russilan was staring at him and was looking for Cara's features, her kindness, her wit. Instead there was only Killian. He felt the unspoken judgement. *You left your sister.* 'We were meant to sail at noon. We are out for a span. When I return, I'd like to talk properly, though. I want to know of you, and the rest of them.'

Struan winced and wrung his hands on his shirt.

'It's only me left, lad,' he said. 'You can't stay? You've only just arrived…'

Killian patted his shoulder. 'I'll hear their tales, at least. There is a school run by Mistress Merrow, in the east,' he said. 'She was good to me, when I got here. If you need anything in this city you ask her and she'll steer you right. It is *good* to see you, old man.'

Struan rose and embraced him again, and Killian found his chest tightening. *Struan. Requin-Port.* The image of his mother at the end of a noose, her legs twitching. The governor coughing blood over a terrified Killian, a knife hilt jutting from his ribs. *Key.*

Killian pulled away and left Struan with a grin, but inside his skull snakes writhed. Arlock Heroneye, the sister who hated him, and was right to do so. The sister he had only ever called *Key.* He did not think about Key, ever. He did not allow himself to think about Key, and the promises he had broken and the promises he had kept. He had promised

Key he wouldn't leave. He had promised his mother he would watch out for her. *All broken.* He had fled, and he had left her behind. She was the crow, he was the cutlass – a mighty skein-mage and a pirate captain who would sail the Crowns. *All of it, lost.*

Out in the pale sunlight of Samurkan, Killian fiddled with the crow and cutlass pin on his hat and then settled it tight on his head and squared his shoulders. Overhead, a gull called and the indifferent smoke from the slave camp spiralled and dissipated into nothing.

6

SMALL GOD ON THE HORSE WATER

'Deep below the lands of Undal and Isken in the northern tunnels, our brethren reported the firewyrms tunnelling. The cavern city of Muhos was lost in its entirety in the third year of the madness. Spider relu of glass and stone emerged in great numbers in the fifth, almost overcoming the Undal Holdfast. Their origin is still unclear. Here in the Crowns we have seen relu of the isles growing unpredictable and at times violent. This summer the holtmaster of the southern isles claims to have bound a relu in service, capable of great feats. This merits cautious investigation.'

– ***Letter to the Council of Isles on the Madness of the Spirits***, Anneli Thirdblood of Holt Suolaa

On the floating dock the younger Evertree Sister Hallis stood flanked by Heavenly Nassin, and next to her a glowering

Cil woman and a hulking hooded warrior in matte-black plate armour, unadorned and utilitarian. The warrior was almost of a size with Heavenly Nassin. The *Hawk* was alive with activity, Timmult and Renard and the Breygars rushing through a throng of heavily armed and scarred humans and Tullioch – the Evertree Sisters' strike force. East of the city the clamour and smoke of the burning slave market drew eyes, but most of the sailors were preoccupied with getting the caravel ready for the open sea. Of the dockmaster there was no sign – Hallis Evertree's presence was enough to send any semblance of the Samurkan authority off on other duties.

'You are late, Captain Heroneye,' she said, and Killian cut a bow. Pollos Twice-Kissed leaned over the rail and Killian gave him wave. He looked perturbed, and disappeared back onto the deck of the ship.

'Some small matters,' he said, and waited expectantly, watching the Cil woman and the warrior. The warrior was muttering something under his breath, face hidden in the shadow of his hood. The woman was armoured in supple black leather and matching cloth, a heavy cloak, and a Cil rune hammer at her side. Killian had never seen one in action but he had heard the stories – Cil hammers could break stone as easily as nutshells. Her hair was a lustrous black and spilled down across her shoulders.

'A change of plan,' Hallis said, and gestured at the newcomers. 'To Caragh's Point to deal with Blue Darrow, yes.'

'And then?'

Hallis opened her toothy maw and her muscly pink tongue flexed as she licked the edge of her mouth. She clicked her teeth and squinted one eye at him.

'The tomb by the Western Antian and the pottery will have to wait,' she said. 'This is the Lady Marion and her protector. They need passage, rather keenly. They have offered to pay your debt to us in full.'

Killian stood still and kept a slight smile on his face, then glanced up at the rail where the soldiers and crew were securing crates and provisions.

'This feels a more private conversation than I'd prefer on an open dock,' he said, trying to keep his voice low, and Hallis flicked her hand in annoyance.

'If your crew think you've no debt then they are fools,' she hissed. 'Burner's Run. They have heard you can cross it. You have told us, and others, you have crossed it. *They* have need to cross it. They have paid *half your debt* in advance for the attempt, Heroneye, over two thousand ducats. Upon their safe return across Burner's Run, they will send word to the Cil ambassador here to release the remaining funds. Should you fail, well... half an apple is better than none at all, eh? So you will take Nassin to deal with Blue Darrow, and then it is the Run for you. Do we understand each other? *Adamant Hand* and *Jade* await you past the breakwater – Captain Tarlis has command of the expedition. He will expect you this eve before you reach Caragh's Point to discuss tactics, but you've miles to go before then.'

Killian stared at the Tullioch, willing her to break his gaze, but she did not. He understood. She thought Burner's Run was a death sentence, or at best fleeing in terror, ship half wrecked and spirit broken. The Sisters had taken half his debt and sold his life for it. They did not believe he could pay them back, or at least not quickly enough to balance the offer of ducats in hand. They did not believe he could cross Burner's Run. *But they don't know what I know.* Killian remembered the wild sea, the look on his mother's face when they crossed that water. *The winter the world went mad.*

Killian relaxed his posture and smiled with his lips tight. The idea of a Cil, not just someone from Cil-Marie but one of the government's agents, on *his ship*, made his eyelid twitch. He scratched at it with a knuckle and tried to plan. *Two thousand ducats. Burner's Run. Certain death.*

'Always miles to go, Hallis,' he said. 'We will meet again soon, I hope.' With a wave he gestured at the ship. 'Aboard then, Lady Marion, Heavenly Nassin, and nameless scary man.'

There was still a gangway lowered as Nassin's mercenaries lugged water and food and weaponry up onto the deck, and they were aboard in quick order. Killian directed his charges to his cabin and then was collared by Pollos Twice-Kissed, the huge Undal's dolorous face still, his eyes a little wild.

'Cast off and get us underway,' Killian said. 'I've to speak to this Cil the Sisters have foisted on us. Get some of Nassin's men on the oar sweeps if you can. Wind is dead in the harbour today.'

Pollos nodded but didn't let go of Killian's shoulder, and instead gestured at the front of the ship. Past the tumult of soldiery and the flustered Breygars. A solitary figure was leaning over the bow of the ship, running a hand through the thick fresh foliage that had been lashed to the bowsprit, boughs of willow and a twist of bramble vine fat with black berries. The figure was diminutive, cloaked and hooded, and Killian felt his shoulders slump when he saw the furred hand.

'Why is there an Antian fondling my green-blessing?' he asked, and Pollos coughed and tilted his head.

'Well,' Pollos started, but Killian pulled at his own face in exasperation and held up a finger, rounding on him.

'I have bloody *Nassin* and his crew,' he whispered, 'who want us to help them fight pirates, and Nassin and his crew *are* pirates! I have a bloody *Cil* woman who has bought our debt from the Evertrees and wants us to take her through Burner's bloody Run, Pollos. Zalan the shipbreaker. The Bloody Crows. All that nasty stuff in the Deep Crowns we said we'd best just *avoid*, all our plans to head west and make some easy money gone faster than spit in a storm. Big Breygar is still contemplating slitting my throat every night we sail since I let Affy Burngull get eaten by those bloody goblins. I've got blood under my fingernails, and in my hair, because I just left a dozen slavers dead who were threatening Miss Merrow. I don't need this, Pollos!'

Killian removed his hat and fingered the worn leather of its edge and tried to catch his breath.

'She's our new tide-mage,' Pollos said gently. 'Petal sent her down. Standard day rate. Petal vouched for her. Do I need to worry about slavers?'

Killian rubbed his eyes and stared at the cloaked Antian, turned his gaze on his cabin door.

'No,' he said. 'Fine. Fine. *Fine.* I need to go and speak to these Cil to see what the bloody burning hell is happening. Get her quartered. Get us out of Samurkan. Get us out of here. We need open water and some time to think. The slavers who saw me are dead, at least. We can worry about that next time we are here.'

Pollos nodded and pated Killian on the shoulder.

'You're doing grand, lad,' he said quietly as Killian turned to leave. 'We'll hit the Horse Water; it'll be grand. Keep your guard up.'

In the end Killian hid for another twenty minutes, helping the Breygars and Timmult and Renard and Pollos cast off. They would have days, if not spans, to discuss Burner's Run. *Idiocy and madness*. Behind the helm he watched Samurkan recede as they picked up a little wind, the *Hawk*'s twin sails catching and pulling taut. He had a better vantage of the docks from here, the fish dock, the stone dock where Isken guild ships were busily unloading, the butcher's dock where a whaler was even then unloading its catch, a wooden crane hauling up the carcass of some grey-blue beast with a dozen fins on each side. He saw the lone Tullioch coral ship, mastless, a hull of worked coral that caught the noon sun in its endless indentations and intricacies. It was perhaps a hundred foot long, with high sides. It was anchored at the far reaches of the inner harbour, as far from other ships as it was possible to be. He could just make out the torsos and heads of Tullioch walking its deck.

The Tullioch coral ships were closely guarded, fast, and few. He had no idea how they propelled through the water. Living beasts, he had heard: skein-magic, coral water jets, underwater oars. *I'd like to see that up close.* Killian cast an eye at the skies but there was no trouble – a solid north-westerly wind that should push them straight to the Horse Water, and the current there should bear them to Caragh's Point. It would take three days, if the winds held and no storms came in. As they emerged from the crab-claw harbour of Samurkan, he caught sight of *Adamant Hand* and *Jade*. Both ships were busy with movement as sails were readied. He did not know them, or their captains – only the reputation, two names of many in the Evertree Sisters' little fleet of smugglers, traders, *pirates*. Mixed crews of Tullioch and human, ruthless where they needed to be but pragmatic above all else. They would leave crews alive, or drop them at the nearest port. No slavery and no butchery, unless either was deemed necessary.

Killian finally admitted defeat and went to his cabin, removing his hat and hanging it on its usual peg as he entered his rooms. He stopped short.

Silver was sat at his desk, drinking a cup of wine. She was wearing a bleached white cotton shirt with a drawstring collar that was loose, and blue trous. Her boots were resting on the edge of his desk, next to a map of the Northern Crowns that had not been open when he had last left his cabin. She smiled at him, nose crinkling, and pushed a wave of blonde curls back from her forehead.

'Captain Heroneye,' she said jauntily, and gestured at his guests. The Cil woman Marion was sat drinking his wine as well in one of the two low armchairs that made up the entirety of his room's furnishing, save for the lidless sea chest full of blades and bows and arrows and the locked sea chest, where he kept his maps and coin. *Which is open,* he noted. Heavenly Nassin stood at the rear of the cabin gazing out through the unshuttered window, hands clasped behind his back. His city attire was gone – now he wore only knee-length trous and a belt of red cloth, his coral-handled dagger tucked into the belt with its blade glinting at his hip. His chest was bare, and he did not look around when Killian entered. Killian sighed and moved forward and poured himself a glass of wine, and sat in the armchair.

'We are well underway,' he said.

'Baal be praised,' a voice uttered from the shadow behind the door, and he almost spilled his wine as he jerked around. The Cil woman's guardian stood behind the door in his matte-black plate armour, his hood down. He was bald, his face and skull painted an eerie pasty white and his eye sockets shaded in black. His eyes themselves were a murky yellow, the whites and irises all tinted. He nodded at Killian and resumed his silent brooding.

'Indeed,' Killian said, and raised his glass to Marion. 'It is *Lady* Marion, Hallis said? Is that correct? I was not aware the Cil had taken to such titles. I thought rank was more the thing.'

The woman Marion smiled thinly at him.

'A mistranslation, perhaps. You may refer to me as Lieutenant, or simply Marion will suffice for our reasons. You seem to know our customs. Odd, for a Russilan.'

Killian smiled at that and took a sip of his wine.

'I spent some formative time in Requin-Port, and learned much. And what *are* our reasons? Hallis said you've paid the debt, substantial that it is.'

Marion looked to Silver.

'This one, *Silver*, is on your crew?'

'An associate,' he said. *Who shouldn't be here.* But they were under sail, a mile or more past the breakwater already. *Bloody fool. Perhaps I can get her off ship en route to Caragh's Point.* 'You can speak freely.'

Marion nodded and set down her wine, and gestured to the table.

'A map of the Crowns, if you please,' she said, and went to loom over his chart table, one finger tapping the head of the intricately wrought hammer at her belt. Silver went to the map chest and returned in a moment with Killian's best map of the Crowns, and he frowned at her. She smirked back at him as she unrolled it. *We will speak of that later.*

'I don't care about this business at Caragh's Point,' Marion said, and at the window Heavenly Nassin clicked his teeth but did not turn around. 'After that, we need to reach the Deep Crowns with all haste. I was told by a source that Killian Heroneye has claimed to have crossed the Run. One of many tall tales about you, Captain, but this one was quieter, and the Evertree Sisters confirmed it.'

'Who told you?' he asked, frowning, but Marion waved him away.

'It doesn't matter. What matters is that only a Russilan captain can do this, perhaps, and your people are not so common. So to speak. We have tried and failed. Zalan himself sent us back, but allowed us to live. Perhaps he sensed our intentions.'

Killian peered at the map. The Deep Crowns were a hundred isles, perhaps more, closely huddled in the centre of the vast circlet that was Burner's Run. A place of strange tides, worse winds. Where Zalan the shipbreaker swam and took his tithes.

'Since Zalan went mad, nobody has crossed the Run,' he said, and Marion tapped the chart.

'Not quite,' she said, and with her finger began to point at small isles in the Eastern Crowns that bordered the Run.

'Here, three years ago. Here, three months after that. Again, again, again.'

Killian leaned back. 'The Bloody Crows,' he said, and Marion smiled thinly.

'Indeed. Three years ago they emerged across the run, black-hulled ships, pirates that leave no quarter. Our only reports being from the few who managed to flee, or happened upon a raid and escaped unseen, that they saw these black hulls heading back towards the Deep Crowns. We need to get into Burner's Run.'

Killian smiled because he didn't know what else to do.

'Lady,' he said. 'The Isken sent four guild ships east to deal with the Crows. None returned. A Kelamor galley with six skein-mages went east, to deal with the Crows. It did not return. What exactly do you expect me to do? Even if we crossed Burner's Run, which is in itself a *question*, you have one scary man with a sword and black armour, and a nice hammer. My ship is not a warship. We are traders, fast ones – but barely armed.'

Marion returned to her seat, taking her wine with her.

'We caught one,' she said savouring the wine. *My best bottle.* He waited for her to continue, brows furrowed, as she took her time. 'A Cil ship that was... patrolling the waters was attacked. The Bloody Crow vessel escaped, our ship was sunk, but they lost a man overboard. A support vessel managed to save him along with a few of our own. We have a name, and a location. Indeed, we already sent one delegation – though that foundered before it crossed the Run, and they captured one of our men. Crow Isle, in the heart of the Deep Crowns is our destination. And we do not need arms, because I am not a soldier, or a spy, or a mage.' Marion smiled at him and finished her wine. 'I am a *diplomat.* Cil-Marie wants to deal with these people, whoever they may be. Before the madness of the gods, the Deep Crowns were hard to reach but not impossible. There is wealth there. Trade, and so on. And they have... one of our people. As I said. Jean du Cilcan, his name is. It is imperative that he is retrieved safely. Hallis Evertree had heard this rumour of yours as well, that you can cross Burner's Run. Several sources, all confident that whilst you may be a liar and a killer, that whilst you may have stolen this ship and killed its captain, that whilst you may be a criminal of every dark inclination, that whilst you may utterly lack morality, ethics, or even a rudiment of education – several of them believe that despite all of this you are a sailor worth your salt, and that you alone can do this thing.'

'You said you've a name?' Killian asked, smiling thinly, and he set down his own wine and stared at the map, ink and parchment belying the intricacy of the world.

'We do,' she said. 'Captain Arlock, of the Bloody Crows. That is all we know. How will you take us across Burner's Run?'

Killian stopped still and stared down at the map and felt the weight of the heron pendant at his neck. He pictured his mother, face hooded, hanging from a Cil rope. His sister fighting to get to her, Killian and Struan and two others holding her back as she railed and screamed and cried. *Arlock. Little Key.* The two of them in the room they shared, comparing by stolen candle-stub light shells and broken blades, scraps of cloth, the treasures of poor children. Promising his mother. *I will look after her.* Fleeing to the docks slick with the Cil governor's blood, and making the choice. Leaving his sister, Arlock Heroneye.

Killian smiled and laughed, and across the desk, Silver stared at him, curious, and he raised an eyebrow to her, and then his glass to Marion. *I found Struan today.* His smile faded. What were the chances, that this day, the day he found Struan after so many years, word of Arlock would reach him? *There are no chances,* his mother's voice whispered in his mind.

'The route and the way across are secret, of course,' he said, toasting the Cil woman, 'but for clearing my debt with the Evertree Sisters, I will get you across Burner's Run. On that you have my word.'

And I'll feed you to Zalan myself.

Kaikatsu stayed at the bow of the ship. There were no lines there to the masts, not right at the very front out past the railing. She crouched in her cloak and made herself comfortable – there was a web of net below the bowsprit and she clambered down into it. The ship left harbour and she sat beneath willow and bramble as salt spray kissed her face, and as the sun dipped they crossed into the Horse Water, one of the great currents that cut through the Crowns. The ship was moving east in convoy with two others, and she let herself drop into the skein.

A tumult of connection but so much *calmer* at sea than the busyness of port. Great connections, currents, lines of sensation between sky and cloud, wind and sea. She could find the intricacy if she focused but instead she let her gaze fall diffuse across the water. Motes of distant fish and beasts, but in that moment, mainly just water and sky. She sighed.

From under her cloak the little god crawled, up onto her shoulder. He chittered, and her senses took him in and all hope of a wide view was lost. The little relu was shaped like a cave mouse, huge ears and a sinuous tail and a body smaller than the palm of her hand. In the skein he was a blazing light, a riot of connections that seemed to dance around him, loose threads that had once tethered him to place and people. She saw him inside and out, from every conceivable angle all at once. A thread of vibrant red energy spun from his heart to her own. She let the skein fall from her eyes and shivered at the exertion, and reached up to pet the little god. His fur was a living cobalt, strands of soft blue metal, and his eyes were shining-bright, smooth orbs of jade. The little mouse scratched at its nose, and its long tail curled around it, a thin strip of sinuous gold. She held him in her hand.

'What do you see?' she whispered, but he did not answer her, and she held him still. *All of his connection, severed. All but ours.*

Kaikatsu hummed in the back of her throat to the little mouse, a wordless song that had calmed her in her youth when her connection to the skein had first manifested, when each night she had dreamt the whole world and each night she had woken screaming. The little god shivered and rubbed at its nose with its paws, and then crawled back under her cloak to the open pouch at her belt padded with soft handkerchiefs. Kaikatsu stared down at her empty hands and then clenched them tight and focused on the horizon. She had spent nearly her whole life below the ground in the

Antian tunnels and enclaves. The humans thought Antian were like dogs, but a mole was closer. The horizon was a blur – her eyes were sharp enough for the proximity of tunnel living, but above ground distance dulled everything to vagary.

The mouse squirmed in its pouch and its head emerged, ears twitching, and Kaikatsu reached a hand down and stroked the silken blue fuzz between its ears, the song of her forebears dying in her throat as she watched the distant blur of a seabird wheel high above them.

'We will find home again,' she murmured, and the little god squeaked, and the *Cutlass Hawk* rode fast on the water.

Requin-Port

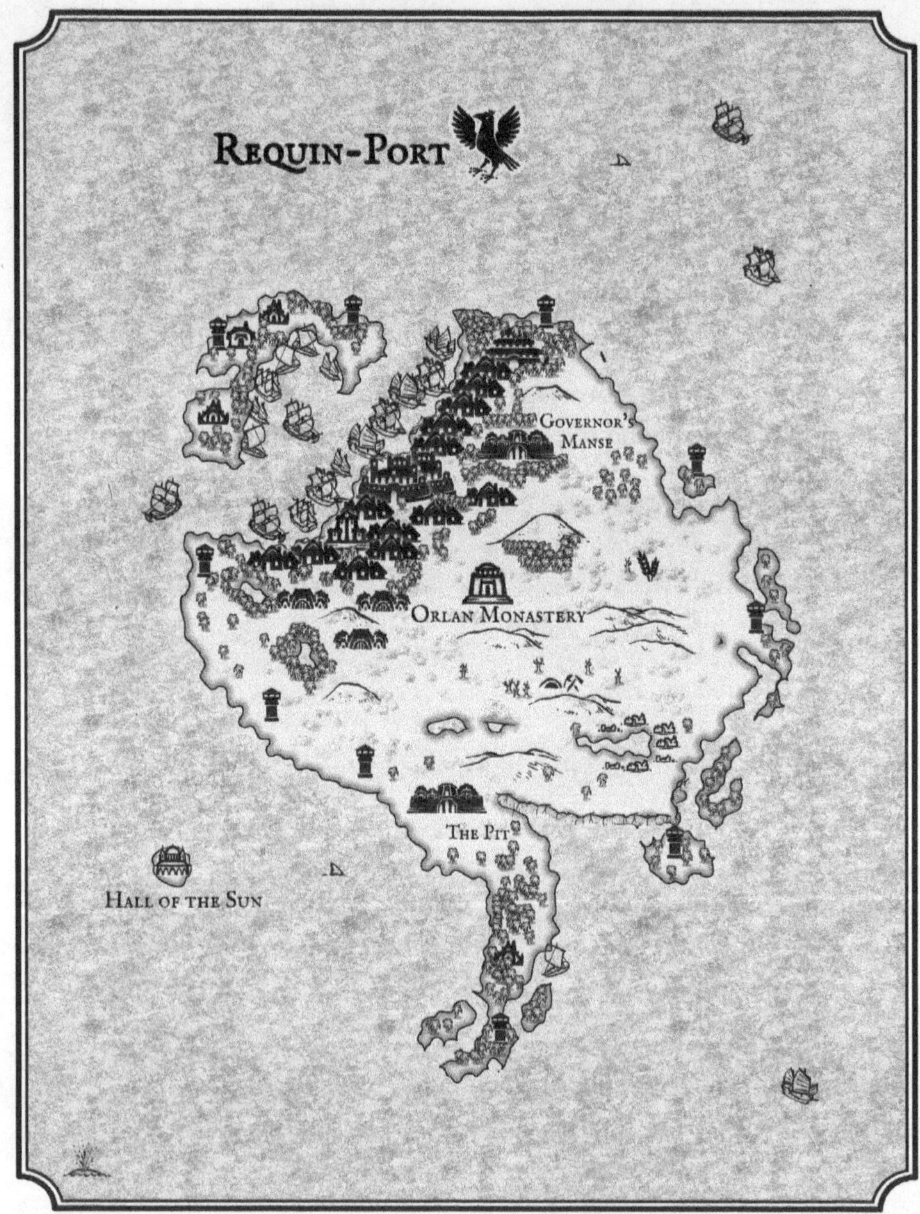

Requin-Port, year 1122 Isken – **From the charts of the *Cutlass Hawk*,** Captain Killian Heroneye

7

A DROP IN THE OCEAN

'"We won't stop, Nashtu. I be the captain, and the Revel Hoard will be ours, and your blood as well!" The rune-scribed cutlass flared with blue flame, the blade weaving through the air as Captain Slip drove the sea devil back. The beast cackled and reached out a hand, gripping the blade, and the ice flames sputtered and died. It hauled the captain off his feet by his throat and snapped his neck with a squeeze, and then spread its wings as it cast his body down. The crew were still. "Captain," the devil Nashtu said, tasting the word. "I like that title."'

– ***The Hundred Deaths of Captain Nashtu,***
R.S. Drissit

The day his mother died, Killian wore his best shirt. He had three shirts: his bad shirt, stained with salt and grime and torn at the waist; his good shirt, cleaner, with only the rip on the left wrist (neatly stitched); his best shirt, a faded green that was long in the body but fit his arms perfectly. It was his mother's favourite, and he only wore it when they visited Struan and Starfinder Russich and the other Russilan for some celebration or mourning.

'We should find Father,' Key said, and Killian huffed and ignored her. *Stupid.* They were in the room they shared with their mother but through the old sailcloth hanging from the ceiling he could hear the other Russilan they shared their rooms with moving. Nell and Hestin, Big Jule, Kettleberry, the diminutive Hawkbone sisters who were twice his age but shorter than Killian, even though his tenth summer had only just passed. Hunger stuck his belly to his ribs but his mother had always found enough fishbones and milk to keep him tall. With a glare at Key he checked himself over again. Belt, trous, shirt. It wasn't late enough in the year to wear his foot wraps. One copper piece with the edge clipped off in a fabric pouch tucked inside his trous. An oyster-shucking knife he had stolen from the fish market hidden in the back of his belt. He had cut himself on it that morning in the pre-dawn blackness, fumbling with it when he awoke from dreams of seabirds wheeling over black water.

'They're going to kill Mum,' Key said, and Killian shoved her hard. She was a stick-thin thing, bird bones and dirt masquerading as a girl. Key fell to the ground without a sound.

'Shut *up*,' he said, and she squinted at him and pulled herself up, and then went to their sailcloth door. 'Jule said they might just take a hand. Might take nothing. It was only bread.'

Key stared at him balefully and he felt his heart sink at the utter hatred in her eyes.

'*I'm hungry*,' she said, her voice a mockery of his own. 'It's your fault.'

Key left the room. Killian sat in silence and pulled the oyster knife from his belt and pressed the blade into the palm of his hand, feeling the tension build so close to breaking through the skin to the blood below. He went to lie down on his mother's pallet, pulled the blanket over his eyes and tried to picture her face. It smelled of salt and straw and her.

Cara Heroneye had been there every day of his life. Cara was beautiful, and smart, and kind. She teased him but always stopped before he was upset. *Not like Key.* Key would find a soft spot and dig until he howled. Cara listened to his questions and answered them. She found him scraps of storybooks to read: Captain Nashtu adventures, Caroban ghost stories. She had taught him his letters, revelled in the stories he told her from the books and from the docks. Cara Heroneye loved him absolutely, and knew every inch of his mind. He had seen her every day of his life, and as he lay beneath her blanket with his eyes squeezed shut and the blade in his hand, he could not bring himself to picture her face, no matter how he tried. *It's your fault.*

'It's time, lad,' a voice called. *Struan.* The bearded man was a barrel, his arms thick as most men's legs. His place was across the warren of slums, close to his work in the whale abattoir, where he lodged with Starfinder Rurich. He wore green as well, and at his neck a pendant with the skull of some beast Killian didn't know. Killian's hand went to his own pendant, the heron skull wrought in iron – the only metal he owned that wasn't stolen.

He wanted the weight of it to comfort him, but it did not. Some of the other Russilan had wood instead of iron or steel, some real bone, and a few wore no skull at all. Killian tucked his pendant in his shirt and joined Struan wordlessly, slipping the oyster knife back into his belt as he stood. He did not think the man had seen, in the gloom.

The Russilan left the slums of Requin-Port in a mournful procession, their best clothes matching the daily rags of the other denizens. There were twenty of them, and Killian and Key were the only children. Key kept her distance from him. As they passed through the mud-slick labyrinth of alleys of the outer slums they were ignored, but once they were within the high city walls of Requin-Port they were glared at and spat upon.

'Go drink!' one man called, a shaven-headed Cil sailor. His compatriots laughed, and Killian glared at them. The lowest of Cil, indentured to some ship, and even they looked down on the penniless Russilan. Destitute, without homeland or god or people. *Go drink,* meaning fall to the Thirst like their ancestors had and drink the sea until they could never drink again. The Russilan had covered the whole archipelago with cities and ships and bright swords until the Thirst took them. Killian kicked at a stone and glared at the sailors.

'Ignore them,' a voice quavered, and Killian forced his eyes forward, quickening his step. It was Starfinder Rurich, one hand on Key's shoulder, and Killian had no time for him. 'Before the sun rose I looked to the sky, my dear boy—'

Killian was fast enough to avoid hearing the end of Rurich's nonsense, fate and life writ in distant stars. *Meanwhile everyone else works.* Anger at Rurich was easier than thinking about the acid ache in his gut and the matching guilt at the base of his skull. The walls of Requin-Port were dressed stone with towers every hundred yards, and inside the city the streets were paved with flagstones and the buildings were tall, stone bases giving way to wooden walls and steep roofs lined with shingle and shale to keep out the driving rain. There was no rain, only a pale blue sky. Inside the walls he could feel no wind. He saw a boy his age with *shoes*, eating a half loaf of brown bread carelessly, crumbs dropping to the street. The eyes of the Cil were upon their procession, and after they entered the walls a retinue of black-clad guards followed them, not trying to be discreet.

'It should be raining if they are going to hang Mum,' Key said behind him, and Rurich shushed her. Killian threaded forward until he was next to Hestin. Hestin who went out at night and slept in the day, with his long hair tied back and a moustache like a Kelamor swordfighter. Hestin who wore a dagger at his hip just a hair's breadth smaller than the legal limit for non-Cil. Only citizens of the empire were allowed long blades. Hestin who didn't work the way the others did, but always had a parcel of food for Cara Heroneye or for the Hawkbone sisters. *Not last span though*. Last span storms had kept the fishing ships in, Struan had no whales to butcher, Rurich only cared for his stars, the Hawkbone sisters were south in the forest gathering mushrooms. Hestin had no food to give. Everyone, an excuse, and Killian and Key hungry and their mother short of work. *Because of me.*

For a month she had asked him to watch Key as she worked the tanneries east of town, where she would return stinking of offal and piss and mud, bone-tired and broken but with money for food. On the third day of the storms he ran out before she left, and she had missed her time and lost her place. Nobody else could watch Key, and his mother wouldn't just leave her. Four days later during a cold drizzle he had told her for the hundredth time that he was hungry, and she had held them both tight, pulled on her thin cloak and left.

That day Killian had run the warrens with his friends, down west and west again through scrubland to the shingle beach where the anchorage was poor and no Cil went. Tellamor, the boy with one eye, said the storm would have washed up all sorts. They found seaweed that was not so bad to chew on, if you had a fresh stream nearby to rinse the worst of the salt off.

When Killian returned that afternoon with his pockets full of shells, two iron nails, and a broken belaying pin, Key had been alone. The storm had broken and slants of weak sun played through the roof of their shack, and he had laid out his prizes on their bed. Key had watched him in silence and he had waited for her to speak, waited and waited and then huffed in exasperation.

'Was *going* to give you a nail,' he had said, and she had burst into tears, because their mother was gone.

Killian forced himself from the memory. *Remembering won't save her.* He sidled up to the whip-thin rake Hestin and matched the taller man's stride.

'Hestin,' he whispered, and the man drew close as they took the last turn towards the docks. 'Hestin… they won't hang her, Hestin. You're a thief. What's the punishment for a loaf of bread?'

Hestin did not meet his eye and kept his pace, his eyes darting around the crowded streets. The group had to squeeze past a cart unloading sacks of corn, another with amphora bedded in straw that bore the intricate stamps of the Isken guilds.

'I'm not a thief, boy,' Hestin said. 'Your mother is a good woman.'

Killian gripped his arm. 'I won't let them hurt her,' he hissed, and Hestin grasped his hand and flexed it back, for anyone watching just a man holding a boy's hand, but he *squeezed* until Killian flinched away.

'*You will*,' Hestin said, 'and I will. They will flog her at best, kill her at worst, and whatever comes, boy, she loved you and she was the best of us. When we get to the square, you look and you look good. Archers on the nearest building, a dozen guards at the base of the gibbet platform, another dozen around the governor and his men. This isn't my first hanging. Three Cil on the platform at least, oh aye. What do you think you'll do with that oyster knife? The one you keep checking in that sorry excuse for a belt? Piss off one, and make it worse for all of us, especially for *you* and your sister. Which is the one thing your mum wouldn't want. So you'll wind your neck in, and hope for mercy on their part. Revenge might come, but you can't save her if she isn't to be saved.'

Killian's heart thudded wildly at Hestin's words. 'Coward!' he spat, and fell back in the procession, his hand aching. *It's your fault.* As they entered the square, he glanced back and saw the stooped, hooded form of Starfinder Rurich following him, inevitable, one hand on Key's shoulder. She was weeping.

It was a bell before the Cil paraded out, and Killian walked the square. The square was walled on three sides, with the fourth a low parapet with a vantage across the teeming harbour of Requin-Port. The gibbet stood resolute on a small stage of stone. The wood of the gibbet was salt-stained and old, but the ropes hanging from it were fresh.

Six nooses stark against a sky that had turned from pale blue to the slick grey of a wet anchor. Hestin had said archers and guards, soldiers and watching eyes. Killian ended up stood with Struan twenty feet from the gibbet stage, and cursed the thief. Hestin was right. There were more Cil than he could count, armed with axe and pike and longswords, armoured in thick leather cuirasses and leather and steel helms. A few of the guards were in heavier armour, plates of metal encasing every limb, cloaks of black trailing behind them as they moved through the crowds. The square was busy, the Russilan contingent a paltry corner of a bustling scene. One man was selling apples, another skewered fingerfish. Killian tried to remember their faces.

With a blare of trumpets a gate in the western wall opened and through it two dozen black-clad guards holding pike and axe. They advanced inexorably to the crowd, who hustled backward, those few that were too slow or hemmed in by others to move at an acceptable pace hastened by barked shouts in Cil and brutal smacks from axe hafts.

The governor arrived. He came to all the hangings, someone had said. He was an old man, with the amber skin of the Cil and piercing golden eyes. He was utterly bald and bedecked in black robes swirling with angular patterns of silver, and at his thick belt a black-headed hammer inscribed with runes hung. Guards preceded and followed him, a ring of steel, and the crowd quieted until he was seated atop the stone dais next to a pale woman in a blue dress. As they spoke to each other, the crowd jolted to life again, the tension palpable.

'What stars did you see last night?' Key asked, and Killian jerked. He had not noticed her sidle up beside him, and she had said nothing but bile at him in the three days since their mother had been taken. He could not bear to hear the pain in her voice.

'Shut up, Key,' he said, a desperate anger the only articulation for his pain he could manage, and she punched him in the gut. By the time Struan pulled them apart Killian was red in the face and his best shirt skewed, a line of bright blood across the back of his hand where her jaw had clamped down. Key bared her teeth at him, victorious.

'There are things you cannot fight, Heroneye,' Starfinder Rurich said in his ear, and then the old man's hands were iron vices on Killian's arms. Killian pushed forward but Struan was there and Hestin, both with hands on him, Hestin reaching roughly to Killian's belt and plucking the oyster knife away. Kettleberry and the Hawkbone sisters had a crying Key in their arms. Rurich gripped Killian harder.

'The stars and the sea tell our fate,' Starfinder Rurich intoned, and then opened his mouth to speak further, the scraggle of his beard and the quaver of his voice both so intimately familiar. Killian struggled against the grip of the Russilan men and stamped his feet but then came a single blare of a trumpet announcing the prisoners and all fell still.

A functionary led them. Killian strained to see, and through the throng he glimpsed the column. Cil, guards, and then *there*. His mother. Paler than he had ever seen, shadows beneath her eyes and a fresh bruise blooming across her jaw. He yelled for her.

She did not hear him. The crowd was a wave of noise as the families and friends and allies of the prisoners all began to call at once. There were a dozen prisoners, and try as he might Killian could not pull free of Struan and Rurich and Hestin.

'Stop!' Struan said at last, gripping Killian's shoulders and forcing him to stillness. 'You stop now, lad. There are words to come, and if you carry on like this they'll have you in a noose alongside her. If you can't be still, I'll knock you down and drag you out of here myself.'

The trumpet blared once more and the crowd fell still. Killian fought, but Struan held him easily. They were a dozen feet from the dais, and finally the chain of prisoners were led upon it. Men, women, and one Antian that was more blood than fur, their arm clearly broken. All of them bedraggled, none of them free from injury. Key was next to him and Killian reached wordlessly for her hand and held it tight without thought, a reflex from a lifetime together. His mother's gaze swept the crowd. She found them and smiled, drawing great gulps of air as she wept. He could not help but cry with her. She stood beneath a noose, and he knew she was speaking to him but he could not hear her. He knew what she was saying anyway.

A man was speaking in Cil, he had a widow's peak of oil-slicked hair and a lustrous green robe stitched with silver stars draped over him. Killian stared at that green and then down at the fade of his own shirt, so pale in comparison. He caught his mother's name amidst the torrent of Cil, and then the unctuous functionary began again in the Isken trade tongue.

'The accused known as: Fai Sellincor, Garet Sellincor, Jonal Harp, Marrideth Bull, Larren Foist, Cara Heroneye, Danal Viln-Ferres, Stromart, Hallis Burn, Siobhan of Wedderburn, Olin, and the Antian known as Failur. The charges are theft and sedition!'

The crowd roared and surged and Killian lost his view. He held on to Key's hand.

When he could see the dais again it was only because a surge in the crowd let him. It had been less than a minute but two men were hanging from nooses, twisting and writhing as they choked. He gripped Key and pulled Struan close.

'She stole bread!' he screamed in the older man's ears, but Struan had no words for him. Key was yelling too, and he was too far away to see, to understand. Someone was screaming, and then a cobblestone flew through the air towards the Cil guards and the screams changed their cadence. Bodies were pushing away from the governor's dais. Killian thrust Key into Struan's arms. The ancient Starfinder Rurich was lost to the crowd. Hestin hovered at Killian's shoulder.

'We should leave!' Hestin shouted to Struan, and Killian took his chance.

He had a brief glimpse of Key's face, pale and shocked, as he drew the dagger from Hestin's belt. The man reacted instantly, but Killian threw himself under the crowd at ground level and scrambled, accepting the kicks and stamps until he found himself up against a railing of wood at the base of the stone dais. Cil guards were laying about anyone who crossed the fence with abandon, grabbing any who did not retreat and dragging them through the western wall gate. Killian held tight to a post and managed to see the dais again. Seven people swinging and writhing, and a noose around his mother's neck and tears streaming down her face as she spoke to a Cil holding parchment and quill, her last words to be eternalised in their records. She kept glancing at the crowd and he screamed to get her attention, not a curse or a threat but a simple plea.

'Mum!' he called, his throat ragged, and she saw him and the roar of the crowd fell away even as bodies pressed against him, hands pulled at him.

Killian's mum saw him and she spoke not to the Cil, but to him alone.

Look after her.

He could not hear her, but he saw the shape of the words, had heard those words so many times.

A Cil executioner kicked the stool from beneath his mother's feet as the functionary kept scribbling his notes, and Killian lunged forward at the nearest guard. An axe haft hit him in the temple and he went sprawling into the crowd, but someone hauled him to his feet and another held his face and looked deep into his eyes, spoke words he could make no sense of. Killian pushed away, and the crowd noise returned. These weren't Russilan rioting, not the drab impoverished dregs. These were the people of Requin-Port, all those non-Cil who had built the city from rock and salt. Killian pushed through them towards his mother as a trumpet blared thrice and the crowd fell still. He heard swords unsheathed, and at the ramparts a dozen archers had arrows nocked in bows.

Killian pushed through the crowd to the rail at the base of the dais, and atop it his mother did not struggle or writhe. Her eyes were open but sightless, and she did not struggle. Her feet were as bare as his own, her hands loose at her sides. She was dead. They were all dead. Killian could not look at her, but could not look away.

The governor rose, and walked away to the western gate along with the pale woman in the blue dress, a matched pair of furrowed brows and sneering mouths as they continued their conversation, the governor waving a lazy hand in disgust at the gathered rabble and not looking at the people within it once. The oily functionary cleared his throat and smiled thinly, appraising the now silent crowd. Three blasts of the trumpets meant the leash was slipped. The Cil guards could maim, could kill, could do as they pleased with impunity. They awaited now only the slightest provocation. Killian gripped the short knife in his fist and forced himself to look at his mother as the Cil man spoke.

'Cil-Marie and the eternal Sun-Masters bring hope,' he said, voice quavering as he tried to project himself. Killian's mum was swaying gently.

'This hope must be guarded,' the Cil continued. 'These criminals sought to undermine the glory of Cil-Marie, and thus Requin-Port, and thus your own futures. Think well on this.'

With nothing further, he turned to leave, a single apple sailing through the sky from the crowd and thudding to the street behind him. He did not look back or stop walking, and Killian did not think about guards, or archers. He did not think about Key, or Struan. He only wanted to sink his blade into that man's heart, a thousand times.

Look after her.

He ignored the flash of memory, those words, and moved towards the Cil. If he was fast enough—

Hestin grabbed his wrist with one hand and hauled him bodily away, twisting the knife from his grip. He turned to fight but Key was there, and as she fell into him he could do nothing but catch her.

The Muruds

The Muruds, year 1134 Isken – **From the charts of the *Cutlass Hawk*,** Captain Killian Heroneye

INTERLUDE

THE SPEAR AND THE POT

'You catch an octopus two ways. You catch him fast with a spear, or slow with a pot. When I was a lad I favoured the spear, but I'm old now. I like the pot. I drop my clay pot on a rope and I wait, days and days, tide and moon, and when I come back and pull it up there is a surprised wriggle in there and then I eat well. You people will learn one day that the spear is well and good, but for the spear you must be in the water; and in the water, there are other hunters. I hope one finds you soon.'

– The final words of Donal Stoneskua, executed 3rd Starsday, Flower, by hanging, Record of executions 1135 Isken reckoning, Druich

Nall kept checking the clouds on the western horizon, a long glance skyward after each pot was thrown back to the sea. He hauled the pots on their long lines of barnacle-sharp rope up into his dog-boat, pausing to pry the largest molluscs from the rough line with his belt knife and eating them fresh from the line. They pulsed in his mouth and he was sure to chew thrice before swallowing down the salt slime of their flesh – his cousin Merrigull had swallowed barnacles whole, and one had clamped its sucker halfway down his windpipe. They'd gotten it out with a flinder of wood, in the end, but the look on Merrigull's face had been enough to teach Nall his lesson. He chewed thrice and swallowed the chunks, and between each line he looked back at the clouds, a bruise of thick purple black blotting over the afternoon sun. He could still make out that sun, a faint perfect circle behind the veil.

Nall was after octopuses, big ones, small ones, whatever came his way. Every pot he checked with his octopus poking stick, and inevitably they latched on and fought and then it was a matter of drawing them out, and as the dog-boat bobbed in the weak surf he would take his belt knife, wide and flat and sharper than a shark's tooth, and drive it deep. Octopuses didn't die fast. The tentacles would wriggle, the beak would snap. It would jet ink that he would try and catch as best he could in a jug. None of it registered much with Nall. He threw it down to the crate with the others. By the time the next jug was raised, his stick would no longer be held tight. He looked back at the storm on the western horizon and chewed his cheek.

'Not right, that one,' he said, and his only companion responded the way she always did. She warbled quietly from her perch at the bow of the boat and he reached down to the bait pot and tossed her a little fish, no more than half a finger. Nall's companion was a cormorant, black slick feathers and a sinuous neck swaying behind a brutal yellow beak. She snatched the fish from the air and steadied herself with her wings, and then warbled again and turned her gaze back to the sea. Nall pulled four more pots but the storm was growing darker and the sun was lost. It was only a short row back around the cove to the nameless hamlet where his family would be waiting, with a worse vantage than he had. The other fishers went windward from the village around the isle so their little sails could carry them back, but Nall's fathers had shown him this spot and he guarded it jealously. When he was a youth he had swum the dark water with a barbed spear and sneered at the old ones with their pots and their patience, but now he had some creak in his bones he understood the world a little better.

None of the octopuses in his cove were poisonous, and that was already an immeasurable relief – the occasional little deathstripe might be found in pots on the windward side, blown down from the far reefs of the Wind Sea. Some of the fools were laying bigger traps there as well, some of them hauling hooked spears on their dog-boats and returning with great fish they had to drag along. But that would need a crew, and Nall only had his bird.

'Fly if you want,' he said, tossing the last of the gathered lines back without collecting their pots. *Lucky ones will have a few days more.* The cormorant spread its wings but then paused and warbled low and opened its beak, cocking its head so one black eye gazed out at the open water. Nall followed its gaze and rubbed at his chin.

The island Nall called home was a windswept mountain jutting from the south-western waters of the Crowns, deep enough in that if he looked north and east he could see the open water that marked the edge of Burner's Run. He had never sailed that way, when he had been of a mind to sail. He lived on Big Murud, had been to four of the little Muruds, and once per year went with the big ship to Requin-Port to trade ink with the Cil. Ships didn't stop at Murud, it wasn't on the way to anywhere except Burner's Run. Working an oar to keep the dog-boat steady Nall blinked.

'Well spotted, girl,' he said, and with his bird he watched a ship cut through the water heading east, heading deeper, heading to where the only isles left were the last few barren stones before Burner's Run. It was a huge ship. It was as large as the largest he had ever seen, and of the same design – high-sided with tightly fitted dark wood, four tall masts, dozens of sails and hundreds of lines, and *movement*. The ship swarmed with bodies, climbing rigging and busying about. It was far enough that Nall could not make out their features but he spat in the water.

'Cil bastards,' he said, and the cormorant croaked and shifted its feet, but Nall could not tear his eyes from the ship. It was magnificent. The sailcloth was catching the wind and she was running fast, fair cutting past Big Murud already. *Wish the boys had been here to see this.* The Cil might be bastards, but Nall's boys loved a new ship. For a moment he glanced back. The storm on the western horizon was now a wall of darkness, and perhaps closer than it had been. There was no time to be home and back close enough for the boys to see. *And if she keeps that clip up we'll have nothing to look at.*

Dejected, Nall sat back and let his oars rest in the wash. The great ship had no oars out, but he could see three horizontal rows that would be oarlocks below deck. He puzzled for a moment and tried to count. *Three decks, maybe twenty locks. Sixty oars?* He knew enough of sailing to know those oars would have four or five men apiece, and he threw his bird another fish as the implication hit him. Even with four men an oar, that was over two hundred bodies, just on the oars. Let alone the ropes. *Let alone the archers, the soldiers.* It was easily triple the number of people than those who lived on Big Murud, on a single ship. *A whole world on the water.*

Nall patted his little dog-boat affectionately and then his cormorant took off flapping and Nall dropped his oars. *Another!* A second ship was hurtling through the water from the windward coast, a sleek sixty-footer with two masts lateen-rigged, huge triangle sails of blood-red cloth that were full of wind and hauling the dark boat below across the water like weight on a line. He knew what red sails meant this close to Burner's Run – the Bloody Crows, Russilan marauders. They passed but never stopped at Murud, never bothered fishermen. *They're after bigger prey.* Nall watched.

It took time for them to intersect. The great ship began to turn about, and Nall saw the brutal ram at its prow, the metal reinforcing its forward hull. It was thrice the length of the new arrival, but the smaller ship was coming with the wind at its heels, and whatever tide-mage rode the Cil galleon had no chance of threading a path that would bring them fast around.

Nall watched in disbelief, forgetting the storm to the west, forgetting his bird and his waiting family. He threw down his little anchor and let the current pull the dog-boat around and then repositioned himself and peered in the failing light. The second ship, the dark shadow with the claret sails – it was not there to talk. It was hurtling towards the Cil galleon, and the deck of the larger ship was now bristling with what must be archers and soldiers. Nall's bird landed back beside him and he absently reached for her, and received a nip to his hand.

'Piss, bird!' he cried, and she only cooed in that thick throaty voice. 'You aren't even any bloody use in octopus season, so you mind your manners or you'll be flying home!'

Nall watched, and behind him thunder rolled and the temperature dropped as a gust of cold air blew down from Big Murud. The minutes of approach were over – the ships were closing together. *The boys won't believe this!* The smaller ship was moving forward as if to collide, and now a hail of arrows split the sky, from here nothing but flecks of darkness against the sky. Again and again every five heartbeats sending a fresh rain of wood and metal. A larger ballistae was spinning up, huge bolts as long as Nall's dog-boat flashing through the air, and then a twist of chain and spikes that just missed the smaller boat's foresail. Nall leaned forward, but he could hear no screams, could hear nothing save the water and the wind, and the thunder. The thunder, again. Closer. He looked back and beyond Big Murud he could see nothing, only dark sky. *Piss!*

Nall began to haul the anchor up and cursed at the bird as he did.

'First taste of excitement in ten year,' he cried, 'and if I stay I'll be bloody drowned! No good, bird, no luck at all!'

The bird croaked a dark and reptilian call and Nall threw the anchor down into the bottom of the dog-boat and threw one last forlorn look at the ships. They were almost level now, and the smaller one with the wild storm winds at its tail had cut to the left. *It'll pass it!*

There was an explosion of noise and a flash of what Nall thought must be lightning, and he dropped an oar. It fell into the water and dimly he knew he should get it, no matter what, but he was dumbstruck. The lightning had not flashed from the sky to the ship, not from the sky to the sea. The lightning had burned from the prow of the smaller ship and exploded a hole the size of a basking shark in the waterline of the Cil galleon.

'What...' Nall said, and then the light flashed again. Purple limned lightning, an explosion of force blasting from the prow of the dark-hulled ship, and then it was passing the Cil Galleon and another, another. Five more cracks of lightning. *A skein-mage? A wizard?*

The bird's furious squawks brought Nall back to his mind and he flung himself at the side of the dog-boat, and Whale's blessing the oar was still close enough, still afloat. He hauled it aboard and began to row as hard as he ever had, his back to his destination and his eye on the open water between him and Burner's Run.

The black-hulled ship was lowering its sails and coming about, and as it did the Cil galleon was sinking fast. Its hull was cracked in a dozen places, and again and again the beams of burning purple lightning spat out. Sailors were throwing themselves into the water and, from the deck of the shadow-hulled ship, arrows were flying at them as they swam. *Swimming where?* Nall grimaced. They wouldn't make Big Murud, not with the currents pulling them to Burner's Run.

'Best we get home, bird!' he called, and he smiled. 'Lot of dead Cil, there. Some magic, that. Boys will *love* it! And might be the currents throw us some salvage, after this storm!'

Nall whistled and watched, shaking his head as the galleon slipped below the water. The cormorant warbled, and behind them thunder rolled as the storm reached Big Murud.

ACT 2

METAL BELOW STONE

Dark now, little one
Sleep below the stone
Wave and tide are only dreams
Salt will keep the bone

'Balm for the waterbound ones that they remember the weight of the sea and know their fate'
– Antian children's rhyme

8

IN SHADOW

'An interesting footnote on the Russilan is the degree to which star charts seem to have held importance, beyond navigation. Many of the tombs uncovered to date have little in the way of decoration, save for their ceilings, which are unfailingly carved with depictions of the night sky. By comparison with the records in the great library in Kelamor, we can precisely date some of these tombs.'

– ***Notes on the Russilan***, Gallo Mancinus

Nassin left them wordlessly as soon as it was clear Killian's discussion with the Cil was dwindling. The hulking Tullioch seemed uninterested. Killian scratched at the dried blood on the backs of his hands. *No time, and miles to go.* He summoned Pollos Twice-Kissed with a shout out the door and had the man show the Cil to her quarters. There were only two real cabins on the *Cutlass Hawk*, Killian's own and then a small simple cell for Pollos. The crew were in hammocks below deck.

'I'm afraid it is rather simple lodging,' he said, bowing, 'but we need access to the chart table in here at all hours so it will be quieter, at least.'

'Blade Mournchild can quarter with the pirates,' Marion said, and Killian smiled at that.

'I think they prefer "free traders", Lady Lieutenant,' he said, and then gripped Pollos by the arm and whispered in his ear. The wide-faced man leaned close, the pitchfyre burn on his cheek taut as he frowned at his captain. 'Keep *Adamant Hand* and *Jade* well in sight, and find out from Nassin if he knows where we anchor tonight.'

Pollos nodded and departed with the Cil woman, and the hulking armoured figure she named Mournchild followed wordlessly. *I'm not looking forward to fighting that one.* Beyond them through the open door Killian could hear the creak of the mast, the shouts of Timmult and Renard as they co-ordinated some line up in the rigging. He let his eyes unfocus for a moment and then set to work. He started by going to his basin and washing his face – there was blood behind his ears, in his eyebrows. He set his cutlass on the chart table and found his cloth and sand and oil, and pulled on a fresh shirt. Silver waited, sitting and watching.

'Rather a lot of blood on your cutlass,' she said.

'No questions, I thought.' He went to the charts and drew his finger across. *Horse water then Caragh's Point then south and east.* He grimaced at the chart, the annotated isles far outnumbered by those with nothing but a faint outline.

'It wasn't really a question,' she said, and he waved his hand at her and stared at the charts. They would need to head south and a little east after Caragh's Point, into the western reaches. *Through the Coracles.*

'Madu,' he said thoughtfully, and Silver blew out a breath.

'I've not heard of Madu. You're angry, Heron.'

Killian shrugged and stared at the map, and then turned to her.

'I left a message with the diggers' guild,' he said, and she shrugged and smiled at him, wrinkling her nose.

'I didn't get it. I came down to see when you might be leaving, and Pollos said right away. I have some work to do and thought I might join you. Lucky I did!'

She gestured at a stack of books and papers and a pile of clay tablets covered in cuneiform Russilan script, all of it piled neatly next to his bed.

'I thought you might not mind some company...'

Killian shook his head and tapped on the charts.

'This isn't a tomb we are exploring, Silver!' he said, and felt his throat tightening. Her face was placid, guarded. 'This is... this is *blood.* We're trailing two pirate ships right now, who go to make war on Blue Darrow. Do you know Blue Darrow? No, no. That was a question. *No questions.* Blue Darrow has burned a dozen islands. Blue Darrow has a bounty on him from the Isken, from the Cil, from Kelamor, even from Undal and Carob. Blue Darrow has spent the last five years preying on ships leaving nothing but blood and bone and timber in the water, and he took Caragh's Point and turned it into his personal fortress, and now the Evertree Sisters want him gone for whatever reason. This will be bloody and dangerous. And beyond that, Burner's Run with this mad Cil woman!'

He slumped. *Beyond that,* he thought, *Arlock. Arlock of the Bloody Crows...* Silver retrieved a book from her pile and opened it.

'We rob tombs, Heron,' she said, her eyes fixing on the page. 'We delve into *Russilan* tombs. It is lucky I came when I did. I would not miss Burner's Run and the Deep Crowns, not for all the gold in Kelamor.'

Killian just shook his head. Silver had seen him robbing tombs, and a few scuffles around those adventures, but she did not know the blood on his hands. *She doesn't know how this will inevitably end.* He tried to picture Little Key as captain of a bloody-minded pirate ship, black-hulled and wild, but all he could see was the gaunt pale girl he had known all his life, until suddenly he didn't.

'You have no idea,' he said, but could find no way to articulate the fear in his gut. He snatched up his sword and clipped it back to his belt. 'The course is set. Any safe port we pass I can drop you, that offer is always there.'

He left her before she could respond and emerged onto the deck. He could see *Adamant Hand* and *Jade* in the distance, both in full sail. The Horse Water was a broad current, a thoroughfare through the northern reaches of the archipelago. There were islands everywhere and little boats, settlements clinging to rock and dirt, seabirds whirling through the sky on their unknown errands. The wind was holding strong and the skies were clear above and ahead, but to the south there was a storm on the horizon. Killian ran a hand through his hair and felt his eye twitching. He spotted Renard.

'Where is the new tide-mage?' he asked, and the slender woman gave him a dour look.

'The *Antian* is in the net under the bowsprit,' she said, not attempting to hide the confusion in her tone. 'You ever heard of an Antian tide-mage, Captain?'

Killian rolled his eyes.

'Petal recommended her,' he said, and then strode off before he could be drawn. To reach the front of the ship he had to pass through Heavenly Nassin's gaggle of soldiers, Tullioch and humans of every size and shape and garb. Some were comparing weaponry; some were playing dice; some were sleeping. There was a canopy set up on the foredeck and beneath it crates and barrels of water and presumably food. Nassin watched him as he walked through, as did the rest of them, conversation continuing but stilted as heads turned to follow him. The black-armoured Mournchild sat apart, cross-legged and hooded. Killian ignored them all and climbed over the rail at the front of the ship and looked down.

The Antian was in the web of netting below the bowsprit, huddled. *Great.*

'Hello there!' he called, and the creature turned its face up to him. 'I'm Captain Heroneye. We need to talk.'

He settled back on the rail and the Antian clambered up and settled next to him. Antian were short and furred, something between dogs and moles in their general appearance, with short tails. Their ears were generally upright, their eyes large and black. This one wore a thick rain cloak of seal hide and beneath it was robed in simple red cotton belted with ship's rope, barefooted. Her fur was a dun dark gold. She carried no weapon.

'I am Kaikatsu,' she said, her voice a low thick hum, and Killian nodded.

'Petal said you know the necessary?' he asked, and the little Antian nodded. She was slight, and to Killian her expression seemed doleful but he had known few Antian in his life, and never well.

'I sailed two seasons with the *Mist Dancer* out of Koch Dara,' she said, 'one season with a whaler out of Druich. I can read tides and wind and reef and storm. I've no talent in healing, but Petal said you've a stitcher aboard already.'

Killian waited, and Kaikatsu waited, and they both sat in silence. A young black-backed gull was flying alongside the front of the ship. With one hand on the rail, Killian reached down and touched the fresh willow boughs tied to the bowsprit.

'Any violence?' he asked at last, and next to him the Antian stayed utterly still.

'Yes,' she said at last. 'I can summon some flame, though the cost is high. I can douse flame, as well.'

Killian nodded and blew a breath through his lips. 'Well,' he said, 'perhaps we won't be needing that, should all go well. Rate is as standard. Berth wherever you prefer – there are hammocks below. Pollos is mate, but if Renard or Timmult tell you to do something that doesn't sound utterly stupid you should do it. The Breygar twins make the rest of our crew. We won't need you on the Horse Water, but the plan is to go upriver a little at Caragh's Point so you will want to look at the maps we have before we reach there. Any issues, let me know. Feel the weather and let Pollos know what you think we are in for.'

Killian rose to leave and the Antian raised her hand.

'Wait, Captain Heroneye,' she said. 'Wait. You have not asked me why I left my holt. Why I left the holdfasts.

Why I left the underground. These are inevitable questions, I have found.'

'Nothing is inevitable,' Killian said, and he looked up to the sky and closed his eyes felt the tension in his shoulders. *Blood and death*. The faces of the slavers he had butchered danced in his mind, masks of claret. Mistress Merrow looking down at him when he was just a boy, soaked in red to the elbow, a street shiv gripped white-knuckle tight in his fist. He could still feel it, the acrid taint in his mouth, the thrill in his nerves. *Why can't I stop?* 'I'm sure we will get to it in time, but if it isn't relevant to reading tide or wind or reef, I have work to be about. Get yourself squared away, and watch for Heavenly Nassin's soldiers. Any trouble, tell Pollos or tell me.'

'You can touch the pattern,' she said quietly, and he turned to her. 'I can tell. I can always tell. It is a knack, I have. It is not so common, this touch. Are you a tide-mage, Captain?'

Killian shook his head and squinted at the ships ahead of them. They were all making good speed, current and wind both in their favour. The *Cutlass Hawk* could catch them, if he chose it to. *Or we could outrun them, if it comes to that.*

'I'm the captain,' he said absently, staring at the water. 'You deal with your pattern. I've work to be about.'

It took two days to reach Caragh's Point. The water stayed calm and the storm gathering on the southern horizon hung steady over the Deep Crowns. In the Coracles the wind was fair and constant, and they made good speed. They passed an Isken guild ship on the first day that gave them a wide berth, and a flotilla of Kelamor galleys with single masts and banks of oars cutting south that *Adamant Hand* kept well back from. Small dog-boats pushed out from islands at the edge of the Horse Water, canoes and small sails trying to catch their ships, aiming to trade. They ignored them all and kept to the deep channels. On the second morning he saw a catamaran with a faded red sail passing, and at its bow a dolphin swam, content to keep pace. He watched them keenly. It was a small ship, perhaps thirty foot long if that. A single sail. *No crew. Simple.*

With Silver he relaxed into the familiar cadence of their previous voyages, and they asked each other no questions. She worked at her books either in his cabin or by the foredeck. The Antian Kaikatsu was a shadow, emerging at the end of the line for food, sleeping in the furthest reaches of the hold, murmuring her weather readings into Pollos's ear. Killian left her to it.

'Antian skein-mages are usually called *witches*,' Silver told him on the first night. 'They usually are only ever seen in groups of three. They work together, channel power together. That is what I heard, at least. A joining of power, a balance of control.'

'Have you ever been to an Antian hold?' he asked, and she pinched his arm. *No questions.* It made their conversations strange long lists of facts and opinions, waiting for the other to offer but never expecting clarity or able to ask directly. 'I'm glad you came,' he told her in the dark of the first night, when the only noise was her breath and the creak of the hull and the gentle wash of the sea against the ship. She did not respond, and he pressed a hand against the wood of his ship and held it and her until sleep took him. He dreamt of his mother again, hanging from the Cil noose for theft and whatever other charges they added. In the dream he and Key were at his mother's feet and behind her there was a field of infinite burning stars, constellations etched in fire, and she was speaking but he could understand nothing.

The Cil woman Marion spent long hours staring at the sea and made occasional forays to talk to Heavenly Nassin, which Killian watched with a keen eye. She had called herself a diplomat but Killian had spent three awful years in Requin-Port, and whatever she called herself she was Cil through and through. *Arrogant. Awful.* The Cil-Marie claimed their great mainland and a dozen 'shield' isles past that, and in theory Requin-Port was the extent of their reach. Pollos brought her food up to her room, and she ate alone, despite an invitation from Killian to join him. He was grateful. *It does not do to dine with someone you plan to kill.* He smiled when he realised, perhaps she felt the same way. Her hooded protector slept in his armour and sat on the deck by Nassin's soldiers, implacable, and ignored all questions or comments. Killian looked at his charts and his maps and scoured his memory of his last, and only, crossing of Burner's Run. *I'm coming, Little Key.* He had broken his promise to her, and lost her. *But it is perhaps not too late.*

At the end of the second day by Killian's reckoning they were a scant few miles from Caragh's Point and *Adamant Hand* led them to anchor in the lee of a small lifeless isle to the north. The isles in this north-eastern area of the archipelago were cold and bereft despite their proximity to the warmer water of the Carob Strait to the north. Some trick of current left them all huffing and reaching for extra layers, and the jut of rock the Evertree Sisters' fleet had chosen as its anchor had no name on Killian's charts. That did not mean much – those charts were old, and the names of the Crown Isles changed with the season as new blood tried to find footing on old land thick with the bones of the dead. Names unspoken were only suggestions.

As they made anchor, a flock of flying creatures circled the boats one at a time before returning to the barren rock and disappearing into some hidden crevice. They were thin with leathery wings and skin and no beaks or feathers, no visible eyes, and from the blunt nubs of their heads through thin slits that he thought must be mouths a keening noise came. All watched, and none knew their name or their kind. Silver made a sketch, and Killian touched the locket at his chest and could only shake his head.

Captain Tarlis of *Adamant Hand* sent a dog-boat, and as darkness fell over the waters Killian, Heavenly Nassin, Marion, and Blade Mournchild were rowed across to the high-sided ship. It had two oar decks and three masts and as Killian clambered over the rail and onto the main deck he could see at least six ballistae battened down near the rails, racks of heavy spears ready at their side, spears with different points – some wide-bladed to tear at sails, some thin and flat to skewer the hulls of thinner-skinned ships or beasts. There were a handful of rope-tied harpoons as well, barbed and vicious for hunting whale or shark or garu. *Free traders, indeed.*

A grizzled whip-thin man stalked the deck like an ancient heron, murmuring to the varied crew as he passed, his hair a wire brush of grey. They had lit no deck braziers or torches, and the only light was the pale reflection of moon on water. He was taller than every other human on the deck, clad in simple black, and the way the crew parted around him let Killian know his identity at once. Killian doffed his hat and cut a short bow.

'I am Captain Tarlis,' the man said quietly, and with a gesture for them to follow strode off to his cabin without waiting for their names. Marion murmured something and Mournchild stood by the rail and rested a hand on his pommel, and grew utterly still. Killian could not see eyes beneath Mournchild's dark cowl, but he thought he heard some muttered words. Killian hurried forward after Nassin, in the hope of leaving Marion in his wake, but the woman was quickly beside him and then with a smile she preceded him into the cabin.

Tarlis's cabin was utilitarian, but pitchers of wine and water wrapped in rope sat on the table with clay cups, and a bowl of wizened olives and pickled octopus tentacles. Killian took a seat between Marion and Nassin and waited. There was one other figure – a short woman with a plait of black hair tied severely tight.

'Lady Marion of Cil-Marie,' Tarlis said. 'Our old comrade Heavenly Nassin. And Killian Heroneye, Captain of the *Cutlass Hawk*. This is Captain Lwell of *Jade*.'

Captain Lwell nodded curtly at them and refilled her clay cup with wine. Her face was a grimace of stone, unreadable.

'A pleasure,' Marion said, but Killian simply nodded. *I'm a small fry, here. A little fish amongst sharks.*

Tarlis loomed over the table and poured wine for the three of them and himself and then unrolled a chart, weighing its corners with some carved wooden blocks that sat on the table, presumably for just this purpose. The chart he presented showed an island, a fat crescent of land with a wide river on the inner curve wending its way from the curve's centre inward and up, mountains along the spine of it, and a settlement marked in red ink. *Caragh's Point.*

'My Lady Marion, the Sisters told me of your deal. Out of respect to you, and with an eye to the future, they thought you may wish to see how we operate. This being free seas, and all, beyond the bounds of any land.'

Marion smiled and ate an olive, delicately removing the stone from her mouth and placing it on the table by her glass.

'I am not a soldier, nor a sailor, Captain,' she said, her thick Cil accent still strange in Killian's ears after so many years away from Requin-Port. 'I am simply someone who needed a ship. But I thank you. I hope you will forgive if any input I have feels rudimentary.'

Tarlis bowed his head to her.

'The Sisters bade me take you into our counsel, and I ask no more than that, Lady. This is Caragh's Point – once a small town and a few outlying farms. It was a Russilan settlement back before the Thirst, abandoned a century or so, and then some guildless traders out of Isken set up shop a few decades after that. Religious types, I think, some sort of monastic retreat. Five summers back Blue Darrow took it, and made it his home port.'

Killian peered at the map; the plumb depths noted in charcoal at different points in the wide bay were thorough.

'Deep anchorage,' he said, 'and protected from the big winds by the mountains. How many ships does Darrow have?'

Tarlis eyed him and drummed his fingers on the table.

'He should have three in anchor,' Captain Lwell interjected. 'He has another three that are currently marauding in the western Coracles. They don't venture so far as Cil-Marie waters, and they steer clear of the Horse Water where the Kelamor and Isken patrol ships might find them. They dance around the little isles and hunt silverfish, any ship they can.'

'How do you know three are in anchor?' Killian asked, and Tarlis sniffed.

'Because,' he said, 'they are waiting to receive *us*. A delegation from the Evertree Sisters to divide up the Coracles. We had a bash with them earlier in the year and both lost ships. We sent a message asking for a parlay, a chance to divide up the Crowns between the Sisters and Blue Darrow. They said to come on this date. And so here we are.'

Killian drank his wine. It was sour and dark purple and had a faint grit to it. He grimaced and looked at Nassin, who simply stared at the map, hands in his lap.

'Here we are,' he echoed, and Captain Lwell drew her dagger. Tarlis unrolled another sheet of parchment with a rough charcoal sketch of a town and a rough-sketched large building with a river running past it.

'Darrow holds the town,' Lwell said, pointing with the tip of her dagger. 'We go in under the peace banner, we get everyone nice and drunk, and then in the dead of night Heavenly Nassin enters the town from the north. There is no good anchorage that way, but your little ship should have a low enough draw to get you well upriver and then you can cut across country to the old monastery. Should be farmland. The river mouth is a good two miles south of the bay where the town and monastery sit, and last we scouted no habitation around it and it is out of eyeline. You wait for sunset. Your tide-mage will need to be sharp, though. If you run into sand bars you'll have to take dog-boats up.'

Killian frowned at the map. 'Surely we should take dog-boats regardless,' he said. 'An unknown river at night is madness.'

'Every foot you sail upriver is a foot you don't have to row or hike,' Tarlis said, and Lwell tapped the map with her dagger blade. It was a silver-bladed piece, with a hilt of antler. She stared at Killian.

'Can you do it, boy?' she asked, and Killian gave her his best smile and took one of the octopus tentacles from their little dish and chewed on it.

'Not met water I can't sail yet,' he said, mainly for something to say.

'So you go in guise of peace,' Marion said, 'and then slaughter them in their cups?'

Her face was inscrutable, and Killian chewed on his octopus tentacle and smiled widely at her.

'They are pirates, Lady,' Tarlis said. 'They are the dregs of these isles. Vicious and mad with blood and gold. The Sisters represent a saner mode of trade. Blue Darrow leaves charred hulks and blood in his wake.'

'It's a classic gambit,' Killian said. 'It's what the Cil did in Concarneau, isn't it? And Requin-Port. And a few dozen more besides. Parlays and trade and peace, and then suddenly a lot of big chaps with heavy weaponry and bad attitudes and a change in control for everyone's best interest. Tale as old as time, and the Shield Isles get another member between old Cil-Marie and the nasty dirty outsiders.'

Marion held his gaze steadily, a twinkle in her eye, and then nodded ever so slightly. *A point won,* Killian thought, and then his gaze was back on the chart.

'You can take my Blade,' she said, 'if he would be of help. He fights like ten men, and has not been blooded in a few weeks. It will do him good, and is a gesture of my... continued goodwill to the Sisters and their organisation.'

Tarlis bowed briefly in gratitude, and Lwell sheathed her dagger.

'After we drop Nassin and his crew, we rendezvous in the fort harbour?' Killian asked, and then felt Heavenly Nassin's meaty hand grip his shoulder, sharp talons digging into the flesh.

'You've a sword and an arm,' Nassin said. 'You'll be with us, Heroneye. All the way.'

Killian's smile froze and he felt a pulse in his chest, a thrill. *Blood and ashes and bone and fire and piss. I need to find Key.*

'I'm not a fighter,' he said.

'I need him *alive*,' Marion said.

Tarlis shook his head and Lwell stared at Killian with no abashment, assessing his every move.

'It took us a while, but we did find out how you got that ship, young Heroneye. We found out *exactly* how. You've a blade and you know how to use it, and you've a thirst a little different than most Russilan. No salt water for you, boy. You want that red, and you'll get it. If you need him alive, Lady Marion, then set your Blade to watching. The Sisters want him with us, lest he do something silly like sail off into the sunrise.'

Marion tilted her head in acquiescence and frowned at the map.

'Have you considered Blue Darrow's plan?' she asked, and Tarlis and Lwell exchanged looks and then Lwell gestured with her knifeless hand for the Cil diplomat to continue. 'He is expecting a peace delegation – how many warriors do you think will reach him, how many weapons? Is he planning to get you nice and drunk and then sink or capture *Adamant Hand* and *Jade*? Vicious and mad with blood and gold, you say. Will he be tricked so easily?'

Tarlis sniffed and picked a pickled octopus tentacle from the bowl and chewed on it, and Lwell sheathed her dagger and shrugged.

'Either way it ends in blood,' she said. 'There are no sureties. In the best case, we might even take his crews for our fleet and only have to kill his officers. In the worst case, we end tomorrow in gull cages hanging from Blue Darrow's walls, waiting for the black-backs to take our eyes.'

Marion smiled thinly and toasted with her cup, and Killian stared at Tarlis and Lwell. *We did find out how you got that ship, young Heroneye.* Killian stared and tried to tell from the set of their faces what they knew, what they could possibly know, but all he saw was scar and skin and sour grimaces.

'Good eve to you all,' Tarlis said at last, and he rose and bowed to the Cil woman. Killian's ears thrummed with blood, and his gut had the sour ache of the taste of violence, and the tingling anticipation on his skin, the thrill of it. He closed his eyes. *A thirst for red. Mistress Merrow taking a shank from a red-wet child. The deck of the* Hawk *slick with blood. A forest under a thousand stars, his bow taut in his hand as he sent arrow after arrow into darkness. The slaver camp, his cutlass dripping. The Requin-Port governor screaming his last and clutching Killian's shirt.*

As the dog-boat rowed them back to the *Cutlass Hawk*, Killian gripped the handle of his sword and stared at the dark of the water, felt the cold of the tugging winds pulling at his hair. He did not look at the stars. The first constellation would be his fate that night – so said Starfinder Rurich in between hacking coughs as he taught Killian and Key in their hovel in Requin-Port. So said his mother before the Cil hanged her. Starfinder Rurich was dead, his mother was dead. *But Arlock is alive.*

Killian did not look up. *My fate tonight doesn't matter.* Tomorrow would be the night for watching stars.

Caragh's Point

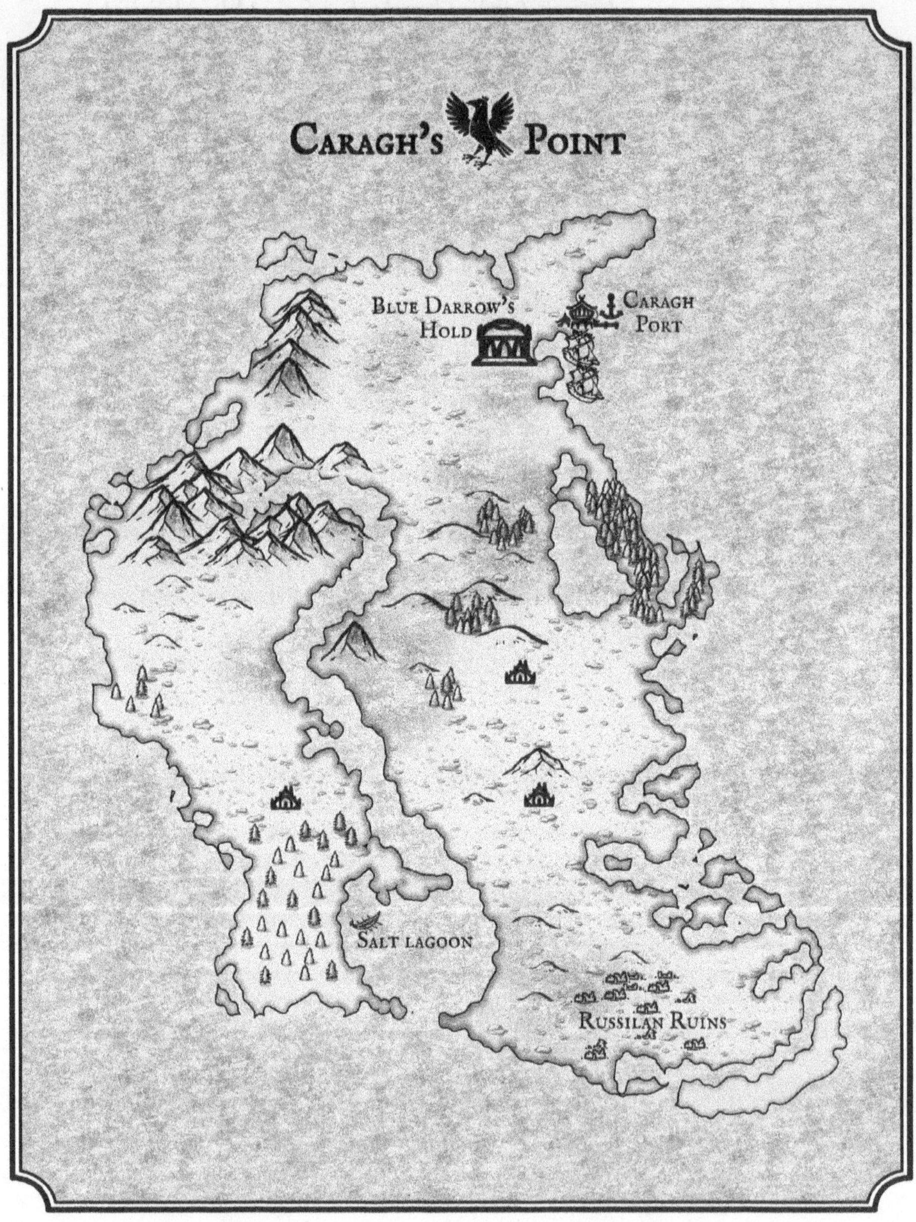

Caragh's Point, year 1134 Isken – **From the charts of the** ***Cutlass Hawk***, Captain Killian Heroneye

9

THE ISLE OF LOST FATE

'The eastern isles on the approach to Ona's imperious mountains are a wild and rain-soaked collection of freeholds and freeports, villages of those who seek utter independence. The clouds that gather over the Wind Sea to the north-east break on Ona's basalt cliffs, and the Eastern Crowns are eternally drenched. The people of Ona are reclusive, and the currents and tempestuous winds deter all but the keenest or most desperate of sailors. There are few riches beyond solitude on offer.'

– ***The Thousand Crowns***, Alwin Brakspear

'Kai, can you get us a read on that weather?' the captain asked, and so dutifully Kaikatsu went to his side at the rail and turned her gaze on the horizon. She did not fall into the skein – to predict weather required a far gaze and a clear eye, and the skein offered neither. A tide-mage did not simply touch the skein and predict weather and wave and depth like a musician reading a score. Many of her roles required analysis and interpretation of the signs the world gave, and the tangled complexity of the skein would only cloud those interpretations. Kaikatsu squinted in the morning light.

Adamant Hand and *Jade* had left with the dawn, and the *Cutlass Hawk* sat alone in the lee of the unnamed isle. Past the isle's shelter she could see the way the wind rippled over the water, whitecaps breaking. She could see five other isles, three small, two larger – none of them Carob's Point. Smoke drifted upward from the forest of the nearest large isle – a hearth or a cookfire deep in the black pines that covered that steep rock. Kaikatsu watched the smoke drift up and then tear away as it rose to the point where the prevailing wind caught it, pushing it deeper into the Crowns, ripping it from smoke to nothingness. There was no cloud above them, and on the far horizon there was no cloud. Only wind.

'Wind is high, for being so early,' she said, and in her robe she felt a scratch as the relu-mouse curled itself closer against the soft fur of her stomach. She shifted her feet and turned her eye to the captain. 'No storm I can see. Thin moon, tonight, a standard tide. If we are to go upriver as you wish, then we should enter when the tide is highest and the estuary as deep as possible.'

Heroneye shook his head and tapped his thumb on the hilt of his cutlass, and peered down at her. *Always looking down.* It was hard for her – for humans and Tullioch, size was a metric of age, age a metric of wisdom, and so her relatively short stature meant many looked at her as simpler, younger, *weaker.* A thing to be protected or ignored, rather than valued. *Many,* she thought, *but not all. Which will he be?*

'Any of the crew giving you trouble, Kai?' he asked, and she wrinkled her nose and scratched her muzzle.

'*Kaikatsu,*' she said, and he raised an eyebrow. 'My name is Kaikatsu. Not Kai.'

Heroneye dipped his head in acknowledgement and smiled.

'I meant no offence,' he said, and she tilted her head. *So strange, these humans.* 'We shorten names as a show of… familiarity. I did not think the practice might not mean the same, to you.'

Kaikatsu pulled her robes closer and stared at the sea.

'Antian names have meaning,' she said. 'To alter one is to change its meaning. We are named and renamed with deliberation and care. We are named again by those we love, and again there is deliberation and care. There is no offence, Captain Heroneye. I simply wish us to be on good terms. You are my captain.'

Heroneye nodded and cast his gaze over the deck, and Kaikatsu followed. Heavenly Nassin and the mercenaries were breaking their fast, a low murmur of conversation. It would be a long day sailing until they reached their destination, and a long night beyond that of violence and death. *What is this ship you have set me upon, Petal?* Kaikatsu knew she did not have the luxury of choice. Heroneye's crew were about, grim-faced as they worked. The big Undal first mate Pollos Twice-Kissed lumbered over to them with chipped clay bowls of porridge. He handed one to Heroneye and then proffered the other to her.

'Porridge, Tide-mage?'

Kaikatsu nodded her thanks and took the bowl and held it in her hands over her stomach, and felt the relu-mouse squirm at the warmth of it through her robes. *It is so much colder here than below.* She shivered and stared at the mercenaries, then up at the sky past the swaying mast. A trio of black-backed gulls were circling above.

'Kaikatsu thinks strong wind but no storm today,' Heroneye said quietly, and the first mate nodded. Heroneye ate some porridge, and between bites continued unhurriedly, as if discussing the weather still. 'I've no intention of losing the *Hawk* on a sandbar in a river we don't know. We'll hit the river mouth where the charts say it is deep enough, and then Kaikatsu, you will say we can go no further. Sandbars. Whatever. I will take the dog-boats with Nassin and his men and run overland. Pollos, you will get the ship turned and ready to leave at full haste. If this nonsense goes south, we need to be out of there.'

Kaikatsu held her porridge and frowned.

'You wish me to lie?' she asked. 'As a tide-mage, my honesty is my reputation. My correct reading. I will struggle to find work if I become known as a liar.'

Heroneye rolled his eyes and looked down on her, but did not drop down to his haunches or stoop.

'It is a river at night, Kaikatsu-mage. Even with a draw as shallow as ours, it is a bad plan. Yes, I am asking you to lie. In darkness and low water with none but ourselves and the mercenaries and the mad Cil-Marie. After this madness at Caragh's Point we will deal with them.'

Pollos Twice-Kissed sighed at that and nodded, then lumbered off back towards the midships. *Deal with them?* Kaikatsu was unsure of the captain's meaning. *Free traders.*

That is what Petal told her of the *Cutlass Hawk*. Free traders who specialised in hunting historical artefacts. Not pirate battles. Not murdering Cil diplomats on the high sea. Kaikatsu hated the Cil; all Antian hated the Cil – they were the bearers of chain and whip, and to the Cil, Antian were no more than things. Kaikatsu sniffed the breeze and tried to hold her calm. *I have my mission. I have my quest. I have my calling*. She knew she could not afford distraction. She would do whatever her captain needed, as long as it let her search.

Kaikatsu turned her gaze back to the water and set down her bowl, and slipping one hand into her robe she gently held the relu-mouse and felt the reassuring warmth of him. For a moment she dropped into the skein.

It was easier, holding the relu, as if it were a conduit. In a moment her perspective shifted. She could see lines of connection between her flesh and the ship, between the tide below. The connection was so thick, vibrant strands of sound and light and feeling in every sense that it was akin to a fog – she could not see far, no more than a hundred feet. *Enough*. It was enough to take in the *Cutlass Hawk*. The intricacies of living beings, the Tullioch and the humans each unique, each species with a vein of similarity in its pattern. In the hold, the scurry of rats – a nest, down below. Next to her Heroneye was like the other humans, but there was a sheen to him – the sheen of one who could touch the skein, with the proper training.

Kaikatsu gripped the rail of the ship and prepared to change her focus, to look outward at the waters, to see how far her gaze might take her, when something else caught her eye. Unblinking she turned towards the captain's cabin. A human with a mote at her hip of sheer concentrated power

– the Cil diplomat's hammer, a weapon made of relu bones. It drew her eye, a density to it, a vibration that sickened her stomach. It was an aberration in the pattern, a tangle. Next to the Cil woman, another figure. *Silver.* Kaikatsu had not spoken to the archaeologist, not yet, but she turned her gaze on her and saw her in more depth than any speech could ever convey, saw traces of connection between Silver and the captain, trailing wavering lines of red and gold that twisted through the wood of the ship and the air and the water below. She gazed at Silver.

Sheen.

With a cold rush Kaikatsu let the skein drop and she rubbed at her eyes. *That hammer is an aberration.*

'The Cil woman's hammer is powerful, Captain,' she said quietly. 'If you are to deal with them, be wary of it. The Cil's hammer is powerful… and the archaeologist Silver can touch the skein.'

Captain Heroneye blinked at her slowly, one corner of his mouth twisting. 'You are sure?'

'I have no reason to lie on either account. You are my captain. This is my ship now. Our fates are entwined, for now at least.'

'For now at least,' the captain repeated, and his grimace faded. 'What holdfast are you from, Kaikatsu? We were hoping to head to the Western Holdfast after this nonsense. That might still happen. Would that be… a good destination, for you?'

Kaikatsu smiled, her muzzle turning upward and her tongue lolling out slightly. *He is a good one.* He did not ask, *are you exiled? Are you criminal?* He did not ask her holt name.

Kaikatsu picked up her porridge.

'I am simply Kaikatsu,' she said. 'I will go where you go – this is my ship, for now at least. You will have no trouble with me at the holdfasts. Now I will go and check the greenboughs, Captain Heroneye, if I may.'

He waved her away and his gaze turned back on the mercenaries lounging across his deck, his face unreadable. Kaikatsu headed towards the bowsprit and her nest in the rope web beneath, and as she clambered down she smiled. Despite the mercenaries, and the cursed Cil woman, it was not so bad a ship. The porridge was salted and glutinous but warm, and as she sat and watched the wind dance over the water she thought of Heroneye and sighed.

I hope I don't have to kill this one.

The moon was a thin sliver of diffuse silver, a haze around it heralding rain. There were clouds, black clouds against a bruised blue sky, and Killian resolutely did not let his gaze linger on the stars. The first constellation he saw would be his fate, and so in the darkness as the *Cutlass Hawk* approached Caragh's Point he let himself look to the moon and the clouds but did not allow his focus to find pattern beyond that.

The ship was running slow at quarter-sail, Timmult and Renard and the Breygars working the lines and Pollos at the helm calling down to them. Kaikatsu crouched on the prow of the ship, and occasionally called back her reading of the current. Heavenly Nassin's men had dismantled their tarp and were checking weaponry or eating, all of them quiet. The big Tullioch himself was stood behind Pollos, and as Killian came to check on their course he took in Heavenly Nassin's raiment. In Samurkan, the Tullioch had worn simple black wool and was unarmed save for his dagger. On the raised aft deck of the *Cutlass Hawk*, he was something from the nightmares of human sailors since time immemorial. A Tullioch warrior, black-scaled, heavily muscled and utterly dangerous. Nassin wore a kilt and vest of cured sealskin studded with black metal, and his coral dagger was cinched tight in a belt of simple rope. In one clawed hand he gripped a spear that was the same height as he, a spear that seemed to be entirely made of black iron. His jaws opened slightly and he clicked his teeth as Killian approached.

'This is you ready for war, Heroneye?' he asked, and Killian shrugged. Killian was dressed as he ever was, knee-high soft boots and shirt and trous of cotton. He had traded his heavy cloak for a short jacket of cured leather lined in wool to keep the cold of the night out, and at his waist his cutlass and hip quiver sat. His shortbow was unstrung and he held it lightly in one hand.

'I told them I'm not a warrior,' he said, and Nassin grunted.

'Not a warrior,' Nassin said, and he sniffed and clicked his teeth. 'A killer, though. Do not worry, Heroneye. Forty of my men, this mad Cil dog with his black armour and muttering, and the crew of *Adamant Hand* and *Jade*. Hang back with your bow. The Sisters simply want to ensure you don't leave before the job is done.'

'Captain,' Pollos said, his eyes on the water and his hands gripping the wheel. Killian and Nassin turned to him, and the ugly man shot Nassin a glance. 'You stand on his deck, you call him *Captain.* Show some respect.'

Heavenly Nassin leaned down close to Pollos and clicked his teeth.

'This spear is star-metal,' he said, voice slow. 'Do you know how you win a star-metal spear, in the Southern Reach? It differs across the seas, tribe to tribe, clan to clan. For some it is inherited. For some it is ceremonial. The Unnamed Knight of the Shardspire, a skein-wreck, a mage who can break mountains, he carries a spear like this. It is a mark of honour, in our people. Where I come from, when your crest fades from yellow and you become an adult, you must swim with nothing but your claws and your teeth into the night and hunt a shark. That is how you earn your spear. Years later, in your prime, some hunt further. The star-metal is only for those who hunt the greatest of hunters, the beasts who swim the deep water. A Carob whale, a white shark, one of the great crocodiles the size of your dog-boats. A creature such as this.'

'You got a point?' Pollos asked, and Killian chewed on his lip.

'My point,' Nassin said, 'is that if a little one picks up a spear, or an untried adult, then yes, he could in theory carry that spear. But it would confer no honour. It would confer no rank. If I was a mewling babe and held the star-metal spear aloft, they would not cry *Heavenly Nassin!* They would fetch my brood-mother.'

'Enough,' Killian said, seeing Pollos's grip tighten. 'Pollos, stay the course. Nassin, go to your troops, take your shiny stick with you. This is my ship. If you want to try and kill me, then by all means do so, but I have no time for this.'

Nassin clicked his teeth, straightened his back, and bowed, then retreated from the aftcastle down to the main deck. Killian followed before Pollos could engage him in conversation. The man was loyal, utterly and undyingly loyal, and unshakeable. *He doesn't need me to hold his hand.* He went to his cabin and found Silver there with one of the cuneiform tablets they had taken from the Skerry tomb, copying the intricate glyphs and writings into her notebook painstakingly. She closed the notebook when he entered. Her rapier was belted at her hip as she sat on a low stool at his chart table. Killian grimaced.

'No,' he said, closing the door. She opened her mouth in a wry smile as if to deflect him, but he went to her and pulled her close and kissed her until she fell into him, and then he pushed her gently down into his chair, her rapier tangling awkwardly with her long legs. 'No.'

Silver's lips parted and there was the faintest twitch at the corner of her right eye, and then she nodded.

'I'll be back with the dawn, and then it is on to Madu and Burner's Run. Read your notes and get some sleep.'

'The Cil woman thinks you can really cross the Run,' Silver said, and he cupped her cheek in his hand and let out a sigh.

'If I live,' he said, 'there are many things I can do.'

He left her at that, and stepped into the night. They were drawing close into Caragh's Point. They were approaching from the south, and from that vantage the island looked small – it was in reality a long curve, but the truth of the map was hidden by the reality of their vision. Pollos steered the ship up the eastward side, and he called out to Timmult and Renard and the Breygars to adjust the ropes as the wind shifted in the lee of the isle. They crawled along the coast, passing a handful of black splotches that could be isolated homesteads. There was a spine of sharp mountains rising along the back arc of the isle, and from them spilled a forest that was utterly black. They found the river mouth easily enough, and it was wider than Killian had dared believe.

'This is more of a lagoon than a river,' he said, and Pollos murmured his agreement. 'Wider than it looks on the charts. Like a sea loch. Get the Antian up here. Stick central and we will give it half a mile if she is happy with the depth, then you fast anchor and we tell them sandbars.'

As they drew into the wide river mouth opening to the lagoon behind, Killian could see the true river stretching north and east, bounded on the seaward side by low hills and on the other side by mountains. Over those low hills lay the monastery where Blue Darrow waited. The *Hawk* inched forward, and he called for the crew to lower sails and bring out the sweeps. Nassin gave them some broad-backed men, so Killian had all six sweeps set, long oars that were oh so slow compared to the wind – but in the shelter of the lagoon, the *Hawk* moved inexorably forward in the darkness, the only sound the synchronised splashing of the long oars, the huff of exertion of the rowers, and the mutters of Kaikatsu as she nudged Pollos to turn left and right, her descriptions of the depth below them as vague as a dream but sharper than any non-mage would ever tell.

'Sandbars,' Killian called out, and the oars pulled in and Big Breygar went to the forward anchor chain, but stopped as Heavenly Nassin stepped in front of her and raised a hand.

'There are no sandbars here, Captain,' he said, and Killian gripped the rail of the aftcastle and looked down.

Everyone looked to him, the forty soldiers armed and scarred, Timmult and Renard and the Breygars, the dark cowl of Mournchild. In starlight he saw their faces, turned to him as if he held answer and knowledge and surety.

'There are sandbars,' he said. 'Our tide-mage has sensed them. We must take the dog-boats.'

Big Breygar moved forward again and this time Nassin reached a hand down and laid it on her shoulder, and the wiry woman was utterly still.

'My tide-mage tells different,' Nassin said, and from the throng of soldiers a man stepped forward with an axe in one hand and a talisman of feathers and intricate leather loops in the other.

'Clear and deep,' he said, his voice thick and strained, and Nassin gently pushed Big Breygar back to the oars.

'Clear and deep,' Nassin said, and he turned back to the prow of the ship and gazed out at the night.

Nassin's tide-mage stomped up the deck and took up post next to Pollos, and Pollos called out for the sweeps to start again. The *Hawk* turned from the lagoon to the river, and the pirate-mage offered no description of depth, only instruction. Killian fell back to the back rail of the aftcastle and looked behind them, the lagoon a mirror of dark and stars that was rippling with the wake of their passage. Killian's thoughts were a wasp's nest, a thousand threats competing. Nassin knew he had tried to trick him, and thus the Sisters. The river might genuinely be too shallow for the *Hawk* – it was a freshwater run, and she would drop perhaps five feet from her normal position on the salt, and not enough time to fix ballast.

Kaikatsu came to him and together they stared.

'I am sorry,' she said, and he gripped his cutlass hilt. 'I did not look at the pirates, closely. I did not think they might bring their own mage. I am sorry, Captain.'

Killian shook his head. 'We are in their currents,' he said. 'Track our course, try and chart the river best you can. When we leave, it may be fast. Be ready.'

They travelled another mile upriver, mountains stark and black to their left, hills to their right. The river was a broad deep thing, more of a sea loch that twisted through the island, and eventually the pirate-mage called a halt and Breygar was allowed to the anchor chain.

'Turned and ready to leave,' he said to Pollos as the pirates lowered the *Hawk*'s dog-boat and the second they had taken from *Adamant Hand*. 'We may come fast. If it works the way the Sisters want, I'll send word and you can take *Hawk* to the main harbour.'

Pollos nodded grimly and patted Killian on the back.

'Luck and good winds, Captain,' he said. 'You want one of us with you? Me or Big Breygar, to watch your back?'

Killian clasped Pollos on the shoulder and nodded to the dog-boats, where in black armour and black cloak the hooded figure of Mournchild stood watching, a rock.

'I have my watcher,' he said, and with that he left to join the boats. He was no longer captain – this was utterly Nassin's operation, and the blades who had sat so idle as the *Hawk* ran the Horse Water were now up and energised, lowering the boats, checking arms and armour. The pirate-mage took the prow of one dog-boat, and Nassin the other, and Killian found himself sat at an oar, Mournchild behind him.

The Lady Marion had emerged from her cabin and leaned languidly over the rail of the ship.

'Take care of my Blade, Captain Heroneye!' she called, and a few of the soldiers laughed. Killian did not respond, but behind him heard a murmur.

'Baal, Morost, Pendar, Tulu, Salaman,' said Blade Mournchild. Killian turned to him and saw only darkness, the warrior's face shielded by his heavy cloak. 'What god do you praise, Captain Heroneye? What Judge do you worship? Do you follow Baal?'

Killian turned back and pulled at his oar and did not answer, and finally he let his eyes up, up to the stars, and they flicked and searched for pattern. *There.* Two stars, one burning bright as any other in the sky and constant, the second a little dimmer, a little off to one side, flickering ever so slightly. *The siblings.*

In his mind he heard Starfinder Rurich. *Or was it his mother?* It was Rurich's wheezing voice, but he could not tell if it was a true recollection, or his mind conflating knowledge and childhood senses. *The siblings represent trust. The siblings represent care.*

On the river pulling hard at his oar, Killian pictured his sister's face when he last saw her. A freckled, sharp-nosed child as dirty as the rest of them, with a furious face but eyes that were so afraid. The details were faded and blurred, the mix of his mother and his sister hard to pull apart, but the fear in her eyes he remembered as sharp as a knife in his lungs. *Because of me.*

'Baal,' he said slowly and clearly, making sure Mournchild could hear, 'Baal is nothing to me, Blade Mournchild. Never even heard his name until I was grown. The Russilan god is mad, did you know that? Perhaps it was a god once, but what use is a god who doesn't answer you? There is the sea below and the stars above.'

They pulled the dog-boats up on the shore of the river where Nassin pointed his star-metal spear, and Killian strung his bow as the pirates formed into loose squads.

'Silent and fast,' Nassin said. 'Someone spots you, blade first. Get 'em down quick. You all know the reward for this. I want Blue Darrow's head on my spear by the time the sun rises.'

Killian followed the pirates, and next to him Mournchild stood, a shadow clinging to his heels. He glanced back downriver but the lagoon and the *Hawk* were lost to him.

They moved quickly over the hills, flocks of sheep woefully bleating and running off into the darkness when the soldiers disturbed them. Killian kept firmly to the back third of the loose column, far from where any ambush might strike. Mournchild ran close to him, never more than a dozen steps away, huffing at the effort of running in full armour compared to the light leather and studs the rest were clad in. They made a motley crew, no uniformity of weaponry. Cutlasses with weighted blades and heavy pommels were prevalent, but many short-hafted boarding axes, and a handful of larger weapons – a Tessendorm two-handed sword as tall as its owner, a bearded axe with two heads and a four-foot shaft. One of the shorter men had something like a ship's hammer in one hand and nothing else, but none seemed worried about them keeping up. Killian saw some shortbows, two crossbows – but no real archers.

'This plan is insane,' he said as he ran, and he did not think any heard it but the dark air and perhaps a sheep, but Mournchild was close to him, next to him within a step and together they ran for a moment. The Uradech warrior had a helm tied to his belt and let out a snort.

'We kill them before they kill us,' he said, 'what is so insane?'

Killian shook his head. They stopped to climb a drystone wall, thigh-sized chunks of stone piled into something that perhaps once had structure. There were many such walls, and low copses of cedar, but they had encountered no shepherds to mind the flocks. *Are there no predators, on Caragh's Point?* Loath as he was to speak to the odd shadow, Killian felt his frustration bubbling over.

'We approach a fortified town with no signal that the infiltration has gone well. No understanding of the layout. No real knowledge of numbers. We are wading into a pirates' nest, two of our own crews perhaps already inside – how are we to tell them apart? It is madness.'

Mournchild laughed and stopped for a moment, reaching a hand down to haul Killian over another wall. The knight put a hand to Killian's chest and then reached up and lowered his hood, and in the starlight Killian could only see a skull and black pits for eyes. Face paint, surely, but it was striking in its oddity, the hollows of cheeks and eyes jet black, the forehead and jaw stark white. The knight smiled, thin-lipped and wide-mouthed, showing rounded teeth.

'You think these men do not know their business. What do you think they have been doing, these last days on your ship? There are signals, there are plans. You simply do not know them.'

Killian looked ahead at the Tullioch and humans moving low between two hills.

'Why would they not tell me?' he asked, and Mournchild shook his head.

'I am not them. Do you tell them your plans, Captain Heroneye? Do I tell you *mine*? Each man must plan, and only Baal above knows all. Perhaps they do not trust you. Your role tonight is to witness, and survive. So stay close to me.'

Killian had no response to the dark knight, so he shrugged himself free of the man's hand and ran onward. Through the valley between two low hills there was a farmhouse, and by the time Killian reached it the forerunners had already slaughtered the men inside. Three bodies piled in the doorway, the pirates not even stopping to search for loot. Simple farmers whose home lay on the wrong path. Killian looked to the sky again but he could not find the siblings, or the warrior. The cloud was coming in thicker, and the thin crescent of moon seemed a mocking smile.

They passed a briar patch and from within a low growl rumbled. They kept running. It was a jaiboar – Killian would recognise that sound anywhere. They kept running straight, no movement towards the beast's lair, no hesitation or fear display that might entice it. Mournchild huffed next to Killian and the beast was soon lost to darkness.

They finally saw torchlights blazing, and slowed their approach. Killian felt cold sweat beneath his jacket, and removed his hat to wipe his brow. His bow was light as a feather in his hand, and his heart beating faster and faster as he took in the scene. A few hundred yards from the dark valley where they crouched, there was a stone wall perhaps ten foot high running right to left. Atop it no torches were lit, but beyond it there was some flame or brazier burning and he could see the monastery. It was easily five storeys of worked stone, an impassive block, unadorned and utterly unnatural. Nassin was kneeling close by and whispering to his fighters. Three of them with bows took off at a low dash towards the wall. They made the base of it with no alarm raised, and Killian lost sight of them in the blackness.

'Monks,' he said, 'or nuns?'

Nassin turned to him, squinting in the darkness. 'Before Blue Darrow, this was a monastery for more than a hundred years. Guildless Isken. What gods? Monks, nuns, both?'

'*Baal, Morost, Pendar, Tulu, Salaman,*' Mournchild intoned beside him. 'The only true god is the five-faced lord of light and dark. The Isken worship goats and coins.'

Nassin peered at the Uradech knight and flicked his forked tongue.

'They worshipped fate,' he said at last. 'The way Darrow's men have told it, if the monks knew enough about when one was born, where one came from, they could predict the future. Prophets. The Isken used to send ships asking for portent and sign. They stopped after enough didn't return. I guess that was sign enough.'

'There are omens,' Mournchild said dolefully, 'but an Isken coin counter would not have the eyes to see one.'

Killian peered up at the sky, but the clouds were pressing close and the blaze inside the town walls was bright enough to dull his senses.

'They didn't foresee Blue Darrow,' he muttered, squinting at the stone wall. Nassin gripped his spear and next to him the pirate-mage spat.

'Perhaps,' Nassin said, and all were silent.

'What is the signal, Nassin?' Killian asked, and felt rain on his face and the wind picking up. *Black skies and rain.* He tried to picture the *Hawk* running smooth down the tight sea loch they had wound their way up as a storm blew over the top of the mountains that ran down the spine of Caragh's Point, and grimaced. *No running from this.*

Over the stone rampart wall the firelight burned brighter and flared high, a column of sparks shooting upward, and a keening scream of utter pain tore through the night air.

As one the pirates ran forward.

10

BLUE DARROW'S HOLD

'For a decade the gods have been mad, and so why do I write to you now? Because their madness is no static thing. The wild wolf of the Ferron roams the acid wastes; Anshuka the bear has withdrawn far to the frozen north; Zalan the shipbreaker has halted all sail travel to the Deep Crowns save by those Russilan with the knack, and he sinks more boats with each passing year; the Whale has been seen to the south, swimming the Doldrum waters where no ship can pass; the Father Dragon has been circling ever westward from the skies of Ona. Our Eastern Holdfast is now under a permanent storm of his creation – their surface crops struggle, and their pumps work day and night to keep the downfall from filling the holdfast from above, even as the sea seeps in from below.'

– ***Letter to the Council of Isles on the Madness of the Spirits***, Anneli Thirdblood of Holt Suolaa

Killian scrambled towards the stone wall of Blue Darrow's fortress. The ground between the dark valley where he and Nassin and the pirates had been crouched to the wall was humps of earth and broken stone, twisted briar patches and gnarled shrubs and the stench of bog. Killian knew his bogs well enough – he sprang from tuft to tuft, keeping the high ground. The scream that heralded their rush forward was still continuing, a wail that went on and on and rose in pitch and intensity. The flaring firelight over the wall burned every star from the sky, and the squat stone tower of the ancient Isken monastery seemed to eat all light, shadows crowding against it.

He reached the base of the wall and behind him Blade Mournchild was plodding through bog and briar in a straight line, no compunction about thorn or sucking mud, an implacable force. Nassin's scouts were already up the wall, and three ropes let down – the forty-strong war party split into three wordlessly; fifteen went left and fifteen right along the base of the wall, lost to shadow almost instantly, the remainder climbing the ropes secured to the wall's top.

'Stick close to me if you want to live, Heroneye,' Nassin said, and the pirate-mage next to him laughed and spat and began to climb. Mournchild gazed up at the wall and pulled his helm from his belt and down over his skull: in the darkness of the wall's embrace it completed his transformation into a nightmare of shadow.

'I was to say the same thing, Heroneye,' he muttered, once Nassin and the mage were halfway up the ropes. 'Lady Marion needs you alive. These lizards want you here, but your blood is Lady Marion's. If this turns sour, stick by my back. If I tell you to flee, flee.'

With that he began to climb, and Killian slung his bow over his shoulder and spat into the dirt. *Stick to my back.* The Uradech madman thought Killian was some milk-wet fool just because he wasn't wearing armour, and much as it galled him, he had to admit it was perhaps useful for the knight to underestimate him. Two pirates remained behind Killian by a dozen feet. *I could cut them down and run.* Scenarios played out in his head. Flee to the *Hawk*; hang back until the fighting was done; kill these witnesses...

He pulled his tricorn hard down on his head and flexed his jaw and began hauling himself up the rope, feet slick against the wet moss that clung to the stone. Mournchild's gauntleted hand hauled him up the last few feet, and Killian crouched low and drew his bow and nocked an arrow. The rampart was deserted save for Mournchild and the pirate-mage, and the three of them crouched and looked below at the square before the monastery and the meek town surrounding it.

Chaos. Screaming. Shadows fighting shadows. Everywhere the ring of steel on steel, the roar of battle. In front of the vast stone edifice of the monastery, a fire the length of a dog-boat blazed brightly, fuelled by a dozen tree trunks. Sixty feet above the flames, three cages hung from long chains from an iron beam that jutted from the corner of the monastery, and within them the source of the screams – two figures lay slumped in darkness, limbs licked by tongues of flame trailing lifelessly through the gaps in the gull cage's bars. The figure in the third cage was still alive, and screaming, and screaming, and their wail overrode the tumult of the battle below and Killian felt his eyes searing at the brightness, but he recognised instantly the etiolated frame of Tarlis, captain of *Adamant Hand*.

'We should leave *now*!' he said, and up wooden stairs to the rampart two men were running, men he did not know. He loosed his bow but the first arrow went wide, and as he fumbled to grab another the pirate-mage next to him roared and a burst of blue flame spat from his hands, driving the two attackers back. Before Killian could raise his bow again, before Blue Darrow's men could bring their cutlasses to bear after shielding themselves from the magical flame, Mournchild was upon them.

The Uradech knight leapt down and slammed into them. The three went crashing through the timber stairway and Mournchild pulled himself up and drew his sword. In the shadow and flickering flame of the courtyard it was nothing but a line, an insinuation of a blade. He waited for the others to stand and saluted them with a strange flourish, touching his sword hilt to his heart and then the faceplate of his helm. Killian ran down what remained of the stairs levelling his bow, the pirate-mage keeping pace, but they were both too slow. Blue Darrow's men went for the knight as pirates did, looking to overwhelm with brutality and strength. They were both large men, and each bore a heavy cutlass, but Mournchild's size belied his speed. With a snaking strike he sent the first cutlass spinning, its owner clutching at his wrist and screaming. The second pirate used the opening to land a blow against what would have been Mournchild's head, but the knight raised an arm and caught it on his steel bracer and sent the sword wide, and then followed through with a one-armed skewer that took the pirate through the ribs. He slid off Mournchild's blade into the dirt, and

Mournchild flexed his shoulder and looked to Killian and then pointed at the battle before them.

'I think we are winning,' he called, and then cautiously stepped forward. From a side street fifteen of Nassin's men arrived and crashed into the ebbing and flowing melee of pirate against pirate. Heavenly Nassin himself was a nightmare of spinning movement, the bulky Tullioch ripping the throat from one of Darrow's own Tullioch with his spear and in the same movement kicking a woman into the roaring flame. He roared as the flames took her, and more than half of the square roared with him. Deeper in the small town, fires were blazing, but no light could compete with the pyre below Captain Tarlis.

Stepping back into the shadows, Killian peered up at the gull cage and tried to work out the mechanism. The iron post it hung from was braced in three places and he saw no mechanism for movement, but each cage hung from a chain. He squinted into the flame and smoke and tried to follow the chains – up to the iron beam, then along, then down into darkness… *There.* He could see the mechanism. High above, Tarlis still wailed, but each wail was broken by a hacking cough.

I could save him.

Killian hesitated, and felt time slow around him. He reached a hand up and gripped his heron skull medallion. Spirals of smoke and cinder dancing through the square, dozens of pirates trading blows; Tullioch and his men, male and female, screaming in rage or pain or defiance. The monastery loomed over it all, dark and ominous and ruinous. He knew he didn't owe these pirates anything, other than gold – *and that was happenstance and bad luck*. Tarlis would leave him in the water for the sharks and the garu as soon as spit. The Evertree Sisters had threatened his ship, his fingers.

Next to him the pirate-mage and Mournchild turned to intercept a trio of Darrow's men armed with boarding axes, and Killian's hand dropped from his amulet to his bow. *I could kill him.* A single arrow through air roiling with flame and the wind flame brought, but he could make the shot. *In the darkness, who would know?*

Killian found himself running, and behind him Mournchild bellowed for him to wait but he ignored it.

'Nassin!' he called as he ran, and the hulking Tullioch plunged his star-metal spear into the thigh of a woman wielding two scimitars and backhanded her into the dirt and then ran to join him. Nassin took in his goal in a moment and the two of them advanced. The gull cage chains led to a panel of iron hooks, and each was secured by a simple bar slipped through its links. In front of the chains a man cowered, a bandana pulled up tight over his mouth and nose. In one hand he held a hammer, the type used to hit pegs into hulls, the type that could break bone as easily as wood.

As Nassin and Killian approached, he lifted it and gestured to the mechanism.

'Any closer I'll burn him!' he called, his voice nasal and heavy with an Isken twang, and Killian loosed an arrow. It took the man in the gut, and Killian slung his bow over his shoulder and drew his cutlass as Nassin finished the pirate with a thrust of his spear.

'If I release it he will drop into the flame!' Nassin yelled, his voice straining to be heard over the roar of the flames and the screaming coughs of Captain Tarlis.

'Get your mage!' Killian replied. 'A thirty count!'

Nassin sped off without waiting, and Killian lifted the dead pirate's hammer and pressed his back to the wall and counted. He had reached ten when Blue Darrow's men came for him. Two of them finished one of the Evertrees' warriors and spotted him, alone, and they stepped towards him warily. One was a Tullioch wearing nothing but a loincloth, a black stone dagger with a coral hilt clutched in its hand. Its scales were white and its eyes a sharp yellow and it hunched down and circled to his right, a practised fighter's cadence to its movements. Its comrade was a bloodied and wild-eyed pirate with a thick beard wearing a vest, dozens of tattoos scrawled across every inch of skin. He held a boarding axe in each hand. They exchanged glances and stepped forward, and Killian spat.

'Fifteen!' he said to them, and they exchanged another glance and the man hurled an axe as the Tullioch darted forward. Killian ducked away from the axe and flashed his cutlass out, bringing the Tullioch's charge short. It had no long blade to parry with and gracefully quickstepped away from his curving slices, but Killian found himself stepping back and back, away from the gull cage chains. He tasted iron in his mouth, an acrid tang, his every nerve a riot of energy as the input around him swelled – the roar of the flame, the shouts of the dying, the stars above them all – he let it all drop away until there was nothing but his breath and the Tullioch and the man.

'Do you even know who I am?' he hissed, and he hurled the hammer at the Tullioch and followed it fast. The Tullioch was stronger than him, bigger than him, heavier than him. It had four fingers on each hand ending in inch-long talons.

It had teeth that could rip flesh, a prehensile tail that could whip and harass. It was built for a life of hard swimming against tide and predator. It was a pirate warrior.

Killian had a thirst for red.

His cutlass flashed out again and again, and fell into an easy rhythm of strike, strike, parry. The pirate man with the beard was circling them but Killian ignored him. Strike, strike, parry. The Tullioch fell back, dagger snaking in its claws as it waited for an opening, for him to overcommit to a strike – and so he did.

He swung harder and let the weight of the cutlass carry through, and as he knew it would the Tullioch darted forward to sink its dagger into the exposed ribs beneath his sword arm. But his swing was a feint, his weight not falling away to jerk back defensively too late but rather continuing around into a spiralling slash. He threw his full weight into the spin, leaping into it and bringing the cutlass down into unguarded flesh. The Tullioch's dagger scored his back but his cutlass cleaved a rent in its shoulder and it writhed away, hissing in agony and spraying blood across the dirt. Killian felt the exultation of drawing its blood but then the scrape of steel behind him sent him scrambling to the ground, flinching from the blow that was sure to follow.

Instead, a wet gurgle and a thump as the bearded pirate hit the ground, and over his corpse limned in firelight the shadow that was Mournchild waved his sword, a spray of blood flicking into the flames of the pyre. Killian threw himself across the ground to the gull cage chains and wrenched at the iron lock bars, unsure which held Tarlis above the inferno, and then Mournchild was there and taking an inch of slack on the weight of the chains and the bars slipped free. Both turned as three cages plummeted down, two holding the dead crashing into the burning logs and immediately lost to sight. The third cage fell ten feet, and then stopped in the dancing riot of fire and began to move, swaying, out of the flame.

Around them the sound of battle slowed as the Evertree Sisters' forces slit throats or accepted surrender from the few remaining pirates. The cage lowered to the front of the monastery where Heavenly Nassin and five of his fighters stood, all of them blooded, and before them shaking with exertion and panting and sweating the pirate-mage fell to his knees, one hand outstretched. Killian felt a twist in his mind as the pirate-mage called upon the skein, a pressure in the base of his skull. The Antian tide-mage Kaikatsu had told him, though he knew it already in hints. *I can feel it.* Was that why the Russilan tombs opened for him? The gull cage slammed to the flagstones at the base of the monastery steps, and Nassin and his fighters gripped it and with his spear Nassin rent the crude lock and hauled Tarlis out.

Killian and Mournchild crossed the field of dead and dying and joined them, and Tarlis coughed and hacked, bootless, his fine shirt and trous charred and blackened, his skin burnt.

'*Darrow*!' he spat, and crouched in the dirt raised a finger to the monastery doors. '*Bring me his head*!'

Nassin turned and rolled his shoulders and flicked his tongue.

'Berrence, Norbau,' he called, 'men to sweep the town, hold this door. We don't know how many they have in there so stick close. We take Darrow, the rest will stop.'

He began to march up the stairs to the monastery doors, and Killian eyed the square, seeking a moment to hide, to stay back. Mournchild's heavy gauntleted fist fell on his shoulder.

'I did not expect to find you interesting,' the knight said, and Killian could only see his eyes through the visor of his helm but they were twinkling. *He is loving this.* 'I think you want to fight. Lady Marion would tell me to keep you here, keep you safe having done your part.'

Killian gripped his cutlass and bared his teeth and felt the war drum in his chest, felt the aching thrill. The twist of skein-sense in the base of his skull faded, but the itch in his palm for his sword hilt did not. He turned back and saw the pale Tullioch he had bested crawling through the dirt and ash, two of Nassin's warriors headed towards it to offer death or employment.

'Lady Marion can go swim,' he said, and shrugging his bow from his back he dropped it by the exhausted pirate-mage and the wheezing Tarlis, and chased up the stairs after Heavenly Nassin.

Mournchild let the little captain lead the way, but it was not long before they were clearly lost. The monastery doors opened into a thin corridor, and then beyond that a central hall of some kind. It was set up for feasting, with a dozen long tables strewn with meat and fruit and bread and barrels of ale in each corner, all of it lit by dancing torchlight that showed the stone of the monastery for what it was – white limestone, greyed with ash and age. There were corpses everywhere. *Pirates.* Mournchild sneered. He had killed seven so far that night and only two had lasted any appreciable time. *My duelling will turn to nothing.* From the banqueting hall a dozen passages spread out, some stairs up, some down, some corridors to kitchens. The Tullioch Nassin tried to keep order, but his men had no discipline and soon they were spreading throughout the monastery, and Mournchild simply shook his head. *Nassin would be good to fight*, he thought, *but if these filthy lizard pirates ever test Uradech they will be sorely treated.* He sniffed and followed the little Captain Heroneye with his bloodlust, the man vibrating with energy, his cutlass tip trailing along walls as he soft-stepped forward.

Mournchild repeated his catechism, the five names of Baal. *Baal, Morost, Pendar, Tulu, Salaman.* Every death of an unbeliever was a boon to his god. Every drop of blood shed in their name a penance he paid for the sin in his heart. They entered living chambers with none living, bunk rooms that stank of whisky and stale sweat. Something like an armoury, racks and piles of spear and harpoon, barrels of arrows.

'Where *are* they all?' Heroneye said, and Mournchild did not respond. They would find the pirates, and they would kill the pirates. Then they would sail past the sea snake, and find Jean du Cilcan.

'You fight well for a sailor,' he said as they climbed stairs. 'Your footwork is good. Where did you learn to fight – Samurkan?'

Three pirates rushed them from a side passage before the captain could respond. The passage they were in was bare stone and lit only by the flickering of the pyre outside through arrow notches. Mournchild felt the bite of steel against his plate before he heard footsteps or had any sense of his attackers, and he chided himself as he beat them to death. His longsword was not ideal for a passage such as this, and his boot dagger unnecessary against such foes. *Fool, chattering away!* he thought, driving his armoured fists into the gut and chest and face of one assailant over and over, the pirate incredulous that his own blows did nothing to penetrate the armour of Mournchild. When that one fell he turned and leapt on the one assailing Heroneye – the third was already down, a cutlass slash across his face and another across his gut. Heroneye was clashing cutlass blade to cutlass blade, and the pirate did not notice Mournchild until he was behind her. With one hand he caught her upswinging sword arm, and Heroneye's blade took her in the chest.

'Baal, Morost, Pendar, Tulu, Salaman,' Mournchild said. 'I should talk less and listen more.'

'Piss!' Heroneye said, his eyes wide, and he crouched to the ground and seemed to shake a moment before standing and bouncing on his toes. 'I learned to fight on a ship. Footwork is everything. Why is an Uradech working for Cil-Marie, Mournchild? Who are you?'

Mournchild drew his boot dagger and tapped it on the vambrace covering his right forearm, and then pointed it down the corridor.

'I am a Blade,' he said, and he took the forward position. To an Uradech that would be answer enough – he was a paladin of the church of Baal, a holy warrior charged with the church's business. *The church must have business with the Lady Marion.* He knew no more, and it was none of this little island rat's business anyway. *You forget yourself, so keen to chatter like a child or a fool.* 'We should descend. I was wrong to allow you to enter this place. This pirate hides beneath his bed, and none of the dead have been any use with a blade. There is no challenge here.'

Heroneye stared at him, and they stood in silence in the corridor.

'*Please*,' he heard, and they both turned their heads. The pirates had ambushed them from a darkened doorway, and past it there was the dull yellow glow of beeswax burning. Heroneye raised a finger to his lips and stepped forward silently, sword raised. Mournchild levelled his dagger. His eyes were tinted yellow that day as it was Tulu's day of worship. *A yellow flame, to yellow eyes.* This was a portent. He muttered a prayer to the godhead Tulu, that day's aspect of the five-faced god. Tulu was the god of nurture. He had laughed that morning applying his dyes – Baal had his irony, that Tulu was the god for a day of blood and destruction. *But to respect nurture in all its forms as one dealt death, was that not a great test of faith?*

'*Please...*' the voice repeated and ahead of him Heroneye carefully peered around a corner and then stopped still and lowered his sword. Mournchild came up to his shoulder and gazed into the room.

It was a stone cell lit by a fat beeswax candle, and the walls and ceiling were covered in scratched constellations that caught the dancing candlelight. Dozens of them etched deep into stone, and lighter lines connecting them, showing how they must move through the sky. There was a single window, an arrow slit thinner than Mournchild's fist. At the edge of the room a figure crouched, shackled by the ankle to a length of thick chain that ran to a fixture in the wall. They were diminutive and sharp-eyed, thin and worn, wearing rags of what once might have been robes. Long matts of hair clumped around their sunken face, and their eyes were peering wells of darkness that absorbed all focus. Mournchild twisted his head and blinked thrice. The robes had faded stripes, a pattern he had seen before. *In Cinnae. The priest of the broken temple.* He had killed that priest with something strange – *was it a wine cup?*

'They are an Isken priest,' he said at last, and Heroneye crouched to his heels and gazed at the emaciated figure.

'Fate tellers,' the captain said, and Mournchild sniffed. *Fool.*

'The Isken count their coins and nothing else,' he said, and he flexed his fingers around his dagger. 'They have no gods, only Judges. They have no church, only guilds. They have no knowledge of Baal above or the eternal fire below. They are lost.'

The monk collapsed back into their corner, and Heroneye gestured at the constellations scratched into the ceiling and walls.

'These were rogues, from Isken,' he said. 'Who is to say what they knew? The Russilan looked to the stars for their fate.'

'For *your* fate.'

Heroneye bristled and turned his gaze back on Mournchild. Higher in the monastery there was a keening wail and a crash.

'I'm taking them,' Heroneye said, and Mournchild stared at him dolefully.

'What use is a priest to an unknown god?' he asked, and he pointed with his dagger. 'I will cut their throat. The blood of a heretic priest is a great blessing. It will strengthen my blade and my arm, and Baal will reward me for our fealty. We have tests yet to endure.'

Heroneye shook his head and grinned and Mournchild held his eye, the beeswax dancing across pools of honey-brown, pupils wide and staring. Blood was spattered across Heroneye's cheek, and Mournchild took measure of the man, the man smiling in this place. *This one is mad.*

'They could be a priest of Baal, you know,' Heroneye said, his tone light, his grip on his sword hilt tight. 'They could have left Isken after that whole little war you two had – that was all about gods, wasn't it? I think we should see what they have to say. If nothing else, some fate telling on deck will while away the evenings as we head towards our certain death. *And* Pollos Twice-Kissed is Undal, and they get a bit funny about slaves and slavers. Won't stand for it. Next heretic priest you can murder, I promise.'

Mad. Mournchild sheathed his boot dagger and recited Baal's five names and went and wrenched the chain fixture from the wall. The monk lay semi-conscious, and they were speaking, but he could make out no words. *Useless.* A cheer cut through the monastery, a roaring shout picked up and amplified outside.

'I think we have won,' he said, and Heroneye went to aid the monk and Mournchild stared from the arrow slit at the black cloud above. *What is an Uradech paladin doing working for Cil-Marie?*

'Church business,' he muttered, and shook his head. 'Baal, Morost, Pendar, Tulu, Salaman.'

Lady Marion will not like this. The Cil woman was impatient as it was, complaining endlessly of complications and intrigues as Mournchild dutifully listened. *Perhaps she can speak to this priest, instead of me.* The thought twisted his thin lips into something like a smile, and he relented. Heroneye scooped up the emaciated priest, and Mournchild led them down to the courtyard, his boot dagger raised, but nobody came against them. A pirate wielding a many-bladed club on the bottom stairwell started towards them but then stopped as a beam of moonlight picked out their features.

'Captain Tarlis is wanting you, Heroneye,' he spat, and without another word spun on his heel and moved off. Mournchild followed dutifully, with Heroneye lagging behind, awkwardly carrying the semi-conscious monk.

They emerged in the courtyard to find the bustle of soldiery. Captain Tarlis sat on a simple stool at the base of the monastery steps, a man tending his wounds from a satchel of unguents and bandages. His shirt was off, and he watched the burning pyre in the centre of the square. Blue Darrow's men were sat cross-legged against one wall of the fortress, perhaps twenty of them still alive, none of them uninjured. The dead were being hauled to the central pyre, two industrious Tullioch stripping them of valuables and weapons and tossing the corpses in like driftwood logs. In front of Tarlis and his simple throne, Heavenly Nassin held his spear to the throat of a man on his knees. *This must be Blue Darrow.*

Blue Darrow was bald as an egg, short and muscled with a face like a butcher's slab, scarred and pummelled. No fresh wounds adorned him. A simple thumb-wide stripe of blue was inked across his skull and face, covering one eye and passing the left corner of his mouth. He was beardless and utterly hairless, and dressed in simple boots, trous and shirt. Tarlis beckoned for Mournchild and Heroneye to join him, and the little captain lay his pet monk gently to the ground and did so, Mournchild dutifully behind him. He looked skyward but the clouds were thick and the fire was bright and hot against his armour. He removed his helm and hooked it on his belt and fell into an easy stance. *They will ask me nothing*, he thought. *They never do*.

'Blue Darrow knew of our plan,' Tarlis said softly. 'He had Lwell and I and the tide-mage Hallafis in gull cages by sundown.'

Heroneye shifted his feet and wiped blood form his face with his sleeve.

'Is Captain Lwell...'

'Dead,' Tarlis said. 'Their cages were lower than mine. I owe you a debt, Heroneye.'

Blue Darrow spat. 'Heroneye, is it? *Cutlass Hawk*?' The man's voice was thin and strained. 'You think the Evertree Sisters will let you keep that ship, little rat? They know what I know, what Tarlis knows, what every sailor in the Coracles, piss, every sailor in the *Crowns* knows. Killian Heroneye is a thief and a pissant. Big talk, a stolen ship. Tarlis, what is this? Your crew came for my head; I took some of yours. It is time for business. Send this boy back to his mother's tit and we can talk.'

Tarlis gazed into the flame and winced as another layer of salve was slathered onto the suppurating flesh of his shoulder. Heroneye leaned forward to Blue Darrow and whipped his cutlass free of its hook, the point of the blade pressing firmly into the man's face until it drew blood. The pirate did not recoil, simply sneered up. Mournchild watched, impassive.

'You mentioned my mother,' he said. 'You mocked my ship. You mocked me. Pissant, is it? Captain Tarlis, can I ask you a favour?'

Tarlis nodded, his eyes still on the flame. 'Heroneye,' he said, 'I am in your debt. Know that. The Sisters saw your value, and I admit I did not. But you are not a boy, or a pissant.'

'I want his head,' Heroneye said, 'and this monk.'

Tarlis did not break his gaze from the flame, and Mournchild considered the back of the little Captain Heroneye. From his post stood behind, Mournchild could see the tension in the boy's shoulders, the shift in his feet. *He is ready to strike.*

'The Sisters—' Darrow began, but Tarlis held up a hand and Nassin silenced the pirate chief with a quick flex of his spear arm, the star-metal weapon lifting Darrow's chin upward.

'The Evertree Sisters are not *here*,' Tarlis said, and he turned his gaze at last from the flame to look at Heroneye. 'Take the monk. Take this one's head. Take my thanks, and a favour for the future. And take a warning.'

Tarlis turned in his chair to look at Mournchild, and Heroneye followed his gaze. Mournchild did not shift, did not stir, and he held his face steady as his masters had taught him with rod and water and flame so many years before.

'This one and his mistress,' Tarlis said, 'they mean to reach the Deep Crowns and Captain Arlock of the Bloody Crows by any means necessary. They reek of desperation.

They will use you and yours hard to do so. Watch your back, Heroneye.'

Heroneye met Mournchild's gaze and Mournchild kept his face schooled in stillness, impassivity. The man simply smiled, the same mad light in his eyes, and then turned with a leap and brought his cutlass down into the skull of Blue Darrow, taking four fingers from the hand raised in mute defence and defiance as his blade fell, and leaving his cleaver buried and the egg of Blue Darrow's skull split and leaking.

Yolk, Mournchild thought, and he considered the darkness. *Eggs for breakfast.* He repeated the names of Baal in his mind and then aloud under his breath, and followed Heroneye mutely as the man collected his cutlass and his unconscious monk and headed back into the monastery to find somewhere to sleep.

This one is mad, he thought, trying to mentally draft his report to Lady Marion. *I like him.*

11

NO QUESTIONS

'The plague that killed the Russilan moved quickly, and killed all who were touched. One account of an island some twenty leagues from the plague's first emergence describes the great efforts of a town to isolate themselves and to fight off unwanted travellers and ships. Despite this, one spring the sickness appeared with its characteristic boils and black veins, and the final note dated from the site is from only a span later. The Thirst took them, and they walked into the water willingly.'

– ***Notes on the Russilan***, Gallo Mancinus

Tarlis had sent a runner to tell the *Hawk* that Darrow's hold had fallen, and by the time Killian was awake and washed he could see the familiar outline of her twin triangular sails cutting into the bay from the thin arrow slits of the monastery. Killian cleaned the blood and ash from his face and hair as best he could from a ewer of tepid water and then examined himself. The score across his back had gouged deep through the leather of his waistcoat, but the shirt below was miraculously intact and the flesh below that only bruised. His cutlass was thick with a clag of scabrous brown. Killian scraped the flat of the blade against a doorframe and then fetched stale bread and some food and some ale from the banquet tables in the central hall.

In the banquet hall there were drag marks where the dead of Darrow's crew had been pulled from the room, trails of scabbed red that the dawn light danced across. When he returned, Mournchild accepted the bread and a handful of eggs – the odd knight had slept on the stone floor in front of the room Killian had chosen, in his armour, and seemed unperturbed and well rested. As Killian opened his door he paused and considered attacking the man. *Would he be surprised?* Having seen him cut through swathes of Darrow's pirate crew Killian was leery to try Mournchild in a fair fight. *I will have to kill him eventually.*

With a sigh he left the morose knight to his eggs, and inside the room, he set down bread and ale and cheese and eggs and used the keys he had found amongst the dead that morning to unshackle the monk. In the light he could make out more of her – he was fairly certain the monk was a her, whatever that meant to a monk.

She accepted the bread and the water mutely and stared at him, clutching at her unshackled wrist even as she ravenously ate. Killian squatted to his haunches. The room he had chosen for rest was some sort of side-chamber, and the sailcloth they had slept on smelled like dust and dry earth, but there was an undercurrent of salt that had brought him a black sleep with no dreams. *No thirst for red, no Thirst for salt water.* As a child he had nightmares of the Thirst, of waking with a parched throat only the sea could sate. Last night had been only blackness, and the sour ale he had found was stale but welcome. He finished his cup and tipped it towards the monk.

'You are free,' he told her, and she stared up at him and chewed on the bread. 'Is it five years, Darrow has held this place? Why are you alive?'

'To tell his future,' the monk said, voice rough. Her hair was a tangle of brown knots and twists, her eyes dark pools. Her lips were chapped and cracked. 'I saw you coming.'

Killian laughed at that. *What else would a fortune-teller say?*

'Come,' he said at last. 'Come down to the bay. I give you your freedom, and passage from here if it is what you wish.'

He led the monk by one arm and Mournchild rose and followed, the corridor a mess of eggshells, his hood raised to hide his face.

'We need to be on our way,' the man rumbled, and Killian waved a hand back at him.

'Where do I look like I'm going, Mournchild? We will get water and any fresh food they have on board, the *Hawk* will be out of here before the sun is high and we can all go swim Burner's Run together. Did you really see Zalan, your last attempt?'

'I saw your snake,' Mournchild said, eyes dull. 'I didn't like it.'

The knight glowered at him and pulled his cloak tighter, and fell into step behind.

The trio exited the monastery, past the embers of the great pyre. Charred bone competed with chain and iron bars and broken weapons for prominence in the remnants of the ash and char, and above them black-backed gulls with vicious cutlass beaks called across an ice-blue sky. There were few clouds, herringbones high and far, moving slow, but closer down the wind was whipping and had a bite to it in the shadow of the monastery. In the morning light Killian could see it better now, a great tower of white stone with a flat roof, the curve of the huge drum tower facing out to the sea, a flat face presenting itself to the inner courtyard. In the darkness the night before it had seemed a great block, but with dawn he could see its curve, could almost feel the wind and storm of the centuries breaking against that great curved wall.

'Russilan monastery,' he said as they walked, and the monk gripped his arm to hold her steady. She was crying, tears running down her cheeks, her face turned to the sun.

'I've not been outside in five years,' she said at last. 'Is Darrow dead?'

Killian grinned at her. 'Killed him myself,' he said, and they walked on slowly. The town was near silent save occasional pirates out searching for breakfast – he figured the townsfolk had fled to the hills or were hidden in cellars, and the few houses that had burned were still sending up thick plumes of black smoke that spiralled through the air with slow intensity. Killian let his feet lead him. He had never been to Caragh's Point before, but the streets would all lead to the most important place – the dock. Mournchild was muttering something about Baal or fire behind them, but Killian refused to let the man sour his mood. *Halfway home, Little Key.*

'I am Captain Killian Heroneye of the *Cutlass Hawk*,' he said to the monk as they emerged onto the dockside, and the monk clung to him as he waved to Pollos – the broad Undal man was throwing mooring ropes down to the lithe Breygar twins who had already clambered down to a space on the long harbour wall that jutted into the bay. The *Hawk* looked undamaged, and he could see *Adamant Hand* and *Jade* and two other ships at anchor further out in the water. It was a wide natural harbour in the lee of the island's low hills, protected from wind and storm. At the bow rail of the *Hawk* the Antian tide-mage was stood between Silver and the Lady Marion, the former languidly leaning on the rail and grinning down at him, the latter's face a storm, arms crossed, fingers tapping the head of the hammer at her belt. His smile faltered.

'The people who took this place are not as bad as Blue Darrow,' he said softly, 'but they are not good people. I can give you passage at least as far as Madu, if you wish – it is not popular, but it is safe enough and you should be able to catch a ship from there to Samurkan, or wherever else you wish to go. Eventually. I can give you a little coin, as well.'

'Why are you doing this?' the woman asked, and Killian met her eyes. In their reflection he saw Blue Darrow, unarmed, Killian's sword in his skull. *Why did I do that?* He saw the Samurkan slave camp alight. *Why did I do that?* He saw a dozen duels, brutal and fast, a hundred shipboard fights before finding the *Hawk*. The governor of Requin-Port an old man asleep in his bed. A shank in a side street near the Samurkan docks. *Such a thirst for red.* He smiled at her and tapped the heron pendant on his chest.

'Why does anyone do anything?' he asked.

Before noon the water barrels were full and deck clear of the accoutrements and detritus of Heavenly Nassin's crew. The hulking Tullioch came and bade a brief farewell, clambering up the gangplank and finding Killian in the midst of directing Renard and Timmult. The Tullioch carried a burlap sack with him and dropped it at Killian's feet, where it clinked loud enough that Renard and Timmult both stopped paying attention to him immediately and stared down at it.

'Captain Tarlis said this is your share,' Nassin hissed. 'It seems he has grown fond of you.'

Killian bowed his head and managed to stop himself from reaching for the bag immediately.

'So my debt with the Sisters is clear?' he asked, and Nassin nodded. His star-metal spear was nowhere in sight, a robe of simple blue wool draped over him rather than the warrior garb he had worn the night before.

'Clear,' Nassin said, clicking his teeth. 'Once those Cil are across Burner's Run. When word of that reaches the Cil embassy in Samurkan, they will pay the second half of your debt. Watch them, Heroneye. They have deep pockets and strange plans.'

Killian proffered his hand, and the Tullioch took it and gripped hard, his claws making their presence felt.

'You hunted a shark for that spear,' Killian said softly. 'Do you fancy coming along for a stretch? I could use some… muscle. It should be fun. A holiday, from the Sisters?'

Nassin clicked his teeth again and snorted. 'Your debt is part paid,' he said, 'not mine. I would not sail Burner's Run, not on your word alone, Captain Heroneye.'

As the Tullioch turned to leave Killian drew close to him.

'A favour,' he said, and Nassin paused and cocked his head. 'Mistress Merrow's orphanage is having some trouble.

If the Sisters can keep an eye, *subtly*, make sure all is well, I will square them on my return. Can you ask them for me?'

Nassin nodded and clicked his teeth in laughter, shaking his head.

'*Subtly*,' he said, but he nodded.

The *Cutlass Hawk* left Caragh's Point as the sun rode high and they sailed south and east. It was two days to Madu, and Killian paced the deck of the ship restlessly, poring over his charts or peering at the water from the aft deck, unnerving whoever was on wheel duty. The weather held, the winds always blowing towards Burner's Run, which meant they could easily catch enough in the lateen rigs to keep them happily in the sweet spot perpendicular to the prevailing wind. Of course, the Crowns were not so simple. There were reefs to navigate, archipelagos of rock and stone that could scuttle them, and the tides and currents danced around each isle and kept his attention drawn. A pack of garu trailed the ship for a day and a night, easily three dozen of the six-foot fish, hooked jaws and sharp teeth and ever-watching eyes. They eventually lost interest. The eastern Coracles were quieter than the northern, and they saw ships but none that drew close. Fishing boats gathered around the larger isles, canoes and catamarans dancing between the smaller. Killian guided them through the deep-water channels but not the widest, not those with the wrong reputation. So close to Caragh's Point it was Darrow's men they should fear, but the *Hawk* was fast, and the routes he chose obtuse. Pirates would go for easier pickings.

The Antian tide-mage Kaikatsu ate alone and spent most of her hours in the net below the bowsprit, emerging only to call guidance on current or tide or wind. The crew were thrilled with their split from Darrow's hold – Tarlis had sent Killian a sack of mixed coins, mainly smaller denominations, and a handful of larger items clearly looted from other ships – candelabra, chalices, three torques of rune-inscribed bronze. He gave the coins out liberally and equally, and Big Breygar held her usual stoic assessment of him as he parcelled out her share.

'Why did you kill Blue Darrow?' she asked, and the rest of them were near enough save Timmult at the helm. They were running smooth. Killian took his hat off and set it on a barrel and adjusted his sword on his belt.

'Pollos, Big Breygar, Small Breygar,' he said, 'Timmult, Renard, Kaikatsu. Me. We have no ballistae. No fire pot throwers. No archers, no soldiers. No muscle. There are ships our size that keep a dozen aboard with bow and blade for nothing but scrapping. We don't have that.'

Renard held a fat silver coin from Undal from the pile of her share of the loot.

'Fewer crew, more pay,' she said, and Killian nodded.

'Fewer crew, more pay. I killed Blue Darrow because once word gets out, any pirate who thinks of chasing us down, of hassling us in port, of pissing in our oats, will maybe think twice. I am building a story. A story of a ship not to be trifled with.'

'Seems to be the story of a captain, not a ship,' Big Breygar said, and Killian gestured to her pile of coin and left them to it. Big Breygar would never love him. *I don't need her to love me.*

The rain came fast that evening, a bank from the north-east pushing in towards Burner's Run. To the east was Ona, a thousand spires of rock surrounded by mountains that rose like fistfuls of spearheads. Above Ona, the Father dragon flew, a great spirit that sent ceaseless rain down. The rain was cold, relentless, and the wind it brought was squalling gusts. They set anchor in the lee of an isle marked on his charts as Narras Rock, uninhabited save for fat seals who clung together on the stone beaches.

'You are quiet,' Silver said to him that night. She found him at the rail staring south-west. They had spoken little since his return. He could tell she was waiting for him to tell her the story of Blue Darrow's hold.

'I am quiet,' he said back, and then scratched at his chin. 'I don't mean to be. The Evertree Sisters, Blue Darrow's hold, this Cil woman. Breygar still won't trust me; she sees everything I do as some self-serving game. I want to speak to the monk now she has had a few days to find her feet. Burner's Run is the hardest sailing there is. I am quiet, Silver. I have a lot to think about.'

Silver drew close to him and pressed her long torso tight to his side, and leaned in close.

'I am your ally, Heroneye,' she said. 'I know you. I see you. We have miles to go – do not shut me out.'

Killian let her stay there, close, and he squeezed her hand and remembered the judder in the hilt of his sword when he drove it into Blue Darrow's skull. *Why did I do that?* Silver did not know him – *how can she know me if I don't know me?*

'There are things I would tell you, Silver,' he said, but he could not bring himself to say more. He left her at the rail and bade Timmult fetch the monk to his quarters. The monk had spent the two days sleeping in a hammock on the lower deck, with Renard plying her with a variety of potions he swore would bring her back to vitality, but five years chained in a single room had left the woman wizened and cowed.

Timmult brought her in on his arm and Killian sat behind his map table. He gestured to a chair, and rose and set a cup of wine and a bowl of olives next to her.

'What say you, then, monk? Are the quarters and Renard's potions to your liking? We have had fair weather.'

The woman gazed at him. 'You want me to tell your fortune,' she said at last, and he tapped his fingers on the map.

'Well,' he said. 'Well, well. Well. Fate worshippers, was what I was told. Diviners of the future, if they knew the past. I saved you from Blue Darrow's pirates, monk. Yes. I would have you predict my future, inasmuch as you can. I have a perilous path to weave.'

The woman cast her eyes downward and took an olive, nibbling at the flesh until only the stone remained. She held it in her hands.

'The Russilan built eight monasteries,' she said, and gestured at the map of Morost's seas. 'One on the isle of Iskander, near Undal, in the Wind Sea. One on the Lello isles to the far north of Carob's Strait, where the Last Ocean begins. One in the southern reach of the Crowns where the Doldrum waters spread endlessly away. One in the shadow of the old fire mountain between Isken and Kelamor. This one here in the northern reach of the Crowns, you call Caragh's Point. One in the Shield Isles by Requin-Port, where Cil-Marie hold sway. And one lost to time and tide.'

'That is seven,' he said, and she smiled but did not elaborate. 'I am Russilan, you know.'

Killian looked at his chart and tried to place those points, and the woman sniffed softly.

'A wolf raised with sheep is a wolf, but it does not know all the ways of wolves,' she said, and he sat back and held his gaze on her. She met his eye, her face tired and sad. 'The Russilan could tell truth and future in the stars above, the patterns they dance relating to the skein below us. Do you know the skein?'

'I know the stars. I know the skein,' he said, and felt the eyes of Kaikatsu meeting his in his memory, the burning intensity of her gaze. *The Antian saw that.*

'We were exiled from Isken, and took up our place. Fate worshippers, you said. Ha. We did not worship fate. We worshipped nothing. We sought to learn how what came before could predict what comes next. But the future is in motion. It is a point in the ocean, not a point on land. It is hard to find, with myriad routes to reach it. And when you are there? A point of the ocean may be many things, as a day or a season turns. It may be calm as a millpond, wild as Burner's Run itself. Tempest or torpor.'

'Tempest or torpor,' he said, and from his chart table picked up a coin. It was a ducat from the north, the jungles of Carob where a great wizard held the throne, the skein-wreck of Belleco. On one side a man's face in profile with a mane of hair, a long bent nose. On the other a stylised jungle cat. He spun the coin and it turned round and round, dancing over the chart, and fell with a shiver with the jungle cat facing up. 'Tempest or torpor.'

They sat in silence, save for the incessant drum of rain on the roof, the rush of wind catching at the furled sails, the steady voice of the sea as the waves spoke to the hull, gently, gently.

'Tempest or torpor?' he asked her, and the monk sipped at her wine and averted her gaze.

'Tempest,' she said. 'But you already knew that, Captain.'

They sat in silence for a long time, Killian's eyes on the map, tracing the locations of the lost Russilan monasteries.

'So the Thirst took the Russilan who built,' he said, 'and your people moved in, and the Blue Darrow found you at such a convenient crossroads on the Horse Water and the northern and eastern reaches. A safe harbour, a strong fort.'

She raised her eye to meet his.

'They saw the Thirst,' she said, and she leaned forward and tapped the heart of the Crowns on his map, the Deep Crowns where the Russilan once dwelt. 'They saw it coming, and they could do nothing to stop it. They saw the madness of the Judges – we did not understand, we did not understand so many of the warnings they left! But afterward, when the smoke hangs in the air, afterward you can read the signs and portents.'

'What use is that?' he asked quietly, and the monk sat back and shrugged, exhausted and broken.

'I knew you would come,' she said, and when he did not speak she closed her eyes. 'As the sun fell from my little window that night I saw a heron with a blood-soaked beak fly low over Blue Darrow's hold and away over the ocean, and as I held my gaze on the point, it fell from my sight, and when darkness came and the stars emerged I saw them. Six dancers.'

'Change,' he said. 'Chance.'

'Luck,' the monk said, and she dipped her head. 'I am tired, Captain. You have my gratitude. I will leave you on

Madu to seek my fate, but before then I will read what signs and portents I may, and help you as I can. Tell me the time and tide of your birth, the place, the year. Tell me your dreams. Tell me all, and I will help you.'

'Before we leave Madu, then,' he said, and he showed her out and he drank the wine and olives he had laid out for her and stared at his charts. *Monasteries and tombs.* His palms itched, and when Silver came to him it all came out. The violence, the faux heroism. Considering murdering Tarlis. Swordfights by firelight. The priest seeing portents and signs. He told it all in a great rush, and Silver sat close to him, their knees touching, and night enveloped the *Cutlass Hawk*. The rain did not stop, and Pollos kept them safe at anchor. The rocks of the Crown archipelago were too erratic for night sailing unless the need was urgent or the route well mapped, and they were past the Horse Water now, onto the little channels and wide passages that made up the eastern reach.

'Every culture thinks they can predict the future,' Silver said at last. Whatever dull remnant of daylight that had been fighting past cloud and rain was lost, and in the darkness they sat close and Killian closed his eyes and felt the weight of the ship around him. 'Every culture that is – or was – has those who read the signs and portents, the stars or currents, deep patterns in the skein or the shape of a skull to determine a person's fate.'

Silver kissed him then, and later as they lay in his narrow bed she ran a finger across his chest.

'The Lady Marion is *interesting*,' she said in the darkness. 'When you were gone she spent some time trying to figure each of the rest of us out. Our motivations. She was not utterly transparent, but I've seen her type before. She would only glare at the Antian, of course, her being Cil. Their prejudices are fascinating, don't you think?'

Silver sighed and let her finger stop tracing, held her palm flat against him.

'That was a question,' she said. Her fingers were long and uncallused, and in the darkness he breathed deep and took in the scent of her hair, her skin, her sweat. The Crowns were cold, the ship was colder, but his cabin was warm with the heat of their bodies and the weight of the thick blanket at their waists.

'No questions,' Silver said mournfully to the darkness. 'I have so many questions, Heroneye. My *life* is questions. That is my calling, my profession, my quest. I am a sage. It is not simply employment. Why of all creatures do only the Antian and the Tullioch and humans speak? And the blue-skinned cannibal Orubor, if you believe in Undal fairy tales. No others. Why did the gods go mad? What is the orb of light that flies from Cil-Marie each night across the Crowns, fast and high, but only this last decade? Where did the Russilan Thirst come from, and where did it go? Can we tell our fates, by star or bone or rite or prophecy? The relu across the world are untethered from place, and are traded – what does a relu *taste* like? Can it love, or speak? Are the Judges made by mankind, or is mankind made by the Judges? Can a Carob whale think as we can, and lacks only a common language with us? Cut a piece from a Barsin squid and the piece will grow a new squid, no matter how small the piece. Which is the original squid? The skein-mages can look deep, up close, can speak, far away. Why is it like this? Every human nation's god differs, but every hell is the same – the unceasing fire below. Why, Heroneye? Is that true for the Antian and the Tullioch? I have so many questions, Heroneye, and every day adds to my list. Where did you get this ship so young, why does Pollos Twice-Kissed love you so, as if you were his son? Who is Mistress Merrow? Why do the Russilan tombs open for you? I have heard of no other being able to do this. What do Marion and her Blade really seek, to travel with a single sword and a ship of ill repute to a place where every soul will surely seek their deaths? Why do you want Big Breygar to love you, to follow you? All of them?'

She paused and her hand clenched into a fist, heavy on his chest.

'Do you love me, Killian Heroneye, or am I simply convenient? Will I ever see my mother again? Have I erred in this path I have chosen? Will we die on Burner's Run? I have questions, Heroneye. *No questions, no feelings, no ties.* I set those rules, not you. No questions, when I first came to your ship. No feelings, when I first came to your bunk. No ties, when I first realised the first strictures were already so hard. Yet here I am, tied to you. Here I am, and I am full of feelings, full to bursting. Here I am, and I have questions.'

Killian lay in the dark with his eyes open. *She does not know me. I do not know me.* He gazed up and in the soft black he felt her breathing, so tense, and he ran a hand through the thick mop of her hair. *Why do I trust you, Silver?* She was a relic hunter, a thrill seeker. She did not know him, and he did not know her. *You should not trust her.* He knew he should not.

'Have you ever eaten honey from Madu?' he asked, and against his chest her fist opened and she laughed and laughed and laughed.

As the sun dipped Kaikatsu took her food and returned to her nest below the bowsprit. The first mate Pollos Twice-Kissed had cut fresh boughs on Caragh's Point, and the thin branches of rowan and hawthorn lashed to the bowsprit hung over her like a forest canopy. It was a good tradition. The Antian had no equivalent – perhaps the jallen flower plucked on ascension days and worn for luck, wilting as more time was spent on the surface. *A reminder to return home*. She ate the food the man Small Breygar had prepared, though she did not understand his name. He was a thin man, and it was a soup of barley and lentils and vegetables, carrot and potato and leek, all of it stained dark red by the pickled beetroot he had spooned into her bowl. She balanced half of a small black loaf on the edge of her bowl and she drank her soup and listened to the water below.

The relu-mouse emerged from her robe and perched on her knee as she crouched in the netting and drank her soup and chewed at her bread. The scent to the rowan and hawthorn was alive, fresh sap and the vegetal suffusion of leaves not yet dying, but no longer alive. She had acquired a thick undershirt of wool from the mate Pollos Twice-Kissed, and with that and her robe she was warm. The cave relu-mouse was a mote of warmth on top of that again, as if she rested a hot cup of tea on her thigh back home in front of the home chimney, listening to her grandmothers recite old stories. In the darkness the cobalt of his fur was utter black, but the orbs of jade that were his eyes shone with a dull light all their own. It wriggled its nose at her soup and she offered it a crumb of black bread, which it held in its small paws but did not eat. *A relu eats feeling,* her grandmother had told her, but she did not know if that were true or just something the old woman had said to fill the silence. It felt true, but feeling was an inadequate word. *A relu is fed by connection,* she thought, and absently she stroked the little mouse.

After she had finished her soup she practised her skein rituals. Every culture had their own – Pollos Twice-Kissed had told her the war mages of Undal tattooed runes in their flesh and could call to the pattern below each rune, flame or force. Their whitestaffs trained in the magic of healing and divination, and focused through staffs of wood from one white tree, recalling named rituals that would reproduce the same results over and over. At home in the holt, the triptych witches would align in their connection and would call on rote patterns by name, names that were so linked to the pattern that to speak them would draw the witches deeper into the skein, would manifest the change they wanted.

Kaikatsu shivered at the thought, despite the warmth of her robe, despite the comfort of the relu on her thigh. Skein-mages all. There was a cost to it, the burning blood, the tang of adrenaline. A skein-wreck could take without giving, but they were legends and stories. Kaikatsu was no legend, no story. *Only me.* A simple mage.

'I could not link with them,' she said to the mouse. It was a bad habit, she knew, but she could not speak to the humans – they were so strange, no cultural reference she understood, all double meanings and side talk. She could not read their expressions, their body language, and the trade tongue of Isken was slow on her lips. *They think me stupid.* If they could understand her speaking the holt tongue of the deep tunnels, quipping mine slang with her holt-mates, always fast! The ritual humiliation of never saying exactly what she meant had left her stoic. 'I have been six summers from the holt now. Do you think the grandmothers are well?'

The relu clambered up her chest and onto her shoulder and pressed itself to her cheek.

'I could not link with the others,' she said again, 'but I have found my way. There is good work here to do.'

Kaikatsu fell into the skein, her vision blurring and then darkness becoming light and dark all at once, layer upon layer of connection and sensation infusing her. She could look in, or out. She had no scars, no staff, no spell words. She only had sensation and the tricks she had learned on the whaler, on the trader, on the hard miles over open water. She simply focused.

'I did not sense a relu at Caragh's Point,' she said, more to practise speaking whilst within the skein than to truly communicate, and the little mouse did not respond. She kept her gaze far from it, instead opening her mind and expanding her senses, loosening her focus and opening herself. She could sense the entire ship and fifty feet beyond it in every direction, could feel so much. Pollos had anchored them in the lee of an unnamed basalt stack. The next morning they would reach Madu. Kaikatsu focused her gaze on the traces leaving the relu, looking for sign.

Since the gods went mad, this relu had lost whatever connection it held to its home. She had found the mouse two years later in the deep mines below her home, but the dry tunnels below the seas expanded into forever, ever outward, ever downward. They were not without peril. She had found the mouse, so lost, so without connection, and she had taken it to her heart. *How far could it have travelled in two years?* She did not know where it came from. No story of her holt told of a relu-mouse.

Kaikatsu breathed out. There was no connection, no thread or limn of light or shiver of vibration or hint of sound linking the relu to any but her, to any place but her heart. *Not here.* As she let her focus drift once more away from the relu-mouse, she stumbled over the knot of Lady Marion's relu-bone hammer, a perturbation in the pattern around it like a knot. It was close. *How close?* Distance was hard to judge, when you were looking at something inside and outside, through other items, people, seeing past and present and motes of future, seeing linkages, seeing—

The relu darted into her robe and a hand gripped Kaikatsu by the arm and pulled her roughly up from her nest below, sending hawthorn and rowan leaves tumbling to the black ocean below as it dragged her through the fresh boughs lashed to the bowsprit. The skein fell from her senses and she fell to the deck in a tumble. Looming over her was the Lady Marion, black leather cuirass embossed with silver scrollwork over black shirt, black trous, black boots, and a thick black cloak with a collar of fur. Her mane of hair was pushed back from her brow, and she sneered down at Kaikatsu. *I know that expression, at least.*

Kaikatsu waited for the lady to speak, trying to marshal her calm. *I will not let her see me panic.* The woman was patient, and it was a ten count before she dropped to her haunches, bringing her face close to the fallen tangle of Kaikatsu's limbs.

'Any Antian who can touch the skein is put down before their seventh summer, where I come from,' she said, and she rubbed a finger at her eyebrow and scrunched her lips. 'You are an oddity, in that regard.'

'We are not where you are from,' Kaikatsu said, and below her robes felt the relu crawl deeper into her wool undershirt, pressing itself against the fur of her belly. 'Any Cil foolish enough to cause bother is put to use, where I come from. We always need fertiliser.'

Kaikatsu slowly unfolded her limbs and sat on the deck. 'What do you want?'

'Perhaps I'm just bored,' the lady said, and Kaikatsu blinked at her and waited a beat and then licked her lips and smoothed her whiskers with one paw.

'You think I am a little Antian slave on Cil-Marie for you to play with in your boredom,' Kaikatsu said, intonation flat. 'Why don't you go and play with your toy knight? Better yet, take a swim. The garu are quite big here, but they won't bother you.'

'They won't bother me?'

The woman drew herself back up to her full height, and Kaikatsu followed, folding her hands below the robes. She could not see Blade Mournchild anywhere nearby. Someone would be at the aftcastle keeping watch, but that was eighty feet away. Her grandmother's voice rang in her ear, the small grandmother with the broken tooth and the scars of a life well lived. *The only good Cil is a dead Cil.* How many of her people, dead at the hands of the Cil?

'The garu won't bother you, Cil,' she said, and she worked on her own sneer. 'Garu have *taste.*'

Kaikatsu walked off, pointedly not looking back, and tried to suppress a shiver as she imagined the hammer of relu bone breaking her. A single blow and then a moment's work and she would be lost to the black ocean.

The blow did not fall, but she stopped. *There.* High in the northern sky, an orb of light the size of her thumb was cutting across the sky. The Cil orb. The light that watched over the Shield Isles surrounding Cil-Marie proper in the west, the light that nobody understood. She had heard it said it spat fire, stole children. That it was a great flying beast festooned in a hundred magical lanterns. That it was a great relu, nearly a Judge, tamed by one of the fabled Sun-Masters of Cil Marie. That it was a ship that sailed the sky.

Kaikatsu watched as the orb sped off into the distance, losing sight of it in a bank of cloud. The rain had dissipated but the clouds were thick. *There is great magic in this world.* She had seen wonders since she left the holt.

'A watchful eye,' Marion said behind her.

'Orbs of light, dead of night,' Kaikatsu intoned, 'hide your eye, take your flight. We know of this thing. Old Ferron magic, from before the Russilan fell to their Thirst. You people are children wielding stolen blades, so proud of how strong you are.'

'A blade is a blade because it cuts,' Marion said, and she snorted in derision. 'What your people know is irrelevant. Your civilisation is irrelevant. You are irrelevant. Nothing but the mewling of dogs and vermin.'

The Cil woman stalked away to her quarters and Kaikatsu went to lower herself to the bowsprit nest she had fashioned, but her eyes would not stop tracing across the dark outlines of cloud. With a sigh she gathered herself over the railing once more and made her way to the lower deck where the crew slept. She found herself a corner and a blanket and curled up small in the darkness, the sound of snores and lapping waves. *I will not be meek*. But she was afraid, and sleep took a long time to claim her.

Madu

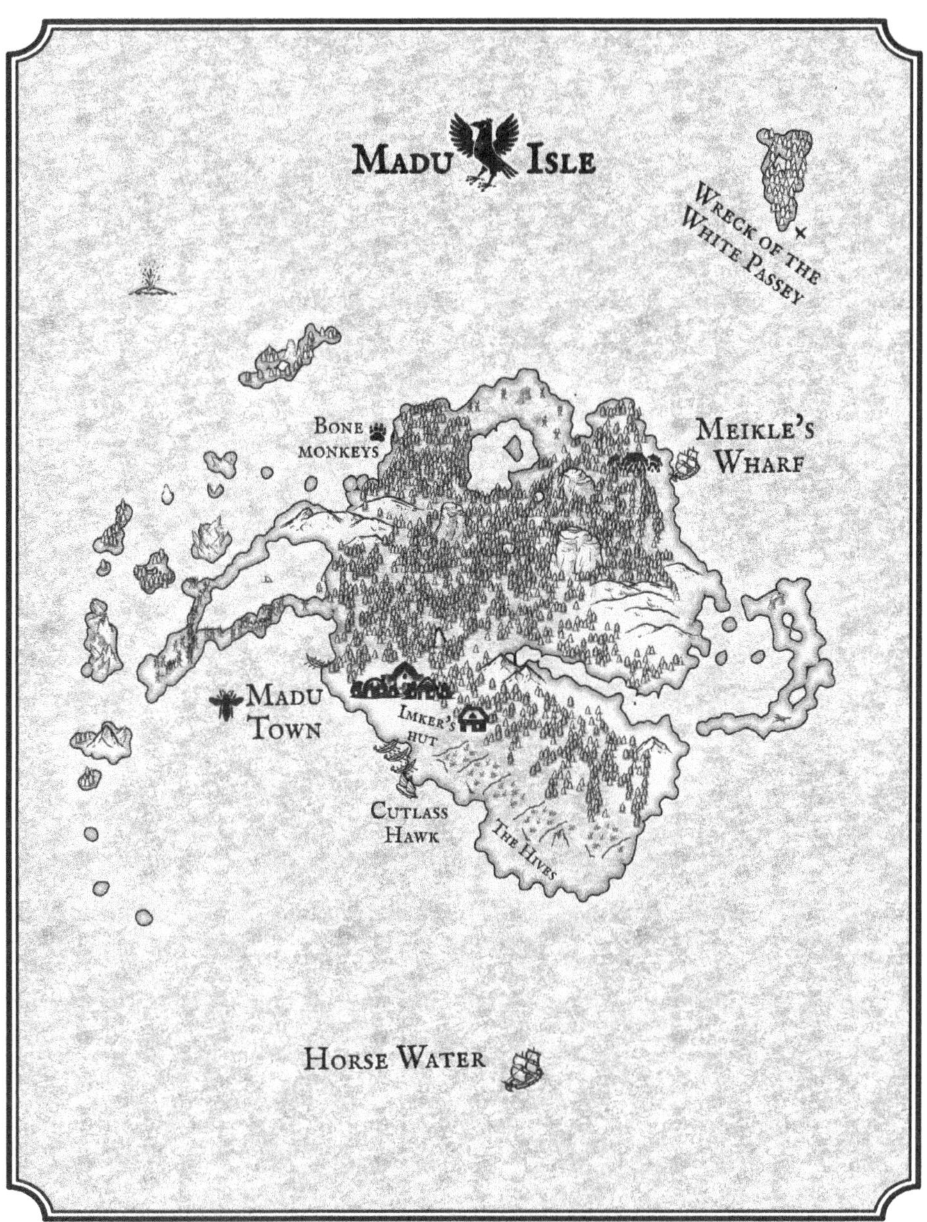

Madu, year 1134 Isken – **From the charts of the** ***Cutlass Hawk***, Captain Killian Heroneye

12

THE ISLE OF THE HONEY-DRINKERS

'Of the Deep Crowns beyond Burner's Run, little is known. That circle of water contains may dozens if not hundreds of isles, and none have mapped it with any accuracy in two centuries. Prior to the madness of the Judges, the route was impassable due only to distinctly adverse currents and wind, with only the Deep Crown ravagers seeming to know the secret to passing. Since 1124 when the gods broke their covenants, the serpent Zalan has added to the danger. No successful crossing by a Strait kingdom ship has been reported.'

– ***The Thousand Crowns***, Alwin Brakspear

'What is your name?' Killian asked, and the emaciated monk did not respond. With the help of Renard he had taken her to where she wanted for her 'reading'. In the pale light of the morning they went to the foredeck and sat beneath the mast.

'I have had many names,' the monk said. 'I was named Sari by my parents. I was named Hassil by my guild. When I left Isken to seek those at the monastery of Caragh's Point I was Sari again, and then with them I was Storm Petrel. We took the names of birds as the old Russilan did. As you do. When I became the abbess, I became simply Petrel. Blue Darrow's men called me witch, and worse things.'

Killian adjusted his cutlass behind him, resting one hand on the hilt.

'I did not realise you were the abbess,' he said. 'To watch them do that to your people... I'm sorry.'

The woman stared up at the sky for a long moment and then met his eye.

'What use is divination, if we could not avoid that fate? That is what you wish to ask me, I think.'

Killian touched the heron skull pendant at his chest.

'I have seen portents, I think,' he said. 'I have dreams of Zalan the shipbreaker. I have dreams of the past. Sometimes I see omens in the crook of a tree, in the pattern of two birds flying. I don't know what is omen, what is portent, what is just a feeling. The Russilan believed you could read your next day's fate by the first star you saw the night before, but I don't know how to do it properly. It never seems to matter.'

'You seek to know your future,' Petrel said, and she put a hand on Killian's knee. 'You ask what all have ever asked. The only truth I can give you is that there is pattern to this world. Fate is... a concatenation of forces. One of those forces is *you*. I could read your death, but you could change it. I could read your life, but you could change it. The skein is not bound by normal time. I do not sense it directly – I've not that gift. But it hints to us, it signals. There is a rhyme and rhythm to the world. When you read a sign and infer a future, your own actions make that future more likely. So the question is, are you reading the signs correctly? If you are not, are you driving towards a future you do not wish?'

The woman, who in the dawn light looked old and wizened and sallow, rubbed her face with her hands.

'These are questions of philosophy. In practice, I have spent decades divining potential fates, sailor – and your fate is no simple one. A heron with a blood-red beak headed towards the sunset. Tell me, then. What stars were you born under?'

So many memories were lost in deep water, or lingering where the light failed so he could see them but only their outline, none of the details. He could always remember the emotion though, the warmth and the love that had never ceased. Killian answered quickly, rotely, surprised at himself at his mother's words returning to him so smoothly after fifteen years.

'I was born at high tide under a new moon,' he said. 'The mountain was the sign my mother saw. My father saw no sign, or did not tell of it if he did. My mother said the day I was born she saw two sparrows caught in a bird-spider's web, and when she saw them, both were alive.'

'Did she save them?' the monk asked, and Killian frowned.

'I… I don't know. I didn't ask; that wasn't the story.'

'What future do you wish for yourself,' the monk asked. She had closed her eyes and from a pouch in her robes produced six tokens of bone, each a different shape – a sickle moon, a star, a circle, a rod, a misshaped knuckle, and a flat oval. All were carved with runes and sigils he did not recognise. *This is ridiculous.* Killian closed his eyes.

'I see my ship with fresh lines and sheets, my crew in a uniform with my crest. I see myself holding a Russilan dagger, dressed in finery, standing at the helm. Silver is with me. We are charting a course into unknown waters. That is what I wish for, Abbess. Not so complicated.'

He looked at her for a response. The abbess did not open her eyes, but cast the bone tokens on the deck and ran her hands over them, muttering indistinguishable words to herself.

'Violence,' she said. 'Past, present, future. I see violence.'

Killian gripped his sword hilt. 'Exploration,' he said. 'Adventure. Love. I am more than a red sword.'

The abbess cast the bones again and they tumbled with a dry clatter. Killian looked at them but could make no sense of the sigils. He felt sick.

'Your past is blood and your present is blood,' she said. 'A heron with a red beak. A heron kills where it must, to feed, to survive.'

With a sudden movement the woman gripped him by his wrists and opened her eyes, staring intently into his.

'I dreamed of you last night,' she said, her voice a whisper. 'I dreamed of you in a great storm at the helm of this ship, with enemies all around you. I dreamed of a heron in flight over calm waters, but beneath the surface something followed, dark and huge. I saw you bleeding under water, I saw you laughing as you cut down your crew, I saw you in fine clothes in a marble hall dancing with beauties, a rapier at your hip. I saw many futures, Heroneye.'

'How does that *help*,' he said, and the monk loosed her grip on his wrists and gently held his hands, and she smiled at him.

'Your fate is not yet locked in stone. There are a thousand endings for you, Heroneye. There are forces driving you towards violence, forces driving you towards death. You must remember that you are a force. When you see a portent you will feel it in your gut. When you *interpret* a portent, think first on the fate you seek, and let it inform you so. I saw betrayal. Your path will not be easy.'

Killian stared at the bone tokens on the deck of the ship, and let his shoulders fall. *Ridiculous, vague. Useless.*

'Thank you, Abbess Petrel,' he said, and he rose to his feet. 'Renard will help you, as much as you need help. I thank you.'

Killian strode away certain of nothing. *Even the fortune-teller would give me nothing.* He had seen palm readers in Koch Dara, card readers, skull readers. He had listened to Starfinder Rurich tell them all nightly about whatever constellation he had peeked in Requin-Port, always describing its attributes in a way that brought hope to the hungry Russilan there.

Killian stood on the deck of his ship. *My ship.*

'What did you think she'd give you, lad?' Pollos asked. Killian hadn't noticed the big man approaching. He shrugged.

'I thought it would be the same as ever,' Killian said, 'and I was right. Vague. I'm sure it would have landed as more ominous if she did not look nearly dead, if she had charts and a bit more showmanship. Do they tell the future where you're from, Pollos? Do they read the stars?'

Pollos leaned next to Killian at the rail and together they stared out at the sea as morning light danced across the water, and he scratched at the pitchfyre scar on his face.

'Undal are utilitarian,' he said eventually. 'Prophecy and fortune-telling is a bit too vague for them. I'm sure some do; I'm sure there is some tradition of it. Undal was made up of slaves from a dozen lands, you know, lad. Old Ferron empire filled it with Cil, with Isken, with old Undal, with folks from Tessendorm. The Orubor elves can read signs and futures, I heard.' Pollos smiled and clasped Killian on the shoulder. 'But then they also eat human flesh and have blue skin, they say. I think you make your own fate.'

'The problem with that,' Killian said, thinking of his mother dead, his sister lost, 'is that makes it my fault.'

Madu was a splodge of an isle almost twenty miles directly east of Burner's Run, a fat low place bounded by basalt cliffs on three sides. The leeward side, inward towards Burner's Run, was a series of low beaches and caves that cut back into the heart of the island. A single mountain dominated the centre of the isle and thick forests of cedar spilled down its sides, and the port was an assortment of low wooden pontoons jutting from a beach of pebbles. The anchorage was shallow, and Killian wanted a quick departure – Madu was a water stop, a town with two things that could generously be called streets, and a single 'inn'. In truth they needed no water, and Marion caught him as he pointed his favoured anchorage out to Pollos. The sky had sat grey all morning, the wind a furtive and ever-changing thing.

'This is a waste of time,' Marion said, and he kept his voice pleasant.

'Information, Lady,' he said. 'I've not sailed the Run in years, and your last attempt ended rather badly. I want to know any word on the Bloody Crows, any word on other ships in the area, and any news of the Run. We will get some stores in as well. From here it is a straight shot to your snakey friend.'

'You speak lightly of your own god, boy,' she spat, and Killian kept his gaze on Renard and the Breygars who were lowering the dog-boat. Silver and Kaikatsu stood awkwardly apart nearby, watching. All of them wanted to go into Madu.

'God of the Russilan,' he intoned, 'great serpent of the depths. Zalan, stormchild. Zalan the shipbreaker. Zalan, tideking. Zalan, what is it? Seagrave? I speak lightly, yes. It is a Judge, Lady Marion. I thought the Cil did not believe in gods. As for calling me "boy", you don't seem to have so many more summers than I. *I* am trying to be civil.'

'We understand power,' she muttered, and straightened her leather cuirass. 'We understand we don't want any to have it over us. It is past time you told us how you plan to cross the Run. Far past time.'

'Trade secret,' he said, and the first dog-boat splashed into the water. Timmult was fast over the side on a rope to make it ready, the Breygars steadying a line a piece at each end to keep it bobbing in the tide. Madu sat before them and the dance of chimney smoke filled the air, the distant ring of what must be a blacksmith's hammer. The

Lady Marion whistled and Mournchild appeared from the aftcastle and loomed next to her.

'It is not a request,' Lady Marion said. 'It is an order. I paid the Evertree Sisters. You work for me. You do as I say.'

Killian watched as a small canoe set out from the pontoon dock. It would reach them in a minute or two – it was not far to the low anchorage he had chosen, and the canoe was long and paddled by a Tullioch and two humans, all of whom handled their craft with diligence. Killian turned back to Marion and then glanced around. Both Breygars, Renard, and Pollos were on hand. Abbess Petrel was staring at the water, waiting to be shipped across to Madu.

'You paid for *passage*,' he said. 'You paid to get across Burner's Run, to find and meet one Captain Arlock of the Bloody Crows. To retrieve one Jean du Cilcan you say is your man. Have I asked how you plan to negotiate release of a prisoner from notoriously bloody pirates? How you plan to convince them not to just send us to the depths? No. I have not. That is your job. You do your job; I shall do mine. Now if you will excuse me, I need to go ask a man about a bee. You can come and join or stay and stew.'

He swung over the side on the line Timmult had used without waiting for her response and clambered down to the dog-boat, and the dour sailor graced him with a smile.

'Cil,' Timmult said resignedly. 'Can't we feed them to the garu? Worse than the bloody Tullioch.'

Timmult massaged the stumps of his missing fingers, even his own mention of the Tullioch driving him into some dark memory. Killian straightened his hat and reached up to help Silver descend down into the dog-boat, and then the frail abbess behind her, but he did not answer. *A garu won't get through plate armour,* he thought, *but it might make a good effort as he sinks.*

Kaikatsu and Pollos remained behind, and the two dog-boats were full. Inevitably it turned into a race between Renard and Big Breygar on the second boat, laden with Mournchild's armour and his mistress's temper, and Timmult and Small Breygar in Killian's boat. They were less than halfway to the pontoon when the canoe from Madu reached them, and all slowed.

'Hail, Madu!' Killian called. '*Cutlass Hawk* out of Samurkan. Traders. Looking for rumour, meat, and mead! How fare you?'

The three in the canoe stared at him and then each other, and the woman at the front of the canoe dipped her head in acknowledgement.

'Hail, *Cutlass Hawk*. Madu welcomes trade. Friendship will be met with friendship, violence will be met with violence. Kill no bee – ignore them and they will ignore you.'

Her voice was nearly lost to the pulling wind, even as close as they were, and water was pulling the canoe and the dog-boats apart. Killian bowed his head and doffed his hat, and waved the rowers on.

'Don't drink the Father honey,' he said to Silver quietly, and she cocked her head and gazed at him, those pale eyes flashing.

'What is Father honey?' she asked, and he shook his head.

'I'll tell you when we leave.'

They made shore easily enough and then the crew dispersed to find meat and mead. The abbess swayed, and Renard held her upright. The village was only a handful of streets, every building made of the cypress trunks, every roof an intricate braid of branches and some sort of weave of grass. They were all single storey, and the people were as varied as the Crowns themselves. He saw the amber skin and silver eyes of Cil descent, skin the colour of burnt umber, skin as moon-pale as his own, two women with the dark complexion more common in Carob and Siobh. There were a dozen children running a game through the town, and everywhere bees and flowers. Fat bees with stripes of gold and black lazily bouncing through the air, filling the town with a warm purring buzz. Every patch of ground that was not path was long grass and wildflower.

'Where are the hives?' Lady Marion asked, and Killian ignored her. A Tullioch with green scales dressed in a pleated skirt of yellow cotton dipped her head and scratched at the frill on the back of the skull.

'You want rumour,' she said, her voice sibilant. 'The Imker will see you when you are ready.'

'This is farewell then, Captain,' the abbess said, and Killian went to her and pressed a small pouch of coin into her hand. 'You have saved me, and with me perhaps all my people learned is not lost. I will return to Isken, to the Archivists' Guild, and tell them what I know.'

Killian dipped his head.

'Renard will take you to the inn,' he said. 'Next ship that is heading to Samurkan, get passage aboard. It should be plain sailing from here. Good seas to you.'

'Good seas to you,' she repeated, and she searched his eyes. 'Do not let fate bind you, Heroneye. Watch the portents.'

She leaned closer and embraced him and whispered into his ear. 'And watch your back, lad.'

Renard led the old woman away, and the Tullioch coughed politely.

'The Imker?' she asked, and Killian bowed and doffed his hat to her. She led them on to the far side of the village. Silver was quiet, eyes wide, a faint smile pulling at her lips. Marion was already sneering, and behind her Mournchild was trailing a gauntleted hand through long grass and staring at the little bees through red eyes.

'Salaman,' he said, and Killian shook his head and leaned in to Silver.

'That man,' he said, 'is mad as a box of frogs.'

'The Imker is harvesting, but he will be with you soon,' the Tullioch said, and Killian nodded his thanks and they waited amongst the long grass and wild flowers. The Tullioch departed, leaving them to their own devices.

'What is this place?' Silver asked, and Killian grinned at her. He had visited Madu before twice, once as a child, and once with a smuggler out of Koch Dara.

'Best honey in the Crowns,' he said. 'They have been here more than a hundred years. Forests are full of bone-monkeys, jaiboar, and the like. But some smart fish figured out the bone-monkeys always avoided the beekeeper's house. And so, they leaned in – now the hives are so extensive you won't catch a bone-monkey for a mile, and the bees make honey and the honey makes mead. Solid anchorage, as well. I think they do okay here. Some... interesting religious practices. But who am I to judge?'

Mournchild glowered at the nearest bee. 'Salaman created the animals,' he said, 'and the insects.'

'Did he?' Silver said. 'How terribly clever of him. Have you seen a bone-monkey, Lady Marion?'

The Cil woman bared her teeth in what could have passed for a grin. 'Of course,' she said. 'Let us finish with this nonsense.'

Moments later from within the house there was a shout of welcome. The Imker's house was the same as the others, squat and unassuming. Mournchild opened a rough door that only loosely fit its setting and waved them inside, and Killian took the lead. Inside the building was empty save a firepit dug into the centre of the floor and blankets surrounding it. A lone man sat cross-legged before the fire, and the smoke rose through an opening in the ceiling. As he entered Killian brushed a bee from his wrist, another from his shoulder. He did not try to extricate the few he felt in the back of his hair below the rim of his hat, though his eye twitched at the thought of them.

The Imker of Madu was a fat man dressed in long shirt and trous of yellow. His beard was black and oiled, but his skull was shaved close and gleamed in the firelight. As well as the fire in the centre of the room fat beeswax candles dripped at every corner, the base of every wall. Wax puddled and pooled around each of these, and several sat atop the rugs surrounding the fireplace.

'Sit and be welcome to Madu,' he said, and from the rear door of the room a small man emerged carrying a dark bottle and a tray of cups. Killian bowed and sat, pushing his cutlass out so it did not tangle in his legs.

'I am Captain Heroneye of the *Cutlass Hawk*,' he said. 'With me the sage Silver of the Samurkan Archaeology and Anthropology Guild, and the Lady Marion who is a diplomat of Cil-Marie along with her guard.'

The Imker nodded at all of this deeply and with a practised ease poured them each a cup from the dark bottle. What came forth was a viscous sweet mead, golden and scented, and Killian raised the cup to his nose and inhaled deeply. *Insane.*

'We offer tribute to our ancestors, who brought the dancing bee across the ocean to this refuge,' the Imker said, his voice bright with delight. 'We offer the Father honey to our guests, as a sign of honour. Drink, and honour those who came before us. Drink, and we will talk.'

Killian raised the cup to his lips and pretended to drink, careful not to let a drop pass his lips. A little touched the lips themselves and he shivered, and waited for the Imker to turn his attention to tending the flame to wipe his mouth on his sleeve.

'We seek to cross Burner's Run,' Marion said, and the Imker stoppered the Father's mead bottle and looked at her, blinking. 'We seek word on the Bloody Crows, and any news you have of the Run.'

'News,' the man said, tasting the word. 'No news, Lady. What would be news? Ships they come and they say, we seek to cross Burner's Run. They honour those who came before, but still they do not return. The Bloody Crows hunt here, they do, they do. But they do not come ashore, do not trade. We saw a ship of theirs ten days past, black of hull and red of sail. It moved north. Hunting, eh? Pirates, eh? That is the cost of freedom. To be free of the sword is to be free of the shield.'

The Imker crawled forward and gathered their cups and placed them on a tray, hesitating at the full cups of Killian and Silver. Mournchild and Marion's cups were empty. He sat back.

'You did not drink the Father honey,' he said, and Killian smiled.

'Imker, take no hurt,' he said. 'I am Russilan. Our dead go to the sea, not the tree. I have drunk the Father mead before, friend. I mean you no hurt.'

The Imker sat back and stroked his beard and then smiled and laughed, then he tipped back Killian's and Silver's cups in swift succession. Marion watched with a sour expression, her tongue working over her teeth.

'I will honour in your place,' he said. 'Now. The inn has food and mead; we have wax and candle, honey and salve, everything you might want.'

Killian rose to his feet and bowed. 'We wanted only information,' he said. 'No news is, in this case, perhaps good news. My crew are buying some stores. I thank you for your kindness, Imker.'

The fat man waved them out, not bothering to rise, his eyes only for his fire and his hand on the mead next to him. Marion followed close behind Killian, and as they emerged into the daylight, with a fingernail she pulled a thick hair from between her teeth and grimaced.

'That mead had *hair* in it,' she muttered, and then she sighed. 'This was a waste of time. Back to the ship, Heroneye. Jean du Cilcan, Captain Arlock. I will have them both. It is time for you to prove your worth.'

Killian couldn't help it. He tried to chew his lips, but a smile broke through regardless as he watched Marion wipe the hair on the outer wall of the house.

'Of course there is hair in it,' he said. 'It's Father mead!'

Marion stared at him dolefully, and Killian waved for them to follow. He walked around the house where the village backed onto the cedar forest. It was sparse so close to the village, but the trees that were there were easily eighty foot tall, each of them resplendent with rough trunks and limbs and a thickness of blue-green needles that carpeted the forest floor. Around each tree, the ubiquitous bees were concentrated. Killian took off his hat and brushed a bee from the brim and then settled it back on his head.

'The Imker doesn't keep hives,' he said, and carefully he stepped forward until he was only a dozen feet from the nearest tree. The others followed and he pointed up. 'A bee will make a hive most anywhere, if you know how to tell it to. These bees love the cedar trees. A little frame, a little encouragement. When a Madu dies, the Imker makes a frame and sets it just *so*.'

They found the shape he was pointing to – in the crook of some low branches, in a loose box of woven branches a body lay, thronging with bees. Honeycomb adorned it, covered it, subsumed it. What flesh could be seen was thick with wax, but most of the corpse was lost to the honeycomb and the thrum of the bees above, only the shape of limb and torso and head.

'Eventually no body is left, only honeycomb,' he said, and Silver let a huff of air through her nose. 'But the Imker knows which comb was whose, I suppose. The Father honey is only for visitors or special occasions. It comes from the last Imker. Of course there is hair in the mead, Marion. Didn't you know how the Madu make honey? I thought you knew everything about the Crowns.'

He turned in time to see Marion fall to her knees and retch, in time for Mournchild's backhand to catch him and send him reeling.

'*I eat of the dead!*' the man howled, and he drew his longsword. His hood fell back and Killian could see frenzy in his eyes, the white of the irises dyed deep baleful red. His skull and face were painted ashen black with white around the eyes and mouth, white stripes across his skull. 'I eat of the *dead*!'

With a leap he moved for Killian but Killian was faster, scrambling up and over a log. The knight cut deep into the tree with his black blade, and then Marion was on her feet and a single blow of her hammer rent the tree trunk in two. The hammer reverberated in the air, shimmering with unspent force, silver sigils and curls on the hammerhead glowing. The buzz of the bees was intensifying. Mournchild fell still, and Marion levelled her hammer at Killian. He raised his hands.

'I...'

'He's sorry,' Silver said, stepping in front of him, one hand on her rapier hilt. 'He's an idiot, and he's sorry. He owes you for this. It was a stupid joke. Burner's Run is close. We should leave now, and put this place behind us.'

Marion spat and Mournchild growled.

'Mournchild,' Marion said, and she slowly lowered her hammer and hooked it on her belt. 'That Imker is a priest, I would say. A bee-worshipping heretic. You have my permission to sacrifice him to your one true god, the five-faced champion of light and life and whatever else you like. *Baal*. Kill the Imker; make it painful and make it quick. Heroneye, sage – back to the ship.'

'I can't let you—' Killian began but Marion rounded on him.

'*Back to the ship*,' she hissed. 'Choose now, and choose wisely, boy. Back to the ship, or I'll kill your sage, the Imker,

I'll burn this town down, and I'll have Mournchild keep you alive enough to get us past that fucking *worm* in Burner's Run before he feeds your cock to the—'

Killian stepped in front of Silver and reached for his cutlass and then there was an explosion of pain at his temple and he fell to the ground, and the last thing he saw before darkness took him was the tops of the cedars swaying in the wind.

13

ZALAN, SEAGRAVE

'I fear. The firewyrms of the Undal Caverns that destroyed the city of Muhos left those stones long ago – where do they travel? If one were to breach the underhold of any of our cities, all would perish. The rotstorm that once blocked the western Wind Sea has now moved to the deep west, the Iron Desert, but surges of its arcane horror still burn across the world, more with every passing season, spawning monsters. Put simply, the threats we know of are great – what others lurk out there, catastrophes of magic once chained and now perhaps moving every moment in our direction?'

– ***Letter to the Council of Isles on the Madness of the Spirits***, Anneli Thirdblood of Holt Suolaa

Killian awoke to rough sea and Silver at his bedside, kneeling on a folded blanket on the floor. She was dabbing at his head.

'Imker,' he said, and she held his hand and pressed her head to his. His cabin was dark, all was dark, and his head throbbed.

'Mournchild killed him,' Silver said. 'Only him. All the crew are aboard. We sailed the day through. It is almost dawn. I thought your head was cracked like an egg, but Renard says it is too thick for that. Your Antian took a look as well. She seemed positive.'

Killian lay in the dark and remembered the smiling face of the Madu chief.

'He honoured us,' he said, and Silver shook her head and reached up, her hand across his chest. She took hold of the heron skull pendant and idly ran her fingers along it.

'It is done, Heron,' she said. 'It is done. We will not return to Madu, not in this life.'

'I could have warned them not to drink it,' he said. 'I could have...'

In the darkness they were both silent until Silver patted him gently and pressed a cup of water into his hand.

'How did Mournchild... how, how did he hit me?' he asked, and even as he said it he realised what must be true. *Mournchild was too far. Marion was unarmed.* Silver had struck him down, to save him from Mournchild's wrath.

'The Imker will make good honey,' she said, voice grim, and she lit a candle with a striker and he saw her. She had tied her curls back into a tight knot at the back of her head, and her usual loose shirt was gone, replaced with a thin jacket of embroidered blue over a vest. The embroidery was hard to make out, but he smiled as he realised the pattern.

'Are those constellations on your jacket, Silver? I see the warrior.'

'Everyone sees the warrior,' she said, and she brought him a plate from the chart table of bread and cheese. He looked at it and felt a roil of acid in his gut, which seemed to join with the pain cascading from his temple. He closed his eye.

'Not in this life, you said. You believe in reincarnation? What are your gods, Silver? That is a good question. Humour me whilst I try and drink this water without throwing up.'

Silver set the candle down and helped him with the cup, and he didn't need it, not truly. He could have picked up the cup and held it to his lips. But she did it so gently, with such care in her eyes.

'I'm from Kelamor,' she said eventually. 'Baal is a popular one. Most worship their ancestors and the nameless creator beyond, though. A bit uninspiring – nameless fire below, nameless creator above. Ancestors watching you take every shit, and if you are a good egg you get to watch your descendants take their own shits.'

'Only someone from Kelamor would step between a knight in plate with a longsword and their victim with nothing but a piss-thin rapier,' he said, and she flicked him on the nose and did not look remorseful when his flinch brought another clear wave of pain down from his temples.

'Only a Russilan would convince a mad Uradech knight to drink honey from a dead heretic priest's arse,' she said, without humour, and he closed his eyes. *A fair point.* He lay back and closed his eyes.

'There was a temple by the water,' she said, one hand rising to stroke his hair. 'The priest talked of tides coming in and out, of lives being like that. You are a wave, but in the end all waves cease and fall back into the ocean. I don't know what I believe, Heron. I know there is magic in this world beyond nature. The relu, the Judges. The skein. They are different from nature, of it but also *apart.* Humans and Antian and Tullioch have been here thousands of years before any history we've written. I've felt the old stones…'

She kept talking, but he fell into a sleep. Not the black abyss of unconsciousness, but the easy calm of someone who is, after long peril, safe.

Killian stepped onto deck at dawn with his tricorn hat firmly pulled down over the black bruise at his temple. He fiddled with the clasp pinned to it; the crow perched on the cutlass, Killian the Cutlass and Arlock the Crow – the pirate captain and the mage. He pictured the little bronze copies he had given the children. *Galli and Nils are better off in Samurkan. Will Arlock recognise the pin?* In truth he had thought her dead, or convinced himself as much. *Did I ever really believe that?* The Cil would have wanted revenge for the death of the governor. Plague went through Requin-Port two years after he left. The madness of the gods. Starvation, murder, assault. Pirate raids. Requin-Port was not a safe place. The weight of it had sat on him for fifteen years. *You abandoned your sister, after promising her. You abandoned your sister, after promising your mother on the day of her death. You left it all, and why?*

He knew why. The thirst for red. For revenge, in blood. It had consumed him. *And now you have Cil on your ship.* The Cil had taken so much from him. *They did not take her. You lost her.*

'A big day,' Pollos said, sidling up to him, and Killian managed a smile. 'Some words maybe? Run will be on us in the hour, only a few more wee isles to pass.'

Killian nodded, and within a few moments the crew had assembled on the deck. Pollos took the wheel and Killian climbed the stairs to the aftcastle next to him and looked down at his crew. The Breygar twins, one judging as ever, the other uncaring. Timmult and Renard who just wanted the sea on the horizon and a fair bit of wage. Kaikatsu peering up at him with her wide eyes, watching, assessing. Mournchild with his hood raised, a shadow in shadow. Marion in her armour and a heavy black cloak, high boots, arms crossed. He thought she looked afraid, her more than any of them. *But then, Zalan has already almost drowned her once.* Finally Silver, leaning louchely against the mast with that foolish rapier at her hip, the silver thread marking the constellations in her jacket catching the dawn light. She smiled at him. *Why am I doing this?* He gripped the heron skull pendant at his neck and squinted at the horizon. He had to find Arlock. *I have to tell her I'm sorry.*

He could see one more isle in the distance, but beyond it was open water. The wind was behind them now, utterly behind, and they were flying fast over water. Running free like this was fast, but unstable, and he cast an eye across wave and water for any sign of a cross-current or rogue wave that would send them reeling, but saw nothing.

'Today we cross Burner's Run,' he said, and there was no cheer. Only expectant silence. High above them a cormorant flew perpendicular to their course, black and oil-slick. He swallowed. 'I've made this passage twice before. I have right to pass, and you with me. When Zalan comes, offer no resistance. When I say, be ready to drop sail fast as you ever have. He'll storm it good to be sure we are serious. Wind won't stick, current won't stick. Kaikatsu – I'll need you at the bow reading current as best you can. The rest of you on the lines. Pollos on the wheel. Mournchild, you stay behind Pollos in case he needs a heavy arm. Lady Marion, Silver, I recommend you wait in the cabin – but if you are on deck, get a line tied on you, and stay the hell out of the way.'

He waited, but there were no questions. Silver smiled at him, and Mournchild immediately moved up to the aftcastle. The knight stopped Killian with a heavy fist placed over Killian's heart, and he leaned close.

'You made me eat of the dead, Heroneye,' he whispered, and Killian peered into his hood but could make out nothing but shadow and grimace. 'There are few greater sins against Baal. I will atone, but you will need to atone before this is through.'

Killian pushed past the knight and made his way to the bow.

'Kaikatsu!' he called. 'I need to speak to you.'

The little Antian scurried up from her nest in the bowsprit and looked up at him, waiting.

'When we reach Zalan,' he said quietly, 'there will be a moment where he assesses us. You will know when. When it happens, you must reach into the skein and activate the pendant at my chest. Do you understand?'

'I do not,' she replied immediately. 'Of course I do not. Let me see.'

The Antian's eyes twitched and her shoulders slumped as she fell into the skein, and Killian felt a tingle in the base of the skull as if someone was watching him.

'The pendant is a key,' he said. 'It holds the key. It has no power, but it is… folded. Locked. It just needs a tweak. That is what I was told. A knot to be unravelled at the right moment. Can you do this?'

Kaikatsu's shoulders raised and she shook her head, looking him in the eye.

'I think so, Captain,' she said. 'I think it would be better if you did it though.'

Killian stared down at her and gripped his cutlass hilt and looked off at the horizon. No more land in sight. White caps, little peaks where a hundred waves were dancing over the sea. The sky was still a vibrant blue but the sea below was iron, a sword blade in the rain at midnight.

'*Next* time I'll do it!' he spat, and then he turned and paced back to the aftcastle. Marion and Silver were both there, both tied with lines to the ship's rail off to one side. *Out of the way.* Marion was pale and breathing heavily, her eyes on the horizon.

In clear sky above, not a cloud in sight, a peal of thunder rolled, and the storm began. The waves grew, and the steady wind from the east died and jumped, instead a gale from the north, then a breeze from the south in the matter of a minute. The waves grew more, more, whitecaps now foaming rollers, and the *Hawk* banked up and down and up and down. From a point a mile ahead of them black cloud pirouetted out and in five minutes the sky was a tempest of dark roiling cloud, lightning dancing within and around the storm-filled sky. The cloud lowered until it was almost touching the mast, and through it all Killian was at the rail yelling orders. The lines had to shift fast, fast to keep the sails tight and facing the right direction.

'Thirds on the middle!' he called, and the Breygars leapt to lower the mainsail to a third of its full extent – some of the gusts were beyond gales now, and if he held it full, the mast would snap like a twig. Up and down, and all direction lost to him. Pollos was keeping them straight into the nearest wave set, but no sooner had they a moment of calm when another set of even larger waves came in at an angle, and he threw himself down the aftcastle stairs to help with the lines. Timmult yelled something at him but it was lost in the storm. Rain was pouring, thick sheets of ice-cold water soaking him to his skin. His hat was gone.

With a crack a line to the aft sail broke loose, the belaying pin snapping free of the rail and rocketing across the ship, a club of sea-hardened wood whipping through the air.

'Breygar down!' he screamed, and the thin man threw himself flat in time to avoid the impact that would have taken his head. The belaying pin instead cracked a deck plank, and then was about to whip out again when Timmult and Renard leapt on the line. Kaikatsu was yelling back to Pollos, yelling the currents, but Killian could barely hear her from the midship. He sprinted up the deck as they fell down the back of another wave and found her lashed to the rail near her precious bowsprit.

'Get to the aftcastle!' he yelled. 'You're useless here, get to Pollos!'

He could hear his own voice. Blinking in a sudden ray of sunlight, the sheets of rain had paused and, above the *Hawk*, the clouds were parting, a circle of blue and gold where only black had been. Kaikatsu's hand took his and she pointed into the water, the punishing waves still raising them up and sending them sprawling back down. *There.*

A ripple of flesh, of stone, of metal. Something below the water. A memory from his childhood – calm water, his mother Cara and his sister Arlock and Starfinder Rurich at their side when they left the Deep Crowns, when they left starvation and sickness to seek a better life. That had been a smaller ship, but Starfinder Rurich had held forth his pendant and there had been something in the water below the ship. He had been sure of it, but in his dreams could never put a shape to Zalan, god of the Russilan. That had been before the gods were unchained, before the Judges of the world went mad.

In the storm around the *Cutlass Hawk* Killian saw his god.

Zalan the shipbreaker, a snake with a body wide as a carriage, rose from the water. Scales of glittering black metal that sparked in the sunlight, a flared head with so many eyes, each a different jewel, no symmetry to be understood. The serpent rose from the water unperturbed by wave or wind, and a tongue of living red crystal flicked between teeth of blue ice, each as long as a man.

Killian stared at Zalan, and gripped the pendant in his fist and ripped it free of his neck, holding it up.

'I am Killian Heroneye of the Russilan. I was born on Deep Crow; I drank from the Well of No End. I am Russilan. My mother was Cara Heroneye. My father was a storm. I am Russilan. Hear me, Zalan, the shipbreaker. Zalan, seagrave. Guardian of the Deep Crowns. Lord of Burner's Run.'

He fell into the skein – it was not a choice. Instead of an immediacy of strange sensation and connection, in the presence of Zalan the skein was an immensity, a vast ocean of power and possibility and future and past. Zalan was a whirlpool, a tornado, sea spout, a burning inferno. He saw the pyre at Blue Darrow's keep but with crystalline eyes; he saw a wave taller than any ship and it whispered his name. Killian flailed and screamed and felt through it all the pain in his hand as he gripped the heron skull pendant. *Focus.*

His mother's voice, as he looked at the stars. She had one arm around him and one around his sister Arlock. They were in Requin-Port and they were poor, and knew nobody except old Starfinder Rurich and the gaggle of Russilan he had pulled around himself. They were sat on the sea wall with the city lights behind him.

'I want to go home,' he had said, and she had held them close.

'You are *home* when we are *together*,' she had said. 'You, and me, and your sister. That is home, Killian.'

Cara Heroneye smiled at her son and turned his face to hers and from her lips a sinuous crystal tongue flitted, forked at the end, and her eyes turned opalescent and on her cheek and brow more eyes of gem opened, more, *more*. Requin-Port fell away. Zalan Seagrave whispered in his mind, a wordless formation of image and sense. *Home. Longing. Family. Connection. Family.* Killian did not know what he was doing but he forced his eyes open and he let the torrent of sensation cover him, engulf him, and then he pushed back to the pendant in his hand and felt it respond to him. It was asleep, and then it was awake.

The skein fell from him, or he from it, and he slammed to the deck. The sea rolled, but Zalan Seagrave sank back into the water, and above them the sky began to clear as clouds of black burst into showers of ice-cold rain and then were lost, part of the ocean once more.

Silver was at his side. He could hear Pollos shouting at the crew, lines, sheets, sail, bearing. Could hear Marion cursing in Cil. Silver was at his side and she pressed her face close to his and when his eyes were open hers were there, staring, hungry.

'What did you see, Heron?' she said, and her voice was wild. 'What did you see?!'

Killian rolled back on the deck and coughed salt water and laughed, and then closed his eyes. *Family. Connection.*

'Home,' he said, and his vision blurred and his body felt as if a great weight were upon it, pressing into his sternum, his bones, his sinews, and darkness claimed him.

Concarneau

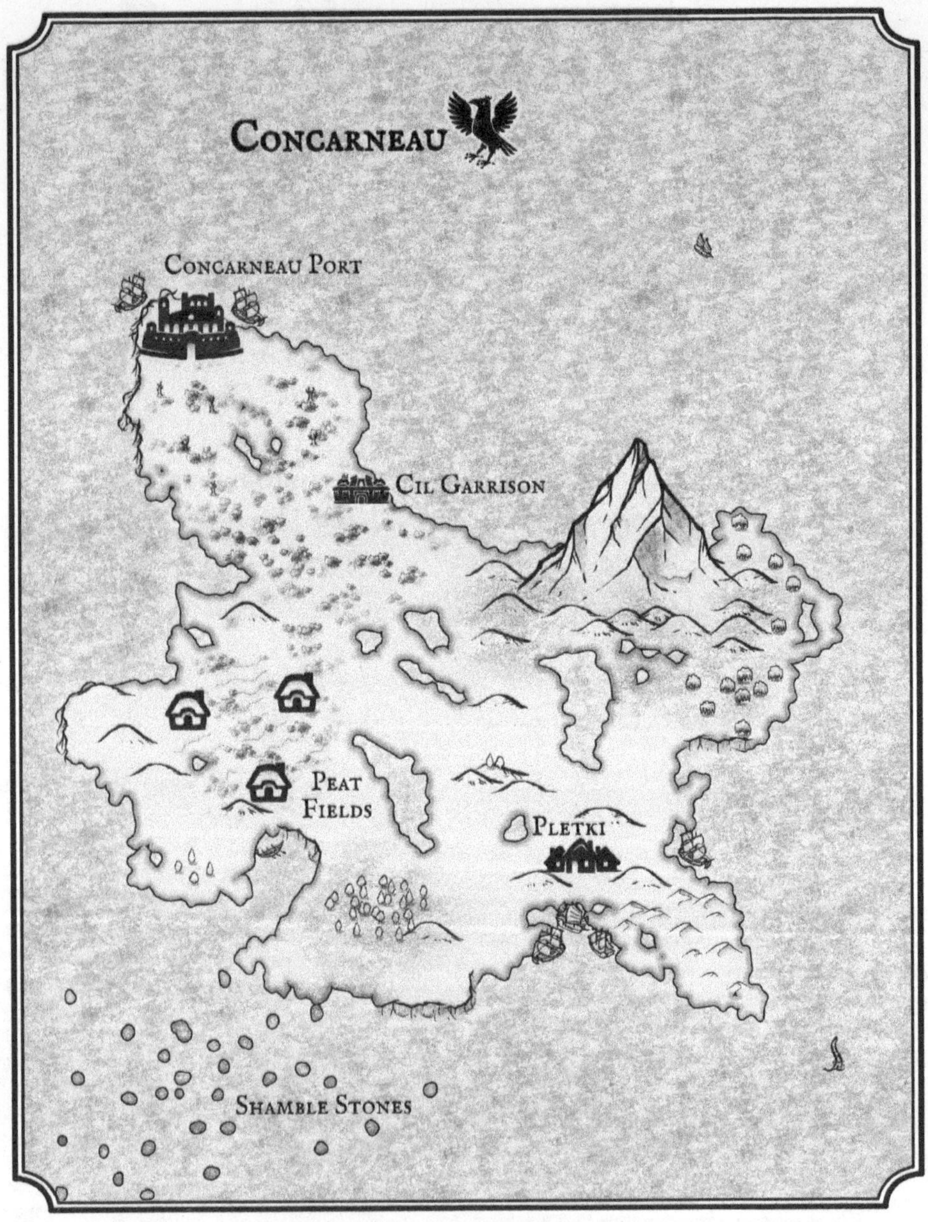

Concarneau, year 1132 Isken – **From the charts of the** *Cutlass Hawk*, Captain Killian Heroneye

INTERLUDE

AN ACORN IN EACH HAND

'A tree sees many things a man does not, and so does a mouse. The mayfly flits but one day. Does he see less than you? The tree sits a thousand winters in one spot. Does he see more? They see different, I say. You see different too. Flit or sit, either way, you see what you see and they see different, as does every person you'll meet. So tell me not of death – every day the world ends, and every aeon it keeps turning.'

– The final words of Darragh Gulltooth, executed 4th Moonbard, Leaf, by beheading, Record of executions 1135 Isken reckoning, Concarneau

In the mingled shade of two oaks Garren set down his pack and his axe and waited. The trees were tall and their trunks were thick with age, and they stood close together. There were few other trees around the foothills of Concarneau – most of the land was given over to wind-blown sheep. There were copses here and there where the land fell to hidden dells, but he was in the foothills of the great mountain, and the wind kept most trees meek and meagre. Not so these. Garren pressed one hand to the trunk of the nearest tree and looked upward to where their crowns mingled and touched, the leaves already beginning to turn to gold as the summer breathed its last. *Who were you planted with, tall one?*

Turning his gaze from the rough bark, Garren took in the vista of the isle of Concarneau. The peat-cutters were still at their work, the bogs now a good dozen feet below the rocky topsoil surrounding them. After generations of slow subsistence harvesting by the locals, the Cil had finally brought in a labour force to strip the peat back. Garren was sure it would be gone soon enough. *And how long until it returns?* He did not know where the peat came from. It was the flesh of the land, and his people had been taking bricks from it since before tales were told, ever since they left Ona and found this empty isle. The Russilan who once lived there had all perished in the Thirst, drowning themselves in the sea. By the time his ancestors' ship had worked its way across the Crowns searching for silence and sunshine, away from the relentless rain of Ona and the shifting presence of the Father Dragon in the clouds above, there was no trace of the Russ left except moss-covered timber and silent stone. *And now the Father Dragon flies ever westward, they say, and the rains come with him.*

Settling his back against one of the tree trunks, Garren could see the mountain of Concarneau and the port in its shadow of the same name. The Cil had named it, after they came. Port and mountain and island, all one name. *Efficient as ever.* His own people had called it Yön Pilvi, the mountain of Night Cloud. The port was a mess of warehouses and long docks, Cil galleons crowding the bay where the anchorage was deepest, and endless dog-boats and small vessels moving on their business. The sky was a brilliant blue, with a stripe of herringbone clouds in vibrant white high above. In the lee of the tree's trunk, he could hardly feel the wind. Casting a glance behind him he saw Concarneau, the mountain, its peak shrouded in a pocket of twisting cloud.

'Mountains make weather,' Garren said, just to hear a voice. His father had taught him that. Up over the mountain all day the clouds danced and tore away, and overnight as the winds died down thick cloud would form so every morning the peak was shrouded again. Every day the winds would tear that cloud away slowly, thick gobbets and streams breaking free to dance over the sea and the islands beyond. The slopes of the mountain were lush, not like the sparse scrubland plains that made up the rest of the land or the black sinking bogs. Mountains make weather, but the Father Dragon kept the rains over Ona ever present. It had sent his people into exile. *What will we do if the rains come?* Rumour said the rotstorm that split Undal and Cil-Marie from the lands west was on the move, a storm a country wide that had sat for centuries now passing miles every day. If the rotstorm could move, if the Father Dragon could fly to Concarneau... Garren shivered and tried to focus on the warmth of the sun on his skin.

He was expecting the others to join soon enough, but he had spent a long span marching the northern tranches of the island, speaking to the farmers and the peat-diggers, the fishermen and the shepherds. It was nice to hear his own voice after a few days of silence. The trail that led to the two oaks was an old one but clear enough, the bracken and bramble of the dark land surrounding the peat bog mainly leaving it be. He saw why soon enough – two fallow deer with thin antlers and white-spotted backs made their way up the trail, past the oaks, onward. *A stream uphill, perhaps,* he mused. Wrapped in the dull brown of his travelling cloak and still and silent, the deer passed Garren by. He waited, and thought on his companions.

Kai from the fishers; Toben from the peat-cutters; Ansa from the town; Margitte from the farms. Each would come with their answers, and their ideas, and their plan. The last moon had seen a dozen more hanged in the port, for varying offences. The Cil had their boot to the neck of the locals, and they were pressing firm. When Garren was a young man he had fought. When the old Premier Clement took too many liberties, Garren had made speeches, had organised. He had fought for freedom. In the shade of the two oaks he bowed his head and remembered the names of those he had lost that bloody summer. That summer, he had learned the difference between a battle and a war. The premier's house had burned and they hanged him from his own gibbet. But with the turn of the moon came ships and soldiers and reprisals. A heavy boot indeed.

And now the young ones come to me to ask, do we fight? Garren shook his head and closed his eyes. Cil-Marie had slowed their push outward decades back, but the last few years suddenly there were warships in Concarneau port, and rumours of 'securing' the Horse Water, of pacifying the Southern Reaches. Garren tried to hold a map of the Thousand Crowns in his mind, as if he flew high above…

He was woken by the snuff of a horse. Blinking in the sunlight, he stared up at the beast looming over him. It was a great dun horse, stamping at the earth and huffing through a bridle. As he sat up in his cloak it backed away, and he could see the rider.

'Hail,' said the man, and Garren pulled himself to his feet. The man had spoken the trade tongue of Isken, and he spoke it well enough. He nodded at the rider and waited. The man wore a stained travelling cloak of grey but Garren could see black leather beneath it. His boots were expensive – you could tell a lot about someone from their boots. These were utilitarian but also of excellent quality, supple leather with no ostentation. Those boots were a year's wage, for a peat-cutter – if they were lucky.

'My Lord,' he said at last, and stood and bowed his head. As he bowed he caught sight of his axe and pack where he had left them, leaning against the trunk of the second tree a dozen feet away.

'You are Garren,' the man said, his expression hidden beneath his hood. Garren raised his head and sighed. *It is over, then.* There was no good reason for a Cil like this to know his name. Turning his gaze to the trees he licked his lips and tried to remember the faces of the friends he had lost when they stormed Premier Clement's house, when they killed the overseers. He remembered nothing but the taste of smoke. He could remember their names, but not their eyes. He could not even remember the premier's final words.

'All fades in time,' he said eventually, and the rider turned his horse about and jumped down from its back. As he dismounted Garren took his measure. The leather beneath the cloak was armour, with silver scrollwork. As the rider pushed back his hood Garren could see his hair was short all around save for the crown, and all of it was tied neatly upward in a topknot. His skin was pale and his cheeks scarred and pitted, and his eyes were lambent flames. The rider led his horse to the nearest oak and rested its reins over a low branch. He did not bother to tie it. *We both know he will not be here long.* The horse snuffed again and pawed at the dirt, and Garren peered.

'Might be a stone in that hoof,' he said, and the man pushed his cloak back and drew a hammer from his belt. It was a simple thing, black metal with a little silver etching on the hammer head. Garren had seen those hammers, had seen what they could do to a man. He looked once more to his axe, and then at the rider – he was a head shorter than Garren, and Garren had a great deal of reach and weight on his opponent. *But I've a few decades on him as well.*

'You *are* Garren,' the rider said, and it was not a question. Garren nodded, and the rider turned to look down at the peat-cutters. 'We caught your man Kai. Banned weapons and seditious material. He gave us your name, you and the other: Toben. That one is fled by boat already. He will not come back. So that leaves only you.'

'He is a young man,' Garren said. *He did not mention Ansa, or Margitte. Tides bless you, Kai!*

'He was a young man,' the rider corrected him tersely. 'I've come to take you to Concarneau for questioning. Will you come, Garren?'

Garren turned to the mountain and smiled. *Ansa and Margitte,* he thought, *I am so sorry.* He knew he could not be sure of what he would say. The Cil had no compunction about questioning a man hard. They would press him, and he would have to give them something, as Kai had.

'Did he die well?' Garren asked, and the rider sniffed.

'You might say so. He went to his death with shouts of rebellion and freedom, but there were none to hear it but his executioners. Tell me. Do you know why these two trees are so close together?'

Garren did not reply. He took a sip from his water skin and then dropped it to the ground, and stared up at Yön Pilvi, the mountain of the Night Cloud. Its peak was almost bare, the last of the clouds almost stripped away.

'The locals used to bury a man of importance with an acorn in each hand,' the rider said. 'Wherever you find two trees in these isles, it means someone was revered.'

'No,' Garren said, and he unpinned his cloak and let it fall to the ground. He had no armour, no weapon. He had not fought in so many years, not with weapons.

'No?'

He shook his head. 'You are wrong. An acorn in each hand is not reverence for some great leader. An acorn in each hand is love. An acorn in each hand is turning a dead thing into life, turning a sadness into a joy that will stand many years. Love, not reverence. It is a tradition we brought from Ona, though the trees were different there.'

The rider flexed his wrist and his eye twitched. 'From Ona, you say.' He sneered. 'Your own words. Ever we are the *invader*, ever we are the enemy. But *your* people came and did just as mine have done. Ever this is the way.'

Garren shrugged and turned to the mountain, utterly away from the rider.

'Believe what you will,' he said. 'Mountains make their own weather. You may clear the cloud away, but more will always come. I will not come with you, Cil, and I'll answer none of your questions.'

He did not ask the rider to bury him with an acorn in each hand. He knew the man would kill him with a single blow and then ride his great horse back to the port. He would believe his work was done. *Ansa and Margitte,* he thought. *I am sorry this has fallen to you.* The hubris of the dominant, to believe themselves so clever, to believe their work complete. Garren knew the work was never done. *More cloud will always come.* High above, the last wisp clinging to the peak of Yön Pilvi was dragged by the wind, and passed out over open water, and below it sped a shadow over the water. He squinted. A heron. *How strange…* Garren closed his eyes and pictured the faces of those he had loved.

He did not hear the strike fall.

ACT 3

THE SEA REMEMBERS

Raorum Raorum found the whale
Raorum Raorum stole the light
Raorum Raorum took his fate
Raorum Raorum banished night

'The tale of Raorum the sun-bringer'
– Tullioch memory song

14

MASKS

'The written language of the Russilan appears to follow a similar structure to that spoken in Siobh, with a similar cuneiform notation. Whilst the language as spoken is dead, syllabic re-creations of some stone tablets have been possible and there appears to have been a robust trading culture. As ever, the great twists of history are rarely written down, but the minutiae of manifests are meticulously logged. Given Russilan maps hinting at the Deep Crowns as the centre of their culture, we should expect greater detail to emerge if ever these lands were able to be explored.'

– ***Notes on the Russilan***, Gallo Mancinus

'Raorum Raorum found us in darkness, in the cold water, and took us.'

The voice was not one he knew. Killian *ached*. He blinked and he was on the deck of the *Cutlass Hawk*, propped on a folded pile of sailcloth in the shade of the aftcastle. In the centre of a deck a Tullioch stood, naked save for an elaborate headdress of feather and beak and bone, a perfect simulacrum of a black-backed gull. From one wrist a stone-bladed dagger hung from a short tether. The Tullioch had blue scales, though the frond at its head was hidden beneath the bizarre headdress.

'What the piss...' he muttered, and propped himself up on his elbows. The sky was a haze above them, dense grey cloud blocking what was left of the sun. He could see the rest of the crew now, arrayed around the strange Tullioch. Mournchild was facing the creature, standing about five feet from it. The Tullioch was a head shorter than the knight, and slim with it. *A child or an old one?*

'We seek Deep Crow,' Marion said, and the Tullioch slapped his chest with his hand.

'Raorum Raorum sought many things,' the Tullioch said, 'to seek is to find, broodmother says. I say, broodmother knows. Deep Crow isn't far. Who is the boss?'

Killian staggered forward and gripped a rope and spat.

'*I'm* the captain,' he hissed. Glancing around he could see islands, *islands!* There were at least a dozen in sight, little islands with wizened old trees and dancing seabirds all around. Everyone turned to him, and then Pollos and Silver were rushing to his side. They lowered him down.

'Boss is the captain, then,' the Tullioch said. 'You can call me Gull, for now. You want the Russilan town, then? Never seen a *new* ship cross the big boss's water. You did well, eh? You Russilan?'

Killian fell to his knees and vomited a thin salt-water bile and then struggled to his feet, Silver and Pollos at either side of him.

'Deep Crow,' he said. 'You are from here, then, Gull? What news in the Deep Crowns, eh?'

Silver squeezed his arm, and Marion circled the young Tullioch, who eyed her without fear.

'He swam up to the ship as we were looking for anchorage for the night,' Silver whispered to him. 'You've been out hours. Pollos didn't want to go deeper 'til you were awake.'

Killian nodded and stared at the Tullioch. Marion reached up and stroked a feather on the gull-shaped headdress, and then she stepped back and folded her arms.

'I am Russilan,' Killian said. 'We seek Captain Arlock and the Bloody Crows. Do you know of her?'

'Raorum Raorum banished night!' Gull exclaimed, and clicked his teeth in amusement. 'Every soul in these waters knows the Bloody Crow. If you are Russilan they will feed and have you, I suppose. If not, they will do the other thing, eh? Gull will come. Gull will show you the way. Late today, though. Morning we sail, eh? Gull will come with dawn.'

The Tullioch strode to the rail of the ship and gave a cheery wave.

'Wait!' Marion commanded. 'Wait. Gull. Have you seen a Cil man? His name is Jean du Cilcan.'

Gull squinted at her and tapped his claws on the hilt of his dagger. 'You know everyone, eh? But then, this is the Deep. Everyone knows *everyone*,' he said, and then he pulled himself up to the rail of the ship and glanced at the water below. Gently he tossed down his gull hat, and it tumbled down to the water. 'Jean is a wild man, I say. But I only met him the once. He will be with the Bloody Crow, oh yes. See you with the sun!'

The Tullioch leapt from the rail of the ship, and Killian collapsed back to the deck.

'Tell!' he said, and Pollos knelt by him, his face contrite.

'Zalan let us through, fair wind and smooth water,' he said. 'Found the first isles an hour or so back, little rocks. Figured these larger ones might be good for the night but I've no mind for weather in here, Captain. No mind for currents, neither. Then as we were arguing about charts, there not being any charts of the Deep Crowns newer than forty years or so in the chest, this Tullioch lad jumped himself over bright as brass.'

Killian nodded and held at his head. There was a persistent ache behind his eyes. Silver pressed a flask into his hand, and when he took a mouthful he almost gagged. It was salty and sweet all at once. He gave her a quizzical look but she just pressed it back to his lips.

'Dawn to Deep Crow then,' Marion called, and without any further word she strode to her tiny room. Mournchild went to the fore of the ship and set himself at a rail, staring out to sea.

'Who or what is Raorum Raorum?' Killian asked, and Small Breygar stopped hauling a line and loomed over the three of them sat on the deck.

'Tullioch lad,' he said. 'Stole fire from a sea monster and made the sun, lad who first found the big Whale those Tullioch are all so keen on. Hero kind of guy, eh?'

Small Breygar wandered off with his line, and Killian shook his head.

'Pollos,' he said quietly. 'Pollos, Arlock is *Key*. Do you understand, Pollos? From what I told you, once. It was a long time ago. Do you remember?'

Pollos Twice-Kissed, once by his mother and once by pitchfyre, knelt and pressed his forehead to Killian's.

'We need to speak, then,' he said, and he hauled Killian to his feet. *He remembers*. Killian felt like weeping he was so tired, but there was a fire in his gut. *Family. Home. Connection*. Zalan had *seen* him. No mention of blood or thirst, no mention of death and tempest.

'What did you see out there? Who is Key?' Silver asked, and he cupped her cheek in his hand and smiled gently.

'I saw a path,' he said. 'The three of us need to speak.'

In Killian's room, Pollos lit a lantern and Killian sank into one of the armchairs. Pollos sat behind the chart table, staring down at the maps in front of him, and Silver retrieved her book bag and perched awkwardly on the other armchair.

'Where to begin?' Killian said, and Silver snorted.

'You told me once,' Pollos said. 'I can tell her, if that is what you are after. Give you a moment to think.'

Killian blinked and turned to his first mate. 'That was ten years ago, Pollos,' he said, and the big man shrugged.

'I remember,' he said. 'What I don't remember, you can set right. We are in it now, and if Arlock is *Key*, then things may get… interesting.'

Silver sat, rapt, her hands clutching her satchel so hard her knuckles were white. Killian stared at them, at her.

'Pollos Twice-Kissed is a good man,' he said, and then he closed his eyes and heard the voice of his old friend, as in a dream.

'He was a boy when they left here,' Pollos said, 'but Deep Crow was suffering. Not a big place, a backwater. Impossible to reach unless you were Russilan, even before Zalan started wrecking ships. Waters too hard to navigate. But a plague came. Not the Russilan Thirst that wiped them out across the isles – something meaner and smaller. A wasting. It took the young and the weak and the old and it left the strong broken. There were not enough hands to bring in the fish, not enough to make the bread. Killian's mother Cara took the chance. Followed Starfinder Rurich, a holy man, in a quest to find a better life out in the Crowns. A city where those who could work would work, to support the others. Cara and her children, Killian and Key. Arlock *is* Key. You understand?'

Through near-closed eyes Killian watched Silver relax her death grip on the satchel and sink back into the armchair. She nodded, waved at Pollos to continue. Killian could picture it so well – the excitement, the hope, the fear of leaving a dying town for somewhere *new*.

'They reached Requin-Port,' Pollos said. 'They sold their ship and used the money to set up a little commune, a place for the Russilan to be safe. A few dozen of them, in total. And they lived there, but times were hard. Cil-Marie had taken Requin-Port, added it to the Shield Isles, and they were keen to make their mark. Russilan weren't trusted. Too *unknown*. The Cil were brutal, as they ever are. Sedition was on the charge list, but they hanged Cara Heroneye for stealing bread to feed her children. Killian promised her to look after Arlock, promised *Arlock* he would be there for her. But he got a chance at revenge, and he took it.'

Killian kept his eyes closed, and sighed. 'I killed the Cil governor of Requin-Port in his bed,' he said, and he still could not tell if he was satisfied with that. *The man needed to die, but the cost was so high.*

'Ten years old and he scaled the governor's walls and put a knife in him, but he was seen. He made the choice to run. To leave, and by leaving keep Arlock safe with the others.'

'I went back three years later and they were all gone,' Killian said.

'Fled on a ship to Samurkan, where Merrow took him in. Then a trader cog, then a smuggling outfit, then a whaler for two seasons. And then he found me, and the *Hawk*.'

'When was this?' Silver asked, and Pollos shook his head.

'Ten years ago,' he said, his voice rough. 'A different name, a different captain. A different aim. For eight years he worked the lines and learned the ship, and then he became captain.'

'Who was the old captain?' Silver asked, and Pollos looked up from the charts and smiled at her, and Killian blew a breath through his nose.

'Irrelevant,' Pollos said. 'But now, we go seeking Arlock. And this Cil woman wants her, and I don't think in a friendly way.'

'Secrets,' Silver said quietly, and she held her fingertips atop her satchel for a long moment, face still. She grimaced and looked to Killian, locking eyes, then nodded. From her satchel she drew out a mask of smooth wood, shaped like a Straits Kingdom Devil – an oval of pale wood with two slits the thickness of coins for eyes, and two curved horns. No other features. Silver gently raised it and it adhered to her face, and she turned to each of them and her shoulders drew in. With the mask on he could not see her eyes or her face at all, only unreadable wood.

'We all have secrets,' she said.

Mournchild had atoned for eating the dead. He had survived another encounter with the idiot snake-god of the Russilan. He had wet his blade with the infidel bee-priest's blood, and he was pure again. In the shadow of the lower deck he had fashioned himself a little privacy, walls of boxed supplies partitioning off a segment of the lower hold. The rest of the crew left him be. The big Undal man had offered him a hammock, but Mournchild did not trust the swaying canvas and slept with it folded up beneath him.

He had removed his armour, and lay in only a loincloth on the hammock, staring up at the wood of the deck above him in the darkness.

'Baal, Morost, Pendar, Tulu, Salaman,' he said, '*Baal, Morost, Pendar, Tulu, Salaman*. I am here to serve the Lady Marion. Why? This place is nothing but beasts and men who are no better than beasts. How long must I serve at the behest of this godless Cil? I do not question the church, I question my understanding. *Baal, Morost, Pendar, Tulu, Salaman*. There are five, and there is one. I would serve. I have atoned.'

'You are here to serve,' a soft voice said, and Mournchild closed his eyes. *Marion*. The lady entered his partition and sat cross-legged on the deck next to him. She was clad in a simple shirt and trous.

'We are coming to the close, Mournchild,' she said. 'This is the place where our fate will be determined. My master has foreseen the hour of my death, and it is not in this place. I tell you this so you understand what is at stake. Jean du Cilcan must be retrieved. Failure is not an option. Arlock of the Bloody Crows must be eliminated. I have the beacon; you have the blade. The church *gave* you to me, to serve *me*, because my master met with them and they saw what he saw. A world of chaos, a world of death and destruction on a scale never seen before. Jean du Cilcan is the key to preventing this. Uradech and Cil-Marie are aligned. The Sun-Masters and Baal are aligned. Morost is not Pendar nor is Baal Tulu nor is Salaman any of the others – each have their role to play to make the greater whole. I need you to serve, Mournchild. Are there any aboard this ship you cannot kill?'

'No,' Mournchild said, with no hesitation.

'Are there any aboard this ship you will not kill?'

'No.'

The lady pressed her hand to his forehead, cool skin against hot and leaned in close.

'The hour of our ascension is here. It is time to put the little pirate in his place. Do you have them?'

Mournchild did not open his eyes, and reached for his belt pouch where it lay by the head of his folded hammock, and took the two little items from within and placed them delicately in Marion's hand.

'You are a good Blade, Mournchild,' she said, voice thick and close to his ear. 'These islands are rife with creatures that deserve no quarter. They seed chaos. They worship false gods. They eat of the dead, and hold nothing but ash where their souls should be.'

'Yes,' Mournchild said. 'Yes, Lady Marion.'

Killian held the mask in his hand.

'Darnielle?' he said, and Silver nodded. 'A mage, and your true name is Darnielle?'

'What is a *true name—*' she started to say, but Killian cut her off with a raised hand.

'I'll leave you two to this,' Pollos said, rising from the chart table. 'This doesn't change what we must do. Find Key. These Cil will pay the other half of your debt if we help them get their man, Killian.'

'The Cil and her pet knight aren't going to be getting their man,' Killian said. 'They aren't going to be *negotiating* with Arlock, if you ever believed that was the plan. They aren't getting this Jean du-*whatever* his name was. Half our debt with the Sisters is nothing to sniff at, but this is all too close. They need to go.'

Pollos simply nodded, and on his way out put a hand on Silver's shoulder.

'Welcome to the crew, I suppose,' he said, and then it was just the two of them.

'We all have secrets,' Silver said quietly. They sat in their respective chairs, not looking at each other. 'Pollos didn't tell me why you two are as you are. How you got this ship. We all have secrets, Heroneye. I just…'

'You just what?' he asked, and in truth he could not tell what he was feeling. 'I left you letters. I dropped you at the door of your guild!'

'Well, I do have a library membership at the Archaeology and Anthropology Guild,' she said, and her mouth twisted. 'Don't hate me for this, Heron. In Isken, nobody knows the true identity of a mage. Only their family. That is what the masks are for.'

Killian held the devil mask in his hand and stared at it. 'Why are you telling me this now?' he asked. 'I don't even know what to do with this.'

'I am on your side,' Silver said. 'I am on *your side*, Heron. Not the guild. Not anything else. You and me, me and you. We can uncover Russilan tombs; we can sail the Crowns. Don't you see? I am on your side and so I wanted you to know, because whatever you are going to do, I am with you. Do you understand?'

'You always knew where the lock stones were. Kaikatsu told me you could touch it, but I thought, just a knack. Like I have. Just a feeling, maybe.'

Silver left her chair and knelt by his and took the mask from his hands and pushed it back in her bag.

'I don't need a mask with you, Heron,' she said. 'Do you know how that makes me feel? A lifetime of hiding who I am, what I am. First in Kelamor, then the guild in Isken, then Samurkan. I wanted you to see me.'

You can't ever see me. The thought came unbidden. Blood, and blood, and blood. *How many dead at my hand?*

'Silver, there are things you don't know,' he said, and she closed her eyes and the lantern dimmed and went out, and then about him points of light danced, one, then another, another, another. Six points of white light each no bigger than a pinkie nail dancing around Silver's head, and then they settled into a familiar constellation.

'The sisters,' he said, and he reached out to touch the nearest light. It felt warm on his hand, insubstantial.

'Luck,' Silver said. 'There are things I don't know. So tell me, or don't. It changes nothing.'

It changes everything.

A knock at the door drew his gaze from hers, and the dancing lights died and the lamp flared back to life in an instant. Silver drew her hands back from his with a squeeze and sat back in her chair.

'Enter,' she called, and Killian closed his eyes and pictured himself with a Russilan dagger at his hip, Silver by his side, at the wheel of the *Cutlass Hawk*.

He opened his eyes as Marion entered, dressed simply, barefoot. She looked between the two of them and curled a lip in disdain.

'This won't take long,' she said. 'I wanted you to have the night to think on it before we reach Deep Crow.'

Pacing over to Killian she reached out her hand and gestured to his own. He raised his palm and she tipped two little brass pins, stylised. Familiar. Pins that matched the one on his hat. A cutlass with a crow perched on the blade just above the hilt. *Galli and Nils.*

Killian held his breath. The red rose, and rose. He could feel the rage in his lungs, his blood, his teeth aching as he ground his jaw.

'Before you do anything stupid,' Marion said, stepping back towards the door slowly and deliberately, 'consider the following. I did my research before I put a foot on this ship. Killian Heroneye with a thirst for blood, but a soft spot for Mistress Merrow who runs the orphanage in the lower tier of Samurkan. Killian Heroneye who always leaves the young deckhands there if he is going on a "heavy job", presumably to save them from the same trauma you had in your own youth. Commendable, I suppose. I am not an idiot, Heroneye. You will not tip Mournchild into the sea and stab me in my sleep and call it a good day's work. If I do not return to Samurkan, if I am deemed *lost*, the children will be sold into the worst pit mine in Cil-Marie. Or perhaps a brothel, I don't know, I left that at ambassadorial discretion. The orphanage will burn, and the old woman will watch and be left on the street. Probably maimed – the agents do tend to be so *zealous* about these things. Galli and Nils, isn't it? Your crew?'

'My crew,' Killian said softly, and every fibre in him wanted to reach for the lidless sea chest full of blades. His gut roiled. 'They are *children*.'

'You must learn to prioritise, Captain Heroneye. In this, your dislike of the Cil and myself in particular, or the lives of your little crew? You must do your duty, as you see fit. Tomorrow we go to Deep Crow, and you are no longer "boss", as that horrible idiot Tullioch said. You will do as you are told. No more games. I return to Samurkan or Cil-Marie with Jean du Cilcan in tow, having had a *chat* with this Arlock character, and in return you get your little crew back, *and* your debt with the Evertree Sisters is cleared. The words you are looking for are: *Thank you, Lady Marion*.'

Killian did not trust himself to move or to speak. He turned his gaze to Silver and she gave an infinitesimal shake of the head, and he felt his cheek split in his mouth as he gnawed his teeth.

'*Restraint*,' Marion said. 'How novel. Perhaps we can save the gratitude for another day. Sleep well, Captain. *Silver*.'

Marion left the room, and Killian stared down at his clenched fist where the brass pins of Galli and Nils were cutting into his palm.

Deep Crow

Deep Crow, year 1134 Isken – **From the charts of the *Cutlass Hawk*,** Captain Killian Heroneye

15

DEEP CROW

'Three Antian holdfasts are known to exist, one in each of the eastern, northern, and western reaches. Their even disposition lends credence to rumours of a further holdfast in Tullioch-held territory to the south, and one Uradech scholar claims historical record of a further holdfast within the Deep Crowns themselves. As ever the Antian remain reticent, and their holdfasts are great edifices of worked stone that invite no approach. Given the Cil-Marie treatment of the Antian people, their defensive posture in these waters is not without merit. Some trade with the Northern Holdfast occurs, though only on the day of the lowest tide. The significance of this is not clear.'

– ***The Thousand Crowns***, Alwin Brakspear

Killian spent a restless night asking Silver for details of her power. He had known his share of tide-mages, but no guild arcanists, and the distinction was unclear to him. Could she throw a man from a ship? Could she shoot fire like Heavenly Nassin's tide-mage? Could she send messages? *Maybe, no, no.* What could she do?

In the end her answers were frustratingly vague, and he was too panicked about Nils and Galli to set any firm plan. In the morning he found Pollos and drew him close and told him, and the Undal man's usually friendly face turned to stone.

'I'll not have any of that,' he muttered. 'We need to get rid of these rats and then go get our crew, I say.'

'Aye,' Killian said. 'But we'll have to do it before they realise she is dead. What do you think?'

Pollos shook his head and then looked to Killian deferentially.

'Your call, Captain. Just say the word.'

Killian patted the big man on the shoulder, and left him to his thoughts. The sky was still full of leaden cloud, but the wind inside the Deep Crowns was strange. He was so used to the ever *inward* direction of the squalling winds of the Crowns, unpredictable in their minutiae yet utterly relentless in their overall direction. This wind was diffident, obtuse: *unknown.* Killian paced the deck. Timmult was sat near the bowsprit playing his reed pipes, a haunting melody, and when Killian passed, the man paused his tune and spat over the rail of the ship.

'That's an old song,' he said, and Killian waited to see if the taciturn sailor had more to say. Timmult rarely spoke without prompt. The man shook his pipes and looked down each reed and then pocketed the set and locked eyes with Killian.

'Renard and I reset the lines after Burner's Run,' he said. 'We should be running at full speed, with a few more repairs we can fit in around the next few days' sail. Do we have a course, Captain?'

Killian stared at the water, and saw a black-backed gull, large and ungainly, slowly drifting towards them. He stared at it for a long moment and tugged at Timmult's hand to draw his eye. A second gull flapped and landed in the water near the first, and slowly they drifted closer. In an explosion of water, a clawed hand wrenched up from below and grabbed the second gull, hauling it beneath the iron water. A moment later, the first gull rose up revealing itself as the ornate headdress of the Tullioch named Gull. He grinned up at Killian and Timmult and waved his prize.

'Time to sail to Deep Crow, eh?' he called, and Killian sighed.

'Throw him a line,' he said to Timmult, and then went to rally the crew. Marion and Mournchild were deep in counsel on the aftcastle, and Silver was having the talk he had asked her to have with Kaikatsu. *We need to be ready.*

With the Tullioch Gull amicably lounging on the rail next to the wheel, they raised one sail and slowly set off through the myriad islands at the edge of the Deep Crowns. Marion kept up a neat barrage of questions for the Tullioch, and when Killian realised her aim he made sure he was close enough to hear Gull's answers. *How many broodmates do you have? Have you ever left the Deep Crowns? Is the city of Deep Crow big? Why do they call it that? Is Arlock as wild as the stories say? How many pirates does she have? How many ships?*

The Cil diplomat was working hard – for every question of the Bloody Crows and Arlock and Jean du Cilcan, there were a dozen more – local fauna, flora, the weather, Gull's favourite foods, his strange fishing technique. Marion's usual cold manner was swapped by an earnest interest and warmth, prolonged eye contact, and follow-up questions. It was unnerving. He learned that Gull had seven broodmates, had never left the Deep Crowns, found Deep Crow to be the largest city he had ever seen (but also the only), had no idea of the provenance of its name, and thought Arlock was rather quiet for one so powerful. He had no idea how many sailors made up the Bloody Crows, but they had four ships in total.

'Impossible,' Marion muttered to Killian when the Tullioch went to the prow to get a better look at their heading. 'They have a dozen ships at least. We lost a galleon off the Muruds not two moons ago. This thing is an idiot.'

'We will see,' Killian said, and then he left before she could rile him. He knew he would only have one chance to rid himself of the Cil. The question was, did he do it on open water, or wait until Deep Crow? If Arlock had a crew of pirates at her disposal, why not let them work through Mournchild's defences?

They outer isles were devoid of people, but the waters around them were teeming with life. Great shoals of glittering fish, a pod of dolphins, all tracking the bow of the *Hawk*. They passed an isle where man-sized crabs with mud-brown shells and mismatched claw sizes all stared at them from the shore, swaying in unison and singing a clicking and whirring chant through their mouthparts. A Carob whale with three antlers, each one at least twelve points, surfaced in their wake, and they had to drop sail and lost perhaps an hour as the Tullioch Gull leapt overboard to try to swim to it, the two creatures eventually settling into a circling pattern around each other. They eventually managed to haul the Tullioch back aboard, and he laughed and smiled at them, utterly unconcerned. The wind was inconstant and feeble, and they made slow pace.

'Look,' Silver said to him, and she drew his gaze to an isle where tall trees bedecked in vines tangled the shoreline. He squinted, and then reeled back as he realised what he was seeing. Bone-monkeys, a dozen at least with their fleshless faces staring, smooth bone showing stark ivory against the dun of their fur.

'The souls of sailors who break their oaths,' Renard commented quietly beside them, and then there was a scoff from Mournchild and she quickly hurried away.

'*Baal, Morost, Pendar, Tulu, Salaman*,' Mournchild intoned, and Killian glowered at the knight. Mournchild smiled a tight smile back. 'Do you think there is such a thing as salvation, Heroneye?'

Killian kept his eyes on the bone-monkeys, and did not answer.

It was deep in the afternoon that they encountered their first vessel. It was a canoe with an outrigger, and aboard it a huge jaiboar corpse was tied, the normally regimented spines on its back haphazard in death. Three hunters were paddling, all of them dressed in hard-worn leathers. They stared at the ship with cold calculation, and Killian did not wait for Marion to give him a course as he knew she would. With Gull at his side he went to the side rail and called down to them as the *Hawk* passed. Gull waved enthusiastically.

'Hail, hunters!' he called. 'A fine prize you have found! We seek open water to Deep Crow. Are we headed in the right direction?'

The hunters conferred, heads close together for a long moment before turning back and staring up at him.

'Have you drunk from the well?' one called, and Killian removed his hat and held it over his heart.

'I have drunk from the Well of No End,' he called, 'though it has been many years.'

Wordlessly they all pointed, their fingers tracing out the heading he had already been on that Gull had provided. The *Cutlass Hawk* was already almost past them, and he bowed in deference and waved his farewell. The afternoon drifted onward, and the wind never lifted to any real speed.

'I remember trees,' he told Pollos in another lull. 'I remember the Well of No End, the docks. Stone towers, I think. What else could there be to remember?'

'Where it is,' Pollos said simply, and Killian wrinkled his nose and swatted the older man on the shoulder. They were alone on the aftcastle at the wheel, and spent a long time in companionable silence before Silver came to them.

'I spoke to Kaikatsu,' she said. 'We can deal with the knight, if it comes to it, as long as we have at least thirty seconds' warning. Enough time to fall into the skein and to make a change in it. She'll put him in the drink, and then he is garu-meat.'

Killian wasn't listening. He reached out and turned her head so she could see the sight that had just appeared from behind a small island: *Deep Crow.*

An isle of dark rock and lush greenery rose from the bleak grey of the water, and Killian grinned. *Home.*

Family. Connection. Zalan had stirred something in him, and the sight of the city made his heart sing. *How long has it been?* The city spread across a wide bay, and above it the most wonderful piece of stonework he or anyone had surely ever seen – the Deep Crow dome, a lattice worked entirely from black seamless stone. *Not towers.* How had he forgotten it?

The dome sat proudly two hundred feet above the tallest building, which was a clocktower attached to a steep-roofed temple. The rest of the buildings were a hodge-podge of styles, Isken columns and flat-roofed Cil square homes, with central common areas. A few squat Russilan granite ziggurats dotted the southern edge of the city. Others were simpler affairs, row after row of little houses and cottages. In and around all the buildings the shadow of the stone lattice dome danced, with the exception of the docks that fell beyond the dome's shadow. Two ships were there, both with black wood hulls as if they had been scourged with flame, and both with furled faded red sails and no other pennant or insignia.

Bells rang as the townsfolk realised they were not alone. In heartbeats the static idyll before Killian was transformed to a scene of chaos and fear. He could see children running, searching for their parents, could see ballistae being wheeled and prepared along the harbourfront and on the decks of one of the ships. On the other ship, no ballistae – instead, a crew of six were wheeling a strange ram of wood and stone and metal tipped with a purple crystal the size of Killian's torso. It was mounted on a ballistae turntable, and slowly they turned it so the crystal was pointed in the direction of the *Cutlass Hawk*.

'Stop,' Marion called up to him from the deck, and Killian nodded at the questioning looks from the crew. They ran to haul the sails in and the *Hawk* quickly slowed to a crawl and then a stop, twisting slightly in the minor current that revolved around Deep Crow.

'What is that?' Killian asked, and next to him Silver held her satchel close to her chest.

'The future,' Silver said. Next to her Marion was ashen-faced, her eyes locked on the long stone and steel-and-wood-worked rods with the crystal tips on the deck of the Russilan ship now pointed at the *Cutlass Hawk*.

'Jean du Cilcan,' she hissed.

A dog-boat came for them. Killian dropped anchor, and the ballistae and the strange rods of metal, stone, wood, and crystal followed the ship's every undulation, a gaggle of stern-faced sailors garbed in simple wool fiercely watching every roll and jump and shift of the ship and adjusting accordingly. One of the crystals was a deep purple, the other a bright orange.

'Have you ever seen crystals like that?' he asked, and Silver frowned but did not answer.

Killian watched the little boat approach, four oars pulling strongly through the water. It was painted a garish blue, and aboard it an older woman in a wide straw hat was standing at the prow, a crossbow perched jauntily on her hip. She was perhaps Pollos's age. As they pulled closer she caught a line Renard threw down and made it fast to her boat's prow.

'I have drunk from the Well of No End,' Killian said, leaping ahead to the probing and protestations that felt inevitable. 'Though it has been some time. This is the *Cutlass Hawk*. I am Killian Heroneye, son of Cara Heroneye. We seek Arlock. Can you bring us to her? We bring a diplomat from, well… Cil-Marie.'

The woman lowered her crossbow fractionally and stared into his eyes and then laughed. Her face was weathered and her cheeks red, and around her eyes deep crinkles and folds were pulled in as she grinned.

'That,' she said, 'is not what I expected. Come on down, fella.'

Killian turned to the crew. *This is it.* Marion and Mournchild waited expectantly.

'Time to finish this,' the Cil woman said, and she pushed past Killian and began clambering down the rope ladder at the side of the *Hawk*. Mournchild followed with a baleful stare, and Killian waited a beat. He began to speak but Pollos waved him down.

'We'll have her ready to run,' he said. 'You take Silver, take Big Breygar, and go make sure Key is okay.'

Big Breygar loosened her cutlass in its hook.

'Who is Key?' she asked, and Killian just shook his head.

'It doesn't matter,' he said. 'Just, watch our backs.' He led Silver and Big down the ladder to the waiting dog-boat, and clasped forearms with the woman with the wide-brimmed hat.

'A pleasure to meet you,' he said, and the woman laughed.

'Don't remember me, handsome?' she asked, and she threw off the line holding the dog-boat in place. Her rowers pushed off and then they were into the placid harbour of Deep Crown, cutting between the two high-sided sloops. 'Have to say I thought *you* were long dead. Would make Cara mighty proud to see her lad running a ship that pretty.'

Killian turned from the ships, from the looming lattice dome and city of Deep Crow, and stared at the woman with the wide-brimmed hat. She smiled at him so softly. There was something about her face he remembered, something about her laugh. He felt instantly at ease with her.

'You gave me a red apple when I broke my sword,' he said at last, the moment of it coming to him – not an image of her face, but a sense of her presence. A friend of his mother. *A friend of mine.* The woman removed the bolt from her crossbow and set the weapon down and leaned forward and wrapped her arms around him, pulling him close. She smelled of salt and sea and black earth and bread and she held him a long moment as the boat bobbed in the waves. From her bench in the dog-boat Marion stared at him, calculating, her eyes glistening.

'Welcome home, lad,' the woman said, and Killian found his throat tight. He forced himself to breathe and turned his gaze from the boat, but could feel Marion's gaze burning into him. *She'll know soon enough.*

They spoke no more. The entire city that had scrambled for ballistae and bow, spear and sword, all of them now watched the dog-boat approach bearing so many strangers. The boat was tied up to the jetty and then it was a long and silent walk through the streets, and he knew at once where they were taking him. *The Well of No End.* The streets were simply paved in grey stone, and the buildings were clean and well maintained. He remembered the chaos of leaving, as a child. Corpses in the street, homes in ruin. *They rebuilt it without us.*

'Is she here?' he asked his mother's friend, and the woman nodded but did not reply. Marion was walking haughtily, as if this were a normal afternoon for her. Silver and Big Breygar hung back at Killian's shoulders, and Blade Mournchild held his black cloak close around him and stayed a respectful but consistent three feet from Marion.

'I'm going to get dinner, but let me know how it goes, eh?' Gull said, and Killian did a double take. He had not noticed the Tullioch in the dog-boat, but with a glance realised that Gull was still wet – he must have swum ashore as they rowed in.

'Thank you, Gull,' he said softly, and he grabbed the Tullioch's sinewy forearm. 'We will meet again.'

'Raorum Raorum took fire from the gods,' Gull said, and he bowed his head at Killian. Drawing close he lowered his voice so that only Killian could hear. 'The gods fought back, though. They did not fight fair. Be careful.'

With that he withdrew, and Killian stared after him, perplexed.

'This might actually be easy enough,' Silver said as they slowly marched through the city. The roads were all so varied, some stone, some packed clay with stone paths alongside, houses in a dozen different styles made of stone or timber. There were no horses, no cows, but Killian could hear goats somewhere nearby.

'They are taking us to the heart of things,' Killian said absently, and then shook himself as he caught the worried look Silver shot him.

'What is this stone net above us?' Big Breygar asked, and they all looked up. Nothing filled the holes in the great stone lattice, and the complex interaction of the sunlight with the clouds and then the stone cast mesmerising shadows across the ground all around them.

'It has been there forever,' Killian said, as if that were an answer. The crowd from the edge of the city had abated as they drew closer to the centre, only a few die-hard onlookers tracking the group from a respectful distance, and as they drew closer to the heart of the city Killian found his gaze drifting, his focus failing. The sky had grown dark and the clouds were blowing free in the dying wind of the day, and he thought he would see stars and so he forced his gaze down. *I will make my own fate.*

'Starfinder Arlock will see you now,' the woman in the wide-brimmed hat said, and she gestured to a stone archway at the end of the road they were walking down and led them to it. 'I'll be seeing you later, Killian. Much to say, much to hear, I think. If you would?'

Killian clasped her hand again, and the woman waved them towards the arch and lingered behind them.

'You will let me speak, Heroneye,' Marion hissed, and Killian shook his head. *Starfinder Arlock?* They stepped through the arch into the heart of the city of Deep Crow, and to the centre of everything, and even though he expected it, Killian stopped dead in his tracks just as the others did.

Ahead of them, a pool of water lay utterly still in the dark of night, the only source of light the reflection of a thousand stars in the black water, cut through by the shadows of the stone lattice above. The pool was set in a huge open plaza surrounded by thick granite walls, with three arches evenly placed admitting access, and between the water and the edge of the plaza there was twenty feet of dark stone on all sides, sending infinitesimal ripples outward.

On the far side of the pool a hundred feet away a throne of driftwood had been placed, so close to the water that the toes of its occupant dangled in the water.

On the throne lounged a pale woman, slender as he was, with a similar long face and high cheekbones. Brown hair swept back from her scowling face. In one hand she held a dagger whose blade was etched in runes that bled a soft blue light, and in the other hand a small book with worn leather bindings. She wore the robe of a Starfinder, black and austere, and as they stepped into the room she ignored everyone but him, her eyes a perfect mirror to his as they locked across the plaza.

'Hello, brother,' she called, leaning forward. 'Have you seen the stars, tonight?'

16

POWER

'Once the relu were spirits of place, creatures of the skein itself – the pattern and the pattern below, manifestations of the spirit of the world. Yet since the winter of madness they change and grow. Some larger, some winnowed. Some have died or disappeared. Some are hurt and wounded, as they never could be before. Some have multiplied, like the glass spiders of the Undal tunnels. Here in the Western Holdfast I have reports that Cil-Marie's bounty for captive relu is ever increasing. We know of their hatred for us. We must ask – what do they do with these captive creatures? Have they weaponised the spirits? In the name of all our siblings in chains under Cil-Marie's hammer, we must find the truth of this.'

– ***Letter to the Council of Isles on the Madness of the Spirits***, Anneli Thirdblood of Holt Suolaa

'I've not looked at the stars yet, Key,' Killian said, his voice carrying across the cenote pool. He smiled, but she did not return it. They all stared at the reflected stars. He felt Marion shifting her feet. *She will be figuring out what that 'brother' means.*

'That is the purpose of the lattice, brother,' Key said, and she gestured to the edge of the cenote pool where intricate markings were etched into the stone. 'If you align your viewing position with the date, the moon, the tide, then it will lead your gaze to a specific constellation, and block out those around it. It is an old method of learning the future, to be sure. I prefer newer methods.'

Arlock stood and removed the black austere Starfinder's robe, folding it gently on the driftwood throne. She wore simple boots, trous and shirt, with a wide belt that had a single dagger thrust through it next to two metal rods, each of which ended in a different gemstone. In those few moments she changed from sage to sailor – he recognised the wear in her boots, the salt stains on her black trous and shirt.

'Ruaridh!' she called over her shoulder, and there was no answer. Arlock began to pace back and forth, her eyes on Killian. *She looks so tired.* The woman with the wide-brimmed hat sighed deeply behind them.

'Let me know if you need anything, Key,' she called, and then she turned to leave. Killian saw Marion's hand tense. *She wants to kill my sister,* he thought, *but she has to find Jean du Cilcan first.*

'Never thought I'd see you working for a *Cil*, *brother*,' Arlock said, and with a kick she sent a pebble dashing into the pool. It fell quickly, and was lost immediately to the dark water. 'Then again, never thought I'd see you at all. Wonders never cease.'

'Who taught you to be a Starfinder?' he asked, and Arlock stopped her pacing and turned on him from across the pool.

'You don't get to ask questions, Killian!' she spat. 'You, who left me alone in a nest of vipers, you don't get to ask me questions. I will do as I will do, and with no input from you. Why did you help these Cil past Burner's Run?'

Killian balked. He held out a hand. 'Key,' he said, 'please—'

She cut him off with a wave of her hand and turned her gaze resolutely to Marion, and Killian felt seawater in his lungs, a heavy weight. *Look after her,* his mother had said before the noose took her. Before the Cil took her.

'We are looking for you, child,' Marion said, and she drew her hammer. It thrummed with potency. Arlock sucked her teeth, and Blade Mournchild let his cloak fall to the ground and unsheathed his heavy grey longsword.

'I am Marion. You will give us the traitor Jean du Cilcan,' Marion said. 'You will bring him to us, and then we will leave. Cil-Marie wants no war with your people, but if—'

Killian unhooked his cutlass and pointed it at Marion, and in the same moment Mournchild raised his longsword and levelled it at Killian. Big Breygar swore under her breath and took two steps back.

'You don't threaten my sister,' Killian said, eyes locked on Marion, and before the Cil woman could answer there was a laugh. Arlock.

'How *protective*,' she said, and then she drew from her belt the short length of metal ending in an amethyst, and she pointed it and from it a beam of purple force exploded and shot across the pool of water, striking stone at the feet of Marion and Killian. The stone cracked. Killian balked.

'I had to find ways to protect myself,' Arlock said, and next to Killian Silver straightened her posture and he could sense her focus. *What is this?* 'This is the latest, I suppose. Certainly the most effective. The Undal rediscovered these a decade back and have been slowly fitting out their army with them, their joke of a navy. The Cil have been rather slower, but they have figured it out. Imagine that, Killian. Every Cil galleon with a dozen of these on deck.'

Another blast of purple light from the wand, this one aimed at the clouds above. It danced upward and eventually was lost from sight. *How far will it go?*

'You want Jean,' Arlock said, 'you want him, but you don't deserve him. Did you see the wands on my ship, Marion? We took it for a test. Do you know how easily a wand like that can split a wood hull? We tested it against a Cil galley, you know. Five beams, and it sank like a stone. The world is changing rather rapidly. I hope you don't get left behind.'

'Key,' Killian said, 'wait—' but his sister did not look at him. She stared at Marion and Mournchild.

'Seize them, bind them, take their toys. Set them in the eye cells.'

From the stone archway behind them a dozen pirates began to slow-step forward. A handful held heavy crossbows ready to fire, and the rest were armed with cudgel or fist.

'I am here as a diplomat from Cil-Marie,' Marion said, and the pirates grew closer to her. Three surrounded Killian as well.

'Lock!' he called. 'Tell your men to back off. It is these two you want in a cell, not us! I need to speak to you!'

Arlock turned and stared at him and tapped the wand in her belt.

'As ever,' she said, 'you disappoint me. You don't know what I want, Killian. You never have, and I think you never will. I think I liked you better when I thought you were dead.'

The eye cells were simple things: a little stone, bars of metal, a huge lock on each. They overlooked the great pool of water these island dregs seemed so obsessed about. Mournchild thought he could cut through the dozen pirates, regardless of crossbows, but Marion gave him the sign and so he let them take his sword and his boot dagger. Each cell was barely big enough for one person and all of them walled on five sides. Lieutenant Marion was on one side of him, and the little captain on the other.

'Arlock of the Bloody Crows is your *sister*,' Marion said, and Mournchild watched the water. Heroneye did not reply.

'What is the pool?' the Breygar woman asked, and Mournchild took a moment to examine the mounting of the bars to his cell door. Given a month he might wear down the stone, but they were not going to bend for him. The fool pirates had left him armoured, and he began to unbuckle the greave from his right shin. *Fools. Baal, Morost, Pendar, Tulu, Salaman.* The godhead would be pleased with him for this little trick.

'It is a cenote,' Heroneye's voice called. 'A hole in the world. We are at the centre of the Crowns, here. Russilan say this is the centre of all things – on our charts, this point is always at the heart. It is a pool that goes down and down forever. There is no bottom.'

'That is impossible,' Silver said, and Mournchild sniffed. There was a pirate left to guard them, some Russilan with no armour or uniform, just a *man* with an old cutlass. *Embarrassing*. Mournchild worked his greave into position, trying to find leverage on the lock of his door.

'We call it the Well of No End,' Heroneye continued, his voice soft. 'All Russilan drink from its waters, at least once. If you swim down, there is no bottom but there are side passages, endless side passages, and if you can swim to them then you emerge in the seas far from here, impossibly far. It is a magical place, Silver.'

'Arlock, Captain of the Bloody Crows, is your *sister*,' Marion said again, and Mournchild heard Heroneye's door rattle as the man shook it. He yelled for the guard, and so Mournchild hurriedly hid his greave behind his back. He wasn't getting any leverage.

'I'm Russilan!' Heroneye yelled. 'Arlock is, as this bloody Cil keeps shouting, my *sister*. I need to talk to her, man! Can you at least ask her to talk to me?'

The guard studiously ignored Heroneye's shouts.

'Those wands on the ship,' Silver called, 'Cil-Marie have them? Truly?'

Mournchild wedged his greave back by the lock mechanism and strained until every sinew screamed and his teeth felt like they would burst. It did nothing.

'We do,' Marion said eventually. 'This last decade we've discovered more than you can possibly imagine. Guard! I need to speak to Arlock *Heroneye*, on behalf of the government of Cil-Marie. Do you hear me?'

The guard walked away around the cenote, ignoring their calls, pausing only to nod at a cloaked figure who entered the room through one of the stone arches. The figure came directly to the eye cells and lowered their hood, revealing a thin balding Cil man of middle years with a wide mouth and a thin beard.

'Marion!' he said, and he waved happily to her. Mournchild stiffened, and strained once more at the greave. *This is the moment!* He felt the gate beginning to shift.

'Jean du Cilcan,' Marion snarled in Summer tongue, the language of the Cil court. 'You have given ship-wands to these *pirates*? And smaller wands as well. What have you done, you fool?'

The man frowned and cast his eyes down. 'I have survived, Lady,' he said, voice stern. 'They have three ship-wands, and two smaller. It has been *years*. I was stalling, so they would keep me alive. They have no idea how to recreate them – their artisans are fine, but materials are scarce. Two of those wands are from the ship I was on. What would you have had me do? Die?'

'Preferably,' she hissed. 'Tell me, traitor. Do you think the Sun-Masters will be pleased you have given our greatest new weapon to a band of cutthroats? I will take you back to them to answer for this, Jean. In chains or in a box, as you prefer.'

Mournchild felt the final shift and knew he was close, so he held back.

'Lady,' he called, 'former or latter?'

'Former,' she said, ice in her tone. 'You are a traitor and a fool, Jean du Cilcan.'

Mournchild threw all of his weight and strength into the gate and the lock burst open, the steel of his greave twisting as it went flying across dark stone.

'My Lady wants you alive,' he said, and then he grinned at the little man who had caused them so much strife. '*For now.*'

Mournchild stalked forward, and the man quickstepped back. The guard was running, yelling, but Mournchild knew it didn't matter anymore. *I will kill them all. Let them all come!*

Jean ducked behind the rushing guard, and Mournchild parried the man's wild swing with one armoured wrist and then punched him in the sternum. He heard the bone crack, and the guard slumped to the floor. Jean du Cilcan tripped and sprawled across the stone and Mournchild licked his lips.

'I have you,' he hissed, and then he stopped. His arm would not move forward. His whole body was gripped as if a great vice were around him, the air itself pressing in at him. He struggled to breathe, his chest only able to expand a mote before air as hard as iron held it. He wanted to scream but had no air left in his lungs, and he managed to strain his eyes to Marion in her cell, confusion writ across her face.

'What are you waiting for, Blade!' she yelled, and then he saw her. *Silver.* The academic, the non-entity with the ridiculous rapier. She sat cross-legged in her cell with a satchel on her lap, and on her face a smooth wood mask with two thin eye slits and devil horns sat tight, surrounded by a mass of wild curls.

'*Swim,*' she said, and Mournchild was thrown through the air and landed in the centre of the bottomless cenote, the

Well of No End. He did not have time to yell, did not have time to fight – he was on land, and then he was underwater, cold salt burning his eyes, filling his lungs. He sank fast and spent a long stupid moment trying to swim, but in his armour it was useless. He began to tear at the buckles and straps of his breastplate, and even as he did so the faint light above was growing dimmer, and his head pounded and his ears burst and he looked wildly for passages to the sides – *the boy said there were ways out!* But it was dark, so dark…

Killian watched Mournchild sink and let out half a laugh, and then from the broken guard's belt a loop of keys floated through the air to Silver's cell. A moment later her door was open and she stepped out, lithe and lanky in her ornate blue jacket, pale devil mask framed by her golden hair.

'You *beauty*!' he yelled, and she looked at him but did not approach. He held out his hand for the keys.

'We did it, Silver!' he said. 'Mournchild drowned, Marion in a cell, the Cil don't get their man. We did it! Give me the key!'

Silver did not give him the key. She went and stood over the weeping Jean du Cilcan and drew him to his feet, and then turned and tossed the key to Marion's cell. Killian pressed his face to the bars.

'*What are you doing, Silver*?' he hissed. 'Silver! Silver! SILVER!'

She did not answer him, and a moment later the Lady Marion stepped out primly from her cell. She reached down and took the cutlass from the guard's limp hands – he had stopped shaking and wheezing, and was either dead or close to it. The lady weighed the blade in her hand and sniffed.

'Find my hammer, Darnielle,' she said, 'and my Blade.'

'I still have the Blade in my hand,' Silver said, voice muffled by her mask, and from the water Mournchild rose, limp and soaked, water sloughing off his armour in sheets as he rose impossibly through the air and was set down next to Jean Du Cilcan. The huge knight coughed and spewed seawater and lay back, blinking.

'A reminder of power,' Silver said. 'Your hammer is in a chest just past that arch. We should leave, now. They may have heard this one yelling.'

Marion heaved Mournchild to his feet and then the small man, Jean du Cilcan, who was muttering and weeping.

'On your feet, Jean,' she said. Killian could only stare. 'Two small wands for the sea witch Arlock, and three ship-wands on the ship in the harbour. That is it?'

'That is it. They will not be able to recreate. I do not think. I do not...'

Marion gripped him firmly by the arm and pulled him along, Mournchild following after with a fearful glance to Silver.

'Kill the boy,' Marion called back as she went to the arch to find her hammer, not even bothering to look at him. Mournchild shot Killian a glance but then they were gone through the arch.

'You said,' Killian started, and the mage Silver stood in front of his cell and raised her hands and he fell silent.

'I said many things,' she replied softly. 'Many of them are true. Many are not. I thought the Russilan tombs would be my key to power, Heroneye. I was wrong. This magic is going to change the world. You have your sister, and your people. Consider this another lesson from the world.'

Silver lowered her hands and Killian fell to his knees.

'*The world doesn't exist to give us lessons*,' he said.

Silver strode from the room and he stared at the water of the Well of No End. It had settled again from Mournchild's tempest, and the stars were writ all across it. *What stars did I see first tonight?* He had not looked. It was too late now.

Three cells along to his left, he heard Big Breygar spit and then rattle her cell door.

'Well,' she said, 'this has gone quite poorly, I'd say.'

17

CUTLASS AND CROW

'Of note are the ravagers, the pirates who thrive within the Deep Crowns and prey on shipping in the northern and western reaches (with the western reaches poor in trade and the southern reaches guarded adroitly by the Tullioch clans). Some of these ravagers claim descent from the Russilan, though others are demonstrably deserters from the Strait kingdom navies, or Caroban privateers. Given the inaccessibility of the Deep Crowns, it could be feasible pockets of Russilan survived the great plague and continue to this day, though no captured ravager has been able to convincingly claim this providence.'

– ***Notes on the Russilan***, Gallo Mancinus

Killian yelled and yelled, and Breygar yelled with him, and their combined din echoed around the plaza of the Well of No End. He yelled his sister's name, he yelled for help, he yelled simply to make noise. After a minute they paused for breath.

'Someone must be coming,' Big Breygar said, and Killian pressed his forehead against the steel bar of his cell. 'Think they will try and take the *Hawk*?'

'I don't know,' he said, and he pressed the heels of his palms into his eyes until he saw stars. 'Shit!'

He yelled more, and at last the guards came. They ran to their man on the floor, and then there was shouting and more running, and bells ringing. *How long since they left us?* It had been minutes. They would need to reach the pier, reach a dog-boat, get to the *Hawk,* and get her underway. *There's still time.*

'Arlock!' he yelled, over and over, and one of the guards came over and punched him in the face through the bars.

'I need to talk to my bloody sister,' he said, and he managed to grip the man's shirt through the bars and haul him close. 'They took Jean du Cilcan! Do you understand? Stop dicking about and get Arlock!'

She was with him a minute later, and the quiet of the Well plaza was now a tumult of light and noise as Russilan pirates began to arm themselves and fan out. Arlock moved through the morass in a straight line, and the pirates moved out of her way. *What power does she have?*

'Key,' he said, 'Key, listen. The Cil were here for Jean du Cilcan. He came to talk to them. They escaped. Key, they'll take the *Hawk*! *Please*. I need to stop them.'

Arlock stared at the guard Mournchild had killed.

'That man has a partner, a child. Has a mother still alive. Will you tell them he is dead because you brought Cil to our home, brother?'

Killian slumped and then rose, felt bile in his throat. *Blood and blood and blood. Family. Connection. Home.* He slammed the bars of his cell.

'Damn you, Arlock,' he said. 'I had to find you! I thought you could deal with the Cil—'

'Me?' she spat. 'ME?! Ah. It is *my fault*. Nothing is Killian's fault. Well I'm sorry to tell you, *brother dear*, it is all your fault. All of it. Mother is dead because you wouldn't stop whining about how hungry you were, and so she stole, and so she was caught. I was left alone because rather than step up to your responsibilities you went off half-cocked and killed the old governor. Was that your big hero moment? And then you left, and everything that happened to me after that for a long time was *your fault*, Killian. You told mum you'd look after me, and instead it was just me and old broken people. You have no idea of my life, Killian. Then you return to us, and bring a *Cil* with you? I've spent the last five years raiding the sea lanes around Burner's Run to dissuade any passage into the Deep Crowns, Killian. We have our city, we have our people. We have food, we have clean air, we have no chains. But you weren't the hero, and so you had to ruin it.'

'Raorum Raorum stole fire from the gods,' Killian said, the strange Tullioch Gull's words echoing in his mind. 'You took those, those *wands*. Magic ballistae? Whatever they are, you took them from Cil-Marie, and more besides. You took that man. What is he?'

'I'd like to go back to the ship,' Big Breygar said, and both of them ignored her.

'He is the one who made those weapons. You are a child, Killian. You are thinking in terms of a ship. What will the Crowns look like when every Cil ship can shoot fire and force like that – can sink another in heartbeats? With three wand-ballistae we sank a *galleon*, Killian, off Madu. With this magic in their hands they will take the Thousand Crowns and turn us all into dutiful citizens. They will take it all.'

'Cil don't expand,' he said, and she pulled a face and rolled her eyes.

'*Cil don't expand.* Listen to yourself. Gods I'd forgotten how *stupid* you are. The Cil have been expanding for a hundred years. The Shield Isles to the west were all independent – Requin-Port, Concarneau, a dozen more. They have moved slowly, but this power will allow them to move fast. So yes, I took it, and I took him. And I would use that power to keep us safe.'

'They are going to take my ship,' he said, and he slammed his open hand against the bars and watched them rattle. '*Cutlass Hawk*. Like we always said. I've got the Cutlass and Crow pins, Key. I'm the captain. You need to let me out. We can still stop this.'

Arlock looked at him and he saw something soften in her eyes for a heartbeat. A man wielding a crossbow ran to her and whispered in her ear, and her mouth twisted.

'You are a fool,' she said. 'I'm taking the *Saltdaughter*. You and your sailor can come with us. Your Cil made it to your ship and they are trying to leave. I could have them burnt from the water right now.'

'We can catch them,' he said. 'Please. My crew. They don't, they aren't… they aren't like me! We can catch the ship. Get you back your man.'

Arlock nodded and gestured at the guard to open the cell.

'We hunt them now,' she said, 'but Jean du Cilcan is the key to making those weapons, and with him, Cil-Marie will turn these isles to ash and stone. I will burn your ship and everyone on it rather than let him go back to the Cil.'

Killian rolled his shoulders as the cell door opened, and an unshaven man with dark eyes pressed his old cutlass into his hand. *Blood and blood and blood.*

'It is good to see you, Key,' he said.

Kaikatsu drank tea with the man Pollos Twice-Kissed. Small Breygar and Timmult and Renard were with the dog-boats waiting for the rest to return. Pollos had set the *Hawk just so*. She followed him as he worked, unnerved by the lattice dome of stone that dominated the isle, afraid of the sleek black-hulled ships and their strange weaponry. *I preferred the whaler.*

He explained his work as he went. He was setting the sail and lines so that with just a handful of quick-release movements the ship would be at half sail, already turned to the heading he fancied best. On the lower deck he locked the oar sweeps into place, hidden inside but ready to slide out in a heartbeat if they could spare the muscle for it. The anchor he had lowered was not their main anchor but a smaller secondary, and the rope that secured it was itself secured by a thin line.

'One cut and we are free of that,' he muttered, 'though it's a waste of a good anchor. Good iron, that one. Seen some action.'

With all of that done, there was nothing left but to panic, and so Pollos suggested tea. They brewed it on a little stove of coals on the foredeck, each sat on a coil of rope. The stars above were bright, and even with a haze of thin cloud Kaikatsu could still see them. Pollos prepared the tea from a tin caddy of dried leaves in a charred enamel pot, and when the steam started to rise he lifted the pot from the flame and set it on the rope coil, and poured them each a cup. Kaikatsu took it with a nod of thanks. The night was cold, and she was tired. Her mind was still full of Burner's Run.

'I had never seen a Judge, before,' she said, and Pollos sipped at his tea. 'It was greater than I expected, in so many ways. Have you seen anything like that before?'

Pollos grimaced and stared out at the tinkling lights of Deep Crow.

'Once,' he said, and he traced the scar on his cheek. 'When the gods went mad, the winter the Judges' chains broke – I was a soldier, if you can believe it. A Judge we thought was long dead came back, the great wolf Lothal. My regiment were evacuating villagers. The winter was *wrong*, too cold, there were Ferron in the north. A lot going on. It doesn't matter. I was a soldier, and I saw it once. I was on watch on a cold night, and at the edge of my sight I saw the wolf. He was in the forest, nearly as tall as the pines at his shoulder, but he was slinking through, quiet like. He didn't turn towards us, didn't look at us. Fur black as coal, streaks of glowing silver, and teeth... gods. Molten black iron. I don't know. They are hard to describe, eh?'

'What happened?' Kaikatsu asked, and she felt the relu-mouse squirm beneath her robes.

'It passed us by. I don't know why, I don't know anything. We made it south, and in the spring the wolf was gone to the west. So was our mother bear Anshuka – three centuries she slept, and then she just left, trailing the great rotstorm behind her. I went to sea that spring for the first time. Wanted to get away from all that, magic and gods.'

Kaikatsu stared at the dome of stone. She had never seen human stonework like it; the lattice seemed impossible. From this distance in the dark she could see no joins. *Is it a thousand smaller stones, or one larger shaped by the skein?*

'How is that going for you?' she asked, and the big man laughed.

'May I see your relu?' he asked, and she froze. Slowly she raised her eyes to meet his. She was still not good with human expressions, but Pollos Twice-Kissed had been kind to her. Gently she opened her robe and reached inside and drew out the cobalt mouse, and it twitched its little nose and stared up at Pollos with eyes of jade. Pollos smiled down at it, and then the mouse twitched again and ran up Kaikatsu's arm and scurried back into the warmth of her robe.

'Thank you,' he said. 'I think this world has magic and gods everywhere. I don't think there is any getting away from it.'

Kaikatsu held her tea and considered Zalan. She had seen it, in the skein, infinite complexity layered over a vague snake-like heart. *Connection.* She had searched the seas for the place where the relu-mouse might have his connection, but when she saw Zalan she saw connection in every direction. There were larger bonds, lines, strings that seemed to end abruptly – but there were a thousand

thousand smaller ones holding Zalan bound to Burner's Run. *Have I been going about this backward?*

With a slump of her shoulders she dropped into the skein and focused on the relu, and saw the recursive patterns that underlaid it, the depth of it like a starfield sharply outlined, and she peered at the edges of it. The connections, all severed, thick lines, wavering loops, and one thin line from it to her heart, a line of liquid gold. She focused and traced her eyes around the outline of the mouse and she found it. *There.* It was a thread of sound and light and vibration, a tentative, weak little thing, green and dancing gold, ephemeral as a thought.

It led from the relu to the heart of Pollos Twice-Kissed.

Kaikatsu let the skein fall from her senses and shivered, and Pollos poured her more tea.

'You all right?' he asked, and she nodded. *We will be.*

'Baal, Morost, Pendar, Tulu, Salaman!' Mournchild hissed There were a dozen pirates between them and the docks, and as they rushed down the silent streets and the bells and shouts began behind them, those dozen had come to readiness. Crossbows, a spear, and so many cutlasses.

'Halt and drop your weapons!' a woman called, levelling a crossbow, and Mournchild spat and turned to Marion. She had her hammer in one hand and Jean du Cilcan gripped tight in the other. The mage Darnielle stood behind her, mask tight to her face. *The mage is Silver. Silver is Darnielle.* Mournchild had not unpacked that – not yet. He was still wet, his lungs ached, and his ears burned with a sharp pain.

She had nearly drowned him with a wave of her hand. He needed to speak to the Lady Marion about that.

'I said, bloody halt!' the woman yelled again, and a crossbow bolt skittered across the stone. Mournchild reached to his belt and gripped his helm. He had left his cloak behind.

'May I, Lady?' he asked, and behind him Marion clucked in her throat.

'Bleed them, Mournchild,' she said, and he slammed the helm down on his head.

It was a close-fitting helm and it was blessedly dry compared to the rest of him. Steel finished in matte black, with a visor he pulled down. The slit for his eyes was thinner than a finger, and over his ears and mouth a dozen small holes perforated the steel so he could hear and breathe. He felt wonderful with his helm on. Mournchild drew his boot knife and stood with arms spread, sword in one hand and knife in the other. He walked forward inexorably, and the woman pirate hurriedly loaded another bolt in her crossbow and started to wind.

The crossbows looked weak, and their aim would be poor in the dark. He decided this, and it was so. Mournchild jerked forward and then rolled to one side away from Lady Marion and their captive. He heard crossbow bolts clatter on the stone of the road. One caught him in the chest as he rose. He felt it like a punch to the pectoral, and he looked down and saw the bolt had pierced his breastplate. It had not broken through the chain shirt beneath, but it was enough to scratch at him, and he growled and made his run.

The crossbow wielders fell back, fumbling with quivers and winches, and Mournchild was left with eight – eight fighters should defeat one, but these were sailors. Half of them didn't even wear boots, let alone armour. Mournchild was a fortress; Mournchild was an avalanche. A cutlass was raised to parry his blow and he let it, and followed with his knife. The ash-blackened blade held by matte-black armour in the night was almost impossible to follow, and the first the pirate knew of it was as it thrust into his chest. Three more were upon him and he accepted blow after blow in order to deal rapturous damage. His sword sang as he drove it through flesh, and he broke toes with brutal stamps of his heavy steel-reinforced boots, and he broke jaws and noses with backhands of his gauntleted fists. The pirates had weapons, but every inch of Mournchild was a weapon. A spear wielder tried to trip him and Mournchild leapt at the man and butted him over and over until the man's skull was a ruin and Mournchild's helm was dripping. He roared. '*Baal, Morost, Pendar, Tulu, Salaman*!'

Flame.

A pirate behind him he had not yet killed exploded in fire, incandescent, and Mournchild turned to see the mage Darnielle with one hand raised, a mote of flame dancing between her fingertips. Marion and Jean du Cilcan were clambering into the dog-boat with Small Breygar and Timmult, and the medic Renard was standing confused in the other. At her stomach she clutched a satchel, and her face was twisted in fear.

'What the hells?' she said. 'Where is the captain, where is—'

Mournchild drove his sword in her gut and then kicked her into the water, and turned his blade on the others. The man Timmult raised his oar and Mournchild simply tilted his gore-soaked head, and with a strangled curse the sailor sank into the boat and sobbed.

'Captain is dead,' Marion said. 'Row, now, row fast.'

Mournchild climbed into the dog-boat and Timmult and Small Breygar pushed off and began to row.

'My sister?' Small Breygar asked, and Mournchild could not remember the man ever speaking before. Mournchild did not answer. His eyes were on the two Russilan ships. On the fore of one a crew were hurriedly loading a ballista. One the other, the giant wands of stone and steel and wood tipped with head-sized crystals were tracking their dog-boat.

'Lady,' he said, and Marion cursed under her breath in Cil. The *Cutlass Hawk* was only a hundred yards away, but it was a hundred yards of open water. *Two volleys with the ballista, perhaps?* Mournchild had no idea of the reload time of those wands, but having seen the pirate Arlock's tiny version crack stone he had no desire to find out.

'Mage?' Marion asked, and Small Breygar did not stop rowing but he asked again, insistent.

'*My sister*?' he said, and behind him the mage Darnielle let out a sigh.

'I will need help, after this,' she said, and then she raised a hand to the two galleys and from her palm mist accreted, water vapour rising from the sea and pouring forth in billows of opaque cloud. The ballista fired and the boat rocked as they all threw themselves flat, but the first shot was wide.

'*My*—'

'*Row*!' Marion cried. 'Your sister is fine, but we are all dead if you don't row!'

Mournchild stared as the sails of the *Cutlass Hawk* began to unfurl and the anchor chain dropped, and a beam of purple light rent the fog cloud pouring from Darnielle's hand and burned into the water a dozen yards ahead of them. He could see the beam shooting onward, fizzing below the water. He caught Darnielle as she collapsed, but her work was done – the two ships were wreathed in thick fog.

'This one is *useful*,' he said, and as they closed on the *Cutlass Hawk* the bells and screams of Deep Crow filled the air behind them, and he allowed himself a smile. In the darkness of the Well of No End he had seen his death, had seen an endless darkness, and felt a presence below, deeper. He had known fear. Not ascension to Baal, not endless fire below – a crushing depth and cold.

But I am alive.

18

HAWK AND SALTDAUGHTER

'The Tullioch-controlled southern reaches that border the endless Doldrum waters to the south are well patrolled by their naval vessels and open to trade, though the long and navigationally challenging crossing of the archipelago is fraught with danger. Despite this, merchants have made their fortune with these exchanges, as the Tullioch capacity to find bounty from the sea is unparalleled. The coronal sceptre of the Prime in Uradech is festooned with pearls from the Southern Crowns, and the weather is reportedly clement and calm compared to surrounding waters. However, any effort to map the southern reach is met with fierce opposition, and all who venture there must submit to a full search of their belongings and merchandise for any maps or navigational charts of the area.'

– ***The Thousand Crowns***, Alwin Brakspear

The *Saltdaughter* flew across the water and Killian stood on the forecastle, burning. Big Breygar was next to him. The *Hawk* was just in view, a few miles ahead. She was running fast – full main and aft sails, and she was cutting closer to the little rocks and islets than he would have unless great need took him. *Where are they running to?*

'They can't cross the Run,' Breygar said, and Killian reached into his belt pouch and drew out the little brass pins he had made for Galli and Nils.

'I don't know what Silver can do,' he said at last. Silver had heard the threats Marion had made to Galli and Nils, and had joined her anyway. *Why?* He knew the answer was simpler than he would like. *Magic. Power.* 'They might try it. They might hope that between Silver and Kaikatsu they can push the wind fast enough to make it. They might count on me stopping Zalan as we follow, to save Pollos and Timmult and your brother.'

'Too late for Renard,' Big Breygar said, and Killian took off his hat and held it in his hands.

When they had reached the docks there was a slaughter of a dozen torn bodies on the quayside, and Renard's body had been floating face down in the water. The *Hawk* had been almost out of harbour, and a desperate crew were scrambling over the *Saltdaughter* to try and make chase. They had both paused at the body, and then both moved on.

'She deserved better than us,' Killian said, and Big Breygar did not disagree. The ships ran fast. *Saltdaughter* was smaller than *Hawk*, but she ran with a full crew on the sweeps and they pulled even as the wind filled her sail. She had less sail than *Hawk*, though. If Killian was at the helm, she would never have caught up. Yet as the pre-dawn shadow gave way to sun, Killian allowed himself a little hope.

'Pollos is letting us catch them,' he said at last, and he went and told Arlock so. She was stood behind the helm, directing her helmsman. It was so strange to stand over her.

'Key,' he said, and she dismissed one of her crew she was commanding and came to him. She looked up at him, face serious. Her ceremonial dagger and robes and book were gone – what remained was a sailor, a belt knife tucked in a sash at her waist. She stood with perfect balance as the ship rolled.

'My ship could lose us,' he said. 'The mate is running it slow. He is waiting to give us a chance.'

'What will that look like?' she asked, tone flat, and Killian scrunched his face. *What would it look like?* He had no idea. He set his hat back upon his head and stared out.

'Let me see some charts between here and the Run and I'll tell you,' he said. 'They have a mage, and the mad Uradech knight, and the Cil woman has a hammer that could break a hull as quick as an egg. I've our tide-mage and three crew on there.'

'Easiest way would be your crew getting off, and us turning that tub to flinders,' Key said, and he winced.

'I thought you wanted your weapon man back,' he said, and she pursed her lips.

'I said easiest. I didn't say that was the plan. Come, see the chart. Tarren, you have the helm. Any big change or if we come up on Illinos Point, you let me know.'

They descended and she led him to the captain's quarters. They were austere. Killian's quarters on the

Hawk were full of maps and trinkets, blades and shells and mementoes. Here there was a cot built into the wall, a chart table with a few basic stools, and a case for charts. A single sea chest. He blew out a sigh as she searched in her charts.

'How did you come to be… well… captain? *Starfinder?* I had to leave, Key. I'm… sorry, for what it is worth. I had to leave – they saw me when I killed the governor. I had to go and then, well. Coming back wasn't easy.'

'I earned it,' she said quietly, rolling out a map. 'I studied under Rurich until he died, and then when Struan and the others wanted to leave Requin-Port for some other halfway house, I made my way back here. I crossed Burner's Run in a dog-boat.'

She stopped and stared at the chart table, and her knuckles flexed white as she gripped the side of it and for a moment her eyes closed. Killian watched.

'Zalan took me down to the deep water and showed me many things,' she said, opening her eyes and relaxing her grip. 'When I woke my little boat was floating in the Well of No End. How did you get a ship?'

Killian had no answer. He tried to remember her as he last saw her, a sleeping child curled beneath a thin blanket, a tangled mane of hair surrounding a face dappled in moon shadow.

Key sighed and laid out four stones to weight the chart and then placed two shells, one black and one white.

'The black is us, the white is the *Cutlass Hawk*.'

Killian leaned over the chart. They were a few hours sailing from the Run, if the winds held. They were headed straight south from Deep Crow, a straight shot. Pollos had held that course all night and all morning so far. Killian traced his fingers ahead.

'What is this?' he asked, and he grinned. It was a series of small islands blocking the path south, an archipelago of some kind.

'Zalan's Teeth,' Key said. 'They have no charts. When they hit that they'll have to turn east or slow down.'

Killian traced his finger back.

'Then when we reach this isle we loop east. They will think we have fallen behind, and when they turn east at Zalan's Teeth, we will catch them fast from the north. We will have full wind behind us, they will be half speed at best. We storm them. Pollos will drop the sail, I'm sure.'

'You're sure?'

'Pollos and I have sailed together for a decade. Pollos Twice-Kissed will do the necessary. You may not like me, Key, but I love you. I've made more mistakes than I can count. This is not to be another.'

'You didn't tell me how you became a captain,' she said, and there was no harsh edge. Just a sister asking her brother. He shivered and tried to find the right words.

'Blood and blood and blood,' he said. 'Same way I do everything.'

Marion kept her hammer gripped tight. If she thought she could sail this cursed ship she would have killed the stupid Undal and the dour sailors and the Antian rat already. The Antian was nowhere to be seen – hiding belowships, surely. *A born coward, like the rest of the rats.* In Cil-Marie Marion had two dozen Antian at her beck and call, always scurrying around her mother's manse at some task or another. She had grown to hate them. If someone had taken her in chains and held her in servitude, she would have cut their throat the first night.

Aboard the *Hawk* Pollos and Timmult and Small Breygar were running themselves ragged pushing the ship onward. Mournchild stood by the central mast, sword drawn, helm on, watching them. The mage Darnielle, *Silver*, had retreated to the captain's quarters, and Marion had thrown Jean du Cilcan into the first mate's quarters and barred the door.

'Lady,' Mournchild called. She went to him. 'Lady, how are we going to cross Burner's Run? We have no Russilan.'

Marion allowed herself a moment of breath, with Mournchild next to her. He would protect her.

'You did well at that port,' she said. 'A dozen dead. You are uninjured?'

He nodded, and she assessed him. His armour was pierced and rent in a dozen paces and the whole thing stank of clotted blood. *But it is not his.*

'You must not act against the mage Darnielle,' she said. 'She is a powerful ally. I am sorry she put you in that water, but I do not believe she is our enemy.'

Mournchild nodded again, and shifted his feet. 'Lady,' he said, 'the Run?'

'I have the beacon,' Marion said at last. She looked out at the water. 'My master saw the day of my death. He had the gift of prophecy, Mournchild. I was in a desert, he said. Sand all around. This is not that day. Burner's Run will not open for us, and we cannot fight a Judge. We need to leave, and our need is great. It is time for us to leave this place, these little people. We have our prize. Gather any of your things you will need. We will go to the aftcastle – that should suffice.'

She found the mage Darnielle in the captain's quarters, loading charts into a satchel. Her mask was off, laid on the chart table.

'You made a good choice,' Marion said, and the woman did not answer her. Instead she stared down at the charts.

'You have seen my power,' she said at last. 'I am not of Cil-Marie. But I can contribute, and I would learn more of this magic. Our agreement was to find the man Jean du Cilcan, and in return payment. I am asking to change our terms.'

Marion looked around Killian Heroneye's room, cluttered with trinkets and books and salt-stained clothes, and she sniffed.

'I do not renegotiate,' she said. 'You will be paid as we agreed. However, a new deal may be met. We are leaving, Darnielle-Mage. You can come with us, and join Jean du Cilcan's research, or you can stay here. Your payment will be waiting in Samurkan, should you ever arrive there.'

Darnielle nodded and placed her mask on her face. 'A few final charts,' she said, and Marion left her to it. As she passed through the door she glanced back and saw the woman stuffing a salt-stained black shirt of Heroneye's into her satchel, and she narrowed her eyes but let the door close.

On the aftcastle the hulking Undal Pollos Twice-Kissed was steering the ship, south and south again as she instructed.

'Isles coming up,' he said gruffly. 'No sign of that ship behind. Think we should turn east around this chain and then south again; they are too close to navigate without charts or patience.'

Marion ignored him, reached into her belt pouch and from within drew the beacon. Behind her Pollos yelled something and the ship began to turn, lines behind hauled and tightened and knots being fiddled with. She didn't listen – she stared at the beacon. She had carried it for nearly two years, since she set out to retrieve the truth of the lost Cil ship, and to retrieve Jean du Cilcan. It was a metal sphere and with trembling hands on the aftcastle she unscrewed its two halves and withdrew the green gemstone within. It was covered in swirling sigils, and she held it in her palm for a long moment and then set it on the deck.

'What is that?' Pollos asked, and she ignored him and drew her hammer. With a single heavy blow she cracked the gem into a thousand pieces. The plank beneath it broke as well, and as the gem broke a swirling vortex of green light burst free and danced upward, upward and Marion felt all of her senses tingle and sizzle. It was skein-magic.

The light faded and Marion stepped back and scattered the broken gemstone with the toe of her boot, and then stared at the skies.

'Why Twice-Kissed?' she asked, and behind her she heard Mournchild climbing the stairs. He had Jean du Cilcan with him in one hand, and her bag of things from her room. Behind him the mage Darnielle followed, a bulging satchel at her waist.

Pollos looked at them all and at the broken green stone, and then he followed Marion's gaze to the sky.

'Kissed once by my mother,' he said slowly, 'and once by pitchfyre. That is the story at least.'

'What is the truth?' Marion said, her eyes still on the low clouds that scudded over Burner's Run to the south. Pollos did not answer, and instead locked the wheel with a loop of rope.

'I need to set the mizzen,' he said, and he pushed past them all. He paused a long moment by Silver and looked at her mask, but she did not meet his gaze.

'How are we leaving?'

Marion pointed to the sky – in the pale light of noon, an orb of light was travelling below the cloud. It was at the edge of sight, but drawing closer.

'We go to the Sun-Masters,' Marion said, and they all stared at the oncoming light.

The first Marion knew of the *Saltdaughter* was when its hull slammed into the *Cutlass Hawk* at full tilt.

Killian was ready, and the moment the *Saltdaughter* hit the *Hawk* he was already mid leap, a rope in his hand from the high central mast. Key had brought the ship in at full tilt, and only at the last second did she turn so that rather than burying her prow in *Hawk's* side, the ship's side rammed into the *Hawk's* hull. The impact was horrifying, a dozen ropes snapping at once, the tear of plank and line and sheet, and the screams of the surprised. As he swung from the rigging of *Saltdaughter* across to *Hawk* he saw the tangle of limbs on the aftcastle – Marion and Mournchild and Silver and Jean du Cilcan. Pollos and Timmult and Small Breygar were at the prow of the ship, already pulling themselves back up, and he could not see Kaikatsu. His crew were pulling weapons from beneath sailcloth, and Killian crashed into the rigging of *Hawk* and slid down a patch of sail, snagging himself on a web of rope halfway up the mast. He scurried down as the ships drifted apart, and saw Big Breygar leap from the rail of the *Saltdaughter* with a blade in one hand. She landed hard against the rail of the *Hawk*, but her brother was there in a heartbeat to take her aboard. Killian looked at his crew and couldn't help but grin.

'Timmult, Pollos'—he smiled—'stop us going under. Small, get a bow. Big, with me. Silver has joined the fucking *Cil*, and she can chuck fire. So heads up. Swords from the other ship are friendlies.'

Killian turned to the forecastle. Marion stood with Silver on one side of her, watching through her mask, and on the other side she gripped the meek figure of Jean du Cilcan. Mournchild was already moving to the stairs. The *Saltdaughter* pulled away from them with a wrench, but Key was sprawled against the *Hawk*'s rail.

'Kill these worms, Mournchild,' Marion yelled, and turned away. Killian saw where she was looking. An orb of light was cutting through the cloud – it was miles off, but closer by the second. *Cil's eye.*

'This,' he called, flicking his cutlass, 'is my ship. These are my *crew.* You killed Renard. You threatened Galli and Nils. You have two choices – swim or die.'

Mournchild descended the steps and spread his arms, a knife in one, his longsword in the other.

'Baal,' he began, and then an arrow shot from behind Killian and hit him in the helm. Mournchild stopped and stared.

'Morost,' Killian continued. 'Something else, a blue one. Nobody gives a shit, Mournchild. Least of all the Cil. Tell me. What could I do to stop you reaching your heaven?'

Killian threw himself forward in a flurry of cuts, every one of them aiming against the hands and wrists – Mournchild's armour was heavy, but the gauntlets were intricate and he slammed his cutlass again and again. Big Breygar was there not with a cutlass but with a long billhook, jabbing and sweeping at the knight's legs until he stamped down on the haft of it and hurled his knife at her. She fell back to avoid it, sprawling across the deck. Switching to a two-handed grip he threw himself at Killian, and Killian could hear the chorus of adrenaline and fear in his ears, the buzz in his skull. The voice of the abbess – *blood and blood and blood.*

He danced back, his footwork always faster on the sloping and ever-changing deck than the hulking knight. The ship was rolling now with nobody at the helm, little waves catching it wrong and sending it into unnatural pitches. At the aftcastle, Silver stepped forward and a mote of fire rose in her hand – it was pointed at Big Breygar, whose attention was fully on tripping up Mournchild so Killian could act. Killian opened his mouth to scream but a blast of wind struck Silver and Marion down, and from beneath the aftcastle stairs the mage Kaikatsu scurried forth, hands raised. Behind the ship the orb drew closer.

'Enough of this!' Mournchild screamed, and he threw himself at Killian with a hurricane of sword blows and there was nothing Killian could do but retreat, retreat. *How much further to the bowsprit?* He was running out of room. He had lost sight of his sister. He could see nothing, only the endless flashes of Mournchild's blade, and then he caught an incoming blow wrong and his cutlass spun from his hands over the rail and into the depths. Mournchild raised his blade.

'I am on a mission from *god, you worm*!' he screamed, and then Pollos Twice-Kissed grabbed him around the waist. The knight threw himself backward and sent Pollos flying, and then looked down. A rope was cinched around his waist. He turned his head at the same time as Killian to see Pollos heaving a dog-boat anchor in his arms, old twisted iron raised high above his head.

'If you're on his ship,' he grunted, shoving the anchor overboard, 'it's *Captain* Worm, actually.'

The anchor splashed and then Mournchild was horizontal as the rope snapped taut and slammed him through the thin wood panel of the side railing, and the sea took him. Pollos and Big Breygar ran to Killian and pulled him up and together they turned to the aftcastle.

Kaikatsu was on her knees, a shield of air and water swirling over her head as a torrent of flame spewed down at her from Silver's outstretched palms. A wall of silence engulfed the ship – behind the aftcastle hanging in the air, unmoving like a squid in the water was the orb of light. It was the size of a carriage, ovoid, and it burned white with a low intensity that pushed the eye away. *Cil's eye*. For a decade the eye had watched the Crowns, had watched Cil-Marie's borders. For a decade Killian had been listening to rumour and story. The silence that came with the arrival of the orb was a pressure, a weight, a pure impossibility that sound could occur. A presence, rather than an absence. The ship lurched, and a moment later an arrow took Silver in the shoulder and she staggered back and Kaikatsu's shield fell, and Pollos ran to her. Killian sprinted for the aftcastle and found Key beside him, a brutal dagger in her hand. Together they ran up the steps. The *Saltdaughter* was circling close, and from her decks beams of purple light burned through the sky, but Killian heard nothing, only caught the glare of the beam of force as it flew past its target and off into the sky beyond.

There was no sound near the orb, only the thick weight of air pressure, and that white light pervaded everything. A second blast of purple light thrust from the *Saltdaughter* and struck the orb and it wavered, but at its base a ramp had lowered through the haze of white light to the rolling aftcastle of the *Cutlass Hawk* below. Silver was pulling herself up it, without a backward glance, and Marion was hauling Jean du Cilcan higher. Next to him he could feel Key scream in frustration as the orb began to rise, and another blast from the *Saltdaughter* was met with a response – a fifty-foot gout of orange-black flame roared from the orb and scorched the foredeck of the ship.

Killian stopped and tried to grab Key. Silver was gone, lost in the light. Marion was gone. *The crew is safe.* He wanted blood, wanted Silver's blood, Marion's blood, but he wanted something more. *Connection. Family. Home.* Killian tried to reach his sister as the orb raised away, as another beam of light rocketed from the *Saltdaughter* past the orb, but she slipped from his grasp and leapt for the ramp, and he lost her to the haze of white light. With an impossible lurch the orb shifted up, away, an arrow loosed from a bow.

Killian heard his own scream as his hearing returned, as the orb fled, and he watched it go. It crossed Burner's Run, and with every moment it flew higher and higher. *South.* With the return of sound came the screams of the burned on the *Saltdaughter*, mixed with the cheers of those who did not understand the price they had paid. Key had said she would rather die than see Jean du Cilcan take his weapons back to the Cil. *And I let her.*

Killian sank to his knees and felt for the first time the pain from a dozen cuts and wounds – Mournchild's marks. Pollos came to him, and Big Breygar, and Kaikatsu crawled up to them and collapsed next to him.

'Standard day rate is not enough, Captain,' she said, and the Breygars laughed. Pollos pulled Killian close and Killian stared after the orb to light departing. Cil's eye driven away, for the first time he had ever heard.

'Where is Starfinder Arlock?' a voice called, and Killian could only shake his head.

'What's our course, Captain?' Pollos asked, and the crew all looked to him.

Killian closed his eyes. 'Our crew need us,' he said. 'Deep Crow, and then Samurkan.'

'Starfinder Arlock?' a voice called again from the other ship, and Killian sank to his knees.

'I need Renard,' he muttered. 'I'm bleeding.'

Timmult and the Breygars carried him to his room then, and laid him in his bed. Under his thin pillow he felt something hard, and when they left him to find bandages he pulled it free. It was a simple roll of parchment, rolled and then folded.

Sorry.
I will see you again.
Silver

Killian laid his head back and listened to the waves and gripped the parchment tight.

19

THE WELL OF NO END

'The world is changing. The gods have descended to madness and old ties are lost, old chains are broken, old paths discarded. We have remained steadfast and safe because of our caution and our alliances, because we seek something different than the humans or the Tullioch. We have worshipped no Judges, though we have paid our tithes as we must. We have worshipped no ethereal spirits like the Baal-cultists of the Strait kingdoms. Our way is the way of Holt and Clan and tooth and claw. I plead of you – assemble the witches, summon the southern holtmaster and his tame, bound relu, and assemble the masters. If we do not act, we may be left behind.'

– ***Letter to the Council of Isles on the Madness of the Spirits***, Anneli Thirdblood of Holt Suolaa

Mournchild sank. His sword had been wrenched from his hands when the anchor took him, as easily as the breath had been wrenched from his body. The water was black so quickly, the ship above falling from sight. His lungs screamed for air, and he wrenched at the rope at his waist but it was thick ship rope and the knot was tight, his gauntlets thick and clumsy. He bled from a dozen wounds, but the blood and the water were both black and the cold broke down the boundary between the sea and his flesh until he was nothing but starving eyes and screaming heart.

Darkness took him. *Baal,* he thought.

'There are many powers and many gods,' he heard in the darkness. The cardinal's voice, smooth and practised, lilting. 'The true godhead has five facets. You will be our Blade, Mournchild. You will accompany Marion of the Cil-Marie. I know this to be the best course. You will be our Blade by being her Blade. Five facets to make one, as a hand closed becomes a fist. The work of the church is never done, Mournchild, and sometimes the unbeliever can have purpose. Marion is one such unbeliever. You will suffer, Mournchild, suffer the infidel, suffer the heathens. You will suffer and through your suffering you will be Baal's instrument in this broken world.'

Memory...

Mournchild did not know why those words returned to him. The last mote of light above faded, the dark hulls of the ships above lost. *Am I still falling?* He could feel no movement, anymore. Only blackness in all directions. The rope was so tight at his waist, cinching his chainmail and breastplate and backplate. At those points alone he could feel his flesh, could be sure he was alive. *But do I still fall?* Mournchild managed to wrench his helmet free and it fell away from him, lost in darkness. The sea would take it, in the end, all its dun metal worn to nothing. The sea would take everything. Removing his helmet made no difference – his eyes were wide and sightless. Mournchild was filled with two certainties. Firstly, if he opened his mouth, he would die. Secondly, he would open his mouth. It was a matter of seconds, not minutes. The pain was incredible, his throat starting to convulse as he tried to force his mouth closed. *Why?*

Why fight?

Mournchild closed his eyes and opened them but there was only blackness, and he felt the anchor rope taut at his waist.

'You will be Baal's instrument,' the cardinal said. There was no distortion of water to his voice; it was a simple quiet surety in the base of Mournchild's skull.

Baal...

Baal, Morost, Pendar, Tulu, Salaman!

'My will shall be revealed in time,' the cardinal's voice said.

In the darkness, a shimmer of impossible light coruscated and twisted. Blue and green, ridges, rows, shapes. *Edges? Is this death?*

Mournchild wanted to pray. His ears ached from the pressure; his skull was a drum, his heart the drummer. Every heartbeat was a spike of pain, but Mournchild knew pain. Heroneye had cut him a dozen times even with his armour and Mournchild bled freely into the water, the blood and the salt mixing, their tides and boundaries unclear.

The light drew closer and curved and danced sinuously, and Mournchild opened his mouth as Zalan, mad god of the Russilan, swam to him. The serpent's maw was open, jagged rows of crystal blue-ice teeth as long as his leg dragging through the water. Dozens of eyes, two great abysses of onyx and so many surrounding them, each eye a different gemstone, all of them reflecting the blue and green light that limned its writhing scales. The water began to fill his lungs as he choked and coughed and the hundred eyes of the great Judge of Burner's Run *saw* him and then he fought no more. He felt himself grow weak, felt all of it fall away save the gaze of the Judge and then a warmth within the cold of the black water.

It sees me...

The pain in his chest, his head, everywhere began to fade. His mind began to clear, and with slow movements he pulled free his gauntlets, and then his vambraces, and then reached down to the ship rope at his waist – but it was gone. The anchor, the ship rope, both gone. The pain at his waist, gone. Mournchild hung in the dark water and Zalan coiled and writhed and saw him, looked *through* him, and he bowed his head.

Thrice now he had seen this Judge. Once from the deck of the *Mendicant Heart*, once from the deck of the *Cutlass Hawk*, and now in the depths below. Entombed in the endless vaults of blind black water, Mournchild felt fear die in him, and he saw and was seen. Beneath endless ocean, the paladin wept.

Zalan, serpent of the Crowns. Zalan, the great Judge. Zalan, the shipbreaker. Zalan, seagrave. Guardian of the Deep Crowns. Terror of Burner's Run. The mad god of the Russilan.

Baal, Morost, Pendar, Tulu, Salaman...
Zalan?

EPILOGUE

THE SIX DANCERS

'The sky tells past and future, tells fate and chance. Every star follows its course, as do we all. If you take the time to watch, you will see that nothing is without pattern. The fish return to their spawning grounds, the whales to their deep coves, the birds south and north and south again. Pattern is the world, from the stars above and the currents below, the skein through it all. Look for the pattern. What is love, but a pattern? Please. Tell them I'm sorry. Look after her!'

– The final words of Cara Heroneye, executed 8th Starsday, Flame, by hanging.
Record of executions 1124 Isken reckoning, Requin-Port

Key remembered holding on to something metal, every sense suffused with white light, some mechanism grating at her arm. How long she held on she didn't know, but then there was a finger pressing at her wrist, and then a boot, and then she fell. The fall was impossibly long. First sight returned to her, and instead of only white light there was light blue and dark blue, spinning, alternating. Then sound came to her, the scream of wind. Then she felt the cold, and then the sea greeted her as only the sea does – brutally, without compunction.

In darkness she clung to a broken spar with one arm and with her other hand clutched her dagger tight. Her dagger was a simple thing, two straight lines meeting in a point, sharp as a razor on each edge – not the hacking dirk or cutlass her crew wore at their belts, not the heavy blade she normally carried. This was the dagger she kept in the back of her belt – an Undal knife, the kind their commandos used in close combat. The kind of dagger designed not to cut rope or any of the thousand things a dagger could do, but to pierce flesh and slink past ribs. A hammer is a hammer because it hammers – *who told me that?* She heard it in her father's voice, Starfinder Rurich's, her mother's. This was a dagger that existed solely to kill. In the Doldrums, there were no waves, no wind, and the water was utter calm. She had fallen south beyond the Crowns and the wind was lost to her.

Key clutched her dagger below the water and tried to keep her eyes moving. There were shapes in the water below, shadows at the edge of her sight. The light was long gone and the water was cold, and Arlock Heroneye hurt. Her ribs hurt, her jaw hurt, and her every heartbeat hammered a flaming spike into the base of her skull. She was bleeding into the water from long gouges in her right leg. Key tilted her head back and looked up at the sky, and between scudding clouds and darkness she could see stars. She tried to focus. *Will it be a shark, that gets me? A squid? A Carob whale? A garu?* She had seen a pack of garu turn a man to scraps before, sinuous fish with hooked teeth and sleek bodies, silver spears that cut through the water. *Something is moving below me.* Key could not bring the energy to search the horizon, anymore. She had been floating for hours, and had watched the sun fade and fall and with it her hope. Despite the motion she knew was below her she stared upward, and lost time. When she awoke the line between water and sky was gone – the dancing cloud was gone, and there was only the darkness and the dancing pins of starlight. The light from a thousand stars reflected on black water, and she was lying in the film between two star-strewn voids, a mote caught between two worlds.

Key could see the Six Dancers, a constellation her mother Cara had always pointed out to her. *The first star you see will be your fate that night.* Luck or change, the dancers meant. Key grimaced and tried to lick her lips, but her tongue was a dry dead thing in her mouth. Dolefully she closed her eyes, and knew if she simply kept them closed, that would be an end. She would fall into the black water below or the stars above and fall until silence took her, or sharp teeth. Instead she let the killing knife slip from her fingers. The knife fell through the water and was gone in a moment and Key brought her hand to her chest and from her tattered and soaked shirt she drew her heron medallion, cold steel slick with salt. She had painted it a garish blue, with an intricate red geometry on top copied from a Russilan tomb on Deep Crow, occult sygaldry whose meaning was lost if ever it held any, even to her with all her studies. In the darkness of the sea the amulet had no colour, and her gaze was for the stars, anyway. She held it and remembered the day her mother had given it to her. *Given them to us.*

Killian had been first to receive his amulet, and Key had been impatient. They had been fighting, always fighting each other even as they never left each other's side, and she had been angry that he went first – as if being a year older made him more important, as if a year made him smarter, or wiser, or stronger. Her mother had calmed them with a smile, and old Struan had been there and the rest, the scant dozen Russilan in Requin-Port living in the slums beyond the fish port, living on scraps and scorn.

'A heron, for a heron,' her mother had said, and then for Key it was the same and the same words again and she was so happy to have something of her own, so angry that Killian had the same. 'A key to home. Starfinder Rurich has blessed them with the old blood.'

Lying in the cold water of the Doldrums, Key gripped her amulet and stared at the stars and waited to die. She had understood her mother's words, eventually, though it had taken her years of searching to find her home. *And now I have lost it.* Above her the stars danced and wheeled and amongst and behind them the mottled swirling dark of pattern lying beyond the light, something at the hint of vision. There was noise, a huff spray of water and a thousand droplets breaking the calm. Weakly she tried to turn, and twenty yards from her the midnight blue of sea and sky were both eclipsed by a shadow, a corrugated wall of living stone. A flame sparked and cast light down the hull of a coral ship, a thousand hues of colour slick with sea spray all gilded by the flame of the torch. From the water Key glimpsed a gap in the hull at the fore of the ship and deep within it an eye was watching her. It was three feet across, an orb in shadow. In the flicker of the torchlight she could see a muddled iris and pupil of black and gold, streaks of the gold shining like living fire as the torchlight caught it. *A whale? A relu?* Key blinked and the eye studied her, and then the coral ship moved closer and the eye was gone. Splashes, noise, and a strong hand under her shoulder.

The Tullioch hauled Key onto their ship and she lay broken and exhausted and bleeding on the deck and though torchlight danced around her she could still see the stars above, and she gripped her heron amulet and clenched her teeth until her jaw ached. The Tullioch were talking, and Key could only think that she had dropped her knife. *A knife for killing.* She pictured her brother's face, the Cil woman Marion, Jean du Cilcan, the mage Darnielle. So many enemies. A Tullioch knelt by her with a waterskin in hand and she gripped his arm, but did not take her eyes from the stars. Six Dancers. Change. Luck.

I'll need a new blade.

ACKNOWLEDGEMENTS

Thank you to Nic and the Head of Zeus team for allowing me to explore more of Morost. Thank you to Oliver for keeping me on track and your endless patience.

Thanks to my editors Charlie and Simon for their insight and enthusiasm and focus. Their help in making this as impactful as possible is dearly appreciated.

Thanks to my wonderful copyeditor Helena for returning to Morost with me – any mistakes remaining are certainly my own.

Thank you to the marketing, publicity, production, art and design, and sales team at HoZ for their support. Thanks to Simon Michele for the cover design and Marcela Bolívar for the illustration on the spectacular UK edition.

Thank you to Captain Jason White (B.S.C, S.S.C, G.S.C) for the nautical sense check.

Thank you to my beta-readers Molly, Adam, Alun, and Anna for catching the nonsense.

Thank you to all the readers who read The Rotstorm series and *Extremophile* for letting me carry on this dream.

Thank you to Abi for always supporting me, Ben for setting my priorities, and to my dad for giving me a love of the sea. And for wee Thomas who has joined the motley crew.

ABOUT THE AUTHOR

IAN GREEN is a writer from Northern Scotland with a PhD in epigenetics. His biopunk eco-terrorism thriller *Extremophile* was one of *Financial Times*' Best Science Fiction Books of 2024 and was shortlisted for the Arthur C. Clarke Award and Dragon Awards. His debut fantasy trilogy The Rotstorm began with the *Sunday Times* bestseller *The Gauntlet and the Fish Beneath*. His short fiction has been widely published and he won the BBC Radio 4 Opening Lines competition, the Futurebook Future Fiction Prize, and was shortlisted for Best Newcomer at the British Fantasy Awards. Find out more at www.ianthegreen.com.